THE HUMBLED

by
IGOR LJUBUNCIC

Book Four of The Lost Words

ISBN: 1512252689

ISBN 13: 9781512252682

Library of Congress Control Number: 2015908143

CreateSpace Independent Publishing Platform

North Charleston, South Carolina

For my readers

ACKNOWLEDGMENTS

You know the drill. Rolling credits: Erin, the CreateSpace editor, so my writing does not come across a total fiasco; Anton Kokarev of kanartist.ru for yet another kick-ass cover; and as always, my wife, who makes sure you get to read a less boring version of the original manuscript.

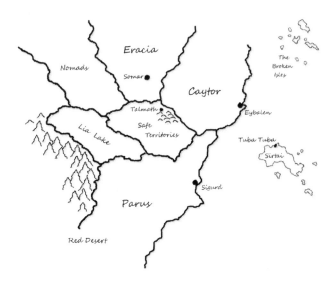

Eracia

Nomads

Somar

Caytor

The
Broken
Isles

Talmath

Safe
Territories

Eybalen

Lia Lake

Tuba Tuba

Sirtai

Sigurd

Parus

Red Desert

PROLOGUE

Calemore rubbed his eyebrow, stepped off a moss-grown stone, and walked toward the seething white mass that was his army. Camped about three weeks north of Marlheim, the eastern force was waiting for him. No, not just a force. A nation.

The whole of Naum was coming against the realms, men, women, children, their livestock. The first wave was comprised mostly of fighting men, but there were would be thousands more coming in their wake, bringing all their belongings and tools and food and seeds for crops. Coming back to their rightful land. The few thousands of years of their exile did not really matter much.

Naum was a colder place than the realms, and it was taking his folk time to realize that. Some still clung obstinately to their thick leathers and furs and sweated heavily in the early summer heat. Others had adapted to the climate, enjoying the sun, exploring the nature.

One of the lookouts spotted him. Calemore was still too far to see clearly, but he knew his cloak gave him away. The lookout whistled, and the camp began transforming. It was as if a gust of wind whipped against forest-floor litter. It shifted, rippled, tiny branches and dried leaves flying.

A collective breath of anticipation and well-practiced fear rolled through the human mass of his followers. Men abandoned their tasks and leisure and snapped to attention before their undisputed master, before their almost deity. Well, for them, he was a god. In every way that mattered.

Calemore's boots crunched over the summer grass in an unnamed valley in the far reaches of the realm called Caytor. He wondered if this region had ever seen a city official come to collect taxes or remind people of their allegiance. South, he had seen a few remote villages, but it was quiet and peaceful and wild in these northern reaches. Animals naturally shied away from humans, but here, they did not have that victim-like behavior like their kin that got them hunted and killed elsewhere. Calemore glimpsed a wolf staring at him from the fringe of a birch forest to the left, its shaggy head almost hidden among the ferns. There was a glint in those eyes, a glint he could admire. Their gazes locked. Calemore blinked. The wolf turned and fled, smart animal.

As he came closer, the soldiers and craftsmen went prostrate. For a tiniest moment, he was surprised by their reaction. He had gotten so used to the nonchalant ignorance of the people of the realms that he had forgotten the abject terror he inspired in his followers.

The fear spread around him in a wave as his troops stopped their lives to acknowledge his arrival. Calemore walked with the bloodstaff in his hand. Younger men had never seen that weapon, not since he had given it to Damian's avatar all those years back, but the fathers and grandfathers in the lot sure remembered. He saw their faces contort, and their expressions pleased him.

He plowed on, and men slithered from his path, almost like ants, crab walking backward on all fours. Calemore let his pale eyes wander over the massive camp, inspecting the order, the readiness. He had not intended to bring the people of Naum to the realms, but it seemed he had to replay the old war to the very last detail, unfortunately. His desire to become a god, *the* god, would not be achieved through peaceful means. He was being forced to exterminate the inhabitants of the Old Lands. He had wished to have their faith and fear, but some things just weren't meant to happen.

There were two armies of Naum marching, converging. This eastern force was going to strike into Caytor. The other one was advancing through Eracia. They would meet in the Safe Territories. By then, Calemore intended to see the one surviving deity killed. If not, the force would move farther south and destroy the third realm. A simple, brutal plan.

In the last war, a similar initiative had failed him. This time, his chances were much better. His enemy was weak, fragmented. His enemy had no magical weapons, few or no Special Children, no recollection of the events of the old war. It would come down to simple brute strength, and for that task, his slave nation was most perfectly suited.

He stopped where he deemed to be the center of this chaotic hive. He gestured, and the men slowly rose, their clothes and weapons and tools creaking and clanging. It sounded like a hill stretching its bones. Not a single pair of eyes in that crowd would meet his. He almost challenged them, but it would be pointless. Tradition was such a beautiful motivator.

He waited until the news of his arrival spread and the leaders of the force were found. Soon enough, the throng parted to let the elders of the tribes come forward. They looked extremely apprehensive. They had not seen him for a few years now, ever since he'd left to complete his father's treacherous affair, and they did not know what to expect. Even though they had prepared all their lives for the march south, the reality of being right there, right then stunned them.

Calemore did not know their names. He did not have to. Whatever he ordered always got done, quickly, with precision, blindly followed. After spending his time with Nigella, he found the notion of such devotion boring. The emotional struggle and all the little doubts were so much more fun.

The most senior elder knelt before him, bowing his head. "We await your mercy."

Calemore was not in the mood for rituals. "You are here. Good. Now, you must proceed south and destroy the people of the Old Land. Just kill them." He raised his hand. "But you will not harm my plaything or her child." Was that what Nigella was, a plaything? Wasn't she?

"How will we know her?" the elder whispered.

Calemore grinned. "I have marked her, and her son. Not only will you keep her safe, you will provide her with whatever she needs. She will be allowed to do as she pleases and go where she pleases. You will give her anything she wants. If she asks you for the hide off your bones, you will give it to her."

The elder nodded. Around him, other tribe leaders imitated the gesture. It wasn't much to ask of them. For someone who knew nothing about free choice, the sacrifice was meaningless. He felt disappointed. The taint of a bespectacled woman and her big teeth was coursing through his veins.

His eyes roamed. "Have you agreed on the division of land?"

"We have," another elder replied. "We have marked the territory for our tribes."

"Good." Calemore did not want his conquest to go sour when his followers decided to bicker over the ownership of captured villages and fields. They might be his nation, but they were still humans, brimming with jealousy, greed, and pettiness.

He noticed an extended hand holding a small, bulging cloth satchel, slightly trembling from the weight of what was inside. Calemore accepted it, undid the knot, and pinched some of the contents between his fingers. It was fine-grained dust, made from the crushed stone of the dead magical barrier markers he had once erected to keep himself safe. A symbol of his strength, vanity, defeat, and patience. He upended the satchel, and the dust winnowed out, blown into the pale, hard faces of his elders. They squinted and wrinkled their noses, but said nothing.

He had made so many mistakes in the war against the gods. He had made so many mistakes in the last century of human life, ever since the Veil of Sundering had come down. He had invested too much trust in his father, not wanting to believe Damian would be willing to risk his own freedom, his life, so he could defeat Calemore. That Feoran revolution; that Adam person; all of it; silly, stupid mistakes.

This time, he would make sure there were no mistakes.

A loud rumble scattered his thoughts. It took him a moment to realize what it was. Thunder. He glanced up. The summer sky was dappled with low clouds, some of them streaked with slate gray, scudding on high winds. He thought he saw a patch of brilliant white bloom inside one of those puffy sky turds. Soon enough, a mockery of a rain erupted, brief and hot. Thick drops slammed the earth, few, heavy, random, and then the rain stopped altogether. No honest Old Land farmer would bless that piss trickle.

However, there was a gasp of delight and wonder in the crowd around him. Calemore remembered his first rain after thousands of years of isolation. None of his men had ever seen precipitation other than snow and ice. For them, this was almost a miracle. He let the cheers continue unabated, let them indulge in a moment of almost childish joy.

I am getting too soft for my own good, he thought. Nigella was poisoning his mind, for sure. Then again, maybe softness was what he needed to win his campaign. His cruelty had not seen him victorious all those centuries back. Perhaps he needed guile and restraint more than he needed butchery. He stroked the smooth, cool length of fused rock-hard glass that made the rod that was the bloodstaff. On the other hand, he yearned to use the weapon in large-scale combat. He wanted to level towns and destroy entire armies with its magical power. He lusted for it. After so long, he deserved some revenge.

His men were still marveling at the rain, holding their hands like supplicants, watching the drops shine and dry on their skin. Others were peering up close at the wet grass or slicked armor, staring like a cruel child might ogle an insect, wondering which of the many legs to pull out first.

Calemore let the moment stretch a while longer. "I am heading south now. You will begin the march first thing come the dawn. Kill everyone."

"We will," the senior agreed.

The White Witch did not wait. He retraced his steps and left the camp. He walked for almost a mile, thinking about the war, about Nigella, about what he must do to become a god. He was so close to achieving his dream it was maddening.

What then? he wondered. What would he do once he won?

He really should not be fretting and worrying. It did not become him. He was beyond human doubt. His moment of weakness annoyed him. At that instant, he wished he were with Nigella, so he could tell *her* what he felt, share his thoughts with her. He wanted to see the expression on her ugly face when she tried to figure out a truth that was beyond her, to understand the enormity of his being. He wanted to know what she had read in the book, and he wanted to feel her body squirm under him.

Most peasants and town clerks had similar passions, he figured. That was a disturbing notion.

Gripping the bloodstaff hard for reassurance, he walked some more, until he got bored. Then he magicked himself to Marlheim, where he knew a hot apple pie and a willing female body would be waiting for him.

CHAPTER 1

Stephan had always considered himself a man with a hunch for bets. Most of the time, he knew a good deal when he saw it. Now, though, he was completely out of his depth.

The High Council meeting was taking place in the office of the shipwrights guild rather than the official headquarters on Gunter's Road. The main reason was the dispute between the dockworkers and the spice traders. It had all started when one of the laborers dropped a cask of saffron into the filthy water of the bay, to much dismay of everyone involved. The shipmaster had been furious, and had the worker whipped, but he had turned livid when the traders demanded he compensate their loss. It had soon bubbled into an insurance blister, and a fight broke out, fists flying, noses bleeding. The dockworkers were demanding protection and higher wages, shipowners refused to be accountable for lost profits when at anchor in large city ports, and the merchants wanted everyone to pay through their noses.

But that discourse was long over.

With the grumbling parties gone, the remaining councillors sat to discuss an even more delicate matter, one that involved pretty much everything.

The fragile political situation in Caytor.

Stephan was holding a letter in his hand, written by Master Sebastian. It informed the High Council of several worrying developments. There was open war between the Parusites and Athesians once again. Emperor James was dead. Lady Rheanna had been detained. It smelled like a disaster.

Stephan had missed most of the intrigue while locked up in Roalas, but he had quickly caught up on all the little plots and schemes and secret deals hammered out during his captivity. He still marveled at the audacity and stupidity of some of his colleagues and wondered what they had intended—and still probably did intend—to achieve.

He looked at the faces round the table, pale, calculating. They didn't like this any better than he did. Most of them had seen at least one of their friends die championing the wrong side. Others had sponsored pretenders for the Athesian throne and were still licking their wounds. Stephan's friend Robin had paid with his life for going over to James. For all practical purposes, the family estates of Councillors Otis and Melville now belonged to the miraculously resurrected Empress Amalia.

Stephan was almost glad to have her at the helm of the crumbling rebel force. Almost. He clearly remembered her conduct during the siege, her obstinate reasoning, and he wondered if she still remained as hard and unyielding as before. One thing was certain: she would have no reason to be friendly toward Caytor, not after supporting her half brother and so many imposters.

It was delicate. It was complicated. It didn't smell of roses.

"What do we do?" He asked the obvious, breaking the silence.

The silence simply flowed back, like mud. No one spoke. They were thinking, more than they had ever done in their lives as politicians, investors, or moneylenders. They were gambling their realm and the best of their fortunes. The past two years had not been favorable to them in any way. Virtually every little deal regarding Athesia had gone sour. Stephan was starting to believe it was a cursed land.

"We do nothing," Councillor Lamprecht said, biting on his pipe.

"Very easy for you to say that," Vareck objected. The man had traveled from Shurbalen for this assembly. He had been one of the strong supporters of Emperor James and was still trying to figure out what he should do with the troops and money he had sent west.

"A wise businessman knows when to cut his losses," Lamprecht countered, unfazed.

"Everything we do risks the peace with the Parusites," Uwe of the cartographers guild said, his fingers busy turning a gilt goblet, the foot making a raspy noise on the hardwood tabletop.

Councillor Doris sniffed, her face contorted with what looked like rage. Stephan did not blame her. She had lost her children to Parusite mercenaries. Ever since coming back, she had championed war against King Sergei. She simply would not relent, and she refused to go back to Monard.

Stephan knew he was among equals, but he felt he had a slight advantage in his favor. None of his hostage comrades had tried to negotiate their freedom or secure the peace. He had been the only one to engage the Athesian hosts in some kind of talks. This gave him a better understanding of what the empress was all about, and so he thought he should lead. Well, a man must not complain if a dire situation led him to fortune.

Only he did not express himself in so many words. His fellow councillors were difficult men and women, highly opinionated, arrogant, and very much displeased for having to count losses in their ledgers. "We should probably ask ourselves, what is it that we want?"

"Trade going back to what it was."

"Athesian land becoming Caytor once again."

"The Parusites must retreat to their own kingdom and stay there."

Stephan grimaced. "Unfortunately, I do not think it's that simple. We should probably contend with the fact King Sergei will not relinquish Athesia. That territory was lost to us twenty years ago." He snorted. "We haven't really ruled Roalas for the past forty."

"Lord Orson tells me the king hasn't accepted his claim for compensation," Vareck said, waving his hand. "It does not bode well for any future negotiation. We should expect no leeway from the Parusites."

"They should be thankful we didn't declare war after the Oth Danesh invasion!" Helmut shouted.

"Well, most of Empress Amalia's soldiers are Caytoreans, so as far as King Sergei is concerned, we probably did declare war." This was Uwe again. Next to him, the head of the glaziers guild was writing something, not really interested.

"What if the Parusites declare war against *us*?" Lamprecht suggested, knowing he was annoying his colleagues. But then, that was his style: cool, dismissive arrogance.

"They cannot," Desmond explained, almost sounding like a teacher. "The nobles have all returned home, and it will be months before the king may summon them again. King Sergei is heavily engaged with the Athesians, and he must not expose his western flank either. I heard he declined a peace offer by the Kataji, so *they* might decide to invade the Safe Territories, or worse."

"I would not worry about Eracians and the nomads right now," Vareck said.

"And I heard," Desmond plowed on, "the king's got rebellion in Pain Mave."

Councillor Evert snorted. "That place was ever a hotbed."

Stephan raised a hand. Too many people were talking, not listening to the others. A typical meeting, except they were discussing the fate of the realm.

"If we go to war," he spoke bluntly, grabbing their attention, "we need armies."

"More losses," Lamprecht teased, clamping his teeth round the bitten end of his pipe.

"If we do not go to war," Doris hissed, "we remain the laughingstock of this nation, of the whole of the realms. There isn't a single brave thing this council has done in the last forty years, ever since the Feoran uprising. We let them take over the countryside. Then Emperor Adam came, and we let him steal our land and people. We let his *son* do the same. No, we invited him! King Sergei unleashed his barbarians into our cities, and we still did nothing. Now, Empress Amalia has detained one of our own, *again*, and we fear displeasing her."

"I am worried about the fate of Lady Rheanna," Stephan agreed.

"She made her choice," Lamprecht said. At that moment, Stephan so much wanted to plow a fist into those yellowing teeth.

"Technically, she is entitled to Athesian lands. Once she married the emperor, the ownership of Athesian lands became hers, too. Now, rightfully, the throne belongs to her, not Amalia." Evert poured himself sherry from a crystal carafe.

Stephan rolled his eyes. This could become a dangerous discussion. He did not want anyone trying to champion

Rheanna's claim for the Athesian throne. That would be political suicide. The very fact the High Council had tried to use Adam's bastard against his legitimate daughter as leverage over future negotiations and demands was justification enough for Amalia to decide she was better off just sending Rheanna's pickled head to Eybalen.

"So we are in agreement then," Lamprecht said, annoying fucker, spanking the table with his hand.

"Please," Stephan said, trying to sound polite. "You're not helping."

Evert pointed at the few ladies in the crowd. "Any businessman must ask himself, or herself, how they can make the best from a situation. *Any* situation. Like during a ball or a large party, toward the end of the evening, when you see a beautiful woman puking excess food and drink quietly in a corner, do you help her, or do you cup a teat when she's defenseless?"

There was a sigh of indignation among the ladies. Doris narrowed her eyes. If looks could kill, she would be skinning the pig now.

"Thank you for that lovely metaphor," Stephan said dryly. "Ever a charmer."

Evert nodded, ignoring the women around him. Some people simply refused to consider the problem seriously. But then, their assets were safe, and they had not spent a year as hostages, wondering if they might die the next morning.

"Things are just happening too rapidly," Uwe said. "Our old allies and enemies are dying like flies. I hear Duke Vincent was assassinated. A rather tricky predicament. Whoever we try to negotiate with might end up dead the next morning. This presents us with a problem. We need to be sure we have a reliable partner who will live on to see their end of the bargain upheld."

Yes, and Commander Gerald is dead, too, Stephan thought. Just a few more months of siege, he could have hammered out a peace, a solid, lasting, favorable peace.

From what reports and rumors Stephan had, King Sergei refused to talk to the Caytoreans. His sister, Sasha was a lunatic. Amalia…no one really knew what she might do now.

But he had not told the assembled council the most worrying part yet.

"If Lady Rheanna meets an untimely end…" Evert's tone was pragmatic. "What do we do with her assets? Do we proclaim her a traitor and seize them?"

"That would be prudent," Lamprecht agreed.

Stephan raked his hair. He was feeling desperate. "Our concern should be seeing Lady Rheanna released safely." He knew he sounded like a hypocrite, but what else could he say?

"The key to this conundrum is King Sergei," Uwe pointed out.

"He does seem inclined toward peace, it's fair to say. After all, he released all of you when he could have easily kept you hostage, or worse." Councillor Baldric stabbed a very pointed stare at Stephan, as if this was all somehow his doing.

"We need to decide what we want," Stephan insisted. "Does the council favor the restoration of Athesian land to Caytor? Or do we agree that we seek peace and trade only? We can then sort all the other details more easily."

"As long as we remain undecided, we won't win any favor with either the Parusites or Athesians." Doris rallied. "Our inaction suits them both. While we may argue about Amalia or James and what they did, they have a much better claim than King Sergei. One thing is certain, Roalas was never Parusite territory."

Stephan breathed into his palm, thinking. If it were that simple for his colleagues to agree on a common cause, there would be no point in having the council, now would it? He tried to imagine what would happen if the High Council threw its support behind Amalia. Or maybe the king. What would happen then?

In a deep corner of his soul, he felt he should be grateful for being alive today, and that gratitude belonged to the Parusite ruler. But there was another corner, soaked in bitterness and national pride, bemoaning decades of humiliation. It went back to Adam, the man who had affirmed the reality of defeat with the Eracians and Caytoreans. The only question was, were they willing to accept it and move on toward a brighter future?

"If we assume we never get Athesia back," he began.

"That land is rightfully ours," Lamprecht goaded.

"If we assume that, then we must ask ourselves, who do we prefer at the throne? Adam's daughter? Or the Parusite king? Do we want religion back in the lives of the small folk?"

Doris squirmed. "The Parusites must not be allowed to control Athesia."

"How can we oppose them?" Uwe again.

"We recruit armies. Simple." Helmut was standing now, drawing attention to his fat bulk.

"Even the simple threat of our intervention could swing the situation in our favor," Desmond said. "The Parusite king relies on our neutrality to complete his conquest. Once he has the whole of Athesia in his hands, we will be facing a much bigger problem."

"We must try to save Lady Rheanna," Stephan told them. "She is the only one among us who managed to gain the upper hand with Emperor James. Otis and Melville tried coercion and trickery, and they paid with their lives. Perhaps we could convince Amalia that she poses no threat. Perhaps Rheanna might give up her claim to the throne in return for her freedom. We might forge an alliance with the Athesians. That way, we could legitimize all the fighting our troops are waging against the Parusites, Athesia becomes our protectorate, so we get our lands back, and that way, we gain power to threaten King Sergei." *And we best the Eracians,* he did not add.

"Will Sebastian support us?" Evert voiced. He was drinking his third cup that morning.

That was a difficult question. The last thing anyone needed was a division between the Caytoreans. But then, it had already started two years back.

Empress Amalia was probably facing the same problem he was, wondering who among her followers might choose greed over loyalty, who might decide that warring was too risky and just go back to being a loyal Caytorean once again. Stephan sure did not favor an outright war, like Doris, but he knew that weakness and indecision would keep Caytor on the losing end against King Sergei.

Recruiting fresh private armies might make sense, too, but paid soldiers were almost always a bad investment. The High Council still had a lot of wealth, but it was draining quickly now that the roads west were closed. Peace in Athesia was imperative. Stephan wished he had Adam for his enemy. The one man who had turned the gangrene in Somar and Eybalen to everyone's prosperity. Now, there was a bunch of crows, fighting over the rotten leftovers.

He looked at his comrades. They all waged their own personal wars; they all had their hidden motives. He would not put it past some of them to have engaged in secret negotiations with this or that ruler. They had plotted against Adam, tried to rally imposters against his bastard. Bloody Abyss, James himself had almost been an imposter.

Stephan didn't like the fact they would have to face Amalia. Women were difficult. The young empress had seen her little empire destroyed, and still wouldn't budge. He had no idea how her defeat might have changed her, but he did not expect any miracles.

Rheanna's plan had been genius. She had gone for the simplest solution of all, marriage. Empress Amalia remained without a husband, and that made her extremely vulnerable and yet immensely powerful. She could easily offer her maidenhood to any of the three realms and see them fight for the privilege. Reconcile with Sergei, marry one of his surviving sons? Reconcile with Eracia, find a suitable noble? Among those who still lived, that was. Offer herself to the High Council?

Who might be a lucky candidate?

A name popped into his head.

Now, if he could somehow convince his fellow councillors that it was the sensible thing to do. He doubted they would sympathize with his logic and ambitions. They all wanted to get richer and more powerful the next summer. That was the one thing that had never changed. Neither the Feoran Movement, nor Emperor Adam, nor all the wars had ever affected that.

Lady Rheanna herself was a valuable asset, but what she stood for was even more critical. If she died, there could be no peace with Athesia. If Amalia killed her, the High Council would be forced to side with King Sergei. No one wanted that. For generations, the religious fools had kept to themselves in their sunny south. Their presence in the heart of the realms threatened everything.

There would be a new civil war, Stephan knew. He just knew. The mercenaries serving Amalia would turn against one another, switching sides as this or that Caytorean paid for their services. The councillors would be forced to commence on a journey of assassinations to keep their agenda afloat. After last year's dreadful experience with the imposters, Stephan could only imagine the magnitude of terror that would gush through Eybalen and other cities.

Lady Rheanna had to live, if only because she symbolized hope for profit.

We take a stance, for a change, he mused. *We go against the Parusites.* Not a pleasant prospect, but then, war never was. Only, for once, Caytor might actually come out as a winner. They had desperately avoided confronting their foes, one after one, and kept losing. This time, it could be different.

He had a plan. He had a scapegoat. What he needed to do was convince his colleagues to cooperate.

Then, a more troubling thought bloomed in his mind. If the empress somehow miraculously agreed to release her hostage, something she had refused to do the last time, what kind of reaction should he expect from Lady Rheanna? Would she be willing to forget the slight? Business as usual? For that matter, few of the nobles released from Roalas had any great love for King Sergei. In fact, most resented him, if only because he stood for something they never would. Worse, women were not as simple as men. They might take this kind of thing *personally*.

The potential for catastrophe was immense. Two women, both with a taste for power, both sniffing round the title of "empress" like hungry dogs. Oh, there was not a bard in Eybalen who could put it in words.

I am the bravest man in the realm, he thought. Because he was going to risk his body and mind and soul for the sake of national prosperity. And his own, of course.

"I might have a solution…" he told the council.

CHAPTER 2

Pacmad stood on the table, holding the shrieking baby above his head. "I have another son!"

The crowd of his tribesmen exploded in a wild, loud cheer. Sonya had to cover her ears to numb the pain of their deafening roar.

Her captor handed the child back to its mother, then hopped down, shaking hands with his warriors. A very emotional display for such a primitive race, Sonya thought. Men ought to be aloof and distant from birth affairs, but she could understand Pacmad's savage pride, even if it concerned yet another bastard, born to a lowly Eracian woman.

Seeing the Father of the Bear gloat over his offspring did not bring her joy. That was her weakness right there, the inability to squeeze babies out from between her legs. Every one born was a potential enemy, one that might interfere with her plans. But a frown similar to hers creased the face of Baroness Richelle, and that *did* bring her joy.

The whore had given birth to a girl. Pacmad had been visibly disappointed, Sonya markedly relieved. Her fear of becoming his second favorite at the court had come undone. Richelle might be a baby smithy, but she gave off rusty products. Like all stupid men, the nomads praised sons, always forgetting it was women who brought them into the world. Now, Pacmad might fuck the baroness again and again, until she whelped him a son, but that gave Sonya enough time to plan and prepare.

Any day now, she hoped, any day now.

The feast began. Sonya moved to her place by Pacmad's side. Two dozen Eracian women were serving food, moving gingerly about the already drunken crowd of nomad warriors, mindful of their ill tempers and groping hands. It was as if the siege around the city did not matter. Pacmad was celebrating the birth of his first Eracian bastard, and he would not let anything spoil his fun.

Sonya stabbed a quick look at the mother. Not a lady, even. Just some common slut, with a big nose on her silly red face. She seemed to be in shock, smiling inanely, probably wondering if the child offered her immunity against beatings or maybe promised her another hot meal or some trinket. Sonya had no idea who she was, and did not care. The woman was irrelevant, meaningless, a peon in a whole different game.

Sonya thought she should feel elated to have been allowed to sit by her captor. He had allowed no other woman nearby. For some reason, he had summoned her and placed her at the same table with his killers. A fleeting thought of a mass rape crossed her mind, but she quickly dismissed it.

Pacmad's eyes were glazed. Was he drunk? She doubted it. He must be pretending. For him, this celebration was all about asserting his power. But it also gave him a splendid opportunity to study his men at their weakest, when they were relaxed, fed, and inebriated.

Sonya realized she was biting her forefinger. She stopped. She was doing that too often lately, and her skin was callused.

"Something on your mind?" Pacmad asked her, looking at her from the corner of his eye.

She cursed herself silently. She could not lie now. "Yes."

He leaned on his right elbow, toward her. "What it is, tell me."

"I am worried about the siege." She stalled, confessing a different kind of truth.

Pacmad clapped his hands. This was a sign for the cooks to remove the crispy goat from the spit and start carving the meat. "Worried? Are you worried that I might win? Or that you might lose?"

The throne hall was unrecognizable, Sonya thought as she gazed around her. There was nothing familiar there. The space was crammed with tables and benches, filled with smelly nomads, the air filmy with soot and smoke from the fires. Once a symbol of national pride, it was now just a filthy altar where the Kataji chieftain humiliated the captive Eracians.

"I am worried that many innocents will die," she stated carefully.

Pacmad grinned mirthlessly. "If your women do their job, the city will stand." He shrugged with his left shoulder. "If they don't, they will die."

Sonya wondered when her brave husband might finally commence his assault against Somar. For the time being, he was tightening the siege, making sure not even a lone warrior could sneak out. The Kataji were completely isolated. Pacmad's efforts at negotiation had failed utterly. Even the promise of treason by some of the Eracian lackeys had borne no fruit. One day, Lord Rotger had simply vanished, never to return. Soon enough, three other traitors had stopped sending their information. The situation seemed rather hopeless for Pacmad. He was outnumbered, and he had a den of Eracian women as fickle allies in the siege. Only a real fool would trust them.

Food levels were still decent, but soon enough, they would run out. With this kind of celebration, sooner than later.

Yet, the general seemed unfazed. Either he was hiding his fear or he knew something else. That infuriated Sonya.

As a loyal wife, she had to assist her gallant husband any way she could. That meant planning patriotic sabotage for when the assault finally came. The city guilds and businesses were firmly behind her. Eracian pride be damned, they all had men to avenge. Pacmad's conquest was grinding to a bloody halt.

But the bastard was smiling, unconcerned, a mongrel.

Sonya was angry at herself for not knowing, angry for not being able to crack his secrets. Even now, after so many months of her most dedicated scheming, he still mistrusted her, still kept things from her, made sure she was jealous and misguided just enough so she could not hope to best him. Her best sex tricks didn't seem to work. Her utter dedication, almost beyond being just a mere act, didn't make much difference. Under any other circumstances, she would have felt privileged to have found such a man, one who truly deserved her respect.

As a soon-to-be queen, though, she was above such trifles. She had a duty to her nation.

Pacmad made a happy sound when a plump servant placed a large tin plate full of steaming goat before him. He picked the hot meat with his fingers, chewed loudly, studied her from the corner of his mongrel eye.

Sonya cracked a perfunctory smile when the woman placed her own portion before her. She picked up the knife and fork and sliced a thin cut.

Pacmad drummed his greasy fingers on the edge of the table. He was staring at her now. She could not read his gaze, and that frightened her a little. Always, always, there was that tiny seed of fear that he somehow knew what she planned, that he had discovered Bart's identity, that someone had told him about her plan. She never forgot he had Richelle and Aileen and all those other whores and that he might choose to replace her with one of them.

Finally, she had to admit, after a year of life-and-death scheming, she was getting a little tired. She could feel the end of it, the day Bart defeated Pacmad, and that hope made her nervous and weak.

"I haven't seen a report on the city's readiness yet," he said in between mouthfuls. There was a thread of muscle or sinew stuck to one of his teeth, and he didn't bother removing it.

So, this was a business meeting after all, she thought. He had not summoned her to partake in the celebration, it seemed. He was torturing her, ever so gently, and this new setting gave him a fresh opportunity. She had to be careful. There were eyes upon her, hundreds of them, women of the city among them. Like her, they had been beaten and raped, but they didn't get to feast with Pacmad. They only had their pain and sorrow. Turning against her could give them respite from their misery. Out of pure envy. Or just simple pettiness.

Ever since receiving Bart's letter, Sonya had made sure she was nice to the other women. They could betray her, and there was no reason to encourage them. Clerks, cooks, even maidservants, each one might choose to give her away, for a favor or out of malice. Sonya had even found a gift or two for Janice, to keep the stupid little bitch appeased.

The worst part was, women had intuition. They could smell something was wrong. All those whores might decide to interpret Sonya's reactions or even facial expressions as a sign of weakness and then use it against her.

Charming Pacmad with his cock in her warm palms, in the privacy of her chambers, was one thing. In public, she was exposed, vulnerable.

She had the numbers imprinted in her mind. "The artisan workshops promise ten new blades and twenty spears every day. The fletchers have over nine thousand arrowheads to deliver. The gates have been strengthened, too."

Pacmad grabbed a pickled onion from a platter and bit into it, juice running down his chin and dripping onto his tunic. "Majestic. How their hearts have turned."

Sonya did not comment. Anything she said would just be wrong. Her plans had to be flawless; they had to be. If not, then she truly didn't deserve to be the queen of her nation.

There was music in the hall, too. Men were sort of dancing, a tipsy gait and flailing of limbs punctuated by grunts and laughter. There were several instruments playing, bags and pipes and strings, each hooting a melody of its own. It sounded chaotic.

Sonya noticed the chair to the left of Pacmad was empty. She didn't know why that was. Other warriors sat on both sides, busy talking and wolfing down meat, unconcerned with the vacant spot. Her tongue burned with a question, but she withheld it. She could not betray her curiosity. Whatever Pacmad did was significant, and soon enough she would learn. His lessons were simple and brutal.

The throne hall doors were closed, containing all that blue smoke within. Then, almost on cue, they opened, and the haze swirled. There was a definite change in the atmosphere. Men stopped making silly noise, their throats turning soft with hums and sighs of wonder. The pipes went silent, too. Sonya frowned. What was that?

Pacmad kept eating his onion, pointedly not looking at her now. Sonya brushed hair from her forehead, annoyed.

The crowd of killers parted, and Aileen came forward.

Aileen, Sonya thought with astonishment, her blood going cold.

Pacmad tossed the half-eaten bulb on the table, leaned back, and burped, a speck flying from his lips. "Aileen, join me," he said nonchalantly.

The young woman was dressed in a thin, sheer gown. White lace and silk and gauze, with a touch of silver. It was a beautiful dress, and it fit her young form all too well. She looked breathtaking and very much half Sonya's age. There was not a single bruise on her face, not a single tear on her cheeks. She looked serene, maybe even content, her eyes were clear and free of pain, and she walked steadily toward Pacmad's side. Eagerly even.

Whore, bitch, slut, Sonya thought. She realized she was gripping the handle of the carving knife too damn hard. Gently, she released her grip, pretending nothing had happened.

Aileen weaved past the slobbering fools and murderers and sat by General Pacmad, opposite Sonya. The chieftain leaned toward her and whispered something. Aileen chuckled. Sonya was forgotten in that moment, forgotten, abandoned, betrayed.

One ugly surprise after another, she thought sourly, all her appetite gone. That little bitch used to cry when he raped her, and now this! What kind of foul trickery was this?

Pacmad spun around quickly. Sonya almost flinched. She thought she saw pure delight cross his features before he made them mellow again, as mellow as his brutal lines could be. "Richelle disappointed me. She told me she would give me a son, but she didn't. Aileen here"—he probed behind him and put a meaty hand on the girl's thigh, not even bothering to look—"she will give me sons. Won't you, Aileen?"

"I will," the little slut said happily.

How do you fight someone half your age and with a healthy womb, Sonya wondered. *With murder,* her mind replied. Her thoughts were dark, thick, gooey, like gelid winter ink. She had never wanted to kill someone so badly. Rip open the girl's stomach and tear out her woman's parts while she watched and screamed and begged. Whore.

She had not expected this. Oh, she had not expected this.

Pacmad dug a finger in his nose, came out with a nugget, and flicked it across the table. It landed in someone's broth, but the warrior didn't notice. "I want you to teach Aileen city business," he ordered.

Sonya kept her lips pressed tightly, making sure no froth of indignation and rage escaped. She had to be careful what she said now. "Trade?" she managed eventually.

The chieftain gestured vaguely. "Everything."

Aileen looked past the man's shoulder. What was that? Sonya did not quite catch that glance, but she remembered holding the girl's hand with Pacmad grunting on top of her.

I misjudged, Sonya thought, on the verge of crying.

There was a sudden commotion in the hall. Several men had cornered one of the serving women. She was trying to fight them off, begging, but they just laughed and hollered. Not quite a rape yet, but close enough.

Suddenly, it was too much. Sonya recalled the day Leopold was killed. She recalled her own violation. Bile rose in her throat, and she gagged, and retched on her plate. Pacmad made a grim face, but that did not stop him eating more meat.

"I'm sorry," Sonya confessed, feeling weak, old, and defeated.

"Something you ate?" he asked casually.

"Maybe she's with a baby?" Aileen supplied happily, her face alight with sincere hope.

Pacmad raised his brows, then shook his head. "Nah. Pregnant women puke only in the morning, I was told."

Sonya wiped her mouth. She drank some wine and sloshed it in her mouth, trying to wash away the acid taste. The fumes rose in the back of her throat, numbing her panic just a little. "Too much smoke," she heard herself say.

The Father of the Bear pursed his lips, looking disinterested. "You have my permission to leave. Go out, breathe some fresh air."

Sonya wanted to tell him she would stay, even if she coughed blood, because she did not dare miss this cruel manipulation. Instead, she nodded, rose, and shuffled out of the hall, surrounded by wild mirth and singing and the soft whimpers of the maid getting raped under a table.

The cool evening summer air slammed her in the chest like a mace. She almost gasped. The stars in the sky turned blurry. No, no, no. She was not going to cry. She was not going to cry. Queens did not cry.

There were dozens of Kataji troops walking about, slightly resentful for being on duty this night, chatting, talking about their simple lives and ambitions, talking about women, food, and battles. Some were gambling. Others were retracing their steps in silence, counting off the minutes till the next shift.

Sonya found herself on a city street, free to roam, free to go anywhere she wanted. With the siege so tightly in place, and the gates shut and chained, Pacmad no longer feared to let his captive women wander about freely. He knew they had nowhere to go. That was a part of it.

The other part was, caged animals never wanted to leave their prisons. They felt safe and sheltered inside. Sonya knew she could run away and hide in a cellar until the war ended. But she could not do it. Not really. The fear of being found and punished was unimaginable. The ever-so-slight doubt of Eracian defeat gripped her soul, an invisible, ghostly tendril. She knew that as long as Pacmad lived, she would never be truly free.

Pacmad had broken her.

She stood there for a while, breathing hard. Slowly, her pain receded, leaving her numb and weary. She wiped the tears that had somehow budded on her eyelashes. She was the realm's queen. Her noble, brave, loving husband was out there, and he was going to save her.

If things were easy, any fool could have done them, she thought. *This task has befallen me, because no one else has the wit and courage to do it. No one. You alone can save Somar, and you must endure the suffering and mockery and all the lies and threats.*

Aileen was a dreadful enemy. Pacmad was smart and ruthless. She would never deny that. He was maybe the smartest man she had ever met. But that was no reason to admit defeat. She could not stop now just because she faced a terrible challenge, a great obstacle.

Get a grip on yourself. You're behaving like one of those whores, she berated herself. *This is unfitting the queen that you are. What would Bart think if he saw you like this?*

She had to be pragmatic. She could never fight age, or the childhood disease that had left her barren. She could never change that. But she had other weapons. She was much, much smarter than Aileen, vastly more experienced and ruthless. The little whore might have a tender, soft pink treasure between her legs, but she knew nothing about court, manipulation, extortion, negotiations.

This is a great opportunity, she tried to convince herself. Pacmad had asked her to take Aileen under her wing and teach her. Mold her. Influence her. In fact, Sonya would have great power over the young cunt. She would be able to steer her in any which direction she wanted, maybe even turn her against the mongrel. Yes, that was it. This was a golden opportunity. Maybe alone she could not defeat Pacmad, but if she had Aileen at her side, even as her unwilling ally, she might actually gain so much more than by acting alone. Pacmad expected deceit and lies from her. He would not expect them from that whore.

Sonya had no idea how much time had passed when she got back in the hall. By then, her cheeks were dry and soft, and her eyes failed to register the fate of several other serving women. They were not her concern right now. Her eyes were locked on Aileen. Her target, her insider. The key to Pacmad's soul. Perhaps through his loins, but still.

This was how a proper queen behaved. This was how a queen took initiative and led, unafraid, undaunted.

Pacmad's eyes narrowed when he saw her enter. He seemed to sense a change in her, but she gave him no chance to explore it further. She grabbed a pitcher of wine and poured herself a cup, one, two, three, drinking happily, pretending to enjoy the birth of another bastard son. With each swallow, it became easier, this pretending, and her darkest thoughts sank deeper, away from Pacmad's prying questions and his penetrating blue gaze. He would never know now.

Tomorrow, she would teach Aileen all about trade. Tomorrow, she would teach the little whore about manipulation. Everything she knew. Everything.

CHAPTER 3

Tanid watched with serene delight as the carts entered the enclosure of his camp. Two families with all their belongings piled in the backs of those wagons, one driven by an old ox, the other by a pair of mules. Children stared at this new world of theirs, eyes big as coins.

Followers came forward to greet the newcomers, the latest pilgrims to join the holy site outside Keron. The rumor of a pious man assembling his own sect was no longer a rumor; it was a hard, solid truth. From all corners of the Old Land, people were flocking to him, disillusioned by war and the empty promises of their rulers. Even in the Safe Territories, some felt they might be better off seeking this religious figure and asking for his blessing. Tanid could not be more pleased.

The Army of the One God counted tens of thousands of souls now, and for the first time in twenty human years, Tanid felt confident. He had a vast, powerful human shield around him.

The small camp had grown, spread, become alive. It was a self-feeding, self-sustaining entity, with men and women growing crops, carpenters building houses, pens for animals, and low sheds where meat could be smoked and cured. They had a palisade, and watchtowers, three wells, and a dozen temples now. The people of Keron often came to trade their goods with Tanid's followers, and sometimes, they stayed, charmed by the mystical, spiritual power of this place.

Tanid had never intended to make himself so visible, so exposed, but it just happened. Well, he was the one surviving god, the god of all, and he understood why people would be drawn to his divine presence. Even if their minds did not know it, their souls felt the ancient magical bond with their creator. It was only natural.

Power begot problems, complications, though. The presence of thirty thousand people outside a town that housed less than half that created a dangerous imbalance. So far, the Parusite king had not challenged him, but his clerks came and went, examining the place, talking to merchants and peddlers and chatty women, writing down reports. Army patrols were often seen trudging down the dusty lanes and through fields surrounding his camp, keeping a close eye on the size and might of the strange faction growing like a wet blister just outside Keron.

Tanid was no fool. He knew he would have to confront— no, talk to—King Sergei, explain the situation, explain the presence of all these people. The camp posed a problem. It choked a trade line but paid no taxes to the crown; it drew away the labor force from other corners of the realm, attracted foreigners who did not swear fealty to the throne in Sigurd. He would understand if the Parusite ruler decided Tanid's holy congregation was a menace, a threat of some sort. Luckily, for now, the king stayed any kind of judgment or action. And that in itself was also quite worrying. But deep down, Tanid was glad for the extra days and weeks, because he still did not feel ready to engage King Sergei. Would the man believe him? Would he be willing to listen? Accept the crazy story of a terrible threat looming over the Old Land? How could he convince the man that peace and unity among all the people who followed the gods and goddesses, who followed him, was imperative?

Tanid did his best to appease the royal spies and soldiers. He made sure no flags were raised, no uniforms sewn, and no songs chanted. He kept his identity as vague as possible. He made sure his speeches focused only on religion, love, and tolerance. He could not allow his good intentions to be misconstrued as a rebellion. There was enough damage as it was. The camp was a big, fat tick, slurping blood from the Athesian countryside, encroaching on new pasture and conquering new hillocks, where fresh timber houses and mills would soon grow.

Tanid wished he could have cooperated with the patriarchs and matriarchs, made his rise to power official. But that just wasn't possible. The world was not ready to acknowledge the presence of a god in its midst, and no matter how much time he spent thinking, pondering, trying to devise some way of making the truth known, he always ended with a bloody disaster smeared across his thoughts.

Well, today was somewhat different.

He saw Ludevit coming toward him. The man walked with a hunch, looking ever so slightly tensed. Tanid skipped a beat. Was there any danger about? For an instant, he felt like a fawn in an open field, exposed.

The other man just shook his head. No danger. Tanid relaxed slightly.

"Your Holiness," Bad Luck Ludevit said, "the priests have arrived."

"Thank you, son," Tanid said. He had avoided the clergy for so many years. He could not anymore. The moment of reckoning was upon him. King Sergei might not be paying much attention to him, but his patriarchs sure were. "Bring them to me."

"Here, in the open?"

Tanid pointed toward the old barn, the heart of the camp. It had become a shrine, and men and women prayed there all the time, feeding him with vital energy. The war with Calemore was coming, and he needed every ounce of it.

He did not expect trouble from the priests, but still he summoned Pasha. The boy might not be the brightest one, but he was shy and quiet, and that made him a perfect companion during discreet meetings. That, and his ability to stop swords and arrows with his flesh.

Soon enough, Ludevit came back, five men in tow behind him. The Special Child had an ax hanging from his waist now, and he did not appear a messenger of peace. Perhaps that was the wrong message to send, Tanid thought with some dismay.

The worshippers at the barn noticed something important was afoot. Quietly, they laid down their offerings and retreated, every last one of them. Tanid was left alone, with an ungainly, indestructible youth for his bodyguard. The five patriarchs stopped some distance away, their faces unreadable.

Leading them was a fat man in a bright-orange gown. His fat bulged under his arms, round his waist, and the cloth was pinned between those big folds, making his torso outlined in clear detail. Sweat budded below his heavy, sagging breasts.

"Greetings," Tanid said amiably. His heart hammered like an entranced smith, banging away.

"I am Under-Patriarch Evgeny," the fat man boomed, his tone rather pleasant, but his eyes were hard. A big hand came forward, the five sausages attached to it wriggling with authority.

My first ordeal, Tanid thought. The patriarch expected him to kiss his hand, to kneel before him, to bow to his holiness, to yield. Tanid refused to do that. But then, he could not tell the man he was all of the gods these men prayed to.

Tanid licked his lips nervously, probably giving off a wrong impression. They were dry with anxiety. "I cannot do that, son," he said at length. "It would be inappropriate."

Under-Patriarch Evgeny retrieved his hand. His face remained impassive, but Tanid could feel ire emanating from his big body. "Some would call that blasphemy. Disrespect toward the gods and goddesses."

Tanid could not budge. "Some would. But they would be wrong. This is a holy place. This camp and all of its people have only one goal, to sustain the faith and praise the gods. We do not measure our love for gods in obedience." He gestured toward the barn's murky interior.

Evgeny looked behind him. "Stay here," he told his four brothers. One of them looked genuinely surprised.

Tanid entered first. Shafts of sunlight streaked between planks, coloring the clear brown interior with golden stripes. Bales of straw had long been cleared. Instead, the floor was covered in charms, gifts, offerings. There was even real gold somewhere there, but no one would dream of stealing it.

"Who are you?" the under-patriarch asked the moment they were alone.

Here it goes. Tanid turned slowly, as if nothing worried him. "My name is Gavril." That was a simple, honest name.

"And where do you come from?"

"The Territories," Tanid heard himself lie. He had practiced this for a long time.

"Why are you not a member of clergy? What is the meaning of all this?" Evgeny stepped forward. Tanid was almost alarmed, but Pasha was standing just behind the fat man, ready to protect him if needed.

"Faith does not require an institution," Tanid rebuked, trying to keep his voice flat. "Faith just requires passion and dedication and pure hearts. That is what we have here. This congregation is not meant to challenge the authority of the patriarchs and matriarchs. It does not diminish the importance of your work. It does not change anything, except give people hope and love. That's all."

Evgeny seemed to weigh that for a moment. "One cannot just claim to speak in the gods' and goddesses' names. That is not right. You must be trained properly. You must be enrolled in a monastery and choose your dedication."

Tanid pointed behind him. "All those men and women have come here because they need faith." He felt silly for apologizing before this priest, but then, he had never expected an encounter with the clergy to be pleasant. He was bracing for far worse.

The under-patriarch deflated suddenly, stepping back. "Religion must have rules, too. By creating this holy site, you have disrupted the normal course of things. Prayer is not a trifle. It must be observed carefully."

No, Tanid wanted to tell him. *Not at all. Any man giving his devotion to the gods feeds me with strength, anywhere, anytime. Shrines and monasteries are human things, meant to give shape to belief so it is not forgotten over the centuries.* "Why does my work bother you?"

The priest grimaced, his jowls inflating like a frog's. He sighed loudly. "Ever since the war against the Feorans, faith in the realms has been greatly weakened. Most of the Safe Territories have been razed, and we are still trying to rebuild all the houses of worship, with great difficulty. Our numbers are scant. Athesia is a godless place, and praise the gods that King Sergei conquered it. Neither the Eracians nor Caytoreans have much love for the gods left. It's only the Parusites who remain righteous." He paused, and then began pacing around Tanid, Pasha shadowing him.

"My brothers and I have worked very hard in trying to rebuild the faith. But the king's efforts are diverted elsewhere, and he does not have money or people to spare. He has stalled my efforts to form a combat clergy, and his contributions to the rebuilding of great monasteries have been…inadequate. I might almost be tempted to suspect he has a sinful agenda. And now this. Amid all our challenges, you have shown up, and you threaten our holy mission."

Tanid was not sure he followed the fat man's thoughts. "I do not understand."

Evgeny pointed in the same direction as Tanid, but his gesture felt greedy. "All those men could have been enlisted as servants of the gods and goddesses, replacing the decimated Outsiders. They could have formed the backbone of the combat clergy. Their donations could have paid for the new gilt roofing for the monastery in Jaruka. Instead, they are wasted here."

"They are not wasted," Tanid replied quietly.

"You are a man of faith?" Evgeny asked.

Tanid nodded.

"Good. But what if you suddenly decide to teach these people…*other* things? Make them believe in other gods. What then?"

Tanid felt as if someone had shone a torch down the dark mouth of a cave, exposing glittering gems embedded in the rock. He finally understood what the under-patriarch was telling him. He did not care anything about Tanid's mission. He cared about power.

Should he be disappointed? Surprised?

"I serve the gods and goddesses," Tanid spoke, trying to sound patient. "My love and dedication are not measured in gold coin or blocks of stone. Just faith, pure faith."

"Gavril," Evgeny chided, "some would say you're a heathen."

Tanid smiled. "I doubt it. All those people out there would disagree with you, son."

"You must address me as Your Holiness," Evgeny pointed out.

"You are equal before the gods and goddesses, like every-one else out there. Pasha?"

"Your Holiness?" the boy croaked, looking uncomfortable.

Evgeny spun, but then he realized the lad had addressed Tanid, not him. His eyes were flinty and sharp now. Fat men had an advantage when it came to hiding their expressions—all that lard covered their muscles, made their skin lax—but the priest could not fool Tanid.

"Holiness is achieved through devotion and sacrifice," Tanid lectured back. "I have earned it. The fact people are flock-ing to me, seeking guidance and redemption when they cannot find it elsewhere, in monasteries in the Safe Territories and other holy places, it tells me something. We follow the gods and goddesses, and nothing you may say will change it."

Under-Patriarch Evgeny was silent for a while. "All right, Gavril, *Your* Holiness, what do you want?"

Tanid tried to suppress his excitement. "I just wish faith to flourish. That is all."

Evgeny wagged a thick finger. "You must want something else."

The god realized the priest was trying to manipulate his defeat into an advantage, make it seem as if Tanid was the one with a hidden agenda. But it was Evgeny who had come to see him. "No, son, you tell me what you want."

Evgeny gestured largely. "I need soldiers. I want to establish a mighty army of faith. I want the combat clergy to rise once more, so it can defend the people from heathens and unbelievers everywhere. We must not allow a catastrophe like the Feoran scourge to ever happen again. We must be able to protect ourselves, to fight against those who would see the faith destroyed, whoever they are." *Much like you have been doing here,* his eyes whispered.

My turn, Tanid thought. The one thing he really needed, to convince King Sergei to seek peace with his enemies so they could unite under him, one god, against Calemore. "I must ask you to petition King Sergei on my behalf. I must see him."

"Why?" Evgeny did not seem to like this proposal.

"This is between me and the gods." Tanid held his gaze.

The priest snorted lightly. "You are a holy man with a mission then. Admirable. I must say I am surprised. I have not met many who claim to have talked to gods or goddesses. Most people hide such truths. We call them Special Children, and they are greatly valued in holy places. They help us in many things."

Tanid avoided looking at Pasha. He did not feel any magic coming from Evgeny, but he could not really know what the man was capable of. Just the fact he knew what Special Children were made him extremely dangerous. Which was why he had avoided the clergy for so long. "I must see the king," he insisted.

"Sure you must. But then, if you were inclined to show favor toward the patriarchs and matriarchs, we might help further your cause, holy man."

A fair compromise? Tanid wondered. Let himself be manipulated into a delicate alliance with these priests? But what other choice did he have? If he posed a threat to their status and power, he could not begin to imagine the danger he posed toward the king. He had no idea how the Parusite ruler might eventually react. He might even decide to unleash his army against him, and then, there would never be unity in the Old Lands against Calemore. He was not selfish enough to allow that. And he dreaded thinking of having to go to Roalas on his own. He still did not feel powerful enough to risk that.

"I could speak favorably in your honor. We could share resources."

Evgeny seemed to like that. "I will assign some of my brothers to serve with you."

No! Tanid breathed deeply. He had to agree. "They will not interfere." A warning and a question.

"We are united in our love of the gods and goddesses, are we not? We share a common cause."

"If you help me convince King Sergei of the urgency of my mission, I will allow some of my followers to go to the Safe Territories and join the ranks of your clergy, be they warriors or priests. And they will help rebuild the holy places, and some of the donations will go to the temples across the land." He caught himself in time, just before he blurted "Old Land." That would have betrayed him right there. *After the war with Calemore, after,* he wanted to add.

"They say a holy man is never poor or hungry, for he has faith," Evgeny intoned.

Tanid did not like the preaching. He was already thinking, hard and fast, about all the possibilities and risks. He was getting himself entangled with the patriarchs. That meant his true identity might be exposed, and what then?

He had to defeat Calemore. That was his real goal. He had to unite these people, to stop them from killing each other in trifling wars, to band their forces and march against the army of Naum. That was all that mattered. If they lost, neither the clergy, nor temples, nor anything else would make much difference.

"We must cooperate," Tanid said at length.

"Yes, we must," Evgeny agreed.

Tanid considered extending his hand, but stopped himself. Priests were not merchants, yet the similarity was uncanny. All of this was his fault, his and of his kin. Once he killed the White Witch, he would change everything.

The fat man retreated from the barn without another word, walking as if he had won a battle. Tanid felt a brief moment of relief, but it fluttered away quickly. The future was chaotic, boiling with uncertainty. He had just wed himself to the clergy. He had made himself vulnerable. He had promised some of his wealth and people when he could not afford to give any away. But it was a necessary sacrifice so he could convince the Parusite king of the real danger to the Old Land—the realms. King Sergei had the most powerful army, and his nation were true believers. Without them, the war would surely be lost. Even gods had to compromise sometimes.

CHAPTER 4

Amalia reached to her chipped ear, touching the corded tissue. Her hair had grown quite a bit recently, covering the ugly scar. She was beginning to look more like her old imperial self.

Her new diary sat open in front of her, its pages filled with blood. Written in ink, drenched in the blood of all those she had sent to their deaths in the past month. Her spring-cleaning was continuing well into the early, warm summer. A necessity. She did not wish to be remembered as a butcher, but she had no intention of making the same girlish mistakes of her past ever again. She was going to be her father's daughter in earnest this time.

She folded the booklet and stood up, stretching, looking around the office. Four men guarded her, trying to look inconspicuous, like ungainly, massive statues chucked into the corners of a room. Two of them were Athesians, the other two Caytoreans, Xavier's men. She could have objected to having them around, knowing all too well they spied on her for that pig-eyed killer, but she never did. They were a reminder of her delicate situation, of her fragile chances. Their presence kept her sharp.

Since James's Last Stand, the Parusites had kept to their barracks, and there had been no new attacks. The enemy must have been decimated just as badly. No one knew for certain the exact numbers, but the toll must have been heavy. The city folk had buried more than ten thousand female bodies in the days after the clash, left behind by the enemy. Soldiers told a rumor of Princess Sasha dying in battle, although she disbelieved it. Amalia did not have that much luck.

The war against the invaders had sort of simmered down, but she had another, more brutal one to fight. One for her own survival.

The army belonged to the warlord, really. Xavier may have helped put down rebellions against her, but she had no doubt he had carefully screened the legions, leaving alive those utterly loyal to him, indebted for having their lives spared. Amalia knew he controlled the officers, and their pay, and he could decide the troops were better off marching back to Caytor after all, if he wanted it. She had to be nice and cooperate.

Keep up her promise of marriage.

She had pushed that ugly deal deep into the recesseses of her soul, but she knew one day, he would demand that she live up to it. So far, she did not know how she might deny him. In a moment of weakness and panic, she had blindly agreed to his proposal. Sobered and more confident now, she cursed herself, but still couldn't think of a wise plan that would leave her army intact and, more importantly, her own head on her shoulders. Would Jarman protect her?

Only if she made peace with King Sergei. Another extortion.

What would Father do? she wondered. How would he handle these men?

She was an empress holding to the tatters of a realm, without a throne, without a proper court, with an army a third of its original size, and green boys for recruits. She had a murderer for a general, a man she loathed and despised and mistrusted to the bone; she had two Sirtai wizards for fickle allies, as long as she complied with their fabulous agenda. Once, long ago, in another lifetime, she had been surrounded by friends, and she had scorned them. Now she had to beg for alms from scum.

She flicked her fingers. "Summon Mayor Alistair. I wish to consult with him," she told Bella, her clerk.

"Right away, Your Highness." The girl put the tax reports on the desk and exited, one of the soldiers staring at her backside. Men just could not help themselves.

Amalia remained standing, thinking. Peace. Peace with the Parusites. Another promise. She had given her word to Jarman. Only she had not done anything yet, except try to solidify her brittle rule. How could she turn this ugly outcome to her advantage?

Ecol was a town recovering from major suffering. There were still hundreds of men in bed, healing slowly. The barracks did not have enough space to keep them all, so citizens had been asked to host them in their own homes in return for some extra flour and a few coppers. Depleted legions needed fresh fodder, and street corners had recruitment stalls side by side with food carts, calling upon Athesians to join the ranks. Amalia had been forced to reduce the allowed conscription age to just fourteen, and that meant most of her new soldiers were sniveling boys with smooth cheeks. True, war had also brought commerce and mercenaries. Word of her victory against the Parusites had made Ecol the bastion of hope, the symbol of resistance, and Athesians were flocking to her side, perhaps because they felt safer around a large army than elsewhere.

Master Guilliam was manufacturing Slicers as fast as he could. Ecol was halfway encircled in a stone palisade, with a row of sharp stakes facing outward. The mines had been reopened, used for ore and masonry, and the builders were hard at work making the abandoned manor house habitable again. Once they refurbished it, it was to become her temporary palace. Not a lot of peaceful gestures, but she did not intend to have to face the Parusite onslaught and their gray monsters without some siege works. Towers, ditches, she would have them all.

Ecol could not fall. If it did, it would be the end of Athesia. It would mean her death. She understood it.

There was a gentle knock on the door. "Enter," she said. Amalia expected the mayor to show his eager face. Instead, she was confronted with the squint-eyed visage of her warlord.

"Your Highness," he said, smiling.

"What do you want, Commander?" she asked, trying not to make herself sound petulant. The soldiers knew nothing of her little arrangement, and they must not know. As far as they were concerned, the warlord was her faithful servant.

Xavier pointed behind his shoulder with his thumb. "Out, lads." The bodyguards left.

Amalia had to admit a tiny tinge of fear in her spine. "Well, Xavier? Be quick about it. I have a meeting with Mayor Alistair."

The Caytorean smacked his lips. "It might be prudent if I was present, too." Then, he inclined his head, looking at her with a funny glint in his eyes. "It's been a while now. When will we officially announce our union?" His hand came up and cupped the air in front of her breasts, an inch away from touching the fabric of her dress and the flesh underneath.

Amalia sighed deeply. Should she feel offended? Not after spending a good portion of the last year posing as Jerrica, subject to humiliation and terror and the simple rudeness of the small folk. "Commander, you have not taken all the facts into consideration."

His face darkened. "What facts?"

She forced a grin onto her face. "We are still in the middle of a war. Our *union* must have significance. You are not noble born. An empress cannot just marry a commoner like that."

He was not impressed. "Your father could."

Amalia did not allow doubt to shatter her resolve. She was desperately scrabbling through her mind, seeking something, anything that would stave off this man without insulting him. She still needed his troops. *I had Gerald, and now I have this swine.*

"My father was a commoner, too, before he made Athesia. He broke all conventions and traditions. I am not in that position. If I were to marry you now, you'd sign your own death warrant. Think of all the councillors in Eybalen. They surely won't favor the idea of a paid soldier stealing their opportunity." There, she had him.

He blinked stupidly. "So what are you telling me?"

You will have to contend with whores until I find a way to dispose of you. "You must be ennobled first."

He was shrewd, but he was totally unprepared for what she had suggested. "I'm listening."

She turned away from him, her breath raw and thin from excitement and fear. She was groping wildly, and ideas were coming together, mad, brutal, unpredictable. "Your loyalty and courage have been noted. With time, you will have won yourself enough sympathy and love that you should be granted a title. My father did not believe in nobility, but we could make an exception."

Xavier scratched his cheek. "I see."

She was not sure if he looked disappointed or eager. Like any true-blooded criminal, he was greedy for more, and he wavered on that thin line between profit and death. His instincts were probably telling him someone like him should be grateful for the power he already had, but he felt compelled to push the limit one more time.

"One more thing, Xavier," she said.

"Yes?"

"If you ever try to grope me," she spoke in an even tone, "I will have your hand chopped off. My promise stands, but that doesn't change anything. You are my subject, and you will behave with utmost respect at all times, in public and in private. Do you understand?"

She feared he might laugh in her face, but her bluff paid off. He swallowed hard, looking grim, like a hungry dog switched on its snout. The warlord sniffed noisily, trying to keep his ire down. "Just to inform you on the restructuring of the army, as you requested. The veterans go into five legions, spread even, officers and squad leaders first. Then we make sure the Athesians and Caytoreans get their equal numbers. We have boys enlisting, but they are worth shit."

Amalia stepped close to the room's window. Brotherly Unity did not have a great view, just rows of houses with their roofs and chimneys and an odd bird's nest. There was a lot of activity in the square. City clerks were hard at work rationing food, metal, and payments, admitting new soldiers and mercenaries, registering newcomers for work.

There was another knock on the door, short and polite. "Yes?"

Bella peeked in, frowning at Warlord Xavier's back; the swine was wearing a cloak made of olifaunt hide, as if he had personally contributed to the death of one of those animals. "Your Highness, Mayor Alistair is here. Your Sirtai adviser also wishes to see you."

Amalia groaned. She wasn't in the mood to talk to Jarman now, to listen to his portent of doom. "I will see the wizard later. Please show the mayor in." She looked at Xavier. "You may leave, Commander."

"Your Highness, one more thing." Bella still hovered with her face in the doorway crack. "There's a messenger from Pain Daye. He says it's urgent."

Of course it is. Everything was urgent, it seemed. "Take his message, then."

Bella grimaced, her freckled face scrunched like a fig. "Your Highness, the message comes from Guild Master Sebastian. It's for you only."

Amalia arched a brow. She saw Xavier turn toward the clerk. She thought she saw a fresh coat of annoyance cover his face. As a former employee of James's patrons, he wasn't well liked by Sebastian, she knew. The fools had tried to kill the guild master, and the man nurtured his grudge like a rare flower. He might be a Caytorean, and he might betray her one day for the interest of his nation, but he would bring Xavier down first. They shared that much in common.

Pain Daye was important. Lady Rheanna had been kept there until recently. She should arrive any day now under heavy escort. Amalia had delayed making any decisions about James's widow. She knew nothing of her affiliation, her motives. The woman was a mystery, and she intimidated Amalia ever so slightly.

"Bring him in."

Xavier turned to leave.

"Stay, Commander." She wanted him present when she read the letter. If she could somehow use Sebastian's information against him, she wanted to make sure he had no time to scheme.

Amalia wondered about Rheanna. Her claim to the Athesian throne was pure nonsense. In fact, James had had no right to it really, even as a man and an elder child. Bastards were not allowed to inherit, as simple as that. But with Emperor Adam, nothing was simple or easy. What mattered was, he had been well liked, and by consensus, he could have been chosen, just what the councillors did when they brought James to life. Exactly that.

If they wanted, they could retract their support for her. Or they could insist on championing Rheanna's cause, ignoring her. Amalia knew this was a very painful battle that awaited her, which was why James's widow still had her pretty head attached to her shoulders. She had to make the woman throw her support behind her. And spare her life in return. A fair deal.

Bella moved aside to let a rider enter. He was shadowed by two sentries, but a quick wag of a finger from the warlord stopped them at the threshold. Bella pointed at her records. Amalia shook her head. She would need no minutes for this.

The man bowed slightly. "Your Highness. Commander."

Amalia realized something was wrong. "Speak."

She could hear the man's complicated swallow blob down his gullet. "Lady Rheanna has escaped."

Lady Rheanna has escaped...

Silence. It stretched and stretched. The messenger just waited, sorry and miserable.

"Details." Amalia remembered to make her lips move.

"As you instructed, she was sent here under heavy patrol. Master Sebastian even had a decoy convoy leave two days prior.

But her column was ambushed not three days away from the mansion. Lots of men were killed, and the others surrendered. Then, these attackers took all their horses so they couldn't pursue, and when the news finally got back to Pain Daye, it was already too late. Master Sebastian did send hunting parties everywhere, and he sent a few of us on fast horses to Ecol. I don't know what happened since." He handed her a rolled note, sealed with Sebastian's sigil.

Amalia looked at the warlord. He was one of the few men who knew about Rheanna's captivity. His own men had been responsible for carrying news and instruction back and forth.

Which meant someone in her circle of trust had spoken, or betrayed her.

If Xavier was party to this plot, his face didn't show it. Instead, it was grim, dark, bubbling with indignation. He was squinting madly. "I will look into this," he growled.

"Thank you. Ask the inn staff for food and lodging," she told the messenger. The man excused himself faster than an arrow, glad to be gone.

Inside, Amalia was very, very worried. But she could not let it show. Part of her cherished this mess. Just moments ago, she had been fumbling for an edge, something she could use against the swine. Now, almost religiously, this had happened.

"I am disappointed, Commander," she chided in her best voice.

Xavier was hardly looking, his squint was so fast and narrow. "I *will* find who did this. I will make myself a new cloak from their skins."

"A beautiful threat," she said. "Meaningless. Worthless. You failed."

He spun toward her. He opened his mouth, then closed it wisely. "She will be found and brought to you, I swear."

Amalia nodded emptily, turning away from him. She could hear noises outside the chamber. Must be Mayor Alistair getting grumpy and impatient. Such perfect timing. It would leave no time for the warlord to keep making more excuses.

"You certainly will."

Rheanna's escape was a serious matter. Amalia was not quite sure she grasped the implications just yet. *Am I mad,* she thought, *that I can still think clearly instead of sinking to the ground and crying hysterically? A woman who would rival me for the Athesian throne is now free, and all I care for is the look of defeat on Xavier's face?*

Perhaps she was in shock, and her mind was numb to pain and truth. Maybe it would hit her when she went to sleep today, and she would fret until dawn, fighting useless, exhausting, repetitive gray thoughts. Then, she was relieved, honestly relieved, that she would not have to face that fat-ass widow and battle her wit. She was certain the woman was very sharp and highly manipulative. After all, she had managed to convince her half brother to marry her. She had succeeded in controlling him when so many other councillors had seen their tame beast turn on its trainers. It was such a consolation that she would face her as a distant enemy. So much easier.

But Rheanna's flight meant something else, too. It meant someone within her camp was a traitor. Someone who Xavier trusted. Or maybe it was the guild master himself?

That should worry her even more. That meant she was exposed. Xavier might turn irrational if he began suspecting plots, if he felt he was threatened and cornered. He might decide to harm her, out of spite, when he felt his own moment of glory was over. Having the swine worried and indebted to her was a great thing, but she must not push him. Not yet. She was still too weak, still trying to consolidate her power, still trying to figure out whom she could really trust.

Master Hector? Timothy? The two Sirtai? She longed for Gerald, even for Theo, for her mother. People she had once taken for granted and whose wisdom and care she had ignored.

A knock at the door, soft like a kitten kneading wool with its paws. *I'll handle Rheanna later.*

"Commander, I am disappointed," she stabbed, her mind swimming. "If you ever wish to become a nobleman, you cannot let this common thuggery be your legacy. If I cannot trust you, then our deal may never bear fruit." Maybe a tad too dramatic, she thought. She was giddy, elated. Worried just a little. *I'm mad.*

He took her tirade very seriously. Either that or he was a genius beyond reckoning. He was breathing heavily, she noticed. A dangerous, armed man, and she might have overplayed her hand.

Xavier spat on the carpet. "I will handle this," he almost threatened and barged out.

The chatter died outside. The mayor seemed a little confused, but his head was preoccupied with town matters. He smiled politely as he entered, a flock of adjutants, scribes, and accountants in his wake. Amalia forced herself to smile, but her mind was thrashing, trying to grasp the enormity of this morning. In between writing her memoirs and discussing Ecol's future, her life had just become more complicated. Her biggest foe was free, and she had traitors in her midst. Worse, she had committed herself to making that swine a hero and a noble, to say nothing of another promise she had given a pair of wizards: to make peace with Athesia's enemy these last two generations so they could fight together against imaginary monsters. She wondered what Father would say of her master plan. He would probably laugh at her.

Only she lived, and that was what mattered for now.

Small steps, humble achievements. That could work for her. The whole empire thing she had tried in Roalas had failed. Perhaps this was the way it should have been done. *Father made his first victory on a hill somewhere. No one thought he would become a legend, then.*

"Mayor Alistair, please," she said and beckoned.

CHAPTER 5

What is the worst kind of enemy one can have? Bart had often wondered. *Who do you fear the most?* Was it a friendly, smiling face shadowing you all the time, leeching your trust? Was it the grumpy rival staring at you from the other side of the battlefield? A jealous woman? A scornful parent? Someone you had never seen but who worshipped your demise like a second religion?

No. For Bart, it was a human baby.

His baby.

That squealing little thing terrified him, haunted him. He was not sure what he was supposed to do. What were men really good for? Fighting, whoring, maybe politicking, he thought. But this whole offspring business was a dark, dreadful affair.

If not for a somewhat knobbly sight of that egg-shaped head, and its shock of fluffy, woolly brown hair, he might have felt content. It was a beautiful summer day, warm, clear, pleasant. The war preparations were going well; there was little sickness in the camp, even less discord. His noble friends and foes were keeping a rather low profile, almost resigned with his status. Not that they would ever stop scheming, but that day, they were quiet, reserved, elsewhere.

Junner was playing backgammon against Edgar. The mercenary was shouting at the old servant, trying to tell him something, but Bart's man was stubbornly holding a hand to his ear. For a change, Bart thought Edgar was about to win that round. Being half deaf had its perks sometimes.

His eyes strayed toward the baby and its mother. His mood soured again. Constance was looking happy, if a little exhausted. Alke was there too, beaming like only a woman could when there was a nipper present. Constance handed Bart's bastard to the maid. Alke hoisted the boy like a war hammer, gushing, making stupid noises.

Bart wanted to escape all this. But he really, really had nothing to do. A dull morning meant he was forced to wrestle with the thoughts of his fatherhood. Well, the fate of all of Eracia really, when it came to that.

The siege camp was almost ready for an attack on the city. Four monstrous trebuchets marred the skyline, poised, waiting to hurl rocks at the walls. The encirclement was complete, and the army had camps and ditches and towers all around Somar. Every day, soldiers kept drilling under the watchful eyes of Commanders Faas and Velten, getting that less likely to die when the moment to liberate the capital came.

Basically, everyone was waiting for him.

What happens when I give the order? he wondered. *Do I get to see my wife's head on a spike above the gatehouse? Does the city burn?*

He knew he would never relent to the nomads. Time for negotiations and mercy was long over. The enemy leader had had his chance to gracefully retreat. The resolution to this ugly business would have to be bloody. Very much so.

What he feared was the time between the assault and the moment they freed the city. It could take hours, days, maybe

even weeks. In that time, the Kataji could systematically kill
every woman and child and set fires to all the houses and shops,
leaving Somar a black, dead ruin. Bart doubted this General
Pacmad would resort to something like that, but desperate men
often made foolish decisions.

The enemy's stubborn refusal to surrender intrigued him.
Why had they not fled when it was obvious they faced an overwhelming force? Had they believed the Eracians would never
muster an army to retake the capital? Did they delude themselves in their chances to win this war? Or to bloody Bart's
nose just red enough to force him to negotiate concessions or
reparations for the three-century-stale evils?

He feared having a madman for a foe. He didn't want Sacred repeated all over again.

What would I have done in Pacmad's place? He clawed at
his conscience, begging for shreds of intuition and guidance.

"Your Majesty!" someone called.

Bart turned. It was one of Faas's captains. He couldn't remember the man's name. "Yes?"

"Commander Velten begs your presence, Your Majesty."

"I will be there shortly," Bart said. The officer saluted and
retreated.

He waited for a while, let his mind clear of silly thoughts.
Once again, his eyes locked on the tiny thing called his son. A
son he could not publicly acknowledge.

Ever since Constance had given birth, they had been forced
to lodge in separate shacks, she surrounded by those pesky, ran-
cid midwives and a score of other women who partook in the
baby-raising mission, he alone and frustrated, with his right
hand as his night companion. Bart wanted to create the proper
impression, even thought he knew no one was fooled by his
sudden act of chastity. Still, it was a must, if only because there

was no need to taunt his nobles and constantly remind them of the gigantic political fiasco he had brewed. His mistress was not helping by being preoccupied with the little thing, always weary, her skin sagging, her eyes like big black coins. She had always been a small thing, and now she seemed even smaller, drained by the pregnancy and child-rearing. Well, except her breasts. He liked them better now.

She saw him. She crinkled a shy, manipulative smile at him. Or maybe it was her "mother's madness." He had heard stories about women going crazy after giving birth. He had never paid that rumor much attention, but he was starting to believe the stories might be true.

I should go there, he thought. *Show that I care.* Pride and worry clashed in a bitter stalemate.

Well, it could not hurt. Could it? He would just talk to her for a moment, then step into the adjacent house, where his officers waited. Damn it. He could not keep being terrified of one little baby.

Marching like a footman stepping into a crossbow range, he approached his mistress. All of a sudden, the other women vanished, just like that. The space cleared, and he felt he should fill it with his presence.

"Isn't he gorgeous?" Constance said, her tone silly.

Bart stared at the creature called his son. It looked like something soaked in brine for too long. They said toddlers looked like their fathers. Well, this child must have had a flat-nosed potato for his sire, because it sure didn't look anything like him.

"Yes." He had to be wary, extra wary. Constance was surely trying to swindle him somehow. Her goals had not changed. Only her tactics.

"I want to name him—"

"No." He cut her off. Junner had told him it was bad luck naming a child in its first year. As an irreligious Caytorean, Constance did not really believe in southern superstition. Neither did Bart. But he did not want his son to have a name. It would make it too personal. Besides, he thought the boy ought to be called after his long-dead younger brother.

Constance was staring at him, he noticed. He pretended he did not really care. He could only guess what she was thinking right now. "The boy needs a father," she whispered.

"He's too young to really care," he reasoned. Constance did not seem to agree. From what he knew, babies really started to pay attention to their surroundings close to their first name day. So he still had plenty of time before he had to begin considering the dangerous legacy of his liaison.

Midwife Irma glided past, scalding him with her eyes. Behind her, Junner was watching and grinning. Edgar looked like he was trying to steal a game piece from the board.

"I have to go, the army, you know," he mumbled. Like a man retreating from a snarling dog, he fled the scene, and was almost too glad to step into the command lodge, only to remember he did not really fancy talking to his staff either.

There was a ripple of salutes, and the two dozen chairs screeched as men rose to acknowledge him. Only the guards stood silent and unmoving.

"Your Majesty," Commander Faas greeted. "We require your consultation."

Bart was glad there was one sane man in this entire camp. Faas had accepted Bart's argument he was not the best man to discuss war affairs, so his ideas were not taken as suggestions, nor directives. There was only one order expected from him.

"Please." Bart sat down. Ever since his arse had gained monarchical status, chairs would magically appear whenever it yearned for a seat. Servants also rushed to offer him drinks and meats. He waved them away.

Colonel Ulrich cleared his throat. He pointed at the city map spread on the table in front of him. Bart could see the tip of the cane was touching the riverfront area. "Your Highness, we know you are concerned a direct assault might lead to heavy casualties. Well, one of my men had an idea. He thought we could try to infiltrate the city through the fish market. Swim upriver under the cover of night, get a few dozen men into the nearby streets. Then, they could cooperate with the women and maybe get the gate unlocked."

"What do you think?" Bart countered immediately. He wanted to hear their opinion first.

Ulrich grimaced. "It's very risky, but it's neat. If we can do this, we save several thousand lives battering the walls down."

"We could just hurl stones from afar, get the walls destroyed," Velten said.

"Yes, but then the nomads can do inside the city as they please," Ulrich disagreed. "We want them engaged heavily on all sides so they're busy manning the walls, and then they don't have time to cause damage or death inside Somar."

Which meant once the battle started, it had to go on until the city was taken or the attack repelled, Bart realized. That was a costly prospect. Sieges were supposed to be a simple, dull affair. One army in, one out, disease, hunger, and maybe a big clash. There were not supposed to be thousands of women and children locked inside, the mothers, daughters, wives, and sisters of the men on the other side of the walls.

No one liked this, Bart least of all. He did not wish to go down in history as the man who made Eracia empty of women. That would be as good as killing everyone and saving them a generation of misery.

"The nomads could have killed them anyhow," a bald-headed major argued.

"But then they know for sure we gonna kill them," another nameless face added.

"This way, they wait. And maybe hope we break." Bart recognized Colonel Maurice.

"What are the risks?"

Ulrich grimaced again. "If our sneak force is detected, the Kataji might construe this as a prelude to an attack and turn on our people. We might have to be ready to attack if the diversion fails."

"Are we ready?" Bart asked.

He heard a cluck of yeses and noes, and then he saw the officers and assembled nobles exchange well-honed political glances, trying to outstare one another. Some favored action; others resented or feared it. Some preferred a peaceful course; others just wanted revenge. There were as many opinions as faces, probably more.

Master of Coin Lorcan did not bother to hide his disdain for the viceroy. "Every day we delay costs us eighteen hundred gold. Our coffers are near empty."

That did not mean the man wanted war, Bart knew. He was just making an effort to be unhelpful. Bart had considered removing him, but he kept him just to confuse his nobles, those opposed to him, at least. He wondered if Junner might not want to earn some extra coin from a few more silent assassinations, but that would not do. Everyone would know and blame him for all those other deaths. Here, at this provisional court, he would have to practice more restraint.

His uncle was sending money, wagons of it, making the Barrin household poorer with each shipment. But there was no other choice. Even the most fervent Eracians would not fight for their nation hungry and penniless.

"Basically, the army is ready. It could be readier," Velten offered. "We can wait awhile longer, but we must make a decision before autumn."

Make a decision. His wife was in the city, presumably alive, held hostage. Liberating Somar meant many things, perhaps also saving his wife from the nomads. That meant making *another* decision, about Constance and his newborn son. He would have to battle these difficult choices, and none seemed simple or pleasant in particular.

Waiting was easier.

Getting rid of Sonya would almost be a blessing. But a tiny part of him wanted to see her, to see her reaction to the news of his stellar advancement, to see that old, familiar scorn, to see envy engulf her as he told her about his bastard. He wanted to see how she would react to his mistress. Then again, he didn't really want any of these to transpire at all. It was a dark, bittersweet torture of his. The same way you fantasized about killing someone familiar, someone you hated. You imagined wielding a large sword, and you saw their head detach from the neck in a flurry of crimson blood, rolling and tumbling in slow motion. Then, you would just walk away as if nothing had happened. As a younger man, he had caught himself daydreaming that scene a few times. Only he had never acted upon it, because he had always feared being discovered, caught in the act and judged. Because he had been a coward, a noble, and a politician, a wretched combination.

Well, now he was leading armies, getting ready for war, getting ready to sacrifice thousands of his countrymen, and he could really order heads decapitated with impunity. Yet, the responsibility, the weight of leadership, had blunted his edge, so to speak.

Make a decision.

Bart realized he didn't have anything smart to share with the staff, nor did he have a decision. In fact, he did not want to be there at all. He didn't want to be anywhere around this camp. He was too distraught to read or write, too nervous to talk to people. He was not in a mood for hunting or poetry or anything really. He felt in a kind of mindless stupor, smothered in lethargy and anxiety.

"Commander Faas," he said, "I would suggest you make sure your men are handpicked and well trained for the infiltration mission. Well trained. And I want volunteers only. Do not send them out yet. However, they should be ready to move within an hour of an order being given." He paused. "That is what I'd recommend, but the decision is entirely yours."

"It shall be so, Your Majesty."

Bart rose, and they all imitated him. The gesture annoyed him. He cleared his throat. "Right. Continue." He exited the house, squinting into the glaring sunlight. Such a beautiful day, but he really couldn't smile.

Edgar was coming toward him, shaking his tuft-eared head. "Your friend is cheating, Your Majesty."

Smile, smile. Almost. "I saw you pilfer a piece off the board, Edgar," he told the old man.

The servant waved dismissively and shuffled away to whatever task had interrupted his fun. Or maybe he had just run out of coins.

Bart felt himself drawn to that rough-hewn table and the polished game board. Junner was carefully counting his winnings, lips moving in a foreign language. The count-turned-viceroy sat down. The wood was undressed, and it wept sap in a few places, snagging at clothes.

"Tell me something, Junner."

The Borei raised his head. "Family problems, Lord Count?"

Bart sighed. He looked around him. There were so many people coming and going, busy and pretending not to pay too much attention to his doings. He was grateful for what little privacy he got in this chaos. At least he had that.

"You could say that."

The mercenary aahed knowingly. "That is why we have many women, Lord Count. Saves trouble. If there are two, you must choose one. Not an easy task. Makes things difficult."

"I can almost believe that," Bart admitted. Sonya and Constance, eating biscuits and sipping hot tea together, chatting, gossiping. One or the other would end up stabbed with a spoon before the tea cooled.

"You have a boy; that is good. Strong blood, strong ties. You have a future now. You have an heir. This is important. Men will respect you more now."

"Not quite." He knew the Borei was all too aware of the political dynamics in the realm.

Junner placed the last coin in a pouch, pulled the cinch tight, and made a complicated knot. Then he deftly and quickly stashed it into one of the many pockets of his hide vest. "Gotta feed my olifaunts now." He stood up, and cursed as the resin drops on the bench sucked on his trousers like a giant limpet.

Bart pointed at the game. "What, we don't have time even for one little game?"

Junner seemed wary. "You want to play against me, Lord Count? Why?"

Bart realized he was grinning, his worries subdued for now. "Why not?"

The mercenary was staring at him very intently. He looked concerned. "You gonna cheat?"

Bart chuckled. "Come on, Junner, what do I know about cheating?"

"Oh, that worries me, Lord Count."

Bart flicked his finger at one of the clerks. The man started, almost dropping his ledger. "Your Highness?"

"Do you have any gold or silver on you?"

The man's eyes went wide. "Your Highness?"

Bart shook his head. "Never mind." He looked back at the Borei. "We will play this game upon honor. You will remember your winnings and losings. And then, afterward, you will go to Master Lorcan and ask him to pay you, should you win."

"No money now, we do not write anything down, just... word of honor?"

Bart chuckled again at the terrified expression the other man was wearing. "Yes. Unless you wish me to ask one of those adjutants to bring me some paper—"

"It is fine. We are men of honor, you and I." Junner had that greedy glint in his eye again.

Bart felt a tingle on his left cheek. He realized Constance was still there, watching him, a mix of forlorn worry and female persistence etched on her pretty face. He ignored her. He did not understand women, or children, but he sure understood how to lose money to a Borei mercenary. With perhaps too deliberate of a motion, he scooped up his pieces.

"You don't mind if I start?"

Junner was leering like a monkey. "No, no, Lord Count. Please. But I'll be watching your hands."

Laughing, Bart set about having some fun and depleting the nation's coffers a tad more, ignoring reality, his wife, his mistress, and his potato-headed bastard of a son.

CHAPTER 6

Sergei pulled on the reins and made his filly stop. She was a new animal, still somewhat unsure about her owner. He had named her Marusya. A fine, beautiful beast with a dark, glossy brown coat.

Riding a horse through the city and out of its southern gate to stand in the field outside was perhaps too much of a symbol of pomp, power, and pride, but today, it was necessary. Very much so. He had a proper entourage tailing behind him, half his court and a sizable body of his soldiers, all dressed for the occasion.

It was not a majestic procession, he had to admit, and the circumstances were almost comical. Roalas was a fairly small city, and it didn't have the space and splendor of architecture that could create or amplify the needed effect of awe. Instead, he felt like a lazy, petty lord who could not be bothered to walk for a few moments at eye height with his citizens.

Theo had told him Emperor Adam would never ride through the city's avenues and alleys, always walk. This humble sacrifice seemed to have resonated with the common people without reducing his might in the slightest. That was something he kept in mind and tried to practice. Only this midday, the occasion called for a horse.

In the field before him, several hundred Athesian soldiers stood, bony, weak, their skin pale like slugs'. Well, these men had lived like slugs for the past year, hidden in dark, dank cellars and dungeons, awaiting their deaths. They were thin, their hair and beards grown absurdly long. They were filthy, their rags a uniform color of stale piss and shit and maybe food leftovers. No one would take them for the once brave defenders of the realm.

They were looking at him, eyes squeezed almost shut, still not quite used to the glare of sunlight beating down upon them. It was warm and nice, but some of them shivered, and others were stooped and frightened, as if the daylight could hurt them.

Sergei had mulled for a long while what to do with these men. Kill them? Let them go? Allow Sasha to continue her pointless hanging rituals? His sister was away, fighting her war against Amalia—unsuccessfully. The city was entirely his to govern. He had pondered for quite some time and then decided on a course of action.

Release the prisoners.

He remembered Amalia clinging stubbornly to her noble hostages. Then, he remembered letting all of them go home without any consideration for the future relations with Eracia and Caytor, choked with grief over the lost of his firstborn. Next, almost as a backlash, he had foolishly harbored the woe council, bringing shame and dishonor to his doorstep. All crucial players, and he had disregarded them, slighted them, ignored them.

On the other hand, Sasha had chosen to vent all her frustration against the several hundred common troops, city watchmen, and soldiers who had surrendered after the fall of Roalas. Their value as hostages was nonexistent. Their strategic importance was nil. He might have gleaned some military information from them, but they could have hardly changed the political picture in any way, and with every day, it was less relevant, and they were less and less useful. Keeping them locked up was meaningless. They were a constant, unneeded reminder to the people of the city that their new king sought revenge. Of all the people he should have kept close by, those weren't the Athesian prisoners.

He intended to rule Athesia properly. That meant peace and courage. Adam's style.

Several hundred emaciated, defeated men would never make any difference in a battle. But the citizens of Roalas were watching, and rumors were already flying. He was going to do what Emperor Adam had done when he had taken the city: offer them mercy. A powerful weapon if you had enough courage to wield it.

Sergei knotted the reins on the pommel, clasped his gloved hands on it. He slanted his head ever so slightly, scanning the crowd, seeking defiance and hatred in those squinting eyes. He was waiting for an outburst of rage, a curse, anything that might make him doubt his decision. But all he saw was terrible weariness. The soldiers were exhausted, defeated, and resigned to their fate.

Sergei looked at Giorgi and nodded. His personal adjutant handed a royal missive to an Athesian harker. This had to be done with a proper ceremony, the king knew.

The other man opened his mouth and proclaimed loudly, "By the grace of His Highness, King Sergei, the king of Parus and Athesia, may the gods and goddesses protect him, you are hereby pardoned for your crime of insurrection against the Crown and released from prison."

If Sergei had ever so slightly expected an excited breath of wonder from the crowd, he was disappointed. There was barely a shrug among the prisoners. A few of them tilted their heads, perked their ears, as if hearing something intriguing, but otherwise, they remained like they were, a forest of brittle human statues, swaying, shivering, scowling.

The silence stretched almost for too long. Then, in the second row, one of the soldiers raised a thin, grubby hand. Giorgi frowned, then glanced at Sergei, uncertain. As far as ceremony was concerned, this wasn't a part of it.

"Speak," Sergei said, surprised at the note of his own voice. It sounded harsh.

"We are free to go, my lord?" the prisoner asked.

Sergei took a deep breath. *My lord.* But he let it slide. "Yes. You are free to go. If you swear a solemn oath that will never raise arms against my people, or me. If you wish to remain in Athesia, then you must also swear fealty to the Crown."

The prisoner let his hand drop. "That's it?"

Sergei waved his hand. "Yes, that is it." He leaned forward in his saddle. "I do not know what ideals you worship, or what you fear, so I cannot ask you to swear in the name of the gods and goddesses. But if you wish to leave the dank cells of the city, then you will promise to live peacefully and abide my law."

"What if we refuse?" an unnamed face shouted.

Sergei could feel his retinue getting somewhat restless. Leather groaned as men shifted their stances, hands going to sword hilts. Anywhere else, this kind of insolence would be considered a grave insult against the king. But Sergei was long past caring about such trifles. Roalas was a dangerous, miserable city. A lack of honor was the least of his worries.

"If you refuse, then you will die," he told the sorry audience.

"Then it's fucking simple, isn't it?" There was a growl in the crowd, and a man went down on his knees.

Slowly, one by one, the former soldiers knelt or bowed, acknowledging his terms. They did not say any wise words or recite any great promises. Sergei did not expect them to do anything of that sort. It would mean nothing. He didn't need empty words. He needed Roalas's sympathy and loyalty. He might lose these several hundred men, they might become rebels in a few weeks, but he would have the respect of the thousands of souls looking on behind him, clothiers, gardeners, bakers, and shoemakers.

"You may not remain in the city, though. You will be escorted to Keron or Gasua, whichever you prefer."

The affair was over, and Sergei was glad to put it behind him. Parusite soldiers moved forward, gently but firmly driving the prisoners toward a long train of wagons waiting some distance away. A bloodless resolution to a sore situation. Sergei hoped there would be no scuffling or mad attempts by a few deranged souls to seize swords from his troops. He did not want bloodshed right after promising these men their freedom and giving them their lives back.

"You have done a very brave thing, Your Highness. I must say I am touched," Genrik, the high scribe, confessed. His usually unforgiving eyes brimmed with regard for his liege.

Sergei nodded. He hoped today's event would go into Genrik's writing. So one day, long after he died, people might read about the mercy and benevolence of King Sergei. Right after reading about Adam the Godless.

That gave him no peace in this life, right then, though.

His son was still very much dead. The campaign in the north had taken a turn for the worse, with a bitter defeat against Amalia's forces. Apparently, the girl's miraculous return had made her that much wiser and harder—and luckier. At least her half brother had died. That was some small consolation, although it meant Sergei would have to negotiate with the High Council now. No one could really predict how they would react to James's demise. There might be a civil war in Caytor. Or they might turn their confusion against him. Sergei did not like the unpredictability of the whole thing.

He turned Marusya around and led back toward the city. Boris's men spread about, their parade lances erect, flags hanging from blunted tops. Well, if needed, those staves could still clear a crowd at full gallop.

The scenes of the city were a colorful blur, his mind too preoccupied to notice any details. Maybe there were more people in the streets than usual, and maybe they were looking at him more favorably now. He didn't really know. He had released those men because it was the right thing to do.

Theo waited for him outside the palace stables. The old man dictated a brutal agenda, and he was never daunted by the challenges of his duty. "Your Highness," he spoke in his lazy voice, "Under-Patriarch Evgeny begs your audience."

Sergei dismounted and handed the reins to Matvey. The clergy was simply refusing to budge. He would never be rid of them until he complied with their wishes, it seemed.

"I shall see him in an hour." He acquiesced wearily.

Sergei felt tempted to let the priest petition him in the court room, but he thought it would be smarter to talk to him in private so he could later deny any demand the clergy made of him. He was not willing to agree to having the patriarchs raise their own holy army with only a loose affiliation to the Crown. That would be risky. He could not let them have it, at least not until he defeated Amalia.

For a moment, he wanted to see Lady Lisa and talk to her, but she had grown distant after learning the truth of her daughter's return. Still, relentlessly, she pushed for peace and reconciliation. Sasha's defeat was a great opportunity for that. Then again, honor called for revenge. The failure in Ecol was a tarnish on his image. Worse, it had much wider consequences than his hurt pride. Any weakness on his behalf was a signal for the Eracians, Caytoreans, nomads, and the tribes in the southern desert to try their luck against him, especially while he was weakened and distracted.

One great battle had gotten him rid of one of Adam's offspring. Perhaps if he made another attempt, he could achieve Amalia's death. Then, it would really be over. But his forces were stretched thin. If he moved any more Red Caps north, he risked leaving the countryside too exposed. He didn't have enough forces to maintain order as well as fight a war, it seemed. Maybe he should muster his lords again.

Sergei threw his gloves on the table and plopped into a soft, massive chair in one of the private studies. Used to be Amalia's, he thought. The corridor walls outside were scarred with deep gouges, as if someone had raked them with giant claws. A sign of a battle, but he could not think of any way an ax or a sword could make those marks.

Timur brought him refreshments, and Genrik sat behind the other desk, ready to scribble truths. Theo took his place next to him. Sergei felt talking to the priests was an entirely Parusite affair, but he wanted the old adviser around, because he was certain Theo would put the good of the city and the realm before anything else. He needed a clear, impartial mind in this meeting.

Soon thereafter, the lardy, massive torso of Under-Patriarch Evgeny squeezed through the doorframe amid much huffing.

Sergei found it fascinating how obese people breathed. They would often make several wheezing notes at the same time, as if they had several throats or noses fighting for air.

This was as private as he would allow himself to be with the priest. His stern upbringing was tugging at his spine, trying to make him bend in subservience and fear. Only he could not summon the old feelings of reverence for the patriarchs anymore.

"Your Holiness," Sergei said.

"Your Highness," the priest returned, out of breath. Timur politely placed a bowl of pear compote in front of the other man.

Sergei sampled his lizard tails and wine. "You wished to see me. I must presume it is urgent?"

Evgeny nodded, his neck wobbling like a gelled eel pie. "Indeed. I believe I must direct your attention to the presence of a holy man named Gavril at the outskirts of Keron."

Sergei paused in midbite and put the sugared cube down. No pleasantries. This was not usually how the fat man went about his business. Normally, he would intone a few vague sayings, speak about morality and trying times, then try to weed cooperation from him. To be so blunt and direct meant he was more distressed than the stretched skin on his jowls let show.

Sergei had tried to ignore the story of a holy lunatic for a while now, hoping it would just go away. But almost like a spot of mold on a wall, it had blistered wider and bigger. He did not have reliable information on the man's activities and intentions, but he seemed to be amassing a large force of followers. In itself, some extra righteousness in this godless land was not a bad thing, but the magnitude of the phenomenon worried Sergei.

Back home, he would have sent one of his dukes and his cavalry to scatter the rabble and hang the leaders. Crazy would-be prophets were nothing new. He remembered the stories of his youth. Almost every summer, there would be a rumor of some peasant getting divine blessing from the gods and goddesses. If the priests showed no interest in taking them away to a temple, they would usually end up hanging from a tree branch after their preachings turned too bitter for the locals or when they started inciting against the nobles.

There was not a wealthy child in Parus who hadn't been told the tale of Mad Monk Fyodor, who had seduced Queen Sveta with his mystic powers. Not even his death had really dispelled the myth among the commoners. This Gavril might keep his influence among the small folk, but the background story was starkly similar.

Twenty years ago, the realms shook when a godless man came and broke all the rules. I do not need a holy man doing the same thing now. "Should I be concerned?"

Evgeny slurped from his own goblet. "I have met this holy man."

Sergei did not like that. He had assumed the priests would be interested in anyone challenging their authority on religion, but he had not expected Evgeny to take a personal interest. "Is he loyal to the Crown?"

The patriarch smiled faintly, as if the very question was blasphemy made by an unknowing child. "When faith shines brightly in one's heart, even the sun's glare is muted. Can we weigh one's loyalty to their ruler against one's love for the gods and goddesses?"

Yes, we can, Sergei thought. "I will not tolerate any insurrection in Athesia. For whatever reason."

Evgeny ahemed, and helped himself to more compote. "I believe this holy man has noble intentions."

Sergei waited. He did not want to appear eager or concerned. He looked at Genrik and noticed the scribe was waiting, pen poised like a headsman's blade. "Noble and *loyal* intentions?"

The priest tapped a silver spoon against his front teeth. "Gavril wishes to see faith prosper in the realms. That is all. He seeks unity among all the people of the realms. After all, we might disagree in our mundane matters, but we are all equal before the gods and goddesses. I am convinced Gavril is an honest man, and he may be blessed."

"What is the purpose of our meeting, Your Holiness?" Sergei pressed.

"Gavril wishes to petition you, my king. He seeks audience with you."

Sergei didn't like this. Instantly, some deep instinct inside him revolted. It wasn't quite fear that coursed through his veins, more sort of a feeling of unease, the kind you have when there's a niggling thought picking at your conscience, vague and persistent.

"Your Highness, may I interject?" Theo piped in. When Sergei said nothing, the old man continued. "It would be prudent if you met this Gavril person. As all reports indicate, he has gathered almost thirty thousand souls at his camp outside Keron. That alone is reason enough to talk to him, if only because he commands a force that dwarfs the nearby town. If you can learn of his intentions, that might help you make the right decision."

Yes, anyone with the ability to muster a following that large in just a few months should not be dismissed lightly, Sergei thought. If the holy man continued unchecked, his righteous army could grow to frightening proportions. Maybe Gavril had innocent intentions. That could happen. But they might get bigger and less innocent as his force grew.

Sergei wished he had time to ponder life's mysteries, to wonder how some nameless pilgrim could become a pivot of so much faith and devotion. But he was too weary to battle philosophy. Gavril could be an ally, and that would be an easy solution to his problems. Or Gavril could be an enemy, and he would have to contend with thirty thousand men who gave him no loyalty.

Athesia was a curse. A terrible curse.

If spy reports were true, three out of every five trade caravans headed for Keron would stop at the farmland outside the town, selling their goods to this strange congregation. There was a steady trickle of people coming from the Safe Territories, drawn to the rumor of holiness budding in Athesia. Even the locals seemed to be attracted. Sergei was losing his own subjects to the faith of a single man, who had not existed just a summer back.

Amalia might be fighting with sword and spear, but at least she had some claim over this land. He could understand and appreciate her effort. He could not grasp what Gavril signified. Or why the priests would throw their support behind him.

Perhaps he was one of their own. A patriarch pretending to be a rogue holy man. Perhaps this was their way of getting their demands answered. This was how they secured gold for the temples and shrines, and fodder for their combat clergy. This could all be a ruse.

He wanted to consult with Lady Lisa. Peace. She would urge for peace, as always. Compromise itched more than saddle sores, it seemed. Brave men compromised, and itched. *Instead of guessing what the holy man wants, why not ask him?* It sounded simple.

Emperor Adam must be cackling in his grave. "All right. I will meet this Gavril."

Evgeny wiped his hand on a silk napkin, rubbing pear juice off his rings. "The gods and goddesses be praised. I shall convey your message, Your Highness."

"I will go to Keron myself," he added. He had to see this holy man's camp for himself.

For a moment, Sergei did not quite feel like a king. More like a prisoner, awaiting his sentence. Not that different from the Athesian soldiers he had freed earlier. He was trapped in this forsaken city.

CHAPTER 7

"Sheldon, come inside!" Nigella shouted, her voice shrill.

"But Mom," her son pleaded. He was lying prone on the grass, almost nose to wing with a large yellow butterfly. The boy was completely oblivious to the terror in Marlheim, but could she blame him?

"Sheldon, right now," she grated.

He oofed but complied, getting up somewhat dramatically and dashing for the interior of her cottage. That left her alone to face the soldiers approaching her home.

Running away was not an option.

Almost overnight, the town had been overrun by Calemore's troops. They had poured over the valleys and hills like a tide. At first, she had almost mistaken their white forms for sheep, thousands of them, rolling over the curves and creases of the land. They had converged on Marlheim from all directions and then entered the town without much fanfare. The few lucky and prudent citizens had fled. The rest had burned.

From what little Nigella knew about wars, soldiers would usually fight, then rape and loot, get drunk and wild on the success of their conquest. They would take time destroying and defacing and humiliating the symbols of their enemy and their resistance. They would carefully pick among the women and take them for playthings.

Not this lot. Not Calemore's soldiers. They behaved as if there was no joy in their task. Almost as if they were compelled to kill the people of the realm, burdened with a grim objective that was tedious and long and unrewarding, almost as if the fall of Marlheim meant nothing to them.

Nigella would have fled, but she remembered Calemore's stern advice.

Do not run.

His words did nothing to alleviate her fear. Worst of all, her own premonition had failed her. She had sensed nothing of this kind coming, read nothing in *The Book of Lost Words* that would have indicated there was a disaster approaching. Maybe, maybe because there was no disaster. Maybe because she was safe.

That did nothing for the random spasms in her belly.

A veil of smoke rose behind the small group of Naum men trudging up the dirt track, curling in broken, sooty fingers, bending this and that way, carried by the summer wind. Marlheim gaped like a festered wound, black, filthy, cracked wide open, and swarming with maggots. Fires had hopped between buildings and whipped across the nearby pastures, leaving charred ruins. Unconcerned by the destruction, the Naum forces camped all around the burned city. Yet more armies were streaming by, some following the roads, others blazing across the green fields, leaving a scarred land in their path.

She had been surprised to glimpse women in that lot. Well, she had expected whores to travel with the soldiers. But the women packed in the backs of wagons and sleds did not seem to be there just for fucking. They had babies and small children, and the drays bulged with home goods and items, the kinds of things pilgrims would carry with them.

Other than observing the quick, brutal fall of Marlheim, she had kept her eyes away from the town. She did not want to witness atrocities, did not want to remember any grisly detail that might haunt her dreams. She needed her conscience clear so she could plan her future.

Only recently, she had happily wondered if she and Calemore might end up together one day. It had been a silly fantasy, a crazy fantasy, but he seemed to like her, and almost respect her, and he sure valued her advice and her cooking. That had to mean something. Her experience with men was drenched in disappointment, but she felt there was something genuine growing between the White Witch and her.

The sight of destruction had warped the happy image she carried in her head.

Still, he cared for her. After all, he had warned her of the impeding attack and promised help. No other man had ever done anything like that.

Nigella stood, palms pressed against her stomach, feeling the muscles fire off with uncontrolled terror. She wished she could be calm. She wished she could face these Naum men bravely. But there was a giant cold fist crushing her chest, making her breathing rapid and short. Calemore had promised she and her son would be safe, but his words felt empty now. Like always, she had given her heart to a man and gotten betrayed, like the fool she was.

Do not run.

There were seven men coming toward her, spread about like birds in flight, arms swinging wide of their belts laden with pouches, knives, and swords. They looked eerie dressed all in white leathers and furs and skins, a pale mockery of their master.

Nigella swallowed. A painful lump rolled down her throat, making a thick noise in her ears. The men stopped ten paces away. A respectful distance, not meant to alarm her, she dared to hope. Her fingers curled round the fabric of her dress.

The man in the center was wearing a sleeveless jerkin of ivory-colored fur. His ruddy, sun-whipped skin was covered in sweat, dripping. He spread his arms, palms up.

Nigella did not know what to do. She waited, carefully watching him.

He moved forward, going down on one knee. She took an involuntary step back, a cool hiss tickling her teeth.

Nothing happened. The man remained kneeling, arms spread.

"I do not understand," she heard herself say, a thin whisper, barely audible.

The warrior blinked, but there was no comprehension on his face. He did not speak Continental. Her gut clenched. What would happen now? She felt dizzy. She wanted to collapse on the ground and cry, but she willed herself to remain standing.

"I do not understand," she repeated, pleading.

The man frowned, then pointed behind him and to the left, toward Marlheim. He waited until she glimpsed in the direction of the town; then he made a palm-down gesture. He pointed toward her, palm-up gesture, both hands.

Nigella rubbed her cheek. It was wet with a tear. "Safety? Am I safe?"

Again, the Naum man pointed at her, then clasped his hands together. Around him, the other six warriors did the same. Her eyes flitted left and right, seeking danger in their movements. But there was no threat there. They tried to appear friendly, she realized. Their gestures were slow, deliberate. A choked gurgle of panicked relief bubbled up in her throat.

The ruddy-skinned leader crooked his thick finger back at himself. He patted the ground in front of him. Nigella was desperately trying to understand his message. But symbolism was a slippery thing. She knew nothing about the Naum civilization.

"Did Calemore send you?" she asked.

The name of her lover did invoke a reaction. Their faces contorted, emotions twitching their rugged, blistered cheeks. She thought she saw fear, deep fear in their eyes, mirroring her own. That sent another blob of relief up her gullet.

"Calemore," the chief warrior repeated, but he said it differently, letters hard and emphasized.

Nigella was glad they could speak, even if they didn't know her language. It convinced her they might find a way to communicate somehow, convinced her a little that these were just ordinary people facing her. From another land, from another culture, still just men.

"Are you here to protect me?" she chirped.

Ruddy lowered his face to the ground. "Calemore," he intoned against the gravel. His six did the same thing. The witch's name reverberated around her, even as Marlheim kept burning in the background, a black haze clotting the sky.

The man straightened. He repeated his earlier gestures, palms up and down, hands clasped. She thought she understood the gist of it. Risking everything, she gave a small nod. *I hope nodding is a good thing in Naum.*

As if to affirm her own body language, the warrior went through the sequence of his motions one more time, then bobbed his hairy cleft chin up and down. Nod, that was good.

He waved his hand at one of the soldiers on his right. Nigella tensed again, uncertain what would happen next. The other warrior removed a pack from his back and undid the knots of the leather straps. He produced a bundle, wrapped in oiled paper, and handed it to his leader.

Ruddy waved the bundle at her, then placed it on the ground before him and waited.

Don't be a coward, she told herself, trying to will her feet to move. But they would not obey.

"Calemore," Ruddy said, touching the wrapped thing.

"Calemore," she agreed. One of her feet jerked forward, then the other. Weak, blood hammering in her neck, her ears, her temples, in the pit of her stomach, she dragged herself close to the Naum man, all too painfully aware of the big ax cinched behind his belt.

Her trembling hands picked up the bundle, and she withdrew. There was a sharp, rank smell oozing round the wrapping. Almost like a string doll, she worked her fingers through the folded, creased layers of paper. Inside, there was a soft, poxy white wheel, sweating milky dew on a wad of gauze.

Cheese. Goat's cheese.

Nigella lost control. The sharp knot of pain in her stomach melted. She breathed in hard and laughed hysterically, her vision blurring with fresh tears. She folded, no strength left in her stomach, holding to the bundle with the last ounces of sanity.

The feeling of terror sluicing away was wonderful. She could feel her muscles shedding it off like snake skin, leaving behind tender, raw flesh. The cold feeling drained down her thighs, down her calves, into her feet, and out of her body. She was warm, too warm suddenly.

Cheese.

The Naum people had brought her cheese.

Ruddy took her brittle laughter as a positive sign. Soon, other men were unloading their bags, and they gave her white carrots, beets, apples, and cured meat. So Sheldon and she would not starve because Marlheim was now a town in ruins.

She stared in wonder at this display of aid, knowing they were doing so because Calemore had made them. But it did not change her sense of sad, honest appreciation for these brutal strangers. *Because many years ago, my own people did just the opposite.*

The leader slowly rose to his feet, making sure his action did not alarm her. She remained sitting on the ground, staring at the wealth of food before her. Then, she followed him as he stepped around her and approached the cottage.

Sheldon was inside. That terror came back, fast and sudden.

Ruddy did not go for the door. Instead, he walked over to the rainwater barrel and gently tapped the old staves. He nodded once, looking at her intently.

Nigella frowned, trying to figure out what he meant. *Repair? Repair the leaks?* She shook her head. The warrior reached toward the roof, touching the straw eaves. She shook her head again. Ruddy looked around, searching for items that might need mending. She could not shrug her unease off with his sweaty bulk moving so close to the cabin, so close to her son.

Done with his inspection, the Naum leader moved back to his previous spot. Right then, Sheldon cracked the door open and peered outside, his bright, innocent face alight with curiosity.

"Sheldon, inside!" Nigella snapped, her heart skipping a beat.

Ruddy stopped and turned. He saw the boy.

Nigella heard a whimper stretch thin. She realized it was her own.

The warrior sensed her terror and quickly distanced himself from the boy. When her keening tapered out, he repeated that gesture, hands up, hands clasped. "Calemore," he grated. Nigella nodded dumbly, feeling defeated and dejected suddenly.

"Mom, who are these men?" Sheldon asked.

"I told you to stay inside," she berated without much conviction, exhausted.

"Are these men with Master Calemore?" the boy insisted.

"Go inside!" she begged.

Tiny face scrunched with hurt, Sheldon retreated to the dark interior of her home.

Ruddy was looking at her, she realized. Nigella made herself look at him. He was nodding. *Everything is all right,* the gesture said.

"Thank you," she said, even though she knew he would not understand.

He waited for a while longer. Apparently, his task was done. When he realized she didn't need or want anything else, he waved his hand, and the soldiers began their journey back to the ruined town.

"Calemore," he offered as a way of farewell. She didn't bother responding.

Nigella watched him go. He glanced one last time behind his massive shoulder and then kept plowing away, without turning.

Soon, reality floated back on a wind that smelled like soot and smoke and burned human flesh. She was back in the world where an enemy army was trampling the land dead just a few quick miles away from her serene little farmstead. Marlheim kept bleeding, the human rats kept engorging on its torn intestines, and large columns of soldiers, women, and children kept snaking past, going deeper into Caytor.

She had little love for the people of the realm. They had given her mostly disappointment and scorn in her youth.

Caytor might have been her birthplace, but it had never been her *home*. Still, the carnage in Marlheim was wrong, immensely wrong, no matter how grateful she felt for being alive and safe.

Sheldon would never be able to go back to his press shop. His friends and his master were probably dead, killed by the Naum invaders. The world around them had changed, had become alien and harsh and dreadful. Infested by these foreign people. Could she trust them? What would she do when she felt like hearing Continental again? Talk to Calemore? Would he become her life, her whole life?

Quite often, in her darkest moments, she had yearned for revenge, yearned for justice. Now that she had them in a sick, perverted way, they tasted just like ashes on her tongue, bitter and oily. Deep down, she had craved for pain and suffering upon the Caytoreans, hoping that would somehow undo the wrongs inflicted on her. She had expected the reversal of evil would liberate her.

First, there was Rob's death. Now this. And looming above it all, the bleak hint of a future where Calemore ruled everything. Rob's demise had freed her in a way, given her determination, if not the satisfaction she had once dreamed of. She had grown more resolute in her decision to steer her destiny the way she wanted it. Now, this sudden destruction of Marlheim was a great setback to her ambition, threatening to crush her, make her small and weak again.

No, she could not let death be her beacon.

Nigella wiped the salty streaks off her face, blew her nose on the edge of her sleeve. She stared at the colorful display of foods on the ground before her, a month's supply. She would not starve or lack any comfort, she thought. As long as she ignored the destruction around her.

Her focused desire to see Rob die was just a blunt, morose ghost of a feeling when it came to seeing so many other nameless Caytoreans perish in this white madness. Not what she had imagined. Not at all. And why? Why did they have to die? What was the White Witch planning?

So far, the book would not tell her.

She had to know. Somehow, she had to unravel the future. She had to learn what Calemore planned, and steer herself away from that dreadful vision. Steer *him* away from it. Despite everything she had witnessed, she still believed they could be together. He might be cruel toward the world, but he did like her, and maybe even respected her. That meant something. That gave her hope, hope to keep trying. Maybe she could save him from himself. Maybe then she would redeem her own soul.

Her taste in and choice of men had always been awful. But so had been her struggle with their disappointments. This time, she would not cave in. She would not retreat and surrender. She would not run and hide and cower again. She needed to be strong and brave so she could build a sane life for the two of them. And for Sheldon.

Nigella rose, dusted herself off, and headed back into her shelter, leaving the goods on the dust trail outside. Sheldon would be delighted to lug things about. In the last few days, she had forbidden him to venture away from the cottage, and he was bursting with pent-up energy. Nigella had better things to do. *The Book of Lost Words* was there, waiting to be read.

CHAPTER 8

"There," Sergeant Angelica said and pointed.

For a one-eyed woman, Angelica was fairly keen sighted, Mali thought, squinting toward the horizon. Or maybe her own age and years spent staring at long lines of thin manuscript had dulled hers. Yes, she could see the thin trail of dust behind her army column.

The Barrin plains were coming to life with early summer crops, turning ever so slightly yellow under the beating sun. Rich, fertile land, and it stretched for more than a week in each direction. Normally, the fields would swarm with people, farmers hard at work, wagons going about. Ever since the passage of those strange white legions, the countryside was deserted. The crops would continue to grow, then wither and die with the autumn rains. There were no people to bring the harvest in. The smart ones had fled; the fools stayed and burned.

The northern force did not seem interested in conquering, or if it did, its destination was so far ahead they didn't mind wreaking havoc now and then, mostly now. Villages stood empty, abandoned, torched to the ground. Roads were cluttered with discarded rubbish, human bodies, animal carcasses, and broken tools, left behind in the wake of the huge invading army. Even blind people could easily follow the enemy. At a respectable distance, of course.

The Eracians were trailing their superior foe, a generous week behind. It gave her troops no time to help anyone, but it was enough to arrive at the scene of destruction long after the fires had burned out. The stench of rot and the buzz of flies were big downsides to shadowing your opponent from a hundred miles away. Still, Mali could afford the discomfort. Better that than death.

She dreaded thinking what would happen—or had happened—at the estate itself. She wanted to believe Lord Karsten had ordered a quick retreat of all the surviving men and women and gone south, out of the deadly path of the invaders. She did not relish finding the army command ruined so soon after its birth last year, but as long as people lived, things could be rebuilt.

"What are they doing there?" Major Nolene asked.

Alexa loosened her hair, then collected it in a new bun and pinned it with a piece of wood. "Well, we won't know until we ask."

Mali took a deep breath, thinking. After their brief, bittersweet victory at the Emorok Hills, the Eracian forces had withdrawn as far south as they could, fleeing that massive wall of men. Luckily, her smaller body of men—and women—could move that much faster, and soon they had outdistanced the unknown threat. Then, to her surprise, the enemy had veered to the east, heading toward Barrin and Elfast.

People with more brains than she would have gladly welcomed the chance for their escape and then marched back home, somewhat shamed but very much alive. However, she couldn't do that.

So she had ordered the enemy trailed.

Once again, they were chasing a foe, and they knew nothing of its intentions.

Colonel Alan had openly cursed her in front of her staff and called her mad. She had silently endured his tirade, then thanked him for joining her in the effort. After all, they were both patriots, trying to save their country. He had fumed endlessly, his long, drooping moustache twitching, but the detachment of Commander Velten's army marched side by side with her girls now.

Mali had to know what this army was doing in Eracia. Why was it not heading south toward Somar? Why was it leading toward Barrin, and farther, into Athesia? Were they in league with Adam's daughter? Moving against her son? Were they some strange allies of the nomads? Well, that could explain their presence, as well as the attempt by the Namsue to draw the Eracians so far north. But none of it made any sense really. Who, in the name of the Abyss, were these people?

And why did they lug their women and children along?

Soon after regrouping and moving after the white army, her troops had discovered another clump of madness. They had found entire convoys of women and children, wagons loaded with poultry and livestock, moving after the enemy force. Refugees normally fled armies, but this lot was doing its best to keep up pace after the foe, trudging loyally in the wake of its destruction. Worse yet, the stream seemed endless, and soon, they discovered many more of these tiny groups and large columns traveling south and east, mostly unarmed.

That was the most bizarre part. You would expect troops to protect their logistics trains. You would expect outriders and formations of horsed bowmen moving around the supply wagons, keeping them safe from bandits or enemy units.

But apparently, this enemy did not care about any of that. It seemed certain there would be no one left behind to interfere.

They probably had not counted on the Third Independent Battalion being there.

Which made Mali even more suspicious. If her wild speculations were true, then it would mean the Namsue flight and this invasion were totally uncoordinated. Just by pure luck, her own forces happened to be there, and they had chosen to follow the enemy. So who were these people? Where were they coming from?

The only way to find out was to intercept and, as Alexa said, ask.

So far, Finley, Alan, and she had agreed not to harry these convoys. They had only watched them, counted their strength, and observed their behavior. There wasn't anything spectacular or extraordinary about the enemy. Apart from strange clothing and using sleds as well as wagons to travel the grassy expanse, they looked every bit like the locals. You might almost mistake them for Eracian pilgrims, which made the situation all the more difficult.

One of the convoys was moving about a league away from her screening force, following another farm road. A ruined village was staring at them some distance from the dust trail, baring its black teeth. There was a weird pattern of fire-blasted streaks running through the barley fields. They were coming toward a bridge, still intact. This far north, the Kerabon was a narrow body of water and fairly calm.

Mali was biting on a grass stalk, chewing it, pondering. That lone, unprotected convoy unnerved her. She knew there were dozens more everywhere around, mindlessly plodding southeast. She had no idea if they had spotted her, and if they had, they didn't seem to care or understand the danger.

"Yes, proceed," she ordered suddenly, biting through the stalk and her indecision. She spat the leaf, her saliva coming out frothy and green. "Meagan," she continued, "you will send a hundred girls hard east. They will cross the river near Quick-pelt and then wait on the other bank. The rest, you strike for the left flank—I repeat, left flank. All the way around them. If they try to flee, Gordon, you box them in."

Alexa pointed toward the bridge. "What if they get there first?"

Alan sniffed, drawing attention to his taciturn face. He was beating a dusty glove against his thigh, almost as if flagel-lating himself free of old fury. "You do not think it prudent to involve my men, Colonel?" he berated.

"It's women and children in that convoy. I don't want any incidents."

He frowned, and she thought the shiny skin on his scalp might tear, but it endured, glossy and taut. He was not pleased, but he still bore her a lot of respect since that battle against the Namsue. Well, a lot could be said against men, all the time, but they had their qualities. They might be quick to judge, but they were easy to buy with valor and honor.

"Move out," she said when she realized there would be no more arguing.

The troops spread about, raising their own dust cloud to match the enemy convoy's. They had to know they were being watched by now, she thought. But the enemy kept moving at the same leisurely, stubborn pace.

Mali resigned herself to wait, propping one leg against a field rock, watching, contemplating, seeking traps. But the land gave away nothing out of the ordinary. Barley fields rip-pled—those that had not been crushed underfoot or licked with flame—birds and insects sang, and the wind added its own whispering tune.

Not the ideal country for army passage, she mused. Most of the traffic went farther east, toward the two rich estates. The Kerabon and the Marock made the northern and western reaches of the Barrin estate trickier to cross, because you would need ferries. They were excellent for hauling grain to the capital, but not when thousands of men and women and frisky horses needed to cross to the other side. Which made, yet again, the enemy force's decision to trample here all the more curious. They could have gone farther south and followed easy roads. Or gone farther west, where it was more boring, but without wide rivers to impede the journey. This stubborn, inefficient arrow-straight pilgrimage of death was quite unsettling.

Maybe the enemy had no idea of the terrain they were following. Maybe there was a dire urgency to their march. Or maybe something worse, something she could not even imagine. A thousand questions, no answers. Well, she would have some soon.

She had asked for her old military life back. Now she had a war that even Vergil himself would have found crafty.

As she watched the troops deploy, her thoughts strayed away to another realm, where her son was. She was wondering how he was faring with his Caytorean wife. Was he fighting court intrigue? Was he fighting real battles, just like her? Was he entertaining fat lords in some opulent mansion, discussing trade and lying about his feelings? She had not had any news from Athesia in months. Her return to the realms was wrapped in half a year of lost time.

I could be fighting a wrong war against the wrong enemy, she thought. For that matter, she had no idea what was happening in Somar either. Who was in charge of the realm, really? Who led the Southern Army, if it still existed? Were the Kataji still infesting the capital, refusing to budge?

How can there be an army coming from the north? There's nothing there.

Oh, now the convoy had noticed the Eracians. There was a certain urgency to their pace now, as fast as mules and donkeys and the hairy cowlike creatures they had could move pulling big wagons behind them. Mali signaled the rest of the force to start moving. Finley and Alan pretended to have come to the same conclusion on their own and ordered their own would-be regiments after her. The force of twenty thousand strong left its own impression in the Barrin plains. The veil of dust became a solid cloud.

There was no fighting. The enemy convoy was quickly surrounded, its one-hundred-fifty-odd souls huddling in their carts and around them, waiting.

Mali dismounted, hitching her trousers up. Her arse itched from sweat, and frankly, she wanted to take a dump. She had not squatted in two days, and she was feeling rather constipated.

She stopped about a stone's throw away from the lot, studying them hard with what she hoped were still healthy eyes. Red faces, blistered by the sun. Haggard faces, as weak as any she had seen in her life. Frightened goats were bleating insanely, pulling on their tethers, the women and children around them trying to calm them down. Ducks and other birds were beating their wings against the wire cages.

There were a few men in the lot, mostly with pale long hair. Some looked quite foreign but not unlike folks she had seen from Eybalen or Sigurd. Others belonged in any nearby village. People just like the Eracians, except they were not.

Mali spotted another strange thing. Most were dressed too warmly for the weather. They absolutely stank.

"So what do we have here?" Finley asked, coming closer.

"Identify yourselves," one of the mounted women barked. No one responded.

"Maybe they don't speak our language," Alexa said, frowning hard.

The silence among the foreigners was oppressive. You would expect them to plead or curse or threat, even in their own tongue. But not doing anything of the sort made her wonder what kind of madness she had stepped into.

"Anyone speak any foreign?"

A few men and women muttered unhelpfully, but no volunteers stepped forward.

Mali realized this could be a rather awkward interception. Asking questions, yes, but were they any good if no one could understand them? A northern army, coming from nowhere, with bloody people who couldn't speak Continental. Bloody Abyss. Fuck.

She turned toward her horse, opened one of the saddlebags, and produced a water bladder. She drank in long, slow gulps. The water was tepid and not very fresh, but they would reach the river soon, and if there weren't too many bloated bodies floating in the shallows, they would refill their rations. After the Crap Charge, she felt invincible. Almost.

Someone spoke, but it wasn't in Continental.

Mali stoppered the bladder and wound the rope tightly round the neck, then knotted it twice and shoved it back into the saddlebag. She looked at the terrified crowd in front of her, all of them wearing those hot, heavy white clothes. "Anyone said anything?"

"This one." A rider pointed with her spear.

There was a woman in the lot, short, pudgy, freckled so much she had more freckles than real skin. Her hand was extended, aiming at Mali's horse. Then, she spoke again. Mali didn't quite catch the words, but she understood the intention.

"They want water?" Meagan retorted.

"Might be," Mali agreed. She took the waterskin out and shook it. That word again. "Enta," that's what she thought she heard.

The short foreigner stepped out of the crowd. Men and women sighed with surprise, drawing blades. A collective gasp rippled through the enemy lot, followed by more curses from the Eracians.

"Easy now!" Mali tried to boom in her best commander's voice. "Steady. No foolish things. They are not armed. Stand down. I said, stand the fuck down!"

The last few stubborn soldiers sheathed their weapons and moved back, easing the tension. Only one lad remained, glaring hard at the short woman, his sword raised and poised.

"Could be a trick," he said, licking his lips.

"One of yours, Alan?" Mali asked, approaching the footman.

The bald colonel growled. "Private, get back before I have you whipped."

Mali stepped next to the soldier, but not quite so close he could swing and accidentally hit her. "Boy, put that away."

"Don't like this shit," he moaned.

"No one likes this shit," she agreed. "But you will like it less if you end up dead 'cause of subordination."

That got him listening. He turned his not-so-bright face, glared at Mali, finally figured out her rank, and quickly retreated. Mali knew he would need careful watching afterward.

Soldiers like him turned nasty when drunk, and they didn't seem likely to forget a slight.

The short woman had not backed away. Either she was oblivious to the danger or very brave.

Mali came quite close to her, fighting the smell of her unwashed body. "You want water? Don't you have any of your own?"

But the freckled foreigner was not listening. She moved down the convoy, five carts away. Mali approached, shadowed by her officers. In the back of the wagon, there were several children, lying down, all looking very tired. They might be delirious or barely conscious, she realized.

Mali looked at Alexa. Her friend made an all-too-knowing face. "Gordon, get me a dozen skins, full."

Her captain was too dazed to argue. Soon enough, his soldiers brought forward several heavy goatskins. As soon as she had her pudgy fingers round one, the short woman clambered into the cart, with surprising agility for her bulk, and trickled water down the throats of those children. One of them snapped away; another moaned weakly.

"Fuck," Alexa said in a quiet voice.

"Yes, fuck," Mali agreed. "Our enemy."

Alan was there, his moustache hanging like a pair of curved knives. "What do you propose, Colonel?"

Mali looked away. The landscape was screaming its lust for revenge. The scarred fields, the ruined hamlets. Even the road itself was scarred with tragedy. There was some strange, unknown threat looming over Eracia, maybe all of the realms, and she didn't have the slightest clue what was happening.

This convoy belonged to the enemy, she realized. For all practical purposes, it was a legitimate prize, a succulent target for her soldiers, and they would get to share the spoils, including the women in the lot. That's how it went. There were no rules in war, and no mercy. She, of all people, knew that to be the truth. She needed no reminders.

But seeing those parched children broke her conviction. Damn.

She had no idea what was happening. But burying these one hundred fifty nameless strangers in the fields would give her no answers. Instead, instead...fuck. What would she do now? How could she sort this mess out? Let them be? So they could calmly trudge down the road and settle down on Eracian soil, with its people evicted or butchered? Let them be, so they could alert their own troops of a local army shadowing them from behind? Ignore them? Kill them all?

Why would an army—no, a nation—leave its own country and come here, to her realm? Maybe they were going somewhere, fleeing an even greater danger, risking everything to save their lives? If so, could she blame them for that? Nothing of this made sense. Nothing.

Fuck, she wanted to scream, but colonels didn't do that.

Intercept, ask questions, learn about your enemy, that was what she had ordered this morning. Well, they had captured a bunch of enemy troops, even if they had turned out to be women and children. Mission accomplished, without any losses. What remained was to crack the secrets of their foreign language and weed out the necessary information.

"They come with us," Mali blurted, cursing herself. There, it was done. She had said it.

Alan's brows shot up, making up for their earlier frown. "Excuse me?"

She stepped close, their noses almost touching. "Do you wanna kill some children? Then go ahead. Be my guest. You do it."

He breathed hard through his nostrils. "You are one serious cunt," he growled.

Mali was undaunted. "I will take that as a compliment. Now smile. We're in this together."

Alan bit his lower lip. "All right. We're in this together." He stepped back. "Fine," he announced loudly. "Get them up with the supply train at the back. Watch 'em carefully so they don't escape. We're gonna try to learn who they are and what they're doing here."

One of Alan's majors was not happy with the decision. "What are we going to do with all those other convoys like this? Are we going to capture every one of them and then get them to follow us?"

There's a thought, Mali mused. "We need to figure out what is happening. Until we do, we won't just randomly kill people if they're not posing any threat. If they raise arms against us, yes, we kill them, but if they surrender peacefully, we spare their lives."

"So we harass their supply lines, is that it?" Alexa wondered.

Mali nodded, groping for a plan. "Yes. For now. We cannot possibly engage their main force, but we can make sure their rear is weak and exposed. Might make them reconsider and slow down." *Then, they turn against us.* "Meanwhile we send fast riders to the other realms, try to warn them of this monstrous army. Buys them some time so they prepare some kind of a defense."

"What are we going to do with all the other captives?" the major insisted.

Send them back? "We'll figure something out," Mali said. "Until we know better, no rash decisions."

Soon, the drama dissipated. Several soldiers remained to watch the foreign women give water to their children, but most moved away, disgusted and confused and worried.

Mali stayed, masticating her own doubts and wild ideas. She had fought ugly skirmishes in her past, but none so crazy as this one. You were not supposed to encounter unresisting, quiet women and children with sunburns and suffering from thirst on your first engagement. It just wasn't right.

But this was only the very first of her worries, she realized, not even sure how big the trouble really was.

Lord Karsten would probably not exercise the same sympathy, she thought, not after the enemy army had destroyed his county. What if all the Eracians were killed or expelled by the foreigners? Did their plight not count? Was she not supposed to be fighting for their lives and freedom? Guilt was trying to smother her. She almost gave in, only the flimsy knowledge that murdering unarmed people was dead wrong stopping her. Whatever the outcome, killing that freckled woman would solve nothing.

She went back to consult her officers about the next hop of their hunt, the image of the short, stocky foreigner dribbling water onto a child's cracked lips haunting her.

CHAPTER 9

There were four of them together in the monarchical chamber. It was a bit crowded, but Sonya decided she would endure it. After all, a defender of the realm must bear sacrifice for her own people.

"There's the question of industrial output," Guild Mistress Delphine said. "We must make sure that we can match the general's demand." Then, she bent over the desk and wrote something on a thin strip of paper and handed it to Sonya.

Sonya carefully read the text, then handed it to Giselle and Sinead. The two mistresses almost touched their heads as they leaned close. Finished, Sinead placed the slip above the candle-wick. It caught fire, and the paper curled, turning black. Just before the flame touched her lacquered fingernails, the head of the builders guild let go of the burning parchment. It dropped into the metal bowl holding the fat red taper, joining a dozen crisps lying there already.

Giselle picked up a chalice of wine and sipped. "It is our duty to keep the city safe, no matter who holds it," she piped in, and scribbled with her other hand, the paper held down by a leaded glass carafe. She handed her own note to Sonya.

> My girls have more than five thousand sword
> blades safely stashed away. We will be able
> to distribute them hidden inside bread carts
> prior to the Eracian attack.

Sonya frowned but said nothing. She passed the message to the other ladies. So was the nation's freedom plotted, she thought, most bravely, under the very nose of the enemy.

It was a grave risk discussing treason, anytime, anywhere, especially inside the palace itself. One little slip, and she would die, probably in great agony. But doing nothing would not help her liberate Somar, nor was it conduct befitting a queen.

Her three partners were loyal. She was quite sure of that. All three had lost their husbands and sons to the Kataji and had every reason to loathe the filthy bastards. They were powerful women, with significant wealth, and Sonya's own ambition did not impose on theirs in any way. In fact, they could only gain by being friendly and cooperative with her, because she had status and even greater wealth. Her brave husband was the richest man in the realm. After the war, she would make sure he rewarded the women for their valiant effort. She also made sure the guild mistresses knew that. Their success depended on their commitment to her.

Even so, Sonya was careful not to divulge all her plans, and she often played them against one another, hinting at future promises and honors and favors, every time spinning a slightly different story. Their greed kept them busy, even as they schemed rebellion against the nomads.

Most of all, Sonya kept a careful eye on Pacmad's desires. Should the mongrel try to appropriate any one of these ladies as his concubine, she would have to be cast outside the circle of trust, because she would then become a rival. Luckily, guild masters usually gained their rank at old age, which made their women somewhat old, too. Pacmad seemed fond of younger girls, and so far, he had kept his hands away from the guild mistresses. They did not seem to appeal to his wicked tastes.

Delphine was busy writing again. The woman led the rather grand food guild, and that meant a hundred other smaller trades would obey her instructions. Sonya expected the pie sellers, bakers, milkmaids, and alewives to use their freedom of travel through the city to carry orders of resistance as well as weapons and tools to the widowed Eracian women, who patiently waited for their chance to turn against the nomads.

Sonya extended her hand. The mistress was elaborating on how she intended to use the weapons produced by Giselle's smiths. Most city women were not skilled in fighting, but there were a few old veterans from before Emperor Adam's time who still remembered how to poke flesh with pointy sticks. Others just lusted for revenge and would compensate for any lack of training with brute dedication.

Armed opposition was only part of it, a very small part. When the Eracian assault finally came, the women would mostly focus on barricading the city, preventing the nomads from deploying freely. They would litter the streets with spikes, block alleys with carts, and set fires to barracks and inns housing the enemy, while making sure children were taken out of harm's way. The fires had to be planned carefully so that the blazes did not spread unchecked. The women would poison the food, and the whores would try to assassinate the soldiers and officers in bed. The majority would simply hide in cellars, with enough bread and water to survive a few days.

Sinead did not seem to like the last note. She was writing her own response, the pen scratching furiously. Giselle was talking so that no one would suspect anything was wrong. So-nya did not believe Pacmad had spies eavesdropping on her, but there could always be some common whore listening in, thinking she might wheedle gratitude or mercy from the no-mad chieftain if she overheard a useful tidbit.

"Two buckets of ash for every rooftop," the smith lady was saying, as if disagreeing with the rest. "And we must have a bar-rel of rainwater, too." Those would come in handy if the wind carrying flames licked the wrong buildings.

Marking all of the taverns and houses holding the Kataji and the Namsue was also a big challenge. After the first wave of rape and pillage, the nomads mostly clustered in makeshift barracks in the wealthier areas. But there were many others who had gone into other quarters, expelling the survivors or using them as laborers. When Bart finally came to free her, Sonya planned for the city to be largely intact, with minimal damage. If everything went smoothly, only the nomad scum would burn and choke in the deliberate arson. She would pres-ent their charred, smoldering bodies to her loving husband, and he would be proud of her. The nation would cheer her as their queen—

Sinead was arching a delicate, thin brow. Sonya looked down and picked up yet another note.

> The general will be suspicious if he notices the lack of flour in the warehouses. I can only manipulate the numbers so much. You promised him too much, and now he expects reserves for at least half a year.

Sonya sniffed. She wrote back.

Then make your women work harder. That's
what accountants and clerks are for. Make
them.

But there was a risk there, too. Most of the underlings were
not privy to the plan, so they also suspected nothing. Which
meant the head of the merchants had to lie to her own women,
and falsify the reports so they would falsify other reports, until
it became a mess.

A wisp of smoke rose as Delphine burned another strip of
paper. The room stank.

Sonya wished she could have consulted more of the
guild leaders, but Pacmad was behaving irrationally lately. He
seemed overly paranoid for some reason, so he would let her
meet with the city leaders only in small groups. That meant
repeating this silent ritual over and over. That took time, and
she had no knowledge how long it would be before Bart came
to her rescue. The Eracians were poised to strike any day now.
She did not have to be a great expert in warfare to understand
what those massive wooden monsters signified, the observation towers, and rank upon rank of soldiers. Her husband was
beefing up the defenses relentlessly, tightening his grip harder
every day.

Maybe Pacmad was afraid of Bart. That made her excited
and even somewhat aroused. But that also made *her* afraid. If
the Father of the Bear lost his composure, he could do something unpredictable. She had enough worries as it was, with
Aileen the whore usurping her place. Then, there was that other slut, Viscountess Verina, eying the general with more than
just fear lately. She was another woman handling her captivity
rather too well, and she might become a real threat.

Well, not all news was dire. Linette had finally died from banging her stupid head against the wall so much. One less opponent but not the one that counted. Aileen and Richelle, those were her primary enemies, and she had to keep ahead of them at all times.

Sonya wished she could kill them, but that would just ruin all her other plans. Soon. She had to keep calm and focused. Queens had a terrible burden to bear, as her own destiny showed.

Bibi came in after knocking three times slowly. Sonya cringed. She remembered how she had snubbed the girl a few times in the past, before she had received Bart's later. *Be nice. Be polite.* Yes, she had to remember to show some humility, even toward silly trollops like the secretary.

The clerk nodded at her mistress. Sinead took her report and read. Sonya waited, keeping her face passive of any ill emotions. She thought Bibi was looking at her, but she pretended to be busy staring at the head of the guild of merchants instead.

"This is quite interesting," Sinead said. Sonya didn't like her voice. It was too high.

Sonya almost snapped her fingers impatiently. "Please, dear?"

The report was written in code, as they had all agreed. On paper, it discussed mundane details of the city's production, the coal, cloth, and pottery figures. But the real message was the change in the position of the nomad forces in the barracks and on the walls. Colors denoted the tribes and clans, tonnage signified the troops' strength, names of shops and storehouses stood for origins and destinations. They had to keep track of the Kataji deployment. It was vital before the city's liberation.

Bibi looked over her shoulder, through the open door of the chamber, into the corridor. She was trying to see if any nomad might sneak around the corner and barge into their meeting. Burning of little notes over candle flame would not reflect well on Sonya's position, so she had girls going back and forth with reports and messages all the time, and if a girl saw one of the nomads coming, she would enter and warn them in time. They even had thin cigarettes, the latest fashion with the ladies in Eybalen, so they could pretend to smoke, and hide the burning evidence.

Strange, Sonya thought, staring at a silver box holding those rolled sticks of dried leaves. People had died in their thousands, mothers had to ration porridge to their babies, but you could find stupid little items like these in almost any villa. The Kataji had left them behind, uninterested or unsure how to use them. Primitives.

Another clerk bustled in, pretending to bring in another missive, her face panicky. It read, "General Pacmad is coming."

Heart hammering like war drums, Sonya carefully rose and upended the candle holder into the hearth. There was time, no need to rush. She looked at her fingers, red polish glinting like blood. Steady. Calm. She sat back behind the desk, reached into the silver box, a gift from her captor, and picked up one of the cigarettes.

Sonya had never bothered much about what Eybalen whores did. She had always had her own superior finesse and style. Using that marvelous gift between her legs that never went out of fashion. Now she rummaged through her memory, trying to remember how to light one of these things. Puff? Inhale? But the end caught flame, and she coughed, gray tendrils eddying out of her nostrils and mouth.

Sinead waved the cloud of acrid smoke away from her, blinking rapidly. Delphine looked surprised by the whole idea. Giselle looked like she was considering the same thing as Sonya.

No, it would be suspicious, Sonya warned.

She could hear steps. Soon enough, Pacmad came into view, grinning. He was walking side by side with Aileen. The girl was wearing some thin white sleeveless dress with narrow straps, her nipples showing. There were bruises on her upper arms and shoulders. And what looked like a bite mark at the corner of her mouth. A sweat sheen on her forehead, hair tousled. She looked like she had entertained the bastard with her young, sweet cunt.

"What an occasion," he teased, the glint in his eyes dangerous. "Aileen will join you for consultations. Tell me, is Sonya teaching you well about city business?"

The girl shrugged. "I guess so."

Sonya swallowed, her throat sore from that smoke. Every time she met that bitch, she felt weak, disoriented, frightened. With every little word, every little gesture, Aileen could condemn her, make Pacmad angry. She could not afford to lose his confidence now. But the mongrel only cared for fathering more children, the one thing she could not give him.

He was staring at her, she realized and suppressed swallowing another hard lump. "Smoking?"

She smiled weakly, unsure what to say. But it was obvious he expected her to demonstrate her affection for this new habit. Carefully, she sucked the bitter end of the rolled, vile thing, and it was nothing like the stories. No sweet taste of mountain herbs, no intoxicating lilt of the spirit, just the smell of old grass and foul smoke. Well, what else could she expect from lying Caytorean sluts?

"Eybalen fashion," she rasped, trying to keep tears away, and a monstrous desire to hack like a dying old man.

He rolled his tongue over his teeth. "That stinks."

She placed the cigarette on the desk, and it decided to roll on its own, leaving tiny orange sparks on the gleaming oak. "I am sorry," she admitted.

"You will not do that," he warned.

Aileen pointed. "May I try, please?"

Pacmad shrugged, his muscles twitching. "Yes."

The slut approached the table and picked up the unfinished stub. Then, she pressed it against her whorish lips, pouted, and tried the same thing Sonya had done just moments earlier. *Cough, vomit, you bitch.* But Aileen did nothing of that sort. She frowned, then inhaled once again. Frowned, inhaled. Eventually, she smirked.

"Is this what ladies in Eybalen do?" she asked stupidly.

Sonya mounted a smile of her own. "It is quite popular." Well, it had been just before Leopold's suicide and her imprisonment.

"Can I take those, please?" Aileen was staring at Pacmad with beautiful, young adoration. Sonya wished she could ruin her face with a cheese grater. Take one of those cigarettes and extinguish it against the white of her eye.

Pacmad showed his teeth, face going soft. "Take them. Sonya will provide more when you need."

Sonya made a tiny nod. "Please join us. We are discussing the production output."

The general looked instantly bored. He appraised the women in the room for a long moment, then went out, his footsteps receding. Aileen sat herself right next to Sonya, blowing smoke in her ear. She couldn't stand it anymore, so she coughed, and then gagged on her own spit.

"You don't like it?" Aileen's face was colored with concern.

Sonya blinked the smoky bite away. "Now, sweetie, here's what we did so far," she started, ignoring the jibe. Like every time Aileen joined her for trade discussions, Sonya carefully altered the topics and began a slow, boring lecture.

Pacmad might want to replace her with this young bitch, but fortunately, Aileen wasn't very bright or too keen on studying. She got bored quite often, quickly, and she skipped many of the meetings, probably too busy fucking. Sonya was immensely grateful for that, because it allowed her just enough time to resume planning her realm's defense. With Aileen around all the time, the insurrection would have been almost impossible.

But the Kataji chieftain was rather lenient with the slut. If he saw urgency in her studies, he never showed it, never expressed his anger. Well, she could not unravel all truths and mysteries. She was fighting for her life, for her freedom, for the freedom of her nation, and she would use any chance to better her position. There would be time to ponder Aileen after Somar was liberated. Oh, there would be so much time to repay the whore for all her little tricks, for all the humiliation. They would make it into a song, Sonya promised.

The guild mistresses sat quietly, looking somewhat shocked by this exchange. Delphine was the first to recover. "Lady Aileen, you might want to review these reports, too." She piled a meaningless swath of papers in front of the whore.

Another day slowly bled as they sat and talked. Aileen was asking too many questions, and they were forced to answer her, give her genuine replies about how the city was run, how one could estimate the required yield, how the supply of wood to forges and the casting of bolts and nails all came together. Sonya taught her about trade agreements, about loans, about collateral payments. She even told her an old cautionary tale about a greedy banker and a crazy goatherd who got rich through a simple mistake in a written contract.

Eventually, the slut surrendered and left. By then, everyone in the room was dead exhausted, and Sonya was nauseated from the smoke. She was hungry, too, and she realized her body hurt from tension, muscles drawn taut.

"We will meet again tomorrow. Early morning." The slut usually slept late. That would give them enough time to resolve some of the difficult plans before they were interrupted.

She was tired. She should just go to sleep. It was obvious that Pacmad had other entertainment. Instead, she left the monarchical chamber and went for a stroll through the palace. After all, she had to keep in shape. Sitting around all day long would not make her belly or her thighs any less lumpy. She had to be beautiful and ravishing, and she could not afford to lose to Aileen.

A summer sun was setting, kissing the city rooftops. If her reckoning of time was correct, tomorrow was the name day of Monarch Raven, who had allegedly founded Somar. A week after that, her own. She would be that much older.

Cruel how time favored men and made women uglier. With every new year, she had to work harder to keep her breasts firm, to keep her bottom round, to milk her skins with expensive lotions so that creases would not settle in. Men were valued by their deeds, women by their faces and breasts.

Sonya considered leaving the palace and walking out into the cobbled courtyard. But her sandaled feet took her toward the workshops in the back of the manse, the ghost of a broken toe clicking faintly. She did not know why she chose to go there and stare at hairy men beating lumps of metal, feeding and grooming horses, or cleaning armor. Yet, their smelly, scarred, imperfect shapes gave her solace for some reason. Maybe after Aileen, she needed a dose of ugliness to calm her down.

The courtyard was thick with nomads, but they ignored her, knowing all too well who she belonged to. They didn't even dare look at her the wrong way. Morbidly, she was totally safe among her foes, these unruly, illiterate tribesmen.

Their smells were offensive nonetheless. Disgusting. Animals, just like the horses and dogs slinking around them. She should be repulsed. Perhaps becoming a queen had changed her perspective, made her stronger. After all, if she could not endure the eye-watering stench of brown horse piss, burnt iron, and unwashed bodies, she did not deserve to lead a nation.

From the corner of her eye, she glimpsed another alien presence, a clean spot on a dirty rag of meat and hair and leather and tools. None other than Verina. She had two ladies-in-waiting trailing her. Unconcerned, just like Sonya, the viscountess was strolling, enjoying herself.

What! First Aileen, now this whore. What kind of trickery is this!

Almost in a trance, Sonya moved toward the other slut. Verina saw her and beamed a precise, cordial smile in greeting. "My lady," the slut greeted, as befitting her station.

"Verina," Sonya said, moving closer, blowing two pecks in the air near the woman's perfumed cheeks. "What a strange place we meet."

"My lady, I saw you crossing the corridor. I thought it would be rude if I didn't come over to greet you. I was just coming back from a visit to the park. General Pacmad provided me with an escort of his men so I would be safe."

What game is that mongrel playing? Sonya wondered, fuming. Perhaps he had discovered her and was merely toying with her. Perhaps she was a dead woman, and she did not know it yet. *No!* She could not give up. She could not let doubt smother her. She was a queen.

"I was intrigued, so I came here," Sonya lied. "I have never given the backbone of a functioning palace much thought. Now that I am in charge of providing for this city, this is an illuminating exercise. One must know the fine details to govern with efficiency."

"You are very brave," Verina agreed, radiating nothing but pure sincerity.

Sonya looked to the left. There was an anvil there, a big hammer resting on top of it, a bucket with iron rods on the ground below. She imagined herself dragging Verina by the hair into the smithy, laying her head on that cold, dusty metal, and beating her brains out, like egg yolk from a shell.

She extended her hand. "Dear, we have not chatted in a long time." And she led her inferior away from the noise and bustle, scheming with vigor, thinking how she would defeat this slut, too.

CHAPTER 10

Jarman was almost bored waiting for his friend to return. He sat on a tree stump, an old, charred relic turned black and stone hard by lightning, watching a beetle rolling a dung ball three times its size, his head swimming with thoughts and worries.

There was a noise like someone whipping dried leaves. Jarman raised his head and saw a cloud of litter settle down. Lucas was standing there, back from his spying. He dusted himself off and stepped closer, his tattooed face stretched with worry and weariness.

"It is bad," the senior wizard admitted, striding past.

Jarman pushed himself off the stump and joined his life slave for a walk back to Ecol, a shy league away. It would take them a while to get back to civilization, to the life of politics and intrigue, just enough time to let them talk uninterrupted.

There was a knot of woodsmen coming out of the Weeping Boughs. One lifted a hand in greeting and waved. Jarman waved back. His robed appearance and Lucas's blue face had made them quite recognizable with the people of the town.

Lucas steered away from the cutters, into the wild grass expanse, surefooted and maybe agitated. To see the old Anada preoccupied was unnerving. "The Naum forces are coming closer. They have almost completely overrun northern Eracia and Caytor. The eastern body is lagging behind a little, but that doesn't diminish their threat in the slightest."

Jarman tried to imagine the layout of the realms. So they had just a few more weeks before the armies clashed. Maybe a month, a month and a half. That was all the time he had to make Amalia forge peace with the Parusites. Then, it might be too late.

"Their supply train is stretched awfully long and thin, though. We should be able to exploit that." Lucas stepped over a rock. "Some of them have taken over abandoned villages and planted a few crops that just wouldn't grow in this climate. But most are just plodding on south."

Lucas's magical trips north and back had given both of them a valuable insight into the disposition of Calemore's vast army. The van consisted of troops, a staggering number of them, moving as a landslide, unstoppable. But they did not have any deep strategy or any reserves. They had to forage off the land, and being bent on destruction, their progress was simply not sustainable. The army could not feed itself, and soon it would be forced to slow down.

Following days and weeks behind, was the rest of the Naum nation, women and children and craftsmen, bringing their lives and culture to the realms. Or rather, returning after their ancient banishment. It seemed Calemore simply planned on killing everyone else, then settling his folk on the empty land. But war had its own unpredictability, and it burned more than it saved. His warriors were slowly starving themselves. Their headlong pace was their biggest enemy right now. They might have to wait for their kin to join them before they could resume their advance.

Jarman was not fond of the idea of murdering unarmed people, but he could not really think of an easier way of fighting a superior foe. As long as the nations of the realms remained split and at war with one another, Lucas and he simply did not have enough soldiers to resist the Naum invaders. Slipping behind the enemy lines and cutting off all their supplies sounded like their best hope. That meant sending some of the defenders into the conquered, ruined territory to harry the Naum forces, maybe even make them stop their brutal war altogether. It was almost unimaginable, but he had to believe that. *My visions...*

At the moment, he was not sure Amalia would listen.

She was very frightened, like a cornered animal, and she felt she desperately needed loyal men around her. Jarman could very well guess what her reaction to his idea would be: one of scorn and disbelief, maybe even outright mistrust.

"You should help Amalia," Lucas said suddenly.

Jarman frowned. "I am."

The old wizard shrugged. "Not quite. You are holding her in your debt. She knows that. She begrudges you for that. No one likes being humiliated, and even less being reminded of their helplessness."

Jarman sniffed. "I have saved her life more than fifty times in the past two months."

Lucas shook his head. "You have indebted her fifty times."

"It's the only way to get her to agree to my proposal."

"Well, so far she hasn't made peace with the Parusites, has she? It's pure luck the Athesians won that battle against Princess Sasha. Now, all Adam's daughter can think of is that she has no friends and allies around her, and she resents that. Resents you."

Jarman was not expecting so much insight, so many words from his old friend. It was disturbing. But Lucas was not one to impose his ideas. "I am helping her," he said weakly.

"We have come here to avenge your third mother," Lucas preached. "That does not mean we should let this land burn after we're done. I've seen people burn their crops and houses before fleeing so that the Naum soldiers would not be able to take them for their own. Not a bad war tactic, but if Calemore loses, then what? Caytor and Eracia will be left scarred, ruined. People will just starve. We cannot allow that. It would be immoral."

Which is why the Sirtai never meddled in continental affairs, Jarman thought with some bitterness. No matter what decision he made, it would always have dire consequences. It would cause as much grief and misery as joy and progress. The only question was, did he want to be the one making the grim choices for the sake of pride?

"I will stand by you to the death," Lucas spoke. "But I will not turn a blind eye."

Jarman looked behind him, north. You couldn't tell by the puffy, milky wisps of white clouds moving across the blue sky that there was death and destruction there, so far, yet so close. "Maybe our plan should focus on stalling the enemy. That could work. Force them to retreat."

Lucas stopped walking. "Until they figure out how to work the land and use rain to their advantage. Until they gather enough food to sustain them for a march all the way to the Velvet Sea. Then, there will be nothing left to salvage." He pointed in the other direction, toward the black, silky cloud rising above Ecol, breathed out by its thousand smithies and forges. "The plan should be making Amalia strong and confident so she makes the right decisions. So she trusts you."

Jarman rubbed his nose, but Lucas carried on, like a tireless plow through black soil. "The Naum people will find the Caytorean winter laughably easy to bear. They will carry on fighting through snow and sleet, and then, the chances of our victory will be even slimmer. For now, they are unsure how to treat these realms. For now, they are indecisive and disorganized and hungry. If we are to beat them, then the whole of the realms must stand together. The key to that is Empress Amalia."

Jarman wished he had Lucas's magic so he could whisk himself north and witness the enemy force with his own eyes. But he had not yet earned his tattoos, and he did not expect to earn them anytime soon. But the moment when he might be forced to use magic to cause death might not be that far off into the future. Amalia was the key to this whole affair. He had to stick to that truth.

"So what do you suggest?"

Lucas leaned in toward him. "Remove the human threats around her. Give her breathing space so she can focus on listening to your story and believing it. Help her. Damn the tradition. We are here, in this strange country, already breaking all known rules and customs. One more will not make any difference."

Jarman started walking. "Yes." He wasn't really sure what his answer stood for. But he didn't have the courage to disagree with Lucas right now.

He found Empress Amalia talking to her new legion commanders, Warlord Xavier standing behind her as if he did not belong among the rest of the officers, his eyes firing off those nervous, erratic blinks. There was a dangerous man, he thought. A threat to the empress. But without him, she would probably lose most of the Caytoreans. Their loyalty was something like the mud at the bottom of a river. You could never really know what it might reveal if stirred.

She had the bearing of a frightened animal, he noticed. Most people would miss the little telltale signs, because they were too focused on seeing Adam's daughter in her. Exactly for that reason, Jarman saw a whole different truth. Her burden must be terrible. Jarman could almost sympathize, having Armin Wan'der Markssin, the most famous investigator in known history, for his father. Well, luckily, sadly, he had escaped the test of normal life by becoming a wizard. Chance, really, but one that had saved him a lot of frustration and disappointment.

Now he was wondering if he might have harbored these emotions for a long time, kept them growing like pale mushrooms in the dark, ballooning big and damp and smelly. This revenge was the expected thing to do, was it not? Besides, he could not even contemplate the alternative. Calemore taking over the realms. The ancient war all over again.

So why did he stick to pride and protocol? Well, after ten years at the Temple of Justice, the notion of shedding all the known, wise, and familiar, the clean and orderly and logical, terrified him. He had wanted this affair to be precise and quick, he had hoped to remain aloof and uninvolved, but it seemed it would not work that way. He expected trust and sincerity from Amalia, expected her to believe his crazy tales when he would not even tell her his own life's story.

The people of the realms might be rude, crude, and rather primitive, but they were not stupid. And they could tell a horseshit seller when one came peddling his wares.

"If I may?" he said loudly, stepping close. He knew he was interfering, but at that moment, he could not possibly care any less.

Amalia raised a thin brow, looking suspicious. Behind her shoulder, her chief killer was glaring. When he saw Lucas enter the common room of the inn, his face clenched with hatred. "Yes, Jarman? Can it not wait?"

"It would be advisable if we talked now," he said, trying to keep his voice even. He had mustered courage to do this almost on a whim, and if he stopped now, he might never find it again. Lucas's words were ringing in the back of his head.

Amalia picked up a dark-brown block that stood for one of her legions and placed it in a different spot on a map spread on top of a table. "We will continue this later. Dismissed." The officers filed out. She looked behind her shoulder. "You too, Commander." Xavier grunted and left.

Slowly, her retinue emptied from the common room of Brotherly Unity. Agatha shuffled out last, waddling ever so slightly, her pregnancy showing now. Amalia waited for Jarman to approach, but he gestured toward the glaring daylight outside. She sniffed, but then she decided to follow him.

"Here to remind me of my promise?" she jibed as they came outside. Her face took on a scowl, but he wasn't entirely sure it wasn't because of the sun.

"Not this time," he said, somewhat abashed. "A troublesome meeting?"

Amalia looked at him as if wondering if he was just teasing her. "Most definitely so. It turns out my feeble reign has just become feebler. I do not have too many reliable, trustworthy candidates for promotion. Commander Xavier is trying to get his men in top positions. Naturally, the Athesians are mistrustful, and I cannot blame them. After all, I am supposed to be the empress of Athesia, not a bunch of foreign legions." She sighed, looking weary and almost on the verge of tears. "Why are people so selfish? Even when there's tragedy looming, they will always first and foremost think about themselves?"

That is how Damian made you, he thought. But then, he was probably championing selfishness like a holy cause. "That is human nature."

"Screw human nature," she lashed, suddenly full of fury. "I need help."

He was almost taken aback by her sincerity. "Yes, you do. You also deserve the truth."

Her face turned serious. "It's about Calemore?"

Jarman looked past her shoulder. He could see that half Sirtai walking past near one of the other houses. He was seeing that man too often. But then, magic followed Adam's children, it seemed. There was him, the White Witch, that dead man Rob...

"The threat *is* real," he told her.

"I know," she said simply. "I know."

He took a deep sigh. He wished she would confess all the little details of what she knew about the gods and goddesses and their affairs, what her father may have taught her during his reign. However, it was his time to shrive.

"Once I tell you what I have on my mind, you will probably think I've gone mad. But it's the reason why I'm here. The reason why Lucas and I have come to the realms."

There was no emotion on her face as she watched him, trying to decide whether he was trying to deceive her. "Go on." She had once hinted at his personal motives. Now she deserved to know them.

Jarman was uncomfortable with the attention all around him, men and women stealing glimpses at their empress and her alien robed adviser. Even the guards, who pretended to be focusing on watching the crowd and looking for dangers, seemed as if they were trying to intrude on his confession. Or maybe it was his imagination. Or cowardice.

He opened his mouth and spoke of the day his third mother died.

No one came nearby or dared interrupt, it seemed. People kept their distance, as if they sensed they would be putting themselves at risk if they stepped into the bubble of truth wrapped around Amalia and him. When he finished, he felt weak, exhausted, relieved.

Silence.

"Calemore does not care about your war against King Sergei or your feud with Lady Rheanna. They are meaningless, trifling events of the last two decades. He had planned his return for thousands of years. I believe your father tried to stop him, but he misinterpreted the signs. Emperor Adam made a decision twenty years too early. He tried to forge peace across the realms, but his timing was wrong." He was quite uncomfortable with Amalia's blank, passive expression and her unmoving lips.

More silence.

"I think we must—" He gushed more words into the void.

Amalia raised a finger. "Let me think, please."

He rolled back on his heels, feeling giddy, hopeful beyond hope. But he was betting so much on the minute chance this girl would be able to grasp the enormity of history and magic and his own dreams. If she didn't, then he would have truly failed. There would be nothing more left. Or maybe her desire to survive this war would overcome her lack of trust, he mused.

She was tapping her upper lip with her knuckle, breathing against it, thinking. He could see fear and indecision wrestling across her face. Despite her young age, there was a twinkle of old, hard wisdom in her eyes. She knew more than she let show. Perhaps she understood the situation better than he could even imagine.

"I thought being my father's child would be enough," she said, almost whispered. "I thought I could do just what my father did. Act like him, be like him. But it didn't work. Now that I finally understand the lessons he taught me, I am all alone in this struggle. You're like some terrible villain from a tale, come to haunt me. And you have your own bloody price." She paused, thinking again. "I do not know why my late half brother decided to accept your proposal, but he must have had his own reasons. Maybe he thought he could manipulate you in return. Or control you. Until you told me the story of your mother, Inessa, I had thought you were just trying to bend my will to your wishes, like the Caytoreans and Eracians tried in my father's time. I still find the story quite incredulous." She licked her lips. "But I cannot allow my own pride to defeat me. I understand why my father never responded with war to all the threats and assassination attempts and all the mockery. He fought for a greater cause, and it wasn't weakness."

Amalia almost smiled. It startled him.

"Perhaps there's truth in your words. Perhaps I am a beggar, and I must accept your alms. I will. For the peace and unity that my father fought for." She looked like she wanted to say something else, but she closed her mouth hard.

"My apology would be meaningless," Jarman said. "What matters is that we work together. You will get your own goals; I will get mine. Through selfless acts of sacrifice." *You will shed your pride, young empress, and maybe your ambitions, and I will forget about Sirtai tradition and my own calling.*

That was a fair bargain, he thought.

"So we fight against this divine creature," she said, "while taking care of our own agendas, is that it?"

Jarman had expected shame to blush his cheeks, but there was none. "You get your father's desire; I get my father's desire."

Amalia looked around as if only now she fully noticed they were standing in front of the inn, talking, ignoring the world, clerks and soldiers and men of craft drifting past on an endless journey of chores and duties. As if she was seeing her weak, fragmented realm for the first time.

"You would have me surrender to King Sergei," she said, repeating his old demands. In the past, she would have been furious and defiant. Now there was a resigned, sorrowful look on her face, as if she felt she could have avoided so much pain if only she had consented earlier. Living surrounded by enemies, with no real friends to confide in and trust, robbed one of all that fury, Jarman noted.

He nodded slowly. "Yes. There's no other way. I'm sorry."

Amalia opened and closed her fist. "I guess my reign was doomed the moment the White Witch stole the bloodstaff from me. It is only now that I fully realize my downfall."

"I *will* help you," he insisted. "No more lies. I will lend magic to aid your cause. And you will help me. Lucas and I will make sure you do not fall prey to assassination plots and treachery at your own court. We will remove your foes and rivals. We will give you the peace of mind you need to rule the land, to strike a just agreement with King Sergei. In turn, I ask you keep true to your father's vision. We must defeat Calemore."

"Do you care about us as people?" she asked suddenly. "Do you even care that the realms bleed? Or are you just obsessed with having your vengeance?"

I never consider it much, he wanted to say. He wanted to say something else, but that would be a lie. No. He could not do that. So he just kept his mouth shut, affirming her judgment.

She snorted. "Wizard, you're my best chance, I guess. My duty is to this nation. As its empress, I must save lives from destruction. I must ensure the children will have a future.

Let's just hope the Parusite king shares the same notion of responsibility."

Jarman extended his hand. That was what he was supposed to do, wasn't it, this strange handshake custom? "Lucas will deliver a peace proposal to both the king and Princess Sasha."

Amalia slipped her cold, soft fingers into his grasp and wobbled his wrist. "One thing, Jarman. I will bow to this Parusite king, but I will not accept any injustice against my own people. There will be no retribution, no suffering. The Athesians must be treated fairly. Or I will fight to the death."

Jarman realized he had committed himself to the idea of unity in the realms. Now he was wondering if he could really make peace between the nations. Would King Sergei forget his own vendetta? There was a tricky question. So far, he had shown promising restraint with the subjugated population, but would he be willing to extend the same mercy to Amalia? Stop his successful campaign, forget all about the ruin of his father's reign?

Within just a few weeks or months, the Naum army would sweep the land. It would be too late then. He had to forge an alliance now. He wished he could have more confidence in his goal, but all he had was the sterile experience from the temple, and his own dreams. That would have to do, it seemed.

"You will have a just peace. And respect."

Amalia let go of his hand. "That is all I ever wanted," she said.

CHAPTER 11

Stephan had not so much as stepped over the threshold of the establishment when a squad of pretty girls rushed to meet him, taking his coat and gloves, his new hat, offering drinks from a silver tray. The House of Gentlemanly Pleasure spoke of carnal delights, from its garish red and gilt paint and decorations to its muted ambiance and perfumed air, but sex was probably the last item on the menu.

Patrons came to the house to talk.

Stephan weaved his way through a wall of soft, young flesh, ignoring the charm and the smiles and gentle strokes against his forearm or shoulder. Like any man, he liked the female attention, liked the arousing sensation throbbing in his loins.

He had a regular spot in the establishment, a quiet, partitioned space all to himself and whoever he deigned to bring along. You could be the richest person in Eybalen, but if you did not have a personal invitation from an existing member, you would never get into the House of Gentlemanly Pleasure.

His companion for the evening was already enjoying the free delicacies of the house, slouched like a slug, already drunk. Ever since his captivity, Adrian had taken to some heavy drinking, not relenting even after safely returning home. He was slurping expensive wine as if it were water. Such a disservice,

Stephan thought, because that wine could buy the apprenticeship of some common lad in the city. The invitation card rested on the table in front of him, Stephan's name etched into the soft metal.

The councillor saw him and raised a pudgy, unsteady hand in greeting. The other was clasped firmly round a glass, sloshing red. "Stephan," he called, too loudly.

Stephan grimaced, trying to twist the expression into a smile. The girls at his shoulder followed him like a shadow, eyes fixed on him, waiting for his instructions, his whims. The house owner was a strict master. If you were a fool, you would mistake the dutiful adoration for a chance to grope a handful. But if you did that, you would never see the interior of the House of Gentlemanly Pleasure again. If you wanted to fuck, you went to a brothel.

"Adrian," he greeted in return, sitting down on plush velvet. The fabric hissed under his buttocks. "I see you are sampling the wines."

The drunkard pointed emphatically, philosophically. "Let me tell you. It's not as simple as it looks. Some of these wines taste almost identical."

Stephan looked at a lovely servant. He wondered where one might find a girl this beautiful. He did not remember seeing them anywhere on the streets, nor in any shop, nor even in the city villas. "Any vintage will do, thanks. Some chives and olives, too, please."

She nodded and retreated, swaying with precision. Stephan recalled his captivity at Roalas. All in all, it had turned out to be a fruitful endeavor. He had met a lot of people, earned new friends and enemies, slept his way through both the Eracian and Caytorean delegations, and almost made himself the savior of the realms. Well, at least he had built character.

"How are things going, friend?" he asked Adrian, who seemed to be kissing and licking the rim of a new, full glass.

Adrian put the wine down, untouched. "Things are going in all directions," he said wisely.

Stephan crossed his hands, waiting. Adrian was a drunkard, but he was also a very well-informed councillor with friends in almost every sector of commerce. In the past, he used to be a sour, distant person, and other councillors and merchants had often avoided him unless they had to trade with him. Now, back in Eybalen, he had cast away his somber mood but retained the drinking. For some reason, people liked him better that way. For an even stranger reason, they mistook his new relaxed character for charm. Maybe they considered him harmless or found it funny to spill their secrets to his turgid mind. Maybe they thought they could swindle him, wheedle him out of his gold. For now, Adrian seemed to be winning, having gained quite a following without giving anything in return.

Stephan knew trying to be nice and polite with Adrian would get him nowhere. So he had adopted a different tactic. He had given Adrian access to the house.

In a city where prestige meant everything, having something others could not was a huge bonus.

Adrian's entry might harm his reputation, Stephan thought, but he was willing to take the risk. After all, what he planned went beyond intrigue, gossip, and silly status. He was trying to save his realm from ruin, prevent a civil war, ally himself with Athesia while keeping the Parusites happy, all the while gaining himself the title of "emperor." That went beyond the trifle matter of flair.

"Tell me more," Stephan goaded.

Adrian winked knowingly. "What I overheard is quite incredible. The rumor will spread faster than gleet among sailors." He laughed at his own words while Stephan waited patiently. Adrian could take his time getting to the point, like a nervous lover flirting with a chaste girl, but he would eventually get there, with both hands.

Stephan nodded as the servant put his own drink and nibbles in front of him. He reached for a pitted black olive and placed it between his teeth.

"Lady Rheanna has escaped from Pain Daye," Adrian blurted, too loudly.

Stephan bit into the olive, and almost swallowed involuntarily. Escaped? This was an absolute catastrophe of news. Not because he did not care for the welfare and good health of James's widow. But because it complicated everything and shattered his own plans and ambitions like thin glass.

"Keep your voice down, friend," Stephan advised, smiling woodenly. "Where did you get this information? A reliable source?"

Adrian leaned back, but that only meant juggling his fat a little. "Most reliable."

"Does anyone know this yet?" There would be no way of keeping this secret. But if he had a week head start before the rest of the High Council discovered the story, he could perhaps leverage some of the disaster in his favor.

"Well someone must know. Otherwise, how would they have told me?"

Stephan did not prod. It would be pointless. As far he was concerned, Adrian could use magic to get his knowledge. What mattered was what he should do right now.

"When did it happen?"

Adrian shrugged. "A while back." He emptied the cup he had slobbered earlier. "No one knows where she is."

If Stephan were the banker, he would not be showing his face before getting some strong, powerful allies either. Rheanna had kept her distance from the council for a while, only coming back briefly to confirm her employees and partners wouldn't betray her tust and to make sure the numbers in the books at the year's end looked right. She had spent some time with her father, toured the city, met some delegates, then gone back to her foreign husband. Not the friendliest gesture to her countrymen and her associates. Then again, she must have bet too much of her luck on the council's willingness to appease the late emperor, as well as his military strength.

She must be wondering how the High Council would react to her downfall, and to her newly gained freedom. She must be wondering if they had already forgotten her, or maybe sold her out, stricken her out of the ledgers as an unfortunate collateral loss. She could not be certain her brief captivity had not been supported by Eybalen's finest. After all, Guild Master Sebastian had been the one to hold her hostage.

Or had he?

After all, she *did* escape. Somehow.

"Do you know the details?"

Adrian was waving at one of the beautiful waitresses. "Well. Kind of. She was being taken to Athesia when her convoy was attacked. They killed the soldiers and got her away. She had some strong support there, and they knew she was coming."

If a friend gambler asked Stephan where to place his money, he would heap it in favor of Sebastian. He was almost certain the man was involved in some way. He had switched his allegiance rather quickly, albeit after almost being killed by those fools Otis and Melville. But had he remained loyal to Amalia after James's death? Worse yet, was he playing both sides?

That was what the best gamblers did: spread their coins about, increased their chances of victory.

Or…maybe Sebastian had acted out of necessity. He might have been forced to remain loyal, following Amalia's brutal take-over in the wake of her brother's demise. She was rumored to be killing anyone who opposed her, hanging soldiers without regard for her losses, even though she desperately needed every sword and spear against the Parusites.

If not Sebastian, then who? One of his colleagues in the city?

That only made him even more troubled.

He drank wine. Not the best thing for clarity of mind, but the possibilities threatened to obliterate his senses. This was the wrong thing, happening at the wrong time. Just when he was carefully planning to make himself the handsome scapegoat of his nation.

"I do not like this," he confessed.

Adrian chuckled, wine coming out of his nostrils. "I thought you liked gambling. How about a wager?"

Stephan wondered if his friend might not be less drunk than he let show. Or maybe he had grown used to thinking with his brain steeped in expensive wines. "What did you have in mind?"

"Your guess when Lady Rheanna shows herself, and who with as her supporters."

The waitress was back again, all pearly teeth and honest eyes. "Would you honor us for dinner, my lords?"

Stephan was normally always polite to beautiful women. But he waved her away, maybe too brusquely. If she felt offended, she never showed it, just glided seductively away.

"A thousand gold pieces?"

Adrian nodded, wet lips pursed, with red bubbles of wine in the corners. "Sebastian."

Stephan gritted his teeth. He would have to name someone else now. "Not him. Someone else."

Then, just like during the council meeting in the harbor, another name popped into his mind.

Another worthy candidate.

The safest bet is no bet. If you must choose a side, choose yourself. He remembered the words of the notorious card player Tielo, a man who, according to legend, had never once bluffed in a game. But that was just risky, too risky. Shit. He was not thinking straight. He was reacting, improvising, responding to his fears. That was the wrong way to plan his future.

She already has an ally, he realized. Someone who would risk everything to get her free. Someone who valued her freedom more than peace and unity in Caytor. There was a dangerous, unknown party already involved, and they might not like Stephan's idea.

Adrian was expecting more, but Stephan kept his mouth shut, mind swimming. "What happens now?"

"You will try to keep this story quiet for a while, as a personal favor to me." Stephan tapped the invitation card. "I will try to figure something out."

"What will Empress Amalia do?" Adrian asked. He was trying yet another wine sample.

Stephan steepled his fingers, touching his forehead, rolling the invisible dice of options in front of his eyes, hardly seeing his fat colleague. He was wondering how the empress would react. You could never really know what desperate people might do. After all, half her troops were Caytoreans. If Sebastian abandoned her, and Rheanna declared against her, that would mean open war. That alone might push her into seeking peace with the Parusites or turning to Eracia for help. That would mean Athesia would never become Caytorean land again. And if she survived this turmoil, she would make sure Caytor paid heavily. Ruined trade, lost wealth.

Which meant Lady Rheanna had to be found and controlled. Steered in the right direction. Made to understand the situation and accept the right choices. It seemed there was no escaping the inevitable. Stephan would be forced to get involved.

One empress or another, what's the difference? At least he knew Rheanna and what she could do. Amalia was an unpredictable, unruly child who had ruined her father's peace. She threatened everything.

He was leaping into the distant future, caressing options so vague they were thinner than mist. If he could somehow convince Rheanna to stand by Amalia, despite their differences, he would forge a powerful alliance. He would be able to influence the Parusites and, better yet, his own council.

Opportunities are problems in disguise, he remembered. A Blackwood quote. Or was it Askel?

"I must ask you for a favor, Adrian," he said. "You *must* find Rheanna. You must."

Adrian reached over and snagged an olive from Stephan's platter. "I can try my best."

Stephan wondered if he should offer an extra incentive. Yes, why not. It always paid off to be nice to your friends. "I guess I could find some handsome investments in your businesses after we conclude this affair."

Adrian munched loudly. "Indeed. I was fancying taking over the fish markets."

"How does that work with your other commerce? Fish and paint?"

The fat man shrugged. "It's always something I fancied."

Stephan noted the future debt. "That can be arranged." Then, he remembered something else. Sebastian had been writing to him, gladly sharing information. Now, though, he doubted everything he had read in the man's letters, his interpretation of political situations, his intentions, everything. "I will also need to know who owns Sebastian's loyalty."

Adrian waved for a waitress again, pointing at all the empty glasses in front of him. "How about some food? I'm hungry. I want lampreys."

Stephan did not relish any snaky things. He wanted an honest, simple meal. "I will probably order roast lamb and goose liver medallions." No, he must not be derailed now. "Make sure you find out about Sebastian's intentions."

"If he keeps his head after all this." True, Amalia might decide he should join the long list of councillors and guild members who had thought they could manipulate Adam's offspring and found themselves short of a head. "Darling," Adrian cooed at the woman.

She listened to their choices, pouted prettily, and retreated. Both of them stared after her, unable to help themselves. Strange, Stephan thought, that even in the most complex life situations, a man's brain would always spare a moment to appreciate a nice body. He had almost expected to find such fine poetry in Blackwood's books, but the man was silent on the affair of rumps and eyes and danger.

As they waited for their dinner, the waitress came with a dozen tiny delicacies to whet their appetite. She was helped by a flock of other women just as charming and seductive as she. The house had earned its reputation well. It amazed him every time.

Adrian was busy drinking new wines, so Stephan spent another moment pondering the boiling situation in Caytor. He realized he should probably hire a few mercenaries, just to be on the safe side. He had never really retained any killers, but it looked as if he ought to now.

That was part of his dilemma. Should he wait in Eybalen? Rheanna might come back to the city. After all, she had all her assets here. She had her connections, her customers, maybe some friends. Then, if she returned, she could find herself surrounded by a thousand smiling enemies. Pain Daye was definitely lost to her, unless…unless Sebastian was her secret ally. That might also make sense. Late Emperor James had made himself the famous young ruler there and won the hearts of half the Caytorean society. Perhaps they loved his widow equally well.

He wished he knew what she really planned. She had come so close to getting Athesia back through the simple matter of marriage. No bloodshed, no treachery, just that womanly persistence that wore at rocks better than a hammer. Just like himself, it had all slipped from her fingers in one bitter moment of misfortune. He could imagine her cursing her bad luck, just like he had cursed the unfortunate fall of Roalas and the death of Commander Gerald.

They both could have been heroes. They both could have wed Athesia back into its rightful clutch. And they both had been betrayed by ill timing. Perhaps if they worked together…

Adaption was a businessman's sharpest tool. As an investor, he had to be ready to discard rotten deals and embrace new ones without losing stride. In one breath, with cold, calculated professionalism. That was what all this was. He had considered trying to win Amalia's heart. But now, he had an even better candidate. In fact, he wouldn't be ruling out any option. Rheanna, Amalia, they were both pretty, rich, and powerful.

"Are you going to tell me what you're planning?" Adrian asked.

Stephan wondered if his face had betrayed too much. "Not yet, friend. Suffice to say, I have some ambitious designs ahead of me."

"Worth another bet?"

Stephan smiled. *Why not?* "Definitely." The food arrived, steamy, spicy, and arranged with grace on expensive porcelain platters. He stole a glance at a pale cleavage before the woman straightened up. "Another thousand." For a moment, he remembered his games with Duke Vincent.

"And what is it that you're going to do?"

Stephan wondered how to phrase it. He wanted it to sound grand. Bookworthy. Then again, he did not want to reveal too much. There was always a risk speaking your mind freely around drunk people, even someone like Adrian.

"Get Athesia back," he stated.

His friend did not seem impressed. "So why bet only a thousand?"

Stephan forked a succulent piece of lamb. "Any more than that would just be showing off."

CHAPTER 12

Riding in a carriage was even worse than parading through Roalas on horseback. As a boy, Sergei would often hurt too much from his father's beatings to endure sitting inside a coach for hours, bouncing up and down. Then, as a young prince, no longer worried about King Vlad whipping his backside bloody, he had been forced to grow beyond the measure of his years and prove his worth, and that meant saddling up with Vasiliy's retainers and joining them on the raids into the Red Desert. For the better part of his life, he had lived on horseback, ruling at saddle height above his subjects.

He would have loved going to Keron riding with a thousand men at his flanks. However, old Theo was not vigorous enough for the task. So he sat inside a large, lavish royal carriage, enjoying the view of the world through a small curtained rectangle, the inside gently reeking of decay and bad teeth. Strange how every old person had that, no matter how rich or noble.

Leaving Roalas to meet this Gavril was a delicate task, with a powerful message. Some might mistake it for a weakness, but it was the exact opposite. Sergei could have used pride for a weapon, but he did not recall any one ruler getting any wiser

that way. Then again, bringing the holy man and his followers
into the city felt a little too much like the nomad overtaking of
Somar. He did not want to be remembered as the *second* king
to lose his head by inviting his enemies over within the span
of one year. Leopold would have an exclusive privilege to the
claim.

The only thing that really bothered him was the carriage.

Yesterday, he had departed from Roalas, arrived in Keron
with the first evening stars, and lodged there, fully aware of the
presence of an army of thirty thousand men just a short distance away. The city officials had gone out of their way to accommodate him, frightened and delighted in equal measures.
Now, he was making the last leg of the journey to meet the
holy man.

He was wondering what he might do if things went wrong.
What if the holy man decided to usurp the ruler, right there,
right then? His soldiers were well trained to protect him, but
there was only so much they could do against a whole army of
followers. Even though the secret and shame of that sad incident had died with Vlad the Fifth, Sergei could not guarantee
the patriarchs had truly forgiven the royal bloodline.

He wasn't their favorite champion. They might simply
have conspired to get rid of him.

There were close to a thousand souls in his retinue, though,
mostly fully armed heavy cavalry, with crossbows and lances.
His three squires were all there, bearing standards. The royal
guard rode around the carriage, both Borya and Vitya among
them. For the sake of national peace, he had even allowed a
hundred Athesian soldiers to join the procession, riding at the
back. This was their chance to prove their loyalty.

At that moment, Sergei wished he were back home, with
his wife and children. He missed them. Sometimes, he struggled

to recall the faces of his sons, and he wondered how much they had grown in the past two summers. He wanted to consult with Vasiliy, to hear his wisdom and his sound, practical advice. Well, he could just keep on riding, to Copper Astar, Bridgen, Corama, and then enter Sigurd. That would mean abandoning this war and, worse, leaving Sasha in charge. He was almost certain she would turn the victory into butchery. She would probably stop only after burying the last of the Athesians at the far northern border, and maybe a few unlucky Caytoreans, too, if they made the wrong choice of being around.

That would mean Vlad having died in vain. That would mean so many bad, sad things. So he had to endure his pain and longing and focus on completing this sorry campaign. It was true what the ballads said. The longer the battle went on, the more desperate people grew. In turns, they just chose worse options still, perpetuating everybody's misery.

His impulse called for giving up. So he knew he had to fight on, hard, making difficult choices.

"You look pensive, Your Highness," Theo remarked. His face said it all; he had seen all there was to rulers and their qualms and doubts and intrigues, and he was not impressed.

"Pensive?" Sergei snorted. "I am exhausted."

"Well, perhaps today you will find peace," the old man added.

Or more bloodshed, Sergei thought. He considered saying something witty, but Genrik followed in the second coach, so there would be no one to scribble his wisdom. He closed his lips tight, leaned back, and let the road bumps jab against his shoulder blades.

It wasn't long before the procession halted. Matvey dismounted, came back, and held the carriage door open for him. Sergei stepped out, stretching. His eyes took a moment adjusting to the sunlight, and then he gazed to the left and saw the massive, sprawling city that worshipped the holy man Gavril.

Not that long ago, he had led a daring charge deep into Athesia, with men pursuing the enemy day and night so they would not have any time to regroup or warn their comrades about the invasion. He remembered the Athesian defeat in Keron, quick and brutal. Villages had burned, people had lain in the fields, killed by an endless, boiling wave of troops. His men would not even stop to pillage; they just kept moving north.

One thing Sergei clearly did not remember was the huge blot of houses, chimneys, barns, and low sheds spread before him. This used to be empty land, fields and grass and an occasional tree. Now, his passage was blocked by a city that outsized Keron. Terrifying as much as it was astonishing.

There was a delegation of peasants and workers waiting for him, several hundred, a human wall that did not ooze love and loyalty.

"Borya," he called. The lieutenant of the guard nudged his horse around. "I want to avoid any confrontations. Keep the men alert, but do not draw weapons, and do not respond to provocations."

"Yes, Your Highness," the soldier barked.

Sergei looked at Gavril's camp again. The men were not armed for battle, but they surely did not radiate peace and compassion. They were well tanned, hardy, and confident. Religion was a very powerful motivator. He wished he could feel some of their conviction.

One of the messengers trotted forward and handed his missive to a likely looking leader of the other group. The man frowned stupidly at the letter, obviously intimidated by written words. Still, without saying anything, he was gone, carrying the message into the camp.

Sergei decided to put all slights and humiliations away, to completely ignore them. There was no purpose to protocol and finesse right now. He wanted to see what this Gavril really wanted. Was it power? Recognition? Something else entirely? Sergei had dealt with rebels before. He had put down and repelled his share of insurrections and raids across Parus. He understood how the mob mentality worked and how, sometimes, people simply felt compelled by the circumstances, unable to back down from silly threats and empty bravado. He understood this Gavril might not be looking to challenge his rule, but he could end up doing that if the meeting went sour.

The best way to resolve the situation was to talk to the holy man. In fact, he had already done a great deal by coming over. *Not weakness, strength.*

As he waited, he tried to glimpse past the welcoming party into this new town. There was a lot of activity there, just as you would expect from a living, breathing place, full of commerce and craft. People were going about their business, nourishing and growing the camp. That gave him some small hope. Folk bent on building things tended to be less keen on destroying them.

It wasn't long before a person came forward, so much like everyone else, yet entirely different. He wasn't young or old, ugly or handsome, tall or short, or anything of that sort. There was nothing special about him. Just an average, ordinary person, with the perfect measure of common and noble. He bore with mechanical precision that was almost too artfully sharp to watch. Dressed in a simple gray robe, he was followed by a boy and a reserved fellow with a long, dangling moustache. That one was armed, a large, wicked ax hanging from his hip.

A whole flock of other people trailed behind, keeping their distance, but it was obvious they wanted to be close to this man. He could feel their adoration, rising like desert heat off the sand. There was a palpable change in the atmosphere, suddenly going soft, mellow, and pleasant. He couldn't hear the throats groaning, but it was as if the air had turned savory and fresh. The human wall buckled, parting to let the man pass through.

There was no mistaking his identity.

Sergei noticed even his retinue was charmed by this Gavril person. Soldiers looked that less tense, that less likely to unsheathe their swords and lop heads off. Their eyes glistened, their mouths hanging slightly open, a breath of surprise on their lips. Genrik was almost smiling. Even Theo looked vibrant and cheerful.

Sergei felt a positive beat of good humor spreading through his body, as if he had just sampled the best kumiss. He realized his anger was seeping away. He tried to will himself to be sharp and nervous and assertive, but his muscles would not respond.

"Greetings, Your Highness," the robed person called. "I am Gavril." His voice was clear, beautiful. "I am most honored by your presence. It takes a great man to leave his castle and visit his subjects. Like a willow that bends before the wind but endures long after the wind has passed."

Sergei blinked, feeling enchanted. He had not felt this relaxed in years. "You have quite an undertaking started here."

Gavril looked behind him as if surprised to see the city behind him. "This place is a flower of faith. When there's fertile ground, faith buds and grows. I just showed these people the way. They built it; they made it."

Sergei was honestly intrigued. He had thought Athesia to be a godless realm. Then, in its very midst, there was a place with so much piety and faith that it rivaled the holy cities in the Safe Territories. Maybe it was just as simple as Gavril claimed.

"This city is a mirror of people's needs and fears and questions. This is where they come to find peace and shelter and answers. Through prayer and devotion for their gods and goddesses, they get what they want. They are rewarded for their love."

Sergei could never recall when prayer would get him *that* much peace. If anything, his conviction had eroded over the years, shattering with Vlad's death. But now, seeing this throng milling with purpose and dedication and belief, he almost doubted himself. "Incredible."

Gavril stepped closer, the moustached man and the big boy staying behind. Borya tensed ever so slightly, but it was like a drunk man responding to an annoying gnat, hardly the reaction of a man charged with protecting the king's life. Onward came the holy man, looking totally unconcerned. Soon, he stood inches from Sergei, his face a wreath of honesty and timeless wisdom.

"When people cannot find harmony with their leaders"—he tapped Sergei's chest—"they find it with their gods. Peace in the realms begins with the peace in your soul."

Sergei felt oddly insulted and relieved at the same time. Gavril's clear voice felt like it carried across the crowd, but he was certain no one else had heard those words. "You might have a point, holy man. But I must ask, what is the purpose of your presence here? Does your endeavor jeopardize my reign?" He probably should have phrased the question more elegantly, but he just couldn't spin the words.

"I do not challenge your rule, Your Highness," Gavril said. "On the contrary, I want to ensure you remain the king and that Parus prospers in the years to come."

Sergei blinked. "You do?"

Gavril pointed toward the open field behind the royal procession. "Let us walk. It is too crowded here." Without waiting for Sergei to follow, the holy man stepped into the field off the road, trampling grass with soft, apologetic steps, as if breaking each stalk hurt him personally.

Sergei nodded at his bodyguards. A risky decision, but then, there did not seem to be anyone within a mile, not counting the thirty thousand unaffiliated Athesians living in second Keron just behind him.

He followed Gavril, and soon, they were entirely on their own, surrounded by the chirp of birds and the buzz of insects.

"Your Highness," Gavril spoke, "I must make it absolutely clear. I assure you, I have no bad intentions. You must not treat me as some rival or a foe. Everything I am doing is ultimately in your favor. My followers will gladly be your followers."

If you tell them so, Sergei mused. The offer sounded genuine, noble, everything he could have hoped for. He had come here to see and assess the enemy presence and strength, to learn more about the holy man raising an army under his nose, to evaluate the charismatic religious leader of the new sect. Well, he had just gotten all that in one fell swoop. Only he wasn't that naïve to believe this Gavril would just so selflessly help him.

"You must want something from me?" he asked, almost feeling rude for making a demand from this lovable priestlike character.

Gavril smiled. "Yes. I must ask you to make peace with the Athesians."

Sergei arched a brow. "I have done that. There hasn't been a conqueror as benevolent as myself."

The smile persisted, unbroken, beautiful. "Yes. I must ask you to make peace with *all* of Athesia. With Empress Amalia."

The mention of the girl's name almost spoiled his mood. Almost. His mind started racing, as if freeing its boots from treacle, and he was thinking about Lady Lisa, and how she had proposed similar things, and he started envisioning plots again. There was a slate of them around him, involving the clergy, the defeated empress, her dead brother, even his sister. He was disoriented for a moment, lost.

"Why?" That was probably the best thing to say.

"You will find my words very hard to believe, Your Highness, but you must try. You must try for the sake of your nation and your family and all your subjects. Your war against the Athesians is justifiable and understandable. However, it is misplaced."

Sergei was quiet, studying the holy man. He wanted to believe his perfectly worded mantra, even though there was rage boiling deep in his soul. There was something about his slow, careful manner that made him weigh his response. He realized this wasn't just a pleasant chat with a lunatic, or banter between deadly if polite rivals. This wasn't about who would rule this sorry stretch of a realm, nor about his family vengeance. He could feel something much older, much more primal at hand, even if he could not put his hands around it and describe it.

"Every human has an interest," Gavril added. Sergei frowned at the strange choice of words. "Everyone. You have your own goals, and I am certain that Empress Amalia, as well as Under-Patriarch Evgeny, have their own desires and whims and passions just as sincere and serious as your own. But these needs dwarf against a great collective urgency facing the whole of the world."

Holy preachers always had a flair for drama, Sergei thought. But the taste on his tongue was not one of mockery. "I find your words troubling."

Gavril raised a hand. "Please, Your Highness, I beg you. Do not dismiss them. I am well aware that my speech sounds insane. It is very…well…preposterous. I have spent a lot of time wondering how I might approach you, ask for your audience and petition you with my news, without sounding crazy or hungry for power. I also understand the more I speak, the more you will be inclined to disbelieve me. But I just implore you, listen to me; then decide what you must do."

Sergei sighed. "All right. Continue."

"There is a war coming. A great war. Against an ancient enemy that has returned to subjugate all of the realms. If the people of this land do not unite, we will lose this war. There will be no more Athesia, Caytor, Eracia, or Parus. The realms will be destroyed."

Omens, omens. Sergei was liking this less and less with every passing moment. How could one argue with a person blinded by his religion? It was pointless, even when someone like Gavril spoke their case so eloquently.

"I must convince you," Gavril added.

"That you do," Sergei said. Under the soft, pleasant layer of thoughts inspired by the holy man's presence, Sergei was already considering military action against Gavril's forces. There could be no reasoning with someone convinced of an inevitable, pending doom. The royal troops would have to crush the congregation, utterly and mercilessly. The defeat would have to be complete, even greater than the one inflicted on the Athesians. It pained him to turn his army against religion, but he could not tolerate unpredictable madness. He understood the cost and the risk. He would gift Amalia with time to reinforce her position, making all future battles that much bloodier. Then, he would have to muster his lords again, make Parus weak and exposed for a while. He did not forget the threat the nomads still posed, especially after he had slighted them last year. They might send their troops raiding into the Safe Territories or Sevorod, and he would not be able to stop them. Or the Gowashi might raise their ugly heads once again. And there was no guarantee for any of the small duchies in the south.

It seemed his legacy would have to be one of blood.

He was almost ready to turn and walk away. Order his men back to Roalas. That was what he should do. Yes, he wanted to make peace, he wanted to be like Adam, but that did not—

"Have you ever wondered how your father died?" Gavril said, shattering his thoughts, pinning him cold to the ground.

"What?" Sergei croaked, his voice brittle, thin all of a sudden. A well of old emotions lurched to the surface, like an empty barrel bobbing in the dock waters.

"Your Highness, do you recall the death of your father? Do you remember the return of the few survivors?"

Sergei was beginning to suspect an elaborate trickery. Gavril must have spoken to Evgeny, who had provided him with information about his past so he could use it against him. He had never really considered his people an enemy, but today's meeting was making him fairly convinced.

"Please, I beg you. Do you remember how strange all those dead bodies looked? Peaceful? With clean wounds?"

The stories about legendary Athesian weapons resurfaced, and this time, it wasn't just an empty barrel. There was a black, oily emotion he could not quite pinpoint, but it smothered him, and narrowed down his vision, and made it pulse red with beating blood.

Bloated purple bodies, eaten by flies and worms, and with large, clean wounds as if made by fire and lance.

Stories, nothing more. Empty stories.

But he did clearly remember glimpsing the bodies of the dead nobles, Vlad the Fifth among them, serene and whole as if sleeping.

Sergei tensed. He heard a noise to his right. He could see that dangerous, taciturn man reach for his ax. There was a murmur of surprise and displeasure in the crowd, on both sides, the woolly charm suddenly broken.

"Your Highness, please, take your hand off your sword hilt. Please." Gavril looked like he might cry.

Sergei stopped himself. He breathed hard through his nostrils, almost flicking snot, but he reined in his wild, dark feelings, pushed them back. "What are you saying, holy man?"

Gavril waited until he was certain Sergei would listen to every word. "Your father was killed by a magical weapon. It is called the bloodstaff. That weapon is now in the hands of the White Witch of Naum, the enemy of this land and all its people." Gavril pointed at the ax wielder. "Ludevit is also blessed with magic. He can sense future danger. He anticipated your desire to unleash violence."

Sergei felt like a child being shown some huge, wondrous toy, ten times the size of a large castle, towering, massive beyond comprehension. *Play with it,* the world teased and goaded. Magic. Magic? That was nonsense. That could not be.

He remembered the dead bodies. He remembered the strange wounds. He remembered, later, for weeks on end, Vasiliy's sword champions and engineers using dead pigs to try to inflict that damage, trying to figure out what might have caused those fatal holes. No matter what they tried, nothing would destroy flesh so tidily.

He had pushed those memories away, their significance. He had focused on his need for revenge. Now that he had Roalas in his hands, now that he ruled this sorry realm, there was fresh room for other thoughts and feelings in his soul. And they were telling him that there could be an incredible truth in this mess.

No, it could not be. Impossible.

"I must thank you for your time, Gavril. It has been insightful."

The holy man grimaced, looking panicky and defeated. "No, Your Highness, please."

Sergei nodded once. "I will consider your proposal. Meanwhile, I expect you and all your men to pay homage to the throne in Sigurd. I do not dispute your faith, but this is my land, and there are two things required from all my subjects: loyalty and taxes."

Gavril's face was almost too painful to look at. "I understand the enormity of my claim, but please, Your Highness, do not disregard my story lightly. What would I gain from this?"

Sergei shrugged. "Who knows? I will heed your advice. I will muster my troops. And I will give Empress Amalia one last chance to bend knee and accept my rule. Then, we shall all have unity, and if needs be, we will stand together against other enemies. If not, then her defeat will mark the end of Athesia, magical weapons or not."

Gavril bit his lower lip, a very childish gesture on that ageless face. "I understand. I apologize if my words caused you disquiet."

Sergei relaxed a little, but his mind had closed to kind words and reason. He began walking back to his retinue, all of whom were carefully watching him, judging his motions, trying to figure out what might have transpired. Gavril followed, his feet silent on the grass.

"We are going back," Sergei announced. "I must thank you for your hospitality," he told his host. Not a cup of the poorest ale. That spoke much about the man's intentions. Then again, he could not imagine Gavril indulging his guests with drinks and nibbles. He could sooner imagine Theo being cheerful and funny.

The spell of tranquility and peace was broken. There were two camps staring at one another with a fair dose of mistrust. He had wasted a day and a half on traveling, and would waste just as much going back to Roalas. To what end? To have his conviction prodded by some crazy man? To have old, filthy memories come back to life, to haunt his dreams?

He was not quite sure what to really make of Gavril's words. They rang true and mad at the same time. They felt utterly wrong, and yet he wanted to embrace them. But brave men did not fear difficult choices.

Made by Adam, he would be like Adam. He would offer his neighbors and enemies peace, but if they scorned it, he would utterly crush them. He invited Genrik into his own coach and found himself dictating the summons for his lords. The Parusite army would assemble and ride north once again. This time, there were be no half defeats and half victories. Amalia would get her one chance. He would grant her that much. But after that, there would be no more silly weakness on behalf of King Sergei. In that moment, he thought about his royal hostage. He was seeing new wisdom in Lisa's words. She had always urged him to seek peace; he had just seen it coming from a position of weakness. In a strange, morbid way, his very enemy had counseled him on the best course of action he could have. Perhaps because she did understand what war really meant.

Lady Lisa, I present you with peace, he thought. *The kind your husband would have forged. May the gods and goddesses have mercy on your daughter.*

CHAPTER 13

Calemore sat under a hornbeam, eating an apple. There was a sudden thunderstorm spilling its guts above him, the sky livid and flickering. He knew that his shelter was not the most ideal choice, but his magic would protect him from boiling sap and hot splinters if a lightning chose to strike right there.

The wind was hissing through the branches, stirring them wildly, ripping leaves, making it all look more chaotic than it really was. In the field out there, the Naum people were standing in the rain, enjoying the respite from the summer heat. Even now, they marveled at the precipitation like children. Amazement, hand in hand with the realization of their quest in these realms.

Killing the locals was their primary task. But they had to make sure they did not totally and utterly raze the land, because after all, it was going to be their new home. Once the war was over, they would settle in the abandoned villages and towns and replant the crops. Some of the destruction was necessary, but total desolation was out of the question.

He had ordered his western army to wait at the imagined border between Eracia and Athesia, because the eastern force was severely lagging behind schedule, and it would take several more weeks before it reached Pain Mave. The terrain in northern Caytor was more rugged, more difficult for travel, less bountiful. His troops were making slow progress, often having to spend half the daylight foraging.

In the west, there were some complications, too. A large number of supply convoys was being delayed for some reason, probably lost or gone down the wrong road. He had instructed the soldiers not to destroy any bridges, to allow for a smooth advance. Even so, the women and children and craftsmen might be facing all kinds of difficulties, from weather to food supplies. Although, from what he had seen, Eracia was quite bountiful, with days and days of rich harvest everywhere.

The sky groaned, rumbled, belched. The world turned brilliant white with the flicker of knives in orange and purple clouds, seething, moving low and fast. Rain came in gusts, slanted by the wind, stabbing at people's squinted, delighted faces. Calemore bit deeper into the apple, his lip brushing the slick seeds in the core.

He was hoping the killing in the north of Eracia and Caytor would flush the surviving god out of his hiding. But no. The rat had holed himself up somewhere, probably farther south, maybe in those would-be holy Safe Territories, trying to build his strength. Well, his opponent was getting stronger. All of Calemore's attempts to locate him and kill him had failed so far.

But he would find him and make sure he died.

He threw the core away. Deftly, he rose and dusted his white leathers from crushed grass and dirt, walked out from under the safe, dry cover of the hornbeam into the rainy world. Cold drops slapped him, slicking his hair to his forehead.

The world was covered in a veil of muddy brownish fog up to knee height, almost like a morning haze. The summer rain pounded the dry earth, raising wet billows. Men were dashing about, covering victuals and weapons with tarps, herding livestock back into pens. Large armies had always had one great weakness, and that was roadside supply. They never had enough to support themselves for a long time, so they had to lug animals along and scavenge anything they could find. At the moment, the shaggy milk-giving goats were probably more valuable than the spearmen.

His nation had gotten used to seeing him around once again. The awe was subdued somewhat, still present and hot in their veins, but it had been replaced with a healthy dose of practical military life. You could not be a good smith if you spent most of the time bowing to your master. Someone had to make those tools.

His white boots had grown a second skin, brown and runny like carob syrup. He frowned and kept on walking, crossing the massive encampment. Guard dogs slunk away when he came near, whining in fear.

He was thinking about Nigella too much lately. He was missing her ugly face, her firm body, her pies, and her intrigue. He wanted to spend a day in her small, humble home, chatting, fucking her, trying to piece together snippets of the future that he could use against the remaining god. But even someone like him had only so much time. When he became a god, it might get easier.

Only somehow, it did not feel like it anymore. His eternal dream was spoiled.

By a woman with buckteeth, spectacles, and delicious pies.

Calemore plowed on, ignoring any signs of servitude around him. He was inspecting the force, trying to figure out if the Naum army was truly ready for the massive campaign that awaited it. So far, they had only encountered light opposition, but now, they would be marching south through the realm of Athesia. That foolish cunt Amalia had a few thousand troops at her disposal. The pious Parusite ruler and his kin fielded some more, although the bulk of his army was in their southern kingdom. The Caytorean lords could put up a valiant effort with their private troops.

Not large numbers, by any means, but they were much better organized, they knew the land well, and they had spent the past two years fighting, gaining valuable experience. His troops would crush them all, but there was the subtle, maddening matter of timing. The attacks had to be swift and precise. Otherwise, the enemy might simply decide to retreat, all too aware of the odds against them. That would mean chasing a smaller, nimbler enemy and tens of thousands of refugees across the realms, a futile, exhausting task. Or the enemy might try to starve the Naum men.

Sweeping through Caytor, the eastern army would trample most of that realm. The western army would destroy Amalia and Sergei and then plunge into the Territories. By then, Calemore hoped the surviving deity would be already too weak to resume his war, or maybe even dead. But if needed, his forces would march on farther south, into the scalding land of Parus. He did not relish that, as his troops would suffer there. And the Parusite king had the healthy backing of his vassals, which would make the fighting even more protracted.

He would be forced to leave pockets of enemy troops behind, like the worthless, broken Eracia and the coastal cities in Caytor that would be spared in the first wave, but they could be sorted out later, once he defeated the one remaining god.

Almost like the ancient war.

Almost identical.

He just worried about food supplies, really. His army was superior. The people of the realms were too few, too fragmented to oppose it. Only he needed quick victories, to ensure that the Naum families could claim the land as their own and start tilling it.

Nigella's advice would be invaluable now. She might tell him how to proceed. But all her riddles and answers had given him little insight into the battles waiting ahead. He felt it would come down to brute force and nothing more. It would be slow, costly, messy, but inevitable. Well, he had one weapon that would make all the difference.

The only reason he had not yet used the bloodstaff against the nations of these realms was his lack of knowledge about the god and his whereabouts. He could not afford to expose himself through rash actions. He had waited for so long.

Patience, he had to be patient.

He paused, watching the world through a gray curtain of watery arrows. He saw several elders walking toward him, oiled cloaks bundled over their heads. Like his own clothes, their uniforms had lost their pristine color, turned brown and mucky by the storm. Raindrops were splattering wildly, jumping like grasshoppers.

They approached him and knelt down, knees sinking in the squelchy mud. "We await your mercy."

"Report," he said. On the horizon, plum-colored clouds lined with silver fire were raging, pulsing with light.

"Snomack and Buan tell their own families have not reached the camp site. We sent a scout party north to inspect, but it has not returned either. Nine days now."

Calemore licked lukewarm water from his lips. Two more clans lost, it seemed. Or delayed. Or maybe ambushed. But that was highly unlikely. Every time his troops had come up against the Eracians, the enemy had fled like mice. That entire Barrin estate had just run away south, leaving all their possessions behind. There were no enemy forces north of his position.

But the string of reports was becoming more than just sundry losses. At first, he had valued the occasional missing convoy as the expected, inevitable waste of a gigantic military machine. For all he knew, they might have found a desirable tract of land and remained there. He could not really blame the women and children for losing the sense of purpose after thousands of miles of hard travel to a foreign land. Yet, he needed them. He needed their skill with thread and needle, with seeds, with pottery. And the men needed their families, to reassure them in this quest. Naum was his, in mind and body, but men were men, Damian's feeble creations, and ultimately, they had tiny hearts and little loyalty except to their animalistic desires and fears.

The missing people were having an effect on the army. There was a sense of confusion, and doubt could never be good for war. Then, there was a genuine shortage of goods. Soldiers traveled mostly with battle gear. His troops clamored about the lack of axle grease, buttons, grinding stones, and leather. Some of the formations no longer had butter or eggs, and there was competition and stealing.

Once, Calemore might instill discipline with an exhibition of grisly executions over the tiniest infractions, but he no longer could summon the joy for terror like he once did. A certain woman had numbed his appetite for horror, made it feel trifling and petty. He just could not see a point in murdering human flesh for power. It almost felt pointless. Nigella had truly corrupted his mind.

For countless centuries, a sharp, clear, fanatic purpose had been his one motivation. Now, he entertained doubt in his mind. Perversely, he liked it, liked the imperfect feel of it. He relished discovering new emotions inside of him, but it bothered him that he would suffer the same turmoils and agonies like these human insects.

Damian destroyed the world over one woman's scorn. Now, I am ruining my own ideals, because I have taken a fancy for apple pies.

That just wasn't right.

For a moment, Calemore considered using his magic to go northwest and prowl the field, searching for the missing parties. But he had to use his skill sparingly. Until he knew for certain the extent of his enemy's tricks and power, he had to avoid wasting his magic. The surviving god might have Special Children, or he might be growing in strength. It was really hard to know, but the fact he had lived through quite a few assassination attempts spoke of a worthy opponent. No matter how slim the chances, Calemore had to proceed with caution.

"Send more scouts. Make sure you do not engage any locals if you find them. Avoid combat at all cost, and return at once with reports." The sky rumbled in approval.

The storm wasn't showing any signs of abating. The air was turning cool, and there were rivers coursing through the grass, the downpour too strong for the earth to soak it all in. Bits of rotten fruit and garbage floated on the brown rain snakes, eddying away from the camp's gentle slope. The weather might bog his men down, but at least it would clean their site.

Calemore snorted. Even plans devised over the course of centuries had a tendency to take an unexpected turn. He had never quite considered his men might clamor about lard, nails, or whetstones. Perhaps he should not. He was the leader of a nation. Such trifles should not concern him. He just had to imagine the flow of the army south, see the great clash, watch the enemy god's power drain as faith died. Once again, he blamed Nigella, her simple, modest life. She had enamored him with appreciation for details, for small things, as if they mattered.

The big problem was horses. His nation lacked them, sorely. There were slow, fat dray beasts, good for pulling wagons, but they would not stand riders on their backs, and they didn't like anything that wasn't a steady plod in a straight line. Which meant his scouts had to go on foot. It made them much slower than the continental people, and if spotted, they could hardly run away. Hundreds of men were busy trying to catch and tame anything with four legs, from wild ponies to mules and mill asses, but Naum would not be having cavalry anytime soon.

The Eracians had fled their homes with what they could carry along, and often butchered or burned whatever was left behind, including dogs, sheep, even horses. Calemore was almost shocked by the display of savagery by the humans. They built their lives with so much hard work and pain, and then, they were willing to destroy all that just so someone else could not lay their hands on their abandoned treasures. Now and then, his troops would capture a stable full of healthy animals or find houses intact with cellars stocked high. But the enemy was using all it could to make the conquest more difficult.

Travel was hard for the Naum men. Calemore had used magic twice to repair sapped bridges and had forbidden his troops from damaging any form of transportation. His massive army would need boats and ferries to move south, anything that would make the campaign faster, easier. He had put out wild, errant fires on a dozen occasions so the captured towns would not turn to ashes. But he could not be everywhere, and the wind cared nothing for his strict orders.

Nigella, he wanted to see Nigella. She was five hundred miles away, and he had to nourish his magic. Maybe, after the western army reached its destination, and the eastern force resumed the march south, then he would magic himself to Marlheim.

This war should have been a simple, worry-free affair. His army was larger than anything the realms could muster, more disciplined despite the harsh journey through an unknown land. He had vast magic, he had the bloodstaff, and he had to defeat only one sorry god, who might have some feeble allies in this land. Only somehow, he was rather concerned. Not afraid, no. He would never let himself stoop that low. Fear was for these puny humans. He was troubled. That was it.

His taste for victory, his desire for revenge, his confidence in the Naum nation, all were marred, flawed, chipped, and cracking, bland, pale, uninviting. Corrupted by his strange, inexplicable obsession with an ugly woman.

Ridiculous.

And yet, he knew that he would find peace in her cottage. He knew she would try to manipulate him, and insinuate her silly female dreams, and she would try to piece together hidden truths from the pages of that book, and he would be frustrated and angry and left without any solid answers. But that seemed like the best option now.

He wasn't sure if he should hate himself or his dead father for this weakness. But whatever he was, no matter how perfect he was, there was a gaping hole in him somewhere, and it yearned for human attention.

The rain kept falling. The senior elder was reporting on the camp strength and readiness, listing away problems and shortages, the number of men taken ill, and other boring details. He simply wasn't in the mood to listen to them.

He just turned away and walked on, eyes squinted against the wet whip, churning mud with boots turned irrecoverably shit colored. All this felt wrong. Futile. He was beginning to nourish a yeasty, moldy thought that ancient vengeance wasn't quite as satisfying as he had expected it to be, but he didn't dare ponder on that idea too long.

I will be a god, he promised, and walked through the storm.

CHAPTER 14

I need friends, Amalia thought, so she smiled at Malik. "Did you like my brother?" Saying the word felt strange. "Brother" was not how she had felt about James. Even half that was too much. Whenever she really, truly let her mind consider him, she always strayed toward Father, some former life he had left behind and some unknown woman who had birthed his son. It stung, so she made sure she never pondered too deeply about James. She wished she could know who he really had been, what had motivated him, and what his family might have been like. But he would never tell her that. So she might as well learn about him from his adjutants, officers, and followers. Maybe bond in friendship with them.

The clerk shrugged. "I did, Your Highness."

"Why?" she asked.

Malik shrugged again. "He was a likable sort, Your Highness." They were walking outside the abandoned manor house taking on repairs. There was a whole regiment of craftsmen scrabbling all around and over the stonework, like ants swarming their hill. The whole structure was enclosed in scaffolding, and it was hard to tell what the masons were really doing. But this would become her new residence soon, she thought, a symbol of status.

"He had humble manners, like your common man," Malik continued. "He didn't have any of that arrogance you would find with the councillors and other nobility. Ordinary soldiers could identify with him."

Unlike me, she thought. Maybe she should show them her scars. They would no longer be a weakness; they would be her badge of honor, her shield. "And why did you join him?"

An easy grimace pinched the adjutant's face. "Frankly, we were all rather fed up with the situation in Caytor. Year after year of humiliation. First, we had those Feorans, and they ravaged the realm. Then Adam—pardon me, Your Highness—Emperor Adam came and stole our land. But the High Council did nothing. No one opposed him. The nation was left in shame. And then those pirates came and humiliated us some more. When your brother declared himself, we thought it was like the war twenty years ago. We wanted to be on the winning side this time around."

She smiled softly. Winning side. She had spoken to several officers and aides, trying to figure out who her brother was. Perhaps they feared her reaction, but they all spoke in great favor of his charm and deeds. It was true that death exalted everyone. There was no harm in saying a good word for the deceased, and it also made you feel better about yourself. It cost nothing. Still, she believed there must be an inkling of truth in their stories, if not the intensity.

"Didn't you think you were betraying your country?" she inquired.

Malik rubbed his chin, and it sounded like the paper he manhandled every day. "Well, all the councillors were flocking to his side. How can that be treason, then?"

"And what will you do now? You know I am the Athesian empress. My duty is to the realm my father *stole* from you."

He did not have an answer. She hadn't really expected him to spout wisdom. How could anyone really sum up four decades of national turmoil, disgrace, and bitter competition between the nation's finest in a few quick sentences?

"Thank you for your time, Malik."

He nodded and dashed off, glad to be free.

Amalia paused in the shadow of a ruined buttress being smeared with fresh mortar, blocks of stone waiting near a catapult-like ramp. Workers were having a simple break in the simple routine of their simple lives, dicing and eating, smoking and laughing. When they saw her, they stood up and bowed. Then, they went back to not really worrying. She almost envied them.

Not far off, Jarman glanced toward her and nodded in support. She pursed her lips at him, as if her expression could tell all she felt. Ever since their agreement, he spent more time around her, trying to help her. She should be grateful, she felt, but it jarred her, his presence, a reminder of her weakness and the impeding doom from the north. She still found it hard to believe, but whenever she doubted his words, she recalled the night in Roalas when Calemore stole the bloodstaff and the book, the day he had utterly ruined her. But her mind would not linger long on those black thoughts, shutting itself against the stark white fear that bore into her temples.

She looked the other way. No time for silly, girlish doubts, she swore. "Master Hector."

The leathery man detached himself from the group of officers and stepped in stride with her. She had not yet spoken to him about James, and she wanted his perspective. "Your Highness."

Tread softly, she told herself. *No. Tread hard.* "Why are you here?"

"You called me."

"In Athesia, following me?"

The man snorted. "We never had a heart-to-heart discussion, Your Highness. I expected it would happen sooner or later. Do you really want the truth?"

Amalia looked at Jarman again. He would protect her, he had promised. She needed friends. The best way to find if you had any was to push people into a corner. Everyone was always nice when things were in order.

"Please."

He spat in the grass. "Doing my duty."

She smiled at him. "Isn't your duty to follow the orders of the High Council?"

The former sergeant smiled back. His teeth were in much worse shape than hers. "Rather than answering that, Your Highness, let me ask you something else in return. You must be wondering what all these men will do if they stop liking the Athesian coin one day. Or Caytorean coin. Or any coin. Aren't you?"

Amalia let his rude manners slide. "That thought did cross my mind."

He clicked his tongue as if he had gained a strategic lead in an argument. "You must understand the Caytorean society first, before you can hear my answer. A long time ago, we had our kings and emperors and the like. Wasn't very profitable. We realized power is much better governed when there's a whole lot of people fighting for their own interests rather than uniting under one leader. That way, they keep scheming among themselves rather than cooperating. Keeps everyone busy. Makes things stable and predictable." He paused. "Loyalty became a matter of profit, rather than principle. You follow the man who pays you, and you do not question morality too much."

"That does not sound very noble," she hazarded.

Master Hector laughed. "Killing people when ordered by a king or a councillor is still the same thing. You might sleep better at night knowing you had no choice either way. So no, my duty is not to follow the orders of the High Council. My duty is to protect *my* realm."

"Is this why you joined my brother?"

"I joined your brother because I was paid to do so. With time, I learned to like the lad, a lot. He had spirit and honesty, in his unique way. You may think I'm mad, but you forget yourself, Your Highness. When you became the empress of Athesia, you took our finest hostage. You threatened my realm. We didn't know if you might lead another war against us, like your father did. When our councillors decided to oppose you, many of us figured we should side with Councillors Otis and Melville to fight you. I got gold to train James, but I was there to make sure he did not suddenly become a greedy bastard with an eye for the rest of our land."

Amalia was fascinated. "Do go on, please."

Hector snatched at an annoying fly buzzing near his ear. He missed. "Lady Rheanna made the greatest sacrifice. She got herself into his clutches, a dangerous game if you ask me, but she did prevail, and she made him into a fine husband."

"Why are you *still* here?"

The once head of the Caytorean Military Academy looked at her like she was asking him to marry her. "Where else would I go? Go back to training peasants how to tell left from right? Adjudicate feuds between lords in backward regions?"

She didn't like this, not the mention of James's fat-arsed widow, not the man's casual manner about loyalty. "You expect me to retain your services after this admission?" Not what she had planned when she had summoned him. But then, she had challenged him, and he did not yield, a tough old man with nothing to lose.

He pointed in the general direction of Ecol, his thumbnail black from sword practice blows. "Most lads out there are just paid killers, and they don't give a dog shit about your cause. Some of us do care and want the best for Caytor. Things got out of control with your brother. Now things might get out of control with you, but we are going to make sure you do not threaten our realm. We will support you if you keep true to your brother's promise."

"What is it?"

"Profit for Caytor. Handsome profit. Alliance." He made a pained, forced expression. "Your peace efforts with the Parusites are not encouraging. Your spring-cleaning sure didn't invoke any extra loyalty. Now you're turning your wrath against Lady Rheanna. That will not go down well with the Caytoreans."

Honesty, in the form of a rebuke and a threat. James might have been some honest Eracian, but he seemed to have done quite well keeping everyone happy. He killed some of his patrons, then gained loyalty by marrying Rheanna. Perhaps that was what she needed? To marry some rich, handsome Caytorean, someone who would not remind her of Gerald so she did not get sad every time she looked at his face?

She often forgot she was a young, presumably attractive empress, if not for her scars, without a husband. That was a great tool if she dared use it. However, she felt weak considering it. That was what ordinary women did, and she did not want to be just another maid seeking a strong man to help her and keep her safe. Then again, Father married a Caytorean woman, a commoner, and that made the small folk adore him. He had united his fledgling empire by carefully balancing the factions.

Sacrifice for her nation. Her own love ideals were unimportant.

She steered the subject gently back to her brother. "Did he tell you anything about his life in Eracia?"

Hector scrunched his nose, deep-gorged skin turning into tree bark. "No. He kept it to himself. No one knew anything about his kin. If the councillors did, they kept it secret, too."

Amalia nodded. Finding friends did not quite work for her. Not only was she all alone in this, everyone hassled and threatened her in the process. Jarman's help had its own wicked barb. Her army consisted of mercenaries making sure she did what they wanted while counting the gold she paid. Even this old man didn't bother lying to her about it; he was simply un-afraid. Her face sagged.

"Amalia," Master Hector said in a gentle voice, surprising her, "I'm an old man. I've been fed so much shit in my life, if you put me in a bucket of night soil, you couldn't tell me apart from a dried turd. You seem to have dignity, and that's good. But power does not come to people just 'cause they were born to it. They gotta earn it. You have to prove yourself. If you want your father's respect, then you have to be like your father."

She was confused. "He took land from you."

The master blinked slowly. "He gave us eighteen years of the best trade we ever had. He gave us peace."

Amalia sighed. Peace. Everyone just wanted her to make peace, even if it meant killing thousands just to get it. Forgive everyone, ignore her enemies, placate them. Bow to King Sergei, bow before the High Council, pray for scraps of mercy and gratitude.

She had promised the Sirtai wizard to seek a just agreement with the Parusites. But that meant alienating her fickle allies. If only she could somehow use either of these weaknesses to her advantage. With Caytor behind her, she could maybe force King Sergei to offer greater concessions. Or maybe the threat of Parus could sway the councillors to help her, lest they lose all their hope of future profit and cooperating.

She was tired. Exhausted. She hated all these speculations, games, deals. She hated having to barter with her soul and honor. The worst part was, her imagined truth of how Father had managed the realm was coming undone. She had once simply believed he had ruled fearlessly, tossing bones to his foes and watching them fight over them like rabid dogs. Now, though, she was beginning to suspect the reality might have been different, more complex, more difficult.

Everyone urged me to make peace. Mom, Theo, Gerald. Everyone. They must have known something I missed as a child growing in my father's protective shadow. I should have listened then.

Two years later, with her honor in Ecol's gutters, she was learning the lesson the hard way.

"Make peace," Hector repeated.

Amalia realized she was nearing the city, having lost her sense of time. Her court trailed behind her, all except Agatha, who rode a palfrey. "Sounds simple."

"Do it while you still have the initiative, Your Highness. You're lucky you have that butcher Xavier. That piece of shit likes his gold so much; otherwise you'd be having open rebellion right now."

He had quite an incentive, she thought. "You waited a long while to tell me this."

Master Hector looked serene. "You never asked before."

"You think I should not have kept Lady Rheanna locked up?" she asked, intrigued.

"That surely did not help your position. Now that she's escaped, she made you look weak. And you might have an enemy when she could have been your ally. You seem quite fond of keeping people captive under armed guard."

She deserved the jibe. "What do you think of the Sirtai's omen?"

He bent down, groaning, and plucked a dandelion. He twirled it between his fingers, then puffed, scattering the seeds. "I am not the one to ask about wizardly affairs. I can give you advice on matters of steel and blood and a man's honor. Piss makes for a good thing to cool hot, forged iron, but it's a poor way of soothing one's pride."

In some lunatic reality, I might call this old hound a friend, she thought. But she realized it would never be that way between them. His open admission was his way of distancing himself from her, she knew. He probably believed she was not going to win this war. Rather than being a traitor, he just closed his heart to her. Erased her. Easier to cope, she knew.

"You would not pay heed to his warning of a large foreign army," she pressed.

"I would not. But *you* should. In fact, you'd better hope that army comes, 'cause it's your best chance now. Once the forces of this or that witch descend on the realms, we will be all too busy fighting it together. Might give you a chance to save face, amend old wrongs."

She had such a splendid repertoire of options before her. She could choose between a Caytorean murderer for her champion, a sly Sirtai wizard with his own vendetta, or serving King Sergei, whose family had been orphaned by her own father. And in between, she could hope she might get on friendly terms with James's widow and the whole High Council, both of which she had scorned, snubbed, and insulted on several occasions. She also had to choose a husband for herself, go back on her promise to Xavier, and outlast a war against an incredible, magical enemy force. If all these turned out all right, she might not have a realm left. All the while, she still had not even the slightest idea who had betrayed her and freed Lady Rheanna.

She could not trust anyone, and that made her attempts at friendship even trickier.

For all she knew, the leathery sergeant might have been the one to help the widow escape. He might be blunt and honest now, but that did not mean he was telling her the whole truth.

Father, what do you do when you don't have anyone you can trust? Oh, Father, I miss you. But late Emperor Adam had no answers for his daughter.

"Thank you, Master Hector," she said and dismissed the wiry sergeant.

Amalia woke in the middle of the night, her bladder bursting. She was quite alert, despite the hour, she realized, the flickering images of her dream gone. It was hot and stifling in her room, even though the window was cracked open. Her soldiers warned her against assassins using the opportunity to slip inside, so she had posted a pair of crossbowmen on the roof at night. Sometimes, she could sniff the stench of their smoking or hear them chatter, mostly about women. Ever since James's dead friend Rob had brought his ugly habit from Eybalen, more and more men had embraced it.

Amalia walked to the small privacy chamber built into the corner of the room. Inside, it had a seat made of polished wood, a funnel, and a bent length of pipe connecting to the drain outside. Marvelous invention. You did not have to tinkle into a pot under your bed or brave the night going to a smelly outhouse.

She sat down, the cold pine making her thighs tickle. It only made her urge to pee stronger. Soon enough, she released her belly muscles and groaned softly, and the tin funnel began purring with a metallic, wet sound. Marvelous invention, indeed. Master Guilliam was not just a highly skilled weapons maker. Once she retook Roalas—if she retook it, she reminded herself—then she would have privacy chambers built in every room of the manse, as well as all the guilds and inns.

She was finished soon enough and reached for a rag, hanging on a nail from the side wall, to dry her nethers. Something creaked. She thought it might be a last errant drop, but it did not sound like urine plinking against metal. It sounded like a floorboard being bent by a considerable weight.

Like a human presence.

Her breath caught in her throat. She swallowed a whimper of panic, imagining Calemore standing out there, waiting for her, a pearly smile on his face.

"Your Highness?" someone whispered.

She almost screamed. She realized she had buried her fingernails in her stomach, gripping hard. What now? Shout for help? Would anyone hear? Would anyone be able to respond fast enough? Who was it out there? A friend? A foe? Why would anyone sneak into her chamber? Was it Xavier, come to rape her?

Amalia heard a reedy snivel escape through her clogged nostrils, in and out. Her body was frozen, and she could not move. She was unarmed, and all she had was her dignity pooled round her ankles.

"Do not be afraid, I wish you no harm. Please come out."

Like a puppet, her arms and legs tied to strings and moved by some unruly giant, she rose, pulled up her knickers, rolled the nightgown down, reached with a trembling hand toward the door of the privacy chute, and carefully pushed it open.

A man was standing by her bed, arms spread in a pacifying gesture. "Your Highness. My name is Adelbert. I have helped your half brother in the past."

"Why are you here?" Was it her own voice? It had to be.

"Unfortunately, the presence of your two Sirtai advisers precludes me from meeting you in the open."

"What do you want?" Did she really sound so terrified, so weak?

"I really wish you no harm. I just want to talk. I noticed you have been making all kinds of deals with your people, so I thought it would be prudent if I mentioned my own debt. The debt your family owes me, that is. Your half brother, but now he is dead, so the debt is yours now."

"How did you get in here?" Hadn't Jarman placed magical wards around her?

There wasn't much light from the moon in her chamber, but she could see the expression on the man's face change subtly, as if he had remembered a fond, pleasant memory. "Those two men are very talented wizards, but they are still Sirtai. They have spent too long living in their own beautiful land to really understand the extent of trickery and ingenuity people under dire circumstances may come up with. They protect you against people of the realms and the witch's touch, but they forgot harm might come to you from one of their own. They don't protect against Sirtai magic, you see."

Sirtai? Was this man Sirtai? She vaguely remembered seeing him before around the city, but he was just another member of the household, silent, distant, unimportant. So what was he doing in the room now?

"I will tell them that," she heard herself say, feeling morbidly detached. Drums rolled in the night, but it was just in her heart really, she figured.

"I would appreciate if you kept our meeting secret. I wish you no harm. But late Emperor James promised I could name my price for my assistance. Your Highness, I must know you will respect your dead brother's promise."

She swallowed; it was an effort. "Tell me."

Adelbert made a minute step toward her. She gasped, so he stopped and shuffled back. If he intended to hurt her, he was taking his time torturing her mind first. But there was nothing outright violent or dangerous about him, except that he stood in her magically warded room. Amalia regretted being alone. Agatha was in the nearby chamber, sleeping on her own. Lately, ever since she had become pregnant, she would snore quite often, because she had to sleep on her back, and Amalia preferred silent nights, without noises and grunts. Her bodyguards were just outside, in the corridor.

Right now, she wouldn't have even minded wet, lousy dogs for company.

"I can't name my price," the strange man insisted. "I have not decided on it *yet*. But I wish to know if you are going to honor the agreement."

"How did you help him?" she croaked. She had to know.

The interloper made a tiny smile, a flash of teeth in the night's silvery light. "He needed magical assistance." He paused. "Perhaps, you might require my help, too? I would be glad to assist you, but the price might be higher."

There was this stranger standing in front of her, but she saw Calemore in his place. Teasing her, making demands, threatening her, asking her questions. How much was she willing to sacrifice? Would she give up her maidenhood?

And then, he broke her spirit.

"What do you say, Your Highness? I could help."

Beggars don't get to choose. "Yes," Amalia mumbled. She had no idea what he could ask. But she would say yes to all of them. Jarman, Xavier, Sergei, Adelbert, all the rest. She would buy herself time and make sure she responded when she finally regained her strength and confidence. Or maybe she never would, doomed to remain a beggar her whole life. That was *her* price, perhaps, for her mistakes in Roalas.

She thought she should be resentful, but all she felt was sadness. Maybe she deserved the terror and derision. Make peace. That's all that mattered. Save the realm.

Once, she might have even considered sweet revenge, but even that idea made her weary now. Could she blame the vultures around her for pecking at her soft flesh? Could she blame the animals for sniffing out her fears and chasing her? This Adelbert was no worse than Xavier or Jarman. He just wanted his share. And Amalia, a weak, pitiful thing, should comply so he would not get upset and retaliate. That was the sum of her new life. An empress reduced to a fool.

She thought she should have learned from her mistakes in the capital. Her spring-cleaning should have established her reputation, made her dreaded even. Well, it may have with the common men, but the powerful figures around just kept using her, ignoring her, commanding her about. As if nothing had changed. And maybe nothing had. She was still a silly, frail, naïve girl who knew nothing about politics and survival.

What would Father do in this mess?

"Thank you, Your Highness. That is good enough for me," he said, shattering her resolve, before she could come up with an answer. "I will be going now. We will meet again." He stepped into the shadow by her bed, and then, she realized he was gone. The shadow changed hue, and it was no longer a man's figure there, but old furniture.

Amalia exhaled a long, shuddering breath. Tears came to her eyes. Biting her lower lip in a silent keen of anguish, she sat down on her bed, cursing her cowardice, her inability to fight her enemies, to stand up for herself. She was such a miserable little thing. She did not deserve to be the empress of Athesia. She didn't deserve anything. She was Jerrica the washerwoman again.

Stop it, a deep inner voice tried to tell her. *You're embarrassing yourself. You're Adam's daughter, you saphead.*

But the weak side prevailed, and she curled herself into a ball, lying under the pale moonlight and mumbling, cursing her ugly luck. She wished Gerald was there to hug her, to love her and protect her, but she had no one, just the bored whispers of the two smelly roof guards discussing the breasts and arses of the town's girls.

CHAPTER 15

Mali had the entire Barrin estate to herself, more or less. She was the countess of Barrin. Sort of.

The people who lived at the estate had fled before the strange northern army arrived, leaving behind a frozen moment in life, only partially spoiled by panic, looting, and the passage of time. Most of the property remained strangely intact, apart from valuables and food, which had gone missing. When the Eracian force arrived at the Barrin manor house, her scouts had found several bandits inside, having taken shelter in one of the halls, spitting rabbits over a fire made from broken chairs. The nearby castle, the one she had used for her mock engagements in what felt like a completely different lifetime, also housed a huddle of new inhabitants, of the unsavory kind. They had quickly been rounded up and killed.

Now, it was her new base of operations. Finley, Alan, and she shared the massive premises, trying to figure out what their enemy had in mind. Leaving behind such highly lucrative, highly defensible positions, entirely empty, sounded like madness. Mali thought she could discern a pattern in the enemy's behavior, but it was a flimsy guess. Apparently, they did not seem that interested in tearing down stone and wood. They only cared about humans, it seemed. And they destroyed only what they considered useless.

The army had more than welcomed the respite. After so many months of grueling, boring marches, they were back in something akin to civilization, with drinkable water in the wells, and real beds. At first, Mali had feared letting the soldiers into the lavish mansion, but she had relented eventually. Lord Karsten would have to find it in his heart to forgive the brave defenders of the realm.

Right now, she was sitting on a crate, whetting a knife, watching life roll by in all shapes and forms. The estate was busy with military work and activity, the two not quite always going hand in hand. There was a bunch of strange northern people being herded back north, escorted by a few mounted men. A new patrol was leaving the camp, armed with crossbows and lances. Like the rest, they were tasked with harrying enemy convoys within a day's march of the estate. If the enemy surrendered peacefully, they were sent home. If they resisted or fought, they were destroyed. Mali did not relish killing civilians, but the moment they drew their knives, they became soldiers.

Her own knife did not need sharpening, but she liked the sound of the stone scraping against the edge, leaving dull marks in the metal. With every stroke, a new thought bloomed in her head, making her feel all the more frustrated and confused.

She still held the people of the first northern convoy in custody. After the initial fear and wonder, they had calmed and somewhat accepted their fate and had not tried to mutiny or run away. In fact, they had almost naturally merged with the Eracian army and followed without question. Well, if they did have any questions, they asked them in the wrong language.

Mali was not looking at the leaf-shaped blade. Her hand was working smoothly, systematically, muscles tuned to a decades-old instinct. Every veteran soldier could sharpen their tools in total darkness, tie knots or patch torn clothing with needle and thread. It was almost a gift.

Her eyes were focused not that far away on the muscled form of a northerner she called Curly.

The northern fellow was rather stocky, with a great deal of fat over his muscles, but there was no mistaking his strength. His skin was pale and freckled and red from the sun, but it glistened with sweat like it was oiled. Curly had russet-brown hair, although it sometimes shone dark red. He was handsome in a burly, ungainly sort of way, she had to admit.

Curly was one of the few men in the northern convoy, and it turned out he might be a carpenter. At least, he seemed fond of wood and working with timber, because he helped repair wagons and broken wheels, and now, he was cutting fresh logs to assist in the repairs of broken houses around the estate. No matter how gentle the passage of the enemy force might have been, it had still left a great deal of accidental damage behind it. But Mali could tell mere chaos and deliberate ruin apart.

This enemy hoped to come back to Barrin one day, it seemed.

She put the speculations about her superior foe away and focused on Curly's work. He was sawing through pine, his chest and shoulders bunching, his face locked with concentration. Sweat was dripping from his hooked nose, onto the workman's bench, leaving big, dark stains. An Eracian craftsman was helping, or rather nodding appreciatively at the man's effort. Nods and grunts seemed universal among men everywhere.

Curly noticed her and paused for a moment. They locked their gazes, and he grinned shyly, then went back to shaving timber.

Mali stroked the knife against her whetstone. It wasn't that hot, but she was feeling kind of fluttery. There was a tingle between her legs. There was girlish fascination at work for sure, she thought. After all, this man represented some strange destructive nation that had stumbled bloodily into her world.

There had been no communication with the northerners yet. No one seemed to have figured out their language. Few of the soldiers had tried to crack the mystery of the enemy's tongue, although Finley's men had made a hundred lewd suggestions to the captive women.

I might as well be the ambassador of good faith, Mali thought, rising. She sheathed the weapon behind her belt and stepped toward Curly. He was watching her quite intently. The other woodworker had wandered away some distance, and she had Curly to herself.

"You a carpenter?" she asked.

He paused, frowning, no comprehension in his pale-blue eyes. He smirked weakly.

Mali licked her gums. Then she realized she had not plucked the hair from her upper lip for a few days, and the silly gesture only made her lady's moustache all the more visible. She tucked her tongue back in behind her teeth, where it belonged.

"So what's your name?" No answer. She touched her chest, maybe a bit suggestively. "Mali." She pointed toward his own, all wet and muscled.

"Mali," he said, his voice pleasantly deep.

"Please don't be stupid," she whispered. "Mali." Her finger touched his breastbone, and she arched a brow.

"Mali," he repeated, grinning.

She rolled her eyes. "Handsome idiot, it seems." She shook her head. "No, dolt. Mali. Ma-li." She looked around. There was no one else she could know by name in her vicinity. Then, she realized she should not just point at her more obvious parts. "Mali." She stared at her own finger. "Mali."

His eyes lit. Finally. "Bjaras."

Curly had just become Bjaras, she thought. Well, the name seemed to fit him. "Why are you here in our realm, Bjaras? What do you want from us?"

His brows touched as he tried to comprehend the foreign language, his face a mask of slightly idiotic confusion. Mali watched him intently, savoring his physique. There was nothing wrong with Gordon, but this man had a sort of wild, foreign charm. Unlike most men from the realms, he was smooth, without any hair on his chest and down his stomach.

"What's your age, handsome?" she asked, turning away from politics. He could not understand her, of course. So she pointed at herself again, then began counting off, both palms flexing. She reached the last decade, almost extended her fingers, and decided to drop it off.

He smiled. He pointed at his own chest, then did some of his own finger math. She almost grimaced when she realized how young he was. Well, it didn't matter, did it?

"Hey, you! What are you doing?" Someone bellowed behind her. Gordon. She spun and saw him coming over, striding with that particular long gait men had when they sought trouble. He barreled toward Bjaras and halted too close to his curly head. "What are you doing?"

The northerner tensed. Other things had their universal ring, like violence, it seemed.

"What are *you* doing?" Mali asked him.

"Is this man threatening you?" Gordon asked, staring at his newfound foe. Bjaras was larger, so the captain had to do quite a bit of posturing to match the sweaty foreigner.

"With me," Mali snapped. She stepped away from the carpenter and walked back to her crate. Grudgingly, Gordon followed. He made it look as if Mali had just saved Bjaras from a thorough beating. "Explain yourself."

"That man could be dangerous. He's got that saw. He could have attacked you."

"I was in no danger whatsoever," Mali hissed, her ire rising. "I was actually trying to communicate. Learn about the enemy. The kind of thing leaders do before they make decisions." Occasionally.

Gordon snorted.

Mali arched a brow. "What is this? Are you being jealous? Are you really?"

Gordon waved his hand dismissively. "That man's an enemy for all I care. You can't be having all pleasant talks with him as if nothing happened. Look around. We're in the middle of a bloody war."

"I am talking to another man. Does that bother you?"

He snapped his head left and right, a quick, involuntary motion. "You can't do that."

Mali took a deep breath. "You're presuming too much, Captain." That sobered him. "Captain-whom-I-fuck, captain. However, I do not recall you and I being anything other than an officer and her subordinate."

He made a pained face. Oh, she had struck deeply, she knew. But she had never allowed men to get soppy with her. That was not how the army business worked.

Then, suddenly, he deflated. "So you mean to tell me our…it…means nothing?"

"That is what we agreed upon, Captain." There was no room for love in her life now. No room for distractions, silly emotions, favor, or hesitation. The moment her empathy and care for another soldier muddled her resolve, she would have to resign. Ordering men to their death was a lonely chore.

"So you keep telling me," he rasped, his voice brittle with disappointment.

She did not want to alienate him. After all, he was a valued, trusted, capable officer. She had to be sure in his judgment, in his loyalty. She had to rely on him in battle. Unfortunately, there was no place for youthful romance in that reality.

Some officers liked to keep their distance, or bicker with their staff, so the tensions always hummed high. That was not her style. She liked honesty.

Mali softened her stance. "Gordon, look. We're both free individuals. We both happen to share something rather intimate, unique, and I appreciate that. I truly do. However, that does not mean you can behave like an unruly, love-blind fool. That does not mean I cannot pursue my other interests if they present themselves. We aren't husband and wife. We cannot be."

"Why not?" He really sounded like some infatuated boy.

"Because I'm older than you, I have given up on family, and I will not risk making the wrong decision in combat just so you get special treatment. That won't work. You won't get any privileges over all those girls out there. I like you, Gordon, but I cannot be your wife."

"So nothing is going to change your mind?"

Mali did not want to break his heart. "Let's get this ugly war finished."

Gordon made a sour face, stabbing Bjaras with a nasty look. "What about Prince Lovelocks over there?"

She almost laughed, how silly it sounded, all that poison. For a moment, he looked like a giant toddler, commiserating the loss of a favorite toy to his childhood nemesis. "Bjaras, that is his name, gets his share of affection like any other man on this estate. I never promised myself to you, Gordon. That's how it's going to be." He nodded, looking defeated. But she could see a spark of rancor in his eyes. "And he will not be harmed."

He stood there, face like a slab of stone, probably thinking, or trying to contain his disappointment. But then, he seemed to reach some inner resolve. "I will try harder," he said. "You will see."

She rolled her eyes. That was exactly what she did *not* want to happen. Stupid men to start doting on her. She did not want to behave like some rich whore, playing with her suitors, teasing them, setting them against one another like dogs. For so many years in her military career, she had avoided having men fight over her. Now, in the prime of her age—and probably well past—she had one of her officers declare a love vendetta against a foreigner fifteen years his junior and without a common word between them. Bloody Abyss. Just what she needed.

"I would like to believe you sought me over some important matter?" she said, desperation trying to edge itself into her voice.

Gordon almost grinned, his passion rekindled to a new, maniacal level. Stupid, stupid men, so impulsive, so reckless. "Yes, sir. Meagan's raiders are back, so I thought to inform you. They ambushed a small party, enemy soldiers this time, proper. On foot. They found them near the Vilswock village, trying to collect onions and turnips from the ground. They scuffled, killed three of them, wounded the fourth and captured him."

"Any useful information?"

Gordon shook his head. "Not a word of continental, so they killed him." He shrugged. "But I guess the main body is getting nervous, so they're sending their troops to investigate. If we keep intercepting their convoys, they might decide to send a large force to try to secure the roads. Or fight us."

"They just might," she agreed.

If that happened, she wanted at least the comfort of a castle to fend off the superior enemy. From what she had seen, the foe had no cavalry and no siege weapons. That meant her riders would be able to harass them without fear, and stationing a garrison behind stone walls could be a great tactic, as long as the defenders had enough food and water. That was a part of the problem, because the crops would not harvest themselves.

Alan had his soldiers toiling in the fields, behind oxen and mules, driving plows. They were trying to stockpile their thin reserves, because the winter would surely be unpleasant, even without foreign soldiers threatening the realm.

Finley, Alan, and she had dispatched letters everywhere, trying to warn the world leaders against the new enemy. She had signed one sent to Commander Velten, one for whoever ruled Eracia now, one for Adam's daughter in Roalas, and one for King Sergei besieging the city. She had almost faltered when sending a missive to her son, pretending not to know this Emperor James. He was probably somewhere in Caytor, with his Caytorean wife. She might be bearing his child by now. One message for the High Council, too.

Mali knew she was terribly, terribly uninformed about world events. Ever since going to war against the nomads and then chasing them north, she had lost touch with current affairs. She was basing her knowledge on rumor and hearsay months old, and that bothered her. Ignorance led to the worst decisions.

She hoped to stall the enemy until the messages reached their destinations. Perhaps the nations could put their feuds aside for a while and unite against the common foe. Maybe her son would come riding north, and they would fight side by side.

What a silly thought.

Her thoughts strayed to Adam's love child. She had not spared this girl Amalia too much attention before, perhaps because it pained her to consider all the implications, like her decision to abandon her military career and hide in Windpoint. To know Adam had forgotten all about her, found himself a new wife, and nourished his little empire with surprising wit and so little force. To know his daughter was challenging the world with her silly ideas and heroics when it was James who should have been the emperor. He was such a gentle, kind, honest man. He deserved to lead nations.

"Our strategy remains unchanged." Send the civilians away, confiscate weapons and tools and livestock, destroy anyone who opposed them. Simple, as long as the enemy kept sending tiny parties. She wasn't sure for how much longer her piecemeal luck would endure. Largely, she believed the enemy considered their rear safe, protected, and once they figured out they had a thorn in their backside, they would scratch it off with a big, bloody paw.

She had to find a way to communicate with the northern people. She had to. This war followed no sane rules. She had found the nomad tribes almost too logical by comparison. What kind of lunatics sent their troops charging forth and then had the unprotected families follow at leisure?

A foe that did not expect to leave any opposition alive, she thought. That worried her. She had spared the lives of a hundred of people in a vain hope to try to reason with the enemy, to try to understand their philosophy, their creed. Now she was beginning to suspect that there would be no negotiations, no reasoning. There would be only a total, utmost annihilation of one side or the other. That wasn't a pleasant prospect.

"Sighted another convoy two days northeast from here," Gordon rambled, all her emotional turmoil invisible to his manly eyes. "And another due west, pretty small, looks like twenty folks altogether, but it seems like they got a whole herd of cows following them. Some shaggy kind, the men never saw them before."

In the past few weeks, they had turned back thousands of the enemy women and children, sent them into the desolate reaches of northern Eracia, back into the half-trampled, half-burned fields and around empty, torched villages. They had butchered several hundreds more, leaving them to the birds. That did not feel like brave campaigning at all.

She had to befriend Bjaras. All of his kind, of course. So she could at least understand why she was killing his fellow countrymen and women and why they so blindly rushed to their deaths.

"We will talk later," Mali said.

Gordon hesitated, looked like he wanted to say something quite touching, then decided against it and walked back toward the castle. He looked like he resisted a terrible urge to turn back and glower at the curly haired northerner.

"Sorry about that," Mali told Bjaras, but her fervor was gone. She left him wondering what had just happened and how it all concerned his people.

The rest of his kin mingled with her troops as if they had lived together all their lives. Women helped as best as they could; the children played, oblivious to all the strangeness around them. Once they had realized they needed to drink more water and dress more lightly, the northerners were coping much better. Only one child had died, succumbing to the heat. Like any Eracian mother, his own had wept for a long time.

Soldiers were lazing everywhere, but never for too long, lest Alan caught them and sent them scurrying into the fields. There was a feeling of vigor at the estate, and it almost felt like the last time she had visited here, except now she had an even greater sense of purpose. Fresh, healthier doses of alarm, frustration, and worry, too. The war against the nomads felt like an ancient, forgotten tale.

Then, there was a commotion somewhere ahead of her. She could hear men and women shouting in both continental and that foreign language. She hastened her pace.

In a yard cordoned by wagons and field shops, several of their captives were at a standoff against one of Finley's warriors. Behind him, half a dozen bored soldiers were goading him, cheering him. The man was yelling loudly, words too blurred to comprehend. One of the women was talking back, a yammer of alien sounds. A tiny child clung to her leg, crying.

It did not feel pleasant, and yet, no one was trying to calm the situation, she noted sadly. Novelty was more important than discipline, it seemed. Mali considered interfering, but then she saw Alexa marching through the crowd, pushing men and women aside.

"What's going on here?" her friend bellowed. The audience suddenly realized the fun had taken a new, unexpected turn. Some of the spectators in the far rows decided to go back to their daily duties. The rest tensed, knowing they were caught in the open, without an easy escape route.

"That bitch attacked me!" the soldier was hollering, his cheeks red, spit flying.

"Did I just not hear you say 'sir'?" Alexa spoke, without losing momentum. Her tone was dangerous, her presence impressive.

The soldier realized he had just aggravated his situation. He stepped back. "No, sir. I did not not sir you, sir. No."

Alexa rubbed her face. "I'll forgive you that one, soldier. Now, why did this *woman* attack you?"

He waved a hand dismissively. "Have no idea, sir."

Alexa looked at the woman. She was still babbling in her tongue, pointing. The girl holding to her skirts was crying, face red like a beet, mouth open, tiny teeth poking out randomly. Her friend looked at the child and frowned; then she looked at the soldier. Her hand went to the worn hilt of her sword.

"Did you try to touch her daughter?"

The man paled. "What? Sir? No, no! I didn't. I swear." He raked his hair nervously. "Look, they got these goats, right, and we ain't eating them. Our company didn't get any meat this week, and these foreigners have all their food. That ain't fair. So I figured we could do with some roast goat chops. No, sir, didn't touch no girl. I swear."

Mali clenched her fist so she did not draw her blade against that fool.

More people were converging now, officers included. The original audience was dwindling fast, because no one wanted to be remembered at the scene of the scuffle. Mali stood back, watching, feeling pride for Alexa. If only she had ever forgotten to be the best friend, always following, always shadowing, she could have easily been an excellent army commander.

"You keep to your mess, and if you have any complaints, tell them to your officers. No one touches these people. Now, scarper."

The soldier saluted. "Gladly, sir." And he beat a rapid retreat.

Mali waited until the crowd cleared, leaving behind dust and the crying girl. Alexa saw her and nodded from across the yard. Mali nodded back, coming over. To the left, an officer was clapping his hands, acting busy, rousing an innocent squad of men to work. They just happened to have taken their card game to the wrong part of the estate.

"It will only get more complicated," Mali said.

Alexa spat. "I guess so. You really think we're doing the right thing?"

Mali knelt near the girl. The child stopped sniffing, staring back with eyes the color of a spring lake. "Well, we can keep killing each other until one side runs out of people, or we can try to somehow sort this out in a civil way." She didn't have any trinkets on her except a short string of bone buttons in one of her pockets. She handed it over. The northern mother gave a tiny blink of appreciation. The child's tiny pink hand closed on the gift, hugging it close.

Mali rose, groaning ever so slightly from the pain in her lower back. "Let's hope we can understand them before it all gets too bloody."

Alexa smiled at the foreign woman, then turned back toward the manor house. On the rooftops, men were busy replacing broken tiles and hanging flags. "I have a bad feeling about this."

Mali shrugged. "Nothing like this in the warfare manuals."

The major clicked her tongue. "I miss the times when we had an enemy who played by the rules. Hasn't been one like that since the skirmishes. Who knows, maybe it was always like this, and we got too old and started looking for philosophy in war. Maybe there is none." She looked sideways. "I saw

Gordon looking all grumpy just earlier. Did you two lovers have a fight?"

Mali snorted. "Men. You give them a good time, and they think they own you."

Her friend made a vague face. "He's a decent chap altogether. You might want to consider settling down after this war is over, you know."

Mali did not expect to hear that. All she could think of were those russet locks on Bjaras's head, and his stocky, well-built body. Perhaps she had gone mad, or she had lived too long denying herself love to be able to appreciate it now.

"Yes, maybe after the war is over." For the moment, it was the only sensible thing to say.

CHAPTER 16

With rain gently patting the earth, Bart slammed his soles against a sheepskin mat and entered the cabin. Constance was sitting in a chair near the window, the child nuzzling on her breast, looking smug and satisfied.

Bart realized he hadn't gotten laid in a long, long while now. He felt his cock stir, like a swamp beast raising its nostrils above the pond scum, releasing a tiny bubble of interest. "Am I intruding?" He knew she would be alone. It was quite difficult catching her without her female human shield, but the surly midwives were elsewhere now.

Constance smiled at him, a thin, almost practiced expression. "Not at all." There, that glimmer of hope in her eyes. Gently, she pried the baby from her nipple like a dockworker giving a limpet glued to a pier a firm tug, a droplet of milk running down. With a deft flick of her free wrist, Constance covered herself, and he was denied the sight of her lovely enlarged breasts.

He looked at the door, almost as an afterthought. Lanford was guarding outside to make sure no one interrupted him. "We haven't been together in quite a while," he said, trying not to sound eager. This was a splendid midday. He had no reports from his officers, no pressing affairs. He could just be an ordinary man in a siege camp—as ordinary as a man trying to figure out how to win the affection of his mistress back could be.

Constance made a small prim face. "Raising a son is a very difficult task." She rolled the baby over, patting his back. The tiny arms and legs waddled, almost as if they had invisible strings attached being worked by a drunken puppeteer.

Bart sat in a second chair, all padded leather. He crossed his legs nervously, then uncrossed them. His unnamed son made a sound almost like a burp. Constance aahed appreciatively. Bart watched the baby carefully, wondering if he was going to spew all that milk onto the expensive rug.

"Here." Constance nudged the child in his direction. He almost balked. "Hold him."

"You hold him," he muttered.

Constance jerked her hands forward, a frightful gesture, like a battering ram getting ready to gore a gate. "Bart, don't be silly. Hold your son. Take him. He needs to get used to your smell, to the sound of your voice."

Why? he wondered. That fatheaded thing looked so squishy, so brittle. He was afraid it would slip between his fingers, like a knot of blood sausages, and splatter on the floor. "Perhaps later."

"Please, Bart, hold him," she urged.

"No," he whimpered, almost feeling panicky.

Constance rolled the boy back and laid him against her chest. The boy made a sound like a sheep trying to bleat and regretting it. She looked like she was whispering in the child's ear. Then her lower lip quivered, and he realized she was crying.

"Please don't cry," he said.

"You do not love our son," she mumbled.

Bart wished he were leading an attack into the city right now, personally. "That's not true."

"Then why don't you hold him?" she insisted.

"Because…" He trailed off, uncertain. Why did he not want to hold that child? It wasn't the prettiest little prince in the world, but it was his son after all. Of that much he was certain. He knew that most fathers felt immense pride in their tiny, spongy offspring, and often imagined they saw their own features in their malformed heads, but all he could summon from his heart was a sense of bafflement and estrangement. This child wasn't just the fruit of his loins. It was a terrible chasm between his life now and the one he had shared with Sonya. Until he figured out what he wanted to do, there was no place for other emotions.

But he could not tell that to Constance. She would hate him. "I am afraid," he said. It was a good lie, he thought, especially since it was mostly true. The mechanism of a soft child did not worry him that much. But the bond, the risk, the implications, they all terrified him.

"You don't care about him. You don't care about me," she lamented in a quiet voice that was worse than shouting. "Are you going to deny me forever? Are you going to keep lying about your son?"

"I am a married man," he reasoned. That was a good argument, wasn't it?

"Your wife is in the city," she said. "But I am here."

"It's complicated."

Constance wiped her eyes. "How can I ever trust you again? When you wanted my body, you didn't have any objections then. You did not stop to think about your wife then."

Wait, he thought. *I should be berating* her. *She is the one who manipulated me. Abandoned that lad Ewan and slipped into my bedsheets, because I had money and a title. There it is.*

He tried his best diplomacy. "You ask for my trust, but you still won't tell me anything about yourself."

That got her defiant, red stare lowered. She sniffed, but he thought it was feigned now, and her mind must be racing with a new strategy.

"All I ask for is, let's go back to how we were before."

"I am a mother now. My son is a bastard, because his father will not acknowledge him. I must be prepared to raise him on my own, to find means to support him. You cannot ask me to go back to how we were before, because that reality is gone. Your wife is waiting in Somar. What will she say when you free her?"

Bart kept silent. She had a point. His own life couldn't have gotten any more complicated. Worst of all, no matter how worried he was, deep down, all he really wanted was to have sex with her. He would think about Sonya and the child later. His mind swam with one simple purpose.

"I am sorry," he said. Women liked to hear those words, he knew. "I am still not ready. I will love *our* son," he forced himself to say. "I will. I promise that. But you must be patient. You must give me time to get there on my own. And there's this war we must win."

She bit her lower lip. Not the response she had expected, he figured, but good enough. It was always hard figuring out what women had on their minds. However, he needed no wise men to tell him his chance of rubbing his face against any breasts was out of the question today.

He rose. Saving his disgnity was the blare of a horn outside, a single long note. "I must leave," he said almost nonchalantly. Well, his plan had fallen apart, so going back to the reality of a siege was a simple task. He would have been rather cross if that sentry had sounded the horn in a different scenario, the one where Constance gave herself to him once more.

Frustrated, his sex vibrating against his trousers, Bart stepped out. Lanford raised a brow. "Sir, we have an Eracian force approaching from the north. But I thought you didn't want to get disturbed."

Bart frowned against the lukewarm drizzle. "Let's go."

With the nomad presence reduced to a small pocket around Somar and some blisters of resistance in the west, traffic and news were flowing once again between the two parts of the realm. Almost weekly, a convoy would arrive at the siege lines, usually reinforcements sent by his uncle. Sometimes, they were footmen, sometimes fresh cavalry, still too inexperienced to hold formations. At other times, artisans, whores, and mercenaries came, ready to profess their trades. No matter how dire the situation was, the world had an endless supply of paid swords to offer.

Bart waited with Faas, Ulrich, and Velten. Junner's men were never too far. They could smell opportunity like mosquitoes could smell blood. The drizzle soon stopped, came back again for a short spell, and then ceased again, leaving a wet summer smell in the air. The dust had settled at least, making distances seem shorter, and every detail was that much clearer.

A large body of men was approaching, it seemed, trying its best to raise a veil of dirt and failing, which belittled its size. The force flowed like a slow, muddy tide, spilling over the plains, engulfing the siege lines. He had expected to see soldiers in the lot, but there were mostly civilians, grubby, dirty, too many of them. He frowned.

Straight ahead, a smaller snake was leading into the camp, surrounded by local sentries on horseback. The van consisted of mounted men, followed by at least a dozen chariots and twice as many wagons. Bart could clearly see the emblem of House Barrin painted on the sides and fluttering on flag posts carried by the riders.

It seemed Uncle Karsten had come to visit the battle lines. But then, why all the small folk? Strange, alarming, and annoying. Bart suppressed a terrible urge to go forward and meet the new delegation halfway.

The camp grew noisier as the force got closer: rumor, gossip, speculations, stories, logistical chaos as supply officers began their preparations. For them, each new arrival was a disturbance in a well-paced, well-oiled machine, and they did not like having to rearrange everything all over again. The carriages drew to a halt. He saw an army of liveried servants dismount, open the door, place a wedge-shaped wooden ramp just below. A moment later, the seated form of his uncle rolled out.

Just behind, Lady Elizabeth exited the second coach, her dainty, frail hand resting on the elbow of her trusted Deirdre. Bart watched with growing apprehension as Karsten pushed himself over wet ground, arms as thick as a lumberjack's propelling him forward, faster than most men would walk.

Major Maurice was approaching, his own pace quite hasty. Bart was liking this less and less, and he wished he had left the greeting ceremony to his subordinates. But now, he had to play the brave role of the viceroy.

"Trouble, Lord Count?" Junner said, showing up suddenly.

"Please, not now," Bart snapped.

The Borei chuckled, unfazed. "We will talk later, friend."

Maurice stepped close and saluted, handing a rolled message to his superior. He nodded at Bart, his chin wobbly with sympathy he could not quite give. "Your Majesty," the major was saying, his tone brittle. "Dire news. I do not think there's an easy way to report this. The Barrin and Elfast estates have been overrun by an unknown enemy force arriving in huge numbers from the north under white banners. They do not appear to be affiliated with any known faction, and they seem bent on total destruction. Lord Karsten has tactfully led a retreat south."

Bart blinked slowly. When he opened his eyes, the world was just as it had been earlier. His uncle was deftly wheeling himself around puddles and ruts in the ground, coming closer. The three commanders were reading the message, their faces impassive with shock.

An enemy army? From the north? What?

"Bartholomew!" his uncle shouted. "Well met. I see you have made yourself into quite a man after all."

"Greetings, Uncle," Bart said, feeling small.

Karsten halted a mere pace away, muddy water flying from the metal rims of his wheeled chair. "Officers. I would get up, but my condition precludes me from doing so, he-he. Well, we must assemble a council right now. We have dire matters of war to discuss. Call your staff."

Commander Faas glanced at Bart, looking uncomfortable.

"Please do so," Bart agreed. To his dismay, he noticed his mother was coming over, too. She had that deceptive look of weakness and frailty, but her stride was as steady as any well-trained spearman's. One relative crippled, another quite healthy, both very much sly.

Karsten made a quick turn with his chair, almost running over Maurice's foot. The major had to step back to avoid discomfort to his toes. "Bartholomew, I still can't believe you've made it this far. A viceroy, would you believe it? My dear brother would have been proud to see you now."

Bart sighed. "Uncle, please follow me. No, Major. My uncle prefers no aid." Maurice raised his hands up defensively.

Bart turned his back to his uncle, walking toward the command lodge. He imagined the Kataji bowmen standing on the curtain wall parapet, leering at him.

"Bartie!" his mother called, her voice carrying over the jangle of armor and harness. "Bartie!"

He rolled his eyes and spun around. A very miserable-looking Ulrich ducked out of his way. Bart saw Junner still hovering nearby, watching the Barrin family with keen, professional interest.

"Where's my favorite son?" Lady Elizabeth cooed with all the elegance of a trueborn dame.

The only son left, Bart thought sourly, remembering Elliot and Wilhelm. "Mother."

She grabbed him forcefully, almost clamping his ears, and planted two kisses on his cheeks. She smelled of lavender, like she always had, the smell of his childhood.

"Bartholomew!" Lord Karsten yelled, refusing to be one-upped by the old woman.

An army of slightly stunned and very polite officers followed their viceroy and his crippled uncle toward the command lodge. Bart quickly waved to his mother and watched her being intercepted by Alke and Edgar.

The junior staff was waiting, ready, maps spread on the tables, held down by various implements, weak after-rain sunlight streaming through the windows. Servants were piling food and drinks everywhere, their anxiety reflecting that of their masters.

Bart stepped in, heard a dull clank behind him. Someone coughed quite emphatically. Bart turned to see his uncle barricading the entrance, the wheels of his chair touching the slightly elevated step of the cabin's entrance. He seemed to be waiting for someone to help him. Then, as one of the more naïve captains tried to assist, Lord Karsten got his sweet little victory.

"I can manage on my own, son," he said brusquely and deftly spun the wheels back and forth and back, tipping himself slightly to reduce the weight on the front of the wheels, and edged himself into the cabin, the muscles on his arms bulging and trembling. Commander Faas and Colonel Ulrich followed, severely embarrassed, although not nearly as much as Bart.

"You can throw those maps away," his uncle declared, looking almost bored.

"Why?" Bart asked, fully aware he was being baited.

"There's a much bigger army threatening the realm. It has overrun our land. Within a few weeks, they will descend upon Somar, and this little affair with the nomads will have become meaningless. We will be dead, all of us, dead. You must focus all your effort on leaving to go south."

"You mean we ought to retreat from the capital, Uncle?"

"Do we have any credible reports about this army?" Ulrich inquired.

"I am credible enough, I would say." The lord bristled. "If you need convincing, you can talk to any of the tens of thousands of people who have just fled their homes."

"What is the enemy strength?" Faas snapped his fingers at one of the adjutants, who drew his pen like a warrior unsheathing his sword.

"Hundreds of thousands. Maybe more."

Bart realized he was gawking like a fool. "Larger than the Parusite force?"

Lord Karsten snorted. "Much larger." He gestured. Tobin, his uncle's old-time attaché, stepped forward with all the grace of a patient assistant, well used to the man's tantrums, and handed over a leather book. The crippled man took it and threw it on the table in front of him. "You want numbers, you have your numbers."

"Do we know anything about this enemy force?" Ulrich pressed.

"They did not seem keen on discussing their intentions with us. They were too busy destroying, burning and killing. Whoever they are, they do not mean for Eracia to survive their onslaught. We must be prepared to abandon the realm and flee."

"The implications are dire," Faas mouthed in a low, awed voice.

Bart rubbed his forehead. The implications were catastrophic. Even without some incredible enemy showing up suddenly in the northern reaches of their country, the presence of so many new people around the siege lines complicated everything. There would be so much more crime and disease. Security and discipline would plummet. The civilians were likely to complain and cause trouble, and there would be a grave shortage of food. Bart did not like the idea of having to redistribute the supplies. He liked the fact there would be no more reinforcements and supplies from the north even less. This meant he was going to be forced to ask King Sergei for help, and he hated that notion.

So here he was, waging one of the most important wars in Eracian history, fighting for its heart, and now, he was being asked to give everything up and run away, like some coward.

He imagined Sonya watching the Eracian soldiers turn their tails and flee, leaving the women to their captors. He could imagine the sneer on her face, the perfect expression of contempt, the sum of his life etched into one grimace. He almost physically felt her disdain.

Oh, he was done being a coward.

He closed his eyes. "There will be no retreat."

A low murmur rippled through the crowd, almost involuntarily.

Lord Karsten slammed a fist against one of the wheels. "Bartholomew, this is not the time for foolish ideas. The Eracian nation *must* retreat. We have to go to the Safe Territories. We must distance ourselves from this enemy. Meanwhile, all the leaders of the realms have to be alerted to the threat."

"They shall be," Bart said, his voice calm. "But there will be no retreat." *Not as such.*

"Remaining here is suicide!" the cripple roared.

"Uncle, keep your voice down," Bart warned. "May I see those reports, please?" Faas handed him the ledger. Carefully, Bart opened its pages, reading. Not good. Not good at all. Sonya, Constance, his son, his imposing uncle, the war with the Kataji, and now this. Lovely.

"Colonel Ulrich, I must ask you to assemble a regiment of horses and send them north. Light cavalry only so they can outpace any enemy troops if needed. Now, do we know anything about our northern detachment, Commander Velten?"

The man cleared his throat. "We have not received any news from Colonel Finley for months now. We must presume they are lost. Either defeated by the Namsue or this new army."

"Perhaps this army is in league with the nomads?" Ulrich suggested.

I didn't want to consider that, Bart thought, a sour taste budding in his mouth. "We cannot assume otherwise until we have more credible information." He looked at the outline of the city, surrounded by colored wooden blocks denoting various Eracian units. "We do not have much time. We must liberate Somar. If this enemy force is coming here, and if the reports are true, they will destroy the capital and kill all our women. I will not abandon them to either the nomads or their potential allies."

Lord Karsten tried to interrupt, but Bart silenced him with a raised finger. "After we free Somar, a contingent of volunteers will remain to protect the city. All noncombatants will be evacuated to Paroth and Ubalar, with further plans to evacuate the cities, if needed. Meanwhile, all the crops must be harvested so that no food is left for the enemy. Major…"—he had to remember the name—"Kilian, I want your sappers ready to destroy all the bridges and ferry crossings."

"Yes, Your Highness."

Not a war leader, Bart thought, *and here I am, devising war strategy.* For a moment, he remembered King Sergei doing the same thing during the Roalas siege, after learning Vlad had been kidnapped. He felt empowerment, a steel ball in the pit of his stomach. It was a cold weight, but it didn't feel wrong. He almost liked this no-choice scenario.

"We will act under the assumption this enemy army cannot be defeated in combat. We will prepare to stall them for as long as possible to allow a safe withdrawal of our people south." He looked at his uncle, challenging him to dispute his strategy, but the old man just looked mildly irritated. "Their gains must be slow and bloody." Bart leaned against the table, one of his wrists making a tiny popping sound. "However, we are not leaving Somar. Until the city is freed and the nomad invaders are repelled, we will not be going anywhere." He had decided he would not abandon the women in the city. He owed them that much.

He turned toward the Southern Army commander. "I believe the time for the infiltration mission has come. Your men are fully ready, I presume?"

"They have been for some time now, Your Majesty."

Bart nodded, pushing himself upright. "Good. I guess this war starts in earnest now." He realized he was giddy, swimming with excitement, fear, confusion. He knew there would be nothing good about this turn of events, only more death and suffering, while none of his other problems would go away. His wife was still there, and so was his mistress and her child. No matter how many foes he defeated, they would haunt him.

"They will attack tonight," Faas promised. It was going to be a long, sleepless night for everyone.

Soon, the meeting was over. Nervous officers rushed to follow up on their orders. The rather dull day was becoming a hot, white chaos. He could hear the growing din outside. He wasn't certain how the nomads would interpret the arrival of the Barrin people. Would they be alarmed by so many civilians? Would they bolster their defenses? Well, the time for doubts and wavering was over.

"You certainly have changed, Nephew," Lord Karsten said, remaining in the lodge.

Bart glanced at one of the servants collecting wine cups. "Yes, I have."

His uncle almost smiled. "Well, a refreshing change, by all means."

"Are you certain about this enemy, Uncle?"

The man patted his wheeled contraption, callused hands running over wet metal rims. "This threat is real, Bartholomew. I have no idea where this enemy comes from. I am just as surprised as you are. But the world is vast, beyond the measure of our maps." He wrinkled his nose at the charts and drawings covering the tables. "We all know there are many nations in faraway lands. It is up to us to protect the realm against this new threat. Just as Vergil did in his time."

Bart felt uncomfortable staring down at his uncle, so he sat down. "I will have to ask the Parusites for assistance. But this does not bode well for Eracia. What will happen if our people are forced to cross into the Safe Territories? Will the king construe that as an invasion? Will he treat our plea for help seriously? Will he ever bother responding? I hardly believe your report, and you're here. He might think I've gone insane."

Lord Karsten rolled himself closer and placed one of his strong hands on Bart's knee. "Two years ago, if someone had told me my spineless nephew, the lowest member of the Privy Council, would rise to become the viceroy of the realm, I would have laughed in their faces. Yet, you are here, proving miracles can happen."

"Thank you for the compliment, Uncle."

The old man bahed. "Stop sopping. You do not need my sympathy. You have women for that."

"Sonya is in the city," Bart said, trying to keep his voice flat.

"So, you finally have the chance get rid of her."

Bart sighed. "I will be one to decide the fate of my marriage, not some Kataji chieftain."

Lord Karsten slanted his head. "I hear you have a son. A bastard. To some Caytorean floozy, no less. It seems you have had quite a bit of time on your hands recently. But I guess that shame is a less pressing matter now."

Bart bristled. He looked at the remaining help. "Out, please." The lodge was soon empty apart from the two of them. "There's nothing shameful about what I've done. Frankly, I'm long past caring what you or Mother may think."

"What made you change so much, Bartholomew?"

He shrugged. He didn't really know. It probably did not matter. "I just got tired of the humiliation." He just frightfully hoped he was acting for the benefit of the realm and its people and not his own petty, selfish ideas. "I am a busy man, Uncle. You are welcome to stay, or you may evacuate to Paroth with the noncombatants." A blithe jibe. "However, I must warn you, do not ever dispute me in public, or I will remove your authority and forbid you from joining the staff meetings. Your gold and your affliction do not make you into a holy man." He frowned. "Is there any gold left at all?"

Lord Karsten grinned, hiding his fury. "The gold is safe with us."

Bart stepped behind his uncle and turned his chair toward the exit. "Excellent. I will need finances to keep this war going properly. Thank you for your time, Uncle. We will talk later. Try to keep out of the deep puddles." He propelled the old man out.

Standing in the doorway, he watched the wheelchair roll away, feeling satisfaction in his limbs. *Have I gone truly mad?* he wondered. *But can a madman ever know he's mad?* It did not matter. Eracia was at war, and he had to fight for the nation's freedom. Complications, new problems, nothing mattered. Nothing would stop him now.

He stood there, people around frowning and wondering what their provisional ruler had on his mind. If they could glimpse inside, they would see him thinking about Sonya, standing on the parapet, her face a mask of disdain.

That would not do. There was his one true motivation.

He had finally reached a decision.

CHAPTER 17

There was a loud noise, the sound of a heavy wooden door slamming into a wall, and Sonya woke, her mind sharp and alert. In that instant between reality and dream, before her body could obey, she knew she had been discovered.

It's over, she thought, and a strange calmness gripped her. *I die with dignity, like a queen.*

"Get up. The general wants you," a male voice rasped.

Sonya opened her eyes, blinked away the sleep mist, made sure there were no tears in them, and looked sideways. There was a Kataji warrior blocking the doorway, the smooth leather of his uniform shining in the torchlight seeping from the corridor. The yellow light only accentuated his animallike features, the sharp creases in his whiskered face, the tufts of pelt randomly sewn to his jerkin, the weapons belt studded with knives.

She was having such a beautiful dream. Now, things would get difficult. And painful. She was already bracing for pain. Against her volition, her stomach muscles hardened, her breath getting shorter, with a panicky wheeze riding on top of it. Gently, she slid the thin linen sheet off her body. The soldier was watching her shamelessly, enjoying her curves. Her nightgown did not provide much in the way of modesty.

"I must dress first. You will wait outside," she said, sitting up.

"Come now," the soldier grunted.

Sonya rose. The soldier let her pass, watching her carefully, then followed. There were two more men in the corridor near her, both holding torches. Another stood farther away, with a drawn blade. The nomad warriors smelled of musty hide and old sweat, and it wasn't a soothing scent for her fluttering stomach.

The torchbearers and their armed comrade turned and led, left and right, boots shuffling, sword sheaths scraping against mortar or clinking against an odd piece of furniture. She expected to find more of these beasts around, sleeping, but their filthy mats and pelts were empty.

I'm not the only one roused from sleep, she mused.

Unsurprisingly, her escort led her toward the throne room. However, what did surprise her was the commotion.

There were almost a hundred souls present, in various states of discomfort and pain. Round the perimeter, the tribesmen stood guard, holding swords and spears. Closer to the dais, a huddle of women waited, looking utterly miserable. Their panic was obvious. Sonya discerned a large number of her noble friends and enemies there, which confirmed her suspicion. Pacmad had unveiled their plot.

The Father of the Bear stood near the throne chair, ogling the lot with half a sneer on his face. He looked smug and irate at the same time. She had been around him long enough to recognize the barely bridled violence pulsating through his limbs, the almost imperceptible twitch of his fingers as he longed to release his wrath.

He heard the footsteps of his warriors and glanced her way. Saw her. "Bring her here."

Sonya made sure she did not waver, whimper, or stumble as she approached the other Eracian women. Some were watching her, hope and terror lined in their features. Others just stood there, numb, shocked.

"Are you going to tell me?" Pacmad asked her suddenly.

Sonya stood next to Richelle. She had not expected to see the baroness there. Apparently, giving birth to Pacmad's daughter did not grant her enough immunity against treason, it seemed. Sonya would have been glad if not for a very selfish regard for her own fate. She had to concentrate. Stupor would not do now.

"I am not sure what I should tell you, Pacmad," she said bravely.

He stepped off the dais and approached her. She braced herself for the blow. But he just stood there, unnervingly silent, staring at her, judging her, weighing, waiting for her to lose self-control.

"You will tell me about the Eracian raid," he spoke.

Sonya went cold. "I do not understand."

Pacmad grinned wide. "You will." He nodded at one of his soldiers. The man barked a short order in their native tongue. From across the hall, Kataji warriors started ushering a new audience into the chamber. Unlike the women, the newcomers hardly walked on their own. They dragged their feet; they shuffled and hobbled; others had to be almost carried inside, with a nomad fighter on each side. Soon, they entered the pool of lamplight and candles, and she could discern more details. Bruised, battered, wet men, with crumpled clothes, spattered in mud and dirt, their faces swollen from a beating. Some were manacled, others walked more or less on their own, but they all dripped on the cold white marble, and the flecks of their blood mingled with the red veins in the flagstones.

"Now you understand," the chieftain said, pleased.

Raid? A night raid? She had plotted an uprising against the Kataji for months now, carefully orchestrating the bits and pieces, planning the city's rebellion to the last detail. Now, when it supposedly was happening, she stood paralyzed, helpless, unprepared.

The warriors deposited the prisoners before the women, unceremoniously dumping them on the floor. Some remained upright, but most sagged to their knees. Sonya realized some of the men were wounded, with knife and sword cuts on their arms and legs. One of the Eracians begged for water, but no one paid him any heed. Lady Fidelma began to cry.

Pacmad looked at the enemy soldiers and nodded, satisfied. He turned his piercing blue eyes back at her. "Now, tell me about the raid."

Sonya swallowed hard. "Honestly, I do not know anything about this." She did not need to pretend. She really did not.

The general sniffed. Once again, Sonya bunched her muscles, waiting for his fist to plow into her belly, and again, Pacmad kept his meaty hands at his sides, looking utterly smug, enjoying the moment immensely. Then, he spun quickly and slapped Richelle, hard. The baroness barely had time to wail before she collapsed. Once on the ground, near the wounded men's feet, she began to sob. Sonya dared herself to look. The woman was holding her face, dark-red blood slithering round her fingers like tiny snakes.

It was happening too fast, Sonya thought. She had to gain control of the situation. She had to. Otherwise, Pacmad would render impossible damage on everyone present, including her. Losing her life would be almost too easy, she realized. But what

217217

if he spared her and then threw her into a dark underground cell? What if he denied her all the perks, all the freedom she had? What if he took away the grudging trust he had given her? The horror of that prospect almost made her vomit.

Seeing Richelle bleed was a lovely occasion, but not right now. As a queen, she had a duty toward all of her subjects, even hated whores like the baroness. She suspected Pacmad wanted her to seem happy about it, wanted to expose her ambitions, alienate her from the rest of the women, strike strife and discord among them. That seemed like the best way to undo their plot. Make one of them betray the rest. Which was why Sonya must not let her emotions show.

Instead of gloating, Sonya went down on one knee and brushed matted hair from the woman's swelling face. Drool and sticky threads of blood ran from Richelle's lips and nose to the marble. The baroness held her eyes shut tightly and was sobbing quietly. Ignoring her disgust, Sonya gently wiped the woman's cheek with her sleeve, then dabbed her lower lips.

"Stay there," she whispered.

"Stand up," Pacmad ordered.

Sonya let go of the other woman and straightened, all too aware this monster and his men were watching her, her nightgown too thin to hide her body. She kept her mouth shut, uncertain what the general might do.

"Tell me about the raid," he repeated.

Sonya licked her lips quickly. "I do not know anything about the raid, I swear."

Pacmad scanned the crowd of frightened women. His mongrel eyes rested on Lady Miranda, a lowly merchant from Paroth, if Sonya's memory served her well. She had found herself visiting Somar at the wrong time. "Benis, Cowden, rape her."

Miranda only managed to squeal in weak, stunned protest as the warriors came forward and dragged her to the floor. The other women began crying loudly. Sonya kept her face hard, passive, and pushed her tears deep into her soul. There was no rule that said you could not weep later, much later. It was almost dignified.

The captive Eracians began stirring, trying to struggle free, cursing and spitting. Not all of them. Some were just too tired beyond caring, others injured and dying, others yet too terrified. Sonya could not blame them.

"Leave her be, you scum," one of the Eracians hissed. He got pierced through the gut with a spear. Laughing, the nomads left him on the floor, feebly kicking with his bare feet, spreading blood in curious shapes with his toes.

"Please stop," someone spoke. It was her own voice. Oh, what a fool she was.

Pacmad glanced at her, looking surprised. "Stop?" The men were tearing the clothes off their victim, sniggering, speaking in their tongue, fondling her flesh with their grubby hands. Miranda was gazing at the vaulted ceiling, her eyes wide and glazed. "Stop?" Pacmad repeated. "Cowden, cut her open. Slowly."

The Kataji pressed a knife to the girl's belly. A red line blossomed round the gray steel, trickled away, pooled in her navel. Miranda was breathing in short bursts.

Sonya dropped onto her knees. "Please. I beg you. Please stop. No one doubts your power."

The general raised a finger, and the other warrior raised the blade off the woman's pale skin, waiting for instructions. That gave Sonya a grain of hope. This whole affair was a well-orchestrated terror act intended to get the Eracians thoroughly defeated. That much was plain. But she had no idea what the chieftain would do once he got what he wanted—be it information or humiliation.

"No one? Then what is this? An Eracian army trying to infiltrate my city? A plot behind my back? You whores dare plot behind my back? Maybe you do not doubt my power, but you surely doubt my intelligence and resolve. Cut her."

"Please!" Sonya wailed just as a shrill cry rose below her feet. Lady Miranda began thrashing.

"You fucking coward," a soldier was shouting, ignoring the sheet of gooey red down the side of his jaw. "You fucking nomad rat. You fuck. Once we take the city back, we'll go west, and we gonna fuck every one of your wo—"

One of the guards thumped him on the nape, and the man dropped to his knees. A kick got him flattened. Then, a Kataji warrior was kneeling above him, sword ready.

Pacmad raised his finger again. He was in total control of the situation, enjoying himself immensely. "Is that so? I have a better idea. You get to keep your lives, soldier, but I get to kill these whores. What do you say?" He reached out and grabbed Sonya by her hair forcefully, bringing hot tears to her eyes. He yanked her close, squashing her face against his crotch. "I kill her, and you go free?"

The prone man rolled sideways, blinking blood out of his eyes and mouth, coughing. "Fuck you."

"Kill him." Pacmad looked at the other Eracians. "How about you, brave fighters? You get to choose. Your lives against theirs. We get to rape and kill these bitches, and you go home." He released Sonya, pushed her away. Then he reached randomly into the crowd and caught another, nameless woman. She started whimpering, and her shrill words mingled with the death gasp of the Eracian soldier. "See this whore? I kill her; one of you goes back to your lords outside. Fair deal."

Sonya was rubbing her scalp, trying to vanish the ants of pain, feeble, defiant satisfaction creeping into her battered soul. None of the soldiers would accept the bargain. Not one. It made her proud of her realm, of her brave husband. He had sent these men to their deaths, hoping they would be able to breach the Kataji defenses and rescue her. His attempt might have endangered her, but she could not hate him for that. In fact, she loved him.

Disgusted, annoyed, Pacmad shoved the other woman back to her friends. His eyes were back, boring into her. "These soldiers might not talk, but you will. Tell me about the raid."

Sonya did not rise. She stared up at her captor, trying hard not to look away. She had to be strong. All these months, she had lied and manipulated, and he had believed her. Now that she was telling the truth, he was doubting her.

"I do not know anything about this raid," she repeated.

Pacmad flexed his jaw left and right. He was breathing through his nostrils, trying to contain himself. Suddenly, he smiled. "I believe you." He turned toward the captive Eracians. "You will tell me everything you know, or I will rape and cut them all to bits, right here, right now."

One of the captives raised his manacled hands. "We were sent to capture the gatehouse. That's all. We were supposed to secure the fish market and nearby quarters, open the gates, and let the army enter the city under the cover of night. That's all. That's all."

The Father of the Bear climbed the dais and sat down on the throne chair, frowning, his face creased with deep thought. *Must be another charade,* Sonya wondered. She was feeling she might have sorely underestimated this man. There was just no knowing what he truly planned. Why he so tenaciously held to his prize, the capital city, even as the Eracian forces captured more of the surrounding land and tightened their grip on Somar.

"You want the gates open?" Pacmad retorted. "You will have them open."

The next hour trickled away in a nightmare of flashes and bright images, flickering lamps and torchlight, the coppery stench of drying blood, and the piercing wails of Eracian men dying by sword and knife. One by one, Pacmad had them tortured to death. The women were forced to watch. Some retched, some fainted, and there was wind of an unladylike smell rising from their midst. Sonya could not have cared less.

She kept her eyes fixed on the slaughter, making sure she remembered every little detail. One day, she would tell Bart all about it, and she would demand he exact vengeance on the Kataji. She would make sure the nomads disappeared from the annals of history. She would make sure not a single baby was left to continue their filthy legacy.

Finished with the killings, the chieftain ordered the bodies removed. Grumpy, disgusted warriors began dragging the pieces out of the throne hall, leaving crimson smears on the floor. Sonya watched as one of the tribesmen grabbed Lady Miranda's leg and hauled her out, whistling a tune, weaving a snaky red pattern behind him. Next, the terrified palace servants were summoned, and they began scrubbing, their mute tears dripping on the pink floor.

Pacmad called one of his trusted warriors over. "Arrest all the guild mistresses and bring them to the palace. We'll keep them locked with this lot." He was speaking in continental on purpose so that Sonya could hear him. "I want no one on the streets. Get four thousand archers near the gates, and let's give the Eracians a little surprise." He rose from the throne chair and walked out.

The women were left there, standing, kneeling, exhausted to the bone. The cleaners ignored them, as if they had some dreadful disease. Sonya shifted her weight nervously from one leg to another. She wanted to sit down, but she could not imagine pressing her rump into all that blood.

"Thank you," Richelle said on her left, her voice distorted by the swelling of her lips and her clogged nose.

Sonya turned, astonished. She had not expected that. "It's nothing," she mumbled. The baroness was hard to recognize, her face all mangled up. Sonya felt pity for the other woman. She knew she should be feeling very much satisfied, but that emotion refused to coalesce.

Time stretched. The squares of night air outside turned purple and pink, and dawn broke. With it, the sounds of fighting, the muted hollers of ten thousand mouths yelling and screaming and cursing. There was a huge engagement between the Kataji and the Eracians, she realized, but she could not imagine how the battle was unraveling.

Sometime later, Pacmad returned, looking clean and fresh. His sword was sheathed, restful. His brows shot up when he glanced at the smelly huddle. "You are still here? Oh well. Dismissed. Go back to your chambers. Sonya, stay."

Richelle gave her a worried look as she shuffled away. But if Sonya had expected the other woman to intervene on her behalf, she was disappointed. Swallowing a lump, she waited for the chieftain's whim.

"You are a brave woman," he told her.

"I am honored," she said, her throat raw. She was thirsty. She was hungry. She wanted to sleep.

He snorted. "Come with me," he ordered and led her away. She found herself disoriented, weaving down familiar corridors without any sense of direction, her footsteps echoing against the cold stone, her eyes focused on the back of her captor. She hated him. She no longer wanted to best him; she wanted to spill his innards and watch birds feast on them.

Steps. She wobbled and groaned as she climbed, out of strength, breathless. But she knew she must not falter. Her fingernails scraped against mortar, ruining the delicate polish Janice had finished only yesterday.

Pacmad was waiting inside one of the solars, smiling. She glinted against the sunlight, shielding her eyes. The mongrel was staring toward the South Gate, where a great battle was coming to an end. The Eracian standards seemed to be moving away from the city walls, back toward the siege lines. The fish market, the docks, the narrow streets of the slums growing like weeds round the gate swarmed with the nomad troops. A pall of smoke was rising from several districts, curling in strange black shapes above Somar.

"You really can't get round the idea of not underestimating us," he was saying, not looking at her. "Even after last year's defeat, you still think we are just bloodthirsty primitives. Today, the Eracian leader has learned a painful lesson." He glanced at Sonya, Vergil's eyes mocking her. "I opened the gates for him. Opened them! Let his troops enter the city. And still they lost."

He put a hand on her shoulder, and she almost winced at his hot, greasy touch. "My victory today will go into the war books. They will speak of my utter cunning. How I lured the Eracians into a trap and destroyed them. My troops only lost several hundred men. The Eracians lost thousands. Such a clever snare. The fires to block the streets so the enemy could not flank us, the archers to pin down the reinforcements, my men lurking in the houses, using the confusion to their advantage."

Bart's army seemed to be in full retreat now, horns blaring. Farther away, the massive siege machines were hurling large stones in great, deep lobes, crashing against the rooftops, corner towers, and the curtain walls. She willed the masonry to shatter, to tumble.

The rest of the city was quiet, peaceful, deserted. The women were probably hiding in their homes, waiting for the order to rebel, but there would no such order today, she knew. Pacmad had outwitted her. He might not know of her scheme, but he had effectively ruined it.

Pacmad's hand strayed lower, to her breast, twisting her nipple. She bit her pain away. "The fools think bringing down the battlements will somehow change the situation. They will only learn the red price of my cunning and resolve as they start losing more and more in those narrow streets and dark cellars. Let them come. No one can defeat me."

Sonya was not a believer, but she sent a nameless prayer for her brave, glorious husband. Pacmad's hand probed lower, more forcefully, his breath getting faster.

"Lie down. Spread your legs," he grunted.

She obeyed, because she knew there was nothing else she could do right now. But she would not despair. She would fight. She was the nation's queen, and she would liberate Somar from the nomad clutches.

CHAPTER 18

E wan stood in the grass by the roadside, watching the pilgrims pass him by, reminding of his first visit to the nameless Oth Danesh cities. Some would look at him and nod in curt greeting, others would smile, but most seemed focused on their own journeys. For every mounted man riding a donkey or an old mule, a hundred walked. The procession did not look inspiring. But Ewan knew its power wasn't in the number of blades or horses it had.

He let the last group pass, a flock of sheep grazing and following in a cloud of dust. The guard dog was keeping the animals together, but when it sensed Ewan, it slunk away to a safe distance, tail tucked low.

Soon, the column veered toward Keron, heading north. Ewan climbed back onto the beaten trail and walked into the settlement. From what he had heard, this place had not existed only a year back, and now it was a town even bigger than the other city just a few miles away. You could see people working in the fields, you could hear hammers banging, and there was smoke sputtering from chimneys. Wrapping it all was an invisible layer of energy. Ordinary folk wouldn't spot it, but he felt it in his bones, a kind of resonance in tune with his body.

Ewan knew he had arrived where he should be. His stomach no longer tingled.

Without any hurry, he marched into the town, ignored by the locals. He was not really sure where to go, but he expected his feet to take him to the right shed or shop. Somewhere in this industrious chaos, he would find the source of all this creation.

"Are you here to join us, son?" someone called, and he knew it was directed at him.

Ewan looked at the other person. A man, fairly nondescript, wearing a priest's robes, well worn with use. "Maybe," he replied.

The clergyman frowned. He must have expected more enthusiasm from the newcomer. "May I know your skills?"

Ewan wondered what his skills really were. *Not dying by a sword edge,* he thought. That would be quite useful in the coming days. "I must speak to whoever leads your congregation. You must take me to see him."

"My name is Brother Clemens," the priest introduced himself. "I can assist you with your needs."

"Unfortunately, you cannot," Ewan responded. He tried to keep his tone flat, but he knew he sounded ominous, even dangerous.

The brother sensed the peril, even though he did not understand it. He inclined his head. "As you wish. Please wait here."

Leaning on the smooth rod of transparent glass, he waited. It was a deadly thing, he knew, not quite sure how he knew it. But the instinctive magic inside him that had so far guided him across the world was feeding him ancient truths as it saw fit, suddenly, abruptly, sometimes with clear memories, other times with premonition and bad feelings. *Not my memories,* he reasoned. But maybe they were his after all.

Several children raced across the street between the shacks, fighting with wooden sticks. A repairman was putting fresh roofing on one of the houses, naked to the waist, his skin browned by the sun. Yet more people were coming and going. It felt busy. But not like Eybalen or Shurbalen. There was unspoken urgency to their movement and actions, a higher cause that united them in spirit and body. They probably didn't quite yet understand what was happening.

There would be a terrible war soon.

Ewan noticed a new presence to his left. He turned and saw a small group walking in his direction. In the front, a stocky man led, a wicked ax held firmly in his right hand, just below the head. He seemed quite determined to put it to good use if he had to. Brother Clemens and a large boy walked just behind. Ewan scowled. That lad was…wrong somehow. But soon, he put him out of his mind.

The last person drew all his attention. There was a man like no other, neither young nor old, neither well built nor scrawny, with a sure, graceful gait. His face was serene, perfectly symmetrical, unremarkable, and yet inspiring. Perfect somehow. Even beauty must have its flaws, Ewan reasoned, but the man's visage was just right. Looking upon him, Ewan felt calmness imbue him. His spirit rose. He was cheerful suddenly. His doubts and worry about the future of the realms melted away, leaving behind a pristine crystal drop of innocence. The other man radiated order and logic on a physical level.

Now that is divine, he thought.

Tanid willed himself to step forward. Fear choked him in a tight grip, made him weak, rigid. He almost stumbled. But he could not let anyone see him falter. That would kill the faith. He must be above human emotions.

However, seeing the Special Child who had killed Damian was probably an exception.

There he was, unchanged like that day near the Womb, a thin, poor youth you'd dismiss for a lowly servant on some estate. The most underwhelming appearance for someone who had killed a god. Worse, in his right hand, he was holding a bloodstaff.

How can that be? Where did he get that weapon? Is he in league with Calemore? Or is he Calemore in disguise? Has he found me, and now he's gloating, testing my resolve, torturing me? Or has he sent this boy to do his ugly task? Of course, the White Witch could not kill another deity, because that would prevent him from becoming one. Maybe this child was a Pum'be.

However, if the lad was intent on murder, he kept it well hidden behind a simple expression of wonder, the lethal clawed end of the rod pointed skyward. There was no immediate threat, and Ludevit was silent. Still, Tanid was ready to shove Pasha in front of him if that youth showed any sign of aggression.

He was not really sure how to fight someone like this Special Child. He was not really sure of the extent of his abilities. But that boy was dangerous, extremely dangerous. And he was wielding the most powerful weapon invented in the whole of human history.

So what now? Do I turn away and run? Better to run and live another day than perish to foolish pride here. His death would mean a total defeat of the realms at the hands of the White Witch. Without him, faith would wither and die, and all of humanity would be left without hope. Animals with tools.

What does he want? Why is he here? Where did he get that weapon? Questions rumbled though his head like a wild herd of nosehorns. With each step, he was coming close to a horrible truth, not really certain his magic would protect him. Even Pasha and Ludevit might not be enough, not against one of their own. Tanid had no idea what this other Child could do. *What are his skills?*

Then, there was the temptation. A deep, throbbing, exciting human temptation. To somehow recruit this lad into his growing band of followers. To make him a mighty defender of the one god. With the bloodstaff in his hands, the victory against Calemore would be almost certain. But then, what was Calemore's weapon doing in the boy's hand? *Maybe he has killed the witch, just like he's killed Damian? Maybe this boy is a destroyer of faith?*

Tanid stepped closer. There was no going back now.

"Greetings, son," he said.

Ewan blinked. He had floated in a sort of sweet trance, his emotions a soft, warm mush of eggs and oil. Now they came back. Just the good ones. The rest remained drowning in that creamy bliss, raising an occasional arm or leg in treacly agony.

Ewan rubbed his hand up and down the glass rod. He tried to focus his thoughts on the perfect man in front of him. That strange instinct inside him was coming to life again, trying to speak to him across the chasm of thousands of years and countless lives, telling him a story of ancient battles, of love and war, of the gods and goddesses.

Somehow, he knew. He understood. If a curious bystander had asked him to frame his cognizance into words, he could not. They were slippery, elusive, misty. Like trying to scoop up a waterfall rainbow in your hand. But you knew it was there.

"Greetings, Father," he offered in return, almost instinctively. Damian was his father, in a way, but so was this man. This god.

Brother Clemens was watching him carefully, looking upset. That man with the moustache also seemed disturbed. The
big boy roughly his age was staring at the ground, as if embarrassed to be there.

"We must talk. Alone," Tanid said. He looked at the axman. "It's safe." Back at Ewan. "Follow me, son."

Into the heart of that town they went, past houses made
from fresh timber maybe days ago, sap drying on shaved logs,
past shrines and prayerhouses and open kitchens. The flood of
human traffic was insane. Groups of men, usually a score strong,
were getting ready to depart, loading wagons with dry goods,
blankets, and improvised weapons. Another memory floated
into his mind. That one fatal day in the Safe Territories, when
his friend Ayrton had left with the Outsiders to fight a holy war.

Not much different from what was happening now.

For every follower preparing to leave, more were coming,
arriving, eyes alight with hope. There were women and children in the lot, and some looked like refugees, haggard, poor,
and with threadbare smocks as their only possessions, but you
could feel the fire of prayer in their hearts, sustaining them.

"These men are leaving north," the god was saying. "They
will join the other nations in a fight against the White Witch."

Ewan nodded solemnly. "I have come to join the war."

The god looked at him from the corner of his eye. Even
so, that gaze was piercing. "You will fight against the witch?" It
wasn't really a question.

Ewan waited until the fizzle of ancient truths in his head
cooled to dark-orange sparks. "All the other deities are dead,
are they not? I felt them die."

The god closed his eyes for a second. "I am the last one. I
am the one god left."

Ewan smiled weakly. "What is your name, Father?"

"Tanid," the deity replied.

"I used to be a young brother in a monastery to God Lar, near Chergo, in the Territories. That was a long time ago." Ewan tried to remember the faces of the other boys he had spent his childhood with, but they eluded him. "I have read about you, though. You were the god of weather."

"I still am," Tanid confessed. "But now everything else, too." The god smacked his lips, trying to say something. It was such a human expression, it shocked Ewan. "Please tell me, son…"

"Ewan."

"Where did you find that weapon?"

Ewan sighed. "At the bottom of a lake. Deep in the Oth Danesh land. In their one named city."

Tanid bobbed his head slightly. "I thought Calemore had it."

Ewan shrugged. "He probably does still. There is more than a single example." He wasn't sure how he knew that, but he was certain of it. Ever since reading *The Pains of Memory*, new dark secrets were coming into his conscience, like old bubbles of air trapped in a muddy bottom, stirred free by his actions.

"That weapon is called the bloodstaff." The god was looking at him again, perhaps slightly apprehensively now. "Do you know how to use it?"

Ewan rolled the rod, staring at its distorted, hollow tube. "I believe so."

They reached a barn. For normal people, it would have been just a farm building, old and beaten by the weather. For Ewan, it was a powerful beacon of that beautiful, calm energy that Tanid emanated, an anchor of faith for this town and its inhabitants.

"I will be marching north myself soon," Tanid spoke. "Soon, the whole of the realms will converge in a great battle against Calemore and conclude the war that was initiated thousands of years ago. I would be honored if you joined me, Ewan."

Ewan stared at the barn. "I am a Special Child," he said.

Tanid laid a gentle hand on his left shoulder. "Yes, you are. Do you know what your abilities are?"

Ewan remembered knives shattering against his skin. He realized he had not sipped water or pretended to eat for weeks now, ever since leaving Naman and Raida. "I feel no pain, no cold, no heat. I cannot be hurt, it seems. It is as if I'm spectating someone's life rather than living it myself."

"That is a valuable gift, Ewan. You would be a great asset."

"What can you tell me about my kind? About me? Why do I have these abilities?" His desire to learn about his cursed heritage had withered in the time he had spent among the Oth Danesh, but now it was flaring again, like a forest fire. He wanted to know the secret of his being. He wanted to know why he was doomed to experience a life robbed of feeling. Why he was still trapped in a young, gangly body, why he wasn't afflicted by sleep, exhaustion, and the weather. Why he was forced to remain so alone.

Tanid was silent for a while, a hand pressed to his chin, thinking. "There are no easy answers to what you're asking. I will tell what I know of your creation, of the ancient war. But some secrets are hidden even from me." He paused. "You will join us?"

Ewan looked away, toward the horizon, where puffy clouds were bleeding into the landline. Somewhere to the north, hundreds or thousands of miles away, he would meet this White Witch and defeat him. He now understood his grim purpose: to be the last chapter in an old, sad story. But while the realms would have their happy ending, he was not really sure what he would do.

What then? What would he do? Become the invincible dockworker?

"I will join," he said.

Tanid could hardly hear himself over the fluttery drumming of his heart. He was terrified, giddy, two lumps of nausea jiggling in the hollows under his jaw, threatening to make him gag. He was watching this dreadful Child, wondering what he might do, what kind of untold damage he could wreak with the bloodstaff in his hands.

It seemed Ewan was inclined to fight against the witch, but the realization did not make Tanid happy—only certain the war was inevitable. Before, he could have delayed the march north, always weighed down by his fear of confrontation against Calemore's magic. Now, there was nothing left. He knew he had to leave this place. He had to lead the army of his followers into a bloody clash. In that place inside his head where even the gods had no control over time and fate, he knew that his destiny toward the war had been sealed.

Immense relief, immense terror mingled into a soup of emotions. With Ludevit, Pasha, and now Ewan at his side, he was like a champion of old, marching to battle with his magical weapons, his magical heroes and scapegoats, willing to sacrifice them for the greater good, for his own. But there was no other way.

"You must not call me by my name in public," he said. "They know me as Gavril the holy man."

"Gavril," Ewan repeated.

Tanid scanned the busy crowds around him. His two Special Children were standing some distance away, the burly boy as awkward and clumsy as always, refusing to meet people's eyes. He was much like Ewan, it seemed, impervious to fire and steel. But this Ewan lad seemed at ease with his magic. He looked like someone who had killed before and did not regret it. Pasha could well learn from him, but maybe it was too soon for that yet. He would have to make sure his Children would cooperate and work together in battle. Ludevit would anticipate dangers, Pasha would physically protect him, and Ewan would use the bloodstaff to decimate the Naum forces.

It sounded like a sure victory, but somehow, he was still terribly afraid. He did not want to meet Calemore in open combat. He feared that confrontation; he feared the conclusion to their ancient strife. One way or another, the war Simon and Damian had started would end. Tanid hoped he would live. He wanted to live. He was not going to let go of this exciting new life easily. Not like in the city. This was a human life. The vulnerability, the doubt, they were a curse. But they were also intoxicating.

Only after he won, what then? Where would he go? Walk through the world among his people, answering their prayers? Maybe he deserved more? Maybe he would find a companion and make her into a goddess? He had never been too fond of love like some of his kin, but he understood solitude. He understood the need for someone to reflect your pain, your doubts, your thrills.

Survival is easy, he thought. *What happens after?*

But there were things that even gods couldn't answer. Like the meaning of their own existence.

"It is time for prayer," he told Ewan, pushing the darkness in his mind away. "Do you pray, Ewan?"

The boy shrugged. "Not recently. I have not felt the need."

Tanid steered him back toward his other Special Children, and they met halfway. Brother Clemens was coming toward the barn, getting ready for his ceremony. The entire town was converging here to bask in faith. Tanid could already feel the fresh blossom of prayer in his veins.

"You should pray. Every soul counts."

Ewan seemed to consider it. Then he shrugged again. "So be it."

Soon, the entire town was chanting, making Tanid that much stronger, except for some of the pilgrims already on the road, heading to war. As a bird flew, one could see dozens of convoys clogging the roads, joining others. King Sergei's troops were there too, plodding toward northern Athesia. It seemed the Parusite leader had heeded his advice after all. Or maybe, he was sending troops for war against the Athesian empress. For the thousandth time, Tanid wished he had someone who could foretell the future. But all he could do was nourish doubts.

CHAPTER 19

Nigella had never considered herself overly social. But for once in her life, she longed for an honest talk with another adult. Sheldon was just too young.

The four Naum soldiers guarding her did not speak Continental, and all they could offer were nods and grunts and reserved smiles as they watched her work. She was not quite comfortable with their stares, but she knew she would not be harmed. These men probably did not even dare conceive illicit thoughts in their heads.

Nigella was kneeling on the hill's slope, the grass tickling her legs. She was collecting herbs, the one thing Calemore's soldiers could not provide for her. She had no idea how to describe the subtle differences between cat's-ears, hawk's-beards, and dandelions to men who had probably never seen these flowers before. Nor would she trust men trained to kill people with such a task.

She had seen very few Naum women, and she trusted them even less. While she was more or less certain of what the soldiers were meant to do, she did not know if the women would obey the same rules. Mothers were extremely protective and possessive, and they might decide Sheldon was being fed way too generously while their own babies had rations. The children could also be troublesome and cruel, and she did not want her son mingling with them. No, Sheldon was better off staying close.

All the time, Naum soldiers would bring her fresh goods, fruit, vegetables, even wine. She lacked for nothing, except spices and the special commodities of her craft. Which gave her an excuse to leave her cabin and walk the nearby hills, watching the countryside transform.

Two months since the Naum forces had swept the land, the prospect of the foreign invasion did not look very promising. Marlheim had stopped burning, and a sizable body of noncombatants had moved in, taking over the burnt houses and scorched fields. But they knew nothing about Caytorean weather and plants, and their crops were failing. The winter would be lean, and that worried Nigella.

What if they decided her little hoard was just too delicious to ignore?

Almost daily, a new caravan would arrive into Marlheim, and another would leave, mostly men on foot, marching somewhere south. They carried weapons, and she could not mistake their intent. But she saw many families take to the road, taking their meager possessions with them. They did not look like the proud army of a mighty conqueror.

The town had hardly recovered from the attack. Shops and stables stood empty. The streets were littered with roof tiles, shards of pottery, broken masonry, and cinders. At least the bodies of dead men and horses had been cleared away, probably because the stench had been unbearable, even for these foreigners. Most of the Naum folk still slept under their wagons, while their shaggy oxen pissed and shat in the gutters nearby. Dogs were everywhere, hunting rats, chasing livestock from one improvised pen to another.

Outside the city's perimeter, men were busy cutting trees down, building new houses, but they struggled. Nigella imagined they had done carpentry before, but not with the type of timber that grew in Caytor. The same went for all their other work. They fished in the streams, they herded goats and other hairy animals, they tried to till the cracked soil, but their effort was slow and awkward. Women were there, too, hard at work like their husbands. She had never been good at human affairs, but she could tell intimacy, even from a remote hilltop.

Sometimes, men and women alike would raise their eyes from the withered cabbage and brownish weed and stare at her, squinting their pale eyes against the harsh sun, their skin red and sweating, their bodies lean from too little food. They would look at her and probably wonder who she was and why she got to watch them laboring in the heat. Nigella couldn't mistake their silent glare of accusation, as if all this was her fault.

So she never went down into Marlheim. She almost wanted to. Not so much as to meet the Naum people, not really. But to see up close the reality her lover was carving for her. She felt braver since Rob's death, and the strange new nation intrigued her as much as it frightened her. But those looks stayed her feet far from the lower slopes, far from the misused parcels of onion and carrot, far from the debris and graves and slow ruin. She would not risk it.

Nigella plucked another flower and placed it one of the nine bags hanging from her waist. There were all kinds of insects crawling through the grass, lively, busy, just like the humans. Not far away, Sheldon was fencing against an invisible foe with a dried branch. In his left hand, he was cradling that present from Calemore. Sunlight would often catch in its clear depth, then shine out in a dazzling array of colors. It was beautiful, mesmerizing, and Nigella had no idea what it was. But she had allowed her boy to keep it, for now.

As far as the future was concerned, *The Book of Lost Words* was quite skimpy on advice.

She had probably reached the middle of the text, not that she believed there was any chronology to the riddles written throughout the book. But her understanding of the words depended on reading every single line, and her progress was slow.

Sheldon was making sounds, the *ooh* and *aah* of valiant swordsmanship. Two of the Naum soldiers were looking at him, grinning. If you ignored their clothing, you might mistake them for an ordinary pair of Caytorean private guards. It was disconcerting, she thought, that people bent on so much destruction could be so similar to everyone else.

Her lower back hurt, so she straightened, massaging her kidneys, spreading the tingling sensation around. Then, she bent over again, inspecting the flowers. She always chose undamaged specimens, with whole leaves and without ants and flies burrowing through the petals and heads. When she dried them, she wanted the crushed extracts to be pure.

The vivid story of flickering images from the previous night's reading still flashed in the back of her mind. She couldn't put words to the sensation, but again, it wasn't a pleasant one. Once, she had read for Calemore, ending up confused. Then, she had begun trying to figure out the truth for herself. But now, she believed their two destinies were entwined, and she couldn't tell her own future from that of her lover's. Whatever the book had to tell, it wove a tale of two people. And that made her work doubly hard.

She thought she had seen an empty alley in a big city, with large gray buildings growing to the side of it, windows empty like black eye sockets in an old skull, the sky boiling with purple and silver and skimming past faster than it should. Yet, there was no wind down below, no leaves blowing across the cobbles. Nothing moved in the street.

Then, a figure was there, standing against the raging backdrop of a silent storm, and his cape did billow. She thought she had seen Calemore, but it didn't feel like him. Still, reading through the passage had heightened her sense of urgency, her unease. As if that man didn't belong there. Or rather, the world around him didn't belong where he was.

The sky turned brilliant, too bright to look, and then, the city wasn't there anymore. She just couldn't see it. She remembered reading, words unrelated to the story unraveling inside her head, and the memory of that place was like a vaguely remembered dream, a nagging emptiness. Only later, after she had put the book away and lay dozing in the bed, Sheldon cradled in her arms, did the images float back to her, reassembling into a message. A warning.

That much she was certain of. It was a warning.

She had known Calemore would bring pain to the realms. She had never read anything that would indicate hope or healing on his behalf. *The Book of Lost Words* had always given her discomfort, deep and primitive. But now, it was different. Worse somehow. As if he was going to make the world something else. Change it. Make it less than what it was. As if…

"Mom, Mom!" Sheldon called.

Nigella blinked. She realized she had stood up, staring west. She shook her head and knelt back onto the slope, picking fresh flowers. "What is it, Shel?"

"I defeated the evil wizard," he said, cheerful, unconcerned. The two warriors were still watching him and grinning. One said something in his foreign tongue, and the other gave a gruff chuckle.

Nigella frowned. "Sheldon, come here."

He shambled over, stepping over rocks with goatlike ease. "Yes, Mom?"

She pointed at the soldiers with her nose. "Stay away from those men. Do not encourage them."

The boy shrugged. "But why, Mom?"

She sighed, wiping sweat off her brow. Working on all fours was a very exhausting task. "Because they are soldiers, Shel, and they are dangerous men. They work for Calemore, and you must keep away from them."

"But Uncle Calemore protects us," he objected.

She felt her blood chill. *Uncle?* "He is not your uncle, Shel."

Sheldon shrugged again, apparently disagreeing with her. "But they protect us."

Nigella swept a burdock from his shirt. "Just do as I say."

"They don't mean us any harm, Mom," the boy insisted. "They told me."

Told you? Nigella felt her blood turn to ice. "What do you mean, dear?"

He pointed back at the grinning pair, without shame or fear. "I heard them talk. They asked me what I was going to do with my sword, and I told them I was going to defeat the evil wizard. So they asked me to show them."

Must be the boy's imagination, was her first thought. *Or he may have really talked to them,* came the second, more sinister one. *How?*

Keeping her dread and curiosity at bay, Nigella stabbed a glance at the soldiers. But they missed the venom in her soul. She was angry, mostly at herself, for not paying attention to her son. Bringing him here was a risk, but she had not dared leave him all alone in the cottage. Here, though, there were other temptations, other problems. Unlike her, Sheldon craved companionship. He did not fully understand this war, this madness, and being exiled to the cabin, locked in with his mother, was a confusing punishment for him. She could not really blame him for wanting some attention or new friends. But not these men.

I must have daydreamed, thinking about prophecies, she wondered, trying to keep her anxiety down. She was such a fool. How could she have let that happen?

"I forbid you to talk to them," she snapped, perhaps too harshly.

Sheldon looked hurt. "Why, Mom?"

Nigella plucked a flower with too much force, crushing it. "Do not argue with me, Shel." The other thought crept back into her mind. How did Sheldon understand the soldiers? Children learned languages much faster than adults, for certain, but he had barely spent time around the Naum men.

How?

She wanted to ask her son, to probe, but she wasn't sure she was brave enough to hear his answers.

In that instant, Nigella wanted to pack her things and head back home, right then, but somehow, she found herself kneeling in the same spot, wondering. Maybe Sheldon had a knack for languages, and maybe he had learned a little of their tongue. That was a huge advantage, if she dared exploit it. Through her son, she could learn more about Naum, more about their intentions, their orders, their desires. She could learn what these men wanted, how they lived.

Only did she really dare do that? Did she dare commit herself? Her boy?

Knowing this strange nation could help her understand Calemore's reality much better. She might steal a glimpse into his world, into the great vision he had for the realms, for the people of the land. She might use that knowledge to complement the confusion and omens that the book offered her. Only that meant endangering Sheldon.

She would never do that.

Sheldon was sitting nearby, shoulders slouched, head bowed in that forced sadness that children used to let their elders know they were hurting. He was deliberately avoiding looking at her, but he was waiting for her to soften, just so he could act proud and defiant. Nigella wished she could indulge him—he deserved it after all the hardship she had put him through—but she couldn't let her emotions best her now. Emotions for her son, or Calemore, for that matter.

Nigella flicked an ant climbing on her thigh and moved uphill, toward a new clump of flowers. She bent low, knees and elbows deep in the prickly, smelly grass, carefully examining the petals, the stalks, the leaves.

Her son squirmed, but she ignored him. He patted the ground, but she pretended not to have noticed. Bored and defeated, he rose, still holding that sword stick of his, but it was a forlorn gesture of misplaced manipulation.

One of the two Naum men said something. The other made a rumbling noise of agreement, a man's signature expression worldwide. She stole a quick glance toward Sheldon. Yes, he was watching them, and his big eyes were lit with clarity. He fully understood what they were saying. She ought to be proud of her child, but all she could summon was fear and worry.

Enough, Nigella thought, rubbing her back again. She had collected a fair share of herbs. After she dried them, she would have enough to last her through the winter. Still, maybe she would visit the countryside a few more times before the autumn set in.

Rising, dusting herself off, she spared another glance at Marlheim, a living, breathing scar on the face of Caytor, a reminder of what her lover was doing. She wanted to feel disgusted, repulsed, and terrified by his heartless actions, she wanted to feel sympathy for her fellow citizens, but she could not summon anything of that sort. Her heart was empty of sorrow and her cheeks dry of tears for people who had never quite treated her as an equal. The fact Calemore planned to reshape the realms did not really bother her. Not as such...

What did was her role in the scheme. What would become of her?

She still tried to wrap her mind around the unease left from the last reading. Calemore would change the land forever. He would carve a new reality. And she would have to find her place in it. That was a part she still couldn't fathom. Her future was a dark shadow, a vague swirl of shapes that hinted at bad things to come. She wanted to hope, to believe they would end up together as a couple, chained by love and understanding, sharing passion and ideals. She knew that Calemore was cruel and vain and treated humans worse than insects under his boots, but he also had a soft, gentle side. He could be considerate when he wanted to. He had shown her appreciation, and he was genuinely interested in her. Unlike all the others. No one had ever done her any favors. Maybe he was a wild, violent man, but how was he any different from any other male out there? And he had never lied to her. Of that much she was certain.

Perhaps she didn't deserve a prince from ancient tales. Perhaps she needed a brutal, hard man to complete her. That was her burden, her ordeal, her destiny. She could flee, like she had always done before, slink away from danger, challenge, and confrontation, take the easy way out. Or she could toughen up and face the ordeal. The price of love. No one said it would be simple. Then, no one had ever told her the life of a mongrel in a magic-hating country would be easy. Not after Rob had left her with a child, not after James had broken his promises, never.

It would be fatally romantic, she thought, almost misty-eyed. It would be like no other story told before. There was only one problem.

From everything she had read in the book so far, it seemed her future might never come to be as she imagined. Instead, she would get a more sinister version. One without regard for her love and dreams. Now *that* was the price of love, it seemed. The more she read, the worse it became. The message, ever elusive, cryptic, but unmistakably dark and troubling.

What will become of me, she wondered.

She had to figure it out, for herself. She had to.

Pouches bulging with herbs and flowers, Nigella retreated to her cabin. Sheldon looked at his stick, tossed it away, and followed after his mother.

CHAPTER 20

Stephan entered the bank. He had not entered a bank in years. Once you got sufficiently rich, money sort of started gravitating your way, like lumps of rock cascading down a cliff into a lake, a lake that was your wealth. With hardly a splash, the surface swallowed it all.

Moreover, influential people had cronies to take care of their business, from secretaries, lawyers, and diligent clerks to mercenaries, all of whom had a role in making your money reservoir more efficient, more lucrative. At a certain point, you even became redundant, but the idea of your wealth kept thriving on its own, sustaining itself like a living organism.

Today, though, his visit had nothing to do with money.

A polite clerk in spotless livery led him upstairs to the personal office of one Lord Malcolm.

Father to one Lady Rheanna.

Guild masters would sometimes wait in the lavish foyer outside the man's opulent office. Merchants, traders, shipmasters, and awfully rich businessmen would sometimes wait for weeks before their appointment could be granted. Even then, they might end up being declined at the last moment. Lord Malcolm could afford to disappoint his customers now and then. His institution had enough funds to patron a few slapped wrists and a handful of wasted hours.

Stephan was spared the ceremony of lounging in leather sofas and sipping expensive wine in the waiting room. He was ushered without a word into the den of wealth.

Rheanna's father was standing near a huge floor-to-ceiling window, staring toward the docks. The panes were clear save for an odd gull dropping plastered against the wrought-iron frame. Stephan could see the slight resemblance to his daughter, the same nose, the shame sharp features.

"Where is my daughter?" the man said as a matter of greeting.

Stephan stopped and waited for the clerk to click the doors shut behind him. The moment they were alone, he eased himself into an impressive chair, the expensive leather creaking ominously. He waited for the man to turn and regard him fully.

"I thought you could tell me that," he told the lord when he slowly spun around.

The man snorted. "Councillor, my time is precious. I have postponed several highly important matters to accommodate your visit, with a firm belief you had valuable information to share. If you intend to banter needlessly in rhetoric, we can end this meeting right now."

Stephan grimaced. "I want to help you." *I want you to help me.*

Grudgingly, Malcolm sat down behind his huge desk. It was empty, and it only served to create an impressive distance between himself and whoever sat on the opposite side. "How so?"

"Well, we both want your daughter found. Safe. Protected. And we want to make sure that her interests in the High Council are not compromised."

"I can guarantee that myself," the lord snapped.

"Perhaps. But it would not hurt if you had staunch allies among the councillors."

Lord Malcolm made a weary face. "I see no point in all this drama. We have worked together before, and we know each other's tricks all too well. What do you want?"

Stephan had hoped to draw out the meeting a while longer before making his proposal, but then, sometimes, the other party dictated the pace of negotiations. "I must ask you, do you know what your daughter had in mind when she married Emperor James? Do you know what she intended to achieve?"

Malcolm tapped the polished tabletop. "Not quite, I must admit. She had kept her affairs rather private, even from her father. But that is understandable. I would not expect her to chat about her designs until it was all well under way, or complete." He looked away, toward a ceremonial bookcase on the left side of the vast chamber. "My daughter is a skilled businesswoman," he added.

Stephan leaned on one of the armrests, but his elbow slipped, and his body bobbed awkwardly. He straightened himself. "I think she meant to get Athesia united with Caytor. First through marriage. Then, maybe as a commonwealth. Finally, as one realm. Once again."

"If anyone can do it, it's my daughter," Malcolm announced proudly.

Stephan nodded. "I want to help Lady Rheanna achieve that goal."

The lord was silent for a moment, watching him, thinking. "That would be satisfactory. But then, I would assume the High Council would fully support my daughter's endeavors. Is that not the case?"

Stephan looked at the empty desk. He imagined a glass of some other expensive wine would be there, waiting to be tasted. But the banker didn't seem to get it. Or pretended not to. "If the council really knew what it wanted, our choices would be much easier."

"So you're telling me the councillors might be split in their decision to support Rheanna? Some might decide to favor Amalia, is that it?"

"There are many possibilities," Stephan said carefully. "We cannot possibly control all of them. Or even predict them. Therefore, we should focus on the one we desire and make sure it happens. In this regard, I believe our common interests are fully aligned."

Malcolm smiled, a dry, perfunctory expression with a fixed rate. "You still haven't told me what you want, Councillor."

Some people really didn't have the flair for negotiations, Stephan mused, slightly disappointed. But trying to wheedle something out of someone like this slick banker was not going to work. "Your daughter is a widow. A beautiful, intelligent, powerful, highly desirable widow. Technically, she is eligible to the Athesian throne, which means Caytor gains access back to its lost territories. Well, to an extent. Some might say Empress Amalia has a much better claim." He waved generously. "Going down that route will lead to bloodshed. We will never win a war where Caytorean troops have to fight over *Parusite* land," he emphasized. "All Empress Amalia has to do to defeat us is to bow knee to King Sergei. However, we could perhaps convince Amalia she is better off with Caytor behind her, rather than those religious southerners."

The lord was frowning, looking intrigued. "Continue, please."

Stephan steepled his fingers. "What if your daughter *willingly* relinquishes her claim to the Athesian throne? What if she peacefully offers her full support for the empress? We get the favorable trade deals we have always wanted. We make sure the loyalty of our private armies is never put to a difficult test. And we stifle discord among ourselves, because everyone profits."

The banker touched his chin. "Why would Rheanna give up her claim?"

Stephan grinned, glad he had finally managed to bait the old wolf. "Because she will have found herself another, far more suitable husband."

Lord Malcolm lowered his hand, his fist clenched. "You presume too much, Councillor. Even I would not dare tell my daughter who she might choose to marry. Bloody Abyss, she didn't speak to me for almost a month after I accidentally broached that topic ten years ago."

"I would not expect you to convince her. Or order her. But maybe suggest? She will need friends in the coming months. She will need allies, people she can rely upon. She will direly need support, because she will be hunted. As long as she remains the widow of late Emperor James, she will be a valuable target. For everyone. The moment she removes herself from that perilous position, she will become safe. We must also make sure that Caytor gains as much as it can from this affair."

The banker rose, going back to the window. "Why do you think I would put your selfish needs before those of my daughter, Councillor? What makes you better than any other man out there?"

Stephan grinned again, at the man's back. Another successful bait. "Well, sir, nothing really. But I have been captive in Roalas for a long time, and I have negotiated with Empress

Amalia and her military commander. I know her better than most other councillors."

"I doubt that."

Stephan shifted his weight. He wasn't quite sure how much the council had learned about the situation in Roalas. He had sent a few letters while in captivity, and received some responses in return, far less than he would have hoped to. Most other Caytoreans had not bothered to write, but he couldn't really be sure Commander Gerald had not manipulated them separately, without each of them knowing about the rest. So it was quite possible his friends on the council had shown equal prowess and ingenuity, and he was merely deluding himself about his hostage heroics.

"I will support my daughter in whatever she chooses," the lord insisted, still watching the bay. "Whatever. Only then will I consider the good of our realm. Second to her desires. She is my only daughter. I don't have much in this world. My dear wife is…not well. Rheanna's wishes are sacred to me. You will do well to respect that. And never underestimate her. Or me."

Stephan cleared his throat. "All right, sir. What do *you* want?"

The banker turned, and his face glowed with victory. Stephan realized he wasn't the only one who could bait people with clever remarks and touching stories. He must not underestimate this man. Indeed.

"I want my daughter to be happy."

Stephan nodded carefully. "All right. How do I fit into that scheme?"

Lord Malcolm walked around his massive wooden rampart, approaching Stephan. The man wasn't alarming, but his presence was quite imposing. The masculine counterpart of what his ravishing daughter was. With her, you wanted to press yourself against that supple, warm flesh. With him, you wanted to dust the lint off your suit, stand, and salute.

"You, Councillor, can help me take over all of the Eybalen businesses." There was almost a mad glint to his eye. "I really have everything I need. More than I could possibly want. The only way to entertain myself is to try something new and different."

Stephan pushed the chair back so he could look at the banker more comfortably. "Well, I believe every wealthy man in the city shares the same ambition."

Malcolm shrugged. "I believe you aren't the only potential suitor for my daughter." He shrugged again. "However, you are the most brazen one, I have to admit. No other has dared yet step into my office and ask me to sell him my daughter. They probably think I would construe it as an insult." He walked away suddenly toward a small padded door near the western wall of his office. He turned the gilt handle and pushed.

A man stepped in. He was of average height, middle-aged, with receding hair that reached to his nape in wavy silver threads. It didn't look very clean, that hair, and there was yellow woven through the strands, which could have been old, permanent filth. The man had no right eye, and a scar ran right through his socket, down his cheek and stubbly jaw. He was well dressed, but no one would mistake him for a gentleman.

"This is Bader, the head of my security," the banker announced happily. "When you said you had your own proposal, I thought it would be prudent if I elaborated on my own. I could ask Bader to take a handful of gold from the coffers in the vault below and buy the services of one of those Pum'be assassins. Then, maybe, the killer could handle whatever threat my daughter faces."

Stephan forced himself to smile. "I heard they are no longer offering their services in the realms." He had tried. The moment he had heard about Emperor James. Only the legendary dwarfs would not accept commissions anymore. No one really knew why, but they refused to step anywhere near Parus, Eracia, or Caytor. Or Athesia. In another lifetime, that would have greatly worried Stephan, but he was too busy trying to scheme his way through political marriage.

Lord Malcolm pursed his lips. "Alternatively, I could ask Bader to hire several thousand new swords and paint the city streets bloody. That would ensure some enthusiasm on behalf of the council as far as my daughter was concerned."

Stephan exhaled slowly. "That would not be the best outcome, I'm afraid."

The banker was unfazed. "Indeed. So I will ask you once again, Councillor. Why do I need you? What value do you bring me?"

And I thought I was a good negotiator, Stephan mused. "Well, I believe we should definitely let Lady Rheanna make her own choices, be it Athesia or Caytor. However, we should unreservedly help her, make sure she is safe and well protected, so that she can act without fear. I would be honored to offer my assistance. In return, I would merely ask that you mention my selfless act before your daughter, should the occasion arise."

"Our first worry is to find her," Malcolm insisted.

"I have already put my best efforts to that," Stephan promised. *What do I gain here? A kind word by a crazy father, if that? I have come to this man to get his cooperation. Instead I have pledged myself to his service. For free? Am I mad? Or is this man a genius?*

"Councillor, I have yet to find a man who has impressed me with his wit and daring. Yourself included. But I can appreciate your candor, and your avarice. They are most commendable. Choosing allies in business is a very tricky ordeal. At the moment, I must choose between cowards scheming in the back rooms of their guilds and lavish villas, and you, a brazen, forward, unscrupulous son of a bitch. I guess that will have to do."

Stephan waited, wondering if the man might say something else. Apparently, he would.

"If my daughter chooses to marry again just so she can advance her agenda, then she will make her own decision who might best suit her in that role. One councillor or another, it probably won't matter. You aren't any better than the rest. However, you may choose to prove you're more than just a money-grabbing fop. That's my advice to you, Councillor."

"Thank you," Stephan said, his eyes on Bader. The man was wearing a sword at his hip, and despite an elaborate silver buckle and thread, it looked like a well-used tool.

"Your knowledge of the court intrigue in Roalas could be valuable. Although I doubt it will help much now. Perhaps it can be used to leverage the Parusite threat. Or mellow Empress Amalia's heart. I leave the tactical decisions to you. I would be glad to help finance your endeavor. You will definitely need help. Including troops."

Stephan frowned. "I am not quite sure I am following."

Lord Malcolm pointed at his one-eyed henchman. "Bader will accompany you on your journey. Searching for my daughter while safely lodged in Eybalen smothers the sense of urgency in the task. You will find yourself far more resourceful on the road. I expect you to find my daughter and form a solid plan that will ensure her success. No matter what she chooses."

"You want me to search for Lady Rheanna across Caytor?"

"You expect me to vouch for you before my daughter, Councillor?"

Stephan slumped. He held power in the city. He controlled information. Leaving all that behind would make his work that much more complicated. He did not like the prospect. But then, he had come to this man to ask him for his assistance, to buy his support. Well, he had expected the old banker to just accept his sophisticated story and lend gold. He should have counted on more from the man who had educated Lady Rheanna, the woman who had tamed Adam's son.

"All right, sir. I could do with an excursion. We'll be having autumn storms anyway, soon. The port might close, and it will get quite boring."

The banker walked back to his place by the window. "If you ask me, the most favorable resolution would be to make peace with both King Sergei and the young empress. Alas, that cannot be. And we must not choose the Parusites, because they will never relinquish Athesia. The only way we can ensure the safe return of our lost trade and territories is to win over Empress Amalia. That will be a difficult task for you. And even more difficult for my daughter. Two women fighting for power. That cannot be pretty. There's your opportunity, Councillor. She will need a man's insight into how to resolve this thing. Women are cruel, relentless. If you leave it to her, she will fight Amalia to the death. We don't want any of that."

"King Sergei might be inclined to appease us after the fiasco with the Oth Danesh," Stephan supplied, trying to sound smart and not intimidated.

The banker waved his hand dismissively. "He might, as long as we do not interfere in his conquest. But since we are going to do just that, all the goodwill we might have earned by being a cowardly nation incapable of defending itself will be lost the moment we try to side with Amalia. I'm afraid he knows that, so he might decide to stop his bloody war and reconcile with the empress himself. We must get there *first*. Otherwise, we will have lost not only Athesia but all the men the council had so generously sent to fight with Emperor James, too. And we might end up having another civil war."

Stephan was looking at Bader. The other man had only one eye, but he could stare well. He was doing just that, staring back, without blinking, watching him, judging his reaction to Malcolm's words.

"Do you know why I never replied to your letters, Councillor?" the lord asked.

Stephan narrowed his eyes. "You have received them, then."

"Yes, everyone has. Whoever held you captive made sure they did get delivered. I never responded, because letters get *read*. Do you understand?"

Clever, but it didn't really help me when I was locked in Roalas. "I see."

"You were the only one to send those messages. It shows you have initiative. Maybe even some daring. Backbone. Balls." He cupped his hand against the deep-blue sky of the Eybalen bay. "Definitely greed. I like those qualities in people I choose to conduct business with. It shows character. You have ambition, and it will drive you toward making sure my own needs are fulfilled."

Stephan wiped any smugness from his face. Time for grinning and smiling was over. But he was that much gladder to learn he had been the only Caytorean to try to exploit the captivity to his advantage. Well, their advantage. He had sort of assumed leadership of all the hostages. Not unsimilar to what he was doing now.

"Thank you."

"I like the way you think. So I expect you to use your cunning to help my daughter." Lord Malcolm seated himself again. He looked even sharper and more cunning than before. "You will have ample funds. Soldiers. Anything you need. Just ask Bader." Stephan wanted to speak, but the man resumed as if he hadn't noticed. "Remember, Councillor, when no one suspects you, you are free to do anything you want."

"I will probably need a cover story," Stephan mumbled. He had completely lost control of the meeting.

"We will think of something. The High Council is too divided anyhow. They might not even notice. I've spoken to some of your colleagues recently. I must say I'm not impressed. Guild Master Curtis, Guild Master Uwe, that awful man Dietrich. You have a golden opportunity, Councillor, and you must not squander it."

Stephan sighed, resigned. The leather chair was not comfortable anymore. "I will be ready to depart in two days, I believe. However, I am not quite sure where to go. Your daughter might be anywhere by now."

The banker was silent. Then, he began tsking, slowly, annoyingly, tilting his head left and right, and it seemed he would go on forever. "My dear councillor, I would have expected more from you. Now you do not think I would send you chasing a ghost of a rumor of a story of the whereabouts of my daughter across the realms? In autumn rains and winter blizzards? Do you really think we have time for *that*? You're not Askel journeying across the four corners of the world with a pen in your hand and a song in your heart."

Get to the point, Stephan thought, becoming agitated. He loved the sound of his own voice like the next man, but it was no fun having to endure all this theatrics. "I see. Where should I go then?"

Lord Malcolm leaned forward. "Pain Daye, obviously."

CHAPTER 21

There was a loud knock on the door.

No, no, no! Mali thought, trying to keep her thoughts focused. The thing was, it was somewhat difficult with a cock inside her.

Bjaras was panting on top of her, almost dutifully, his curls all wet and plastered to his forehead, his muscles shiny with sweat and flushed with blood. He was quite heavy, but right now, it felt good, oh so good. He was moving in rhythm with her breathing, so she didn't really need to fight for air. A refreshing change.

Another knock, louder still.

"Wait there," she whispered. Bjaras plowed on. She tapped him on the shoulder. He frowned but stopped. Mali slumped her head against the rumpled sheets, inhaling deeply, trying to clear her head. "What is it?" she rasped.

"There's a battle coming. You're needed, sir." A muffled voice came through the rough planks, almost apologetically. Well, it was hard to miss the nature of the grunts from inside the room. Or the screech of the bed legs sliding across the floor.

Battle? Battle? She groaned. Bjaras was still waiting, propped, his face mildly stupid, like all men in heat. "I will be there shortly." *Go away.*

She nodded at him, almost urgently. The northerner smiled, and then his face turned vague with lust, and he resumed his efficient pounding. Mali felt tingles up her ribs, up her arms, and she felt her eyes roll to the back of her skull, and her legs became custard. She whimpered against Bjaras's hair.

Then, just as she felt she could relax and let that blissful warmth wrap around her, his pace intensified, and she gasped with sweet pain as he climaxed. Damn, he was heavy.

Groaning, Mali pushed him off. He flopped, dazed, disoriented, calm like a baby. The frogskin on his member looked like a forest mushroom. "I have to go," she told him. "You stay here. Understand?"

Of course he did not. Bjaras just raised his brows, which probably meant he was exhausted and not going anywhere. Just as good. She did not want her officers and clerks commenting on the handsome northerner leaving her chambers. Not that she had really tried to be inconspicuous in the past several weeks. Not really.

Mali rolled over and wiped her body dry with an old, musty shirt. Then, she began dressing, knees wobbly, her privates on fire. She missed a trouser leg and almost stumbled into the small nightstand. Somehow she managed to roll the leather up her skin and buckle herself up. Her shirt fought her back, but she won eventually.

"Stay," she repeated and exited the room.

Outside, a red-faced clerk was waiting, trying to look invisible. "Major Alexa wishes to see you, sir."

Mali brushed her hair back. She was winded and thirsty. And still somewhat confused. Her body and mind were not quite ready for anything serious yet. "What battle?"

"Some of those strange northern people again, sir. A patrol from the south."

"Get me some water," she ordered and lurched against a wall. "Please." The clerk walked away toward the small canteen. Mali closed her eyes and breathed slowly, trying to calm herself. Outside the barracks, she could hear a noise intensifying. It didn't sound like chaos, but it wasn't a usual afternoon either.

The girl came back with a large earthen jug. Mali drank eagerly, rivulets running down the sides of her chin, dripping onto her collarbone. "Thank you." Bracing herself, she stepped into the main corridor and climbed down the flight of steps into the entrance hall of Lord Karsten's mansion.

Alexa was standing near an old statue, arms clasped in front of her, but she had armor pads on her. "You sure took your time."

"It was hardly two minutes," Mali complained. "What is happening?"

"We have engaged a large enemy patrol near the village of Narris. Must have come to sniff after their missing convoys. Well, three hundred strong, properly trained and with spears. All infantry, though."

Mali looked up and to the right, trying to imagine the layout of the land. "Where are Finley and Alan?"

Alexa crossed her hands the other way. "The troops are drilling, mostly. Don't know where the two of them might be. I thought to inform you first." Her friend touched an old marble bust, forehead creased with thought. "And there's another force coming, perhaps two thousand strong. We still have about a day and a half before they reach us."

Mali pointed toward the large double doors. The soldier standing guard pushed one of the wings open. Squinting against the sunlight, Mali walked out of the manor, into the large yard, her friend just behind her.

About two score of women were in various stages of handing their mounts to stable grooms. They were all covered in brown road dust and maybe a splotch of blood. It was quite warm, and everyone looked sick from exhaustion. Fat, disobedient fingers tugged at armor straps and cinches, trying to free the heavy, stifling plates. Pieces of metal clanged to the ground unceremoniously, making a solid din.

Major Meagan had already dismounted and was rubbing her face with a wet towel, smearing streaks of dirt round her cheeks. She was still wearing her greaves, one of them dented. Recruits from both her own battalion and the other divisions were running back and forth, carrying swords and spent crossbows and lances still intact. The yard was rather busy. Still more women were coming inside the mansion grounds, arriving in small groups of two or three. Blessedly, they did not look wounded, just dead tired.

"How are you, Meagan?" Mali asked, feeling just a little bit guilty for having had her fun with Bjaras. But she deserved it. Bloody Abyss, she could not be on duty all the time.

The officer huffed. "Too hot. Just too hot. If not for these lads, I'd strip naked."

Mali arched her brows. That was quite a statement from the noblewoman. "Any casualties?"

"Just three women. One fell off her horse, broke her neck. Another got an arrow in her eye. Lucky shot through the visor, imagine that. One of Nolene's corporals was killed by a spearman. Impaled through her guts, wasn't pretty. I think Alan lost half a dozen of his own, too."

Meagan waited for a moment, and when she realized she was no longer needed, she walked away to talk to one of the stableboys. He was trying to remove the saddle from her filly, but the major did not like the way he was treating the animal.

At her side, Alexa undid the strap on her shoulder pad and let it dangle. "This enemy is dedicated, but they are mad, and not very skilled at fighting against cavalry. We stayed away, firing from horseback until we ran out of shafts. Then we'd dash in, poke them, rush out, let them pursue and get weary, circle back, and stab again. Only this larger force worries me."

Mali did not normally approve of Alexa leaving on raids, but she needed her most skilled officer to be in command when her troops met the enemy soldiers. Just as she had feared, they had started showing up, more often and in larger numbers, coming back northwest to inspect the delay in their rear forces. Three hundred men was a respectable body to send on a reconnaissance mission, but hardly any risk to her girls. Two thousand, however…

She had been quite certain the patrols would get much, much bigger. And they had.

The time to figure out the enemy's intentions was running out. So far, no one could really understand the northerners. Well, she was too busy fucking one. That counted for something, didn't it? After all, she was trying to reconcile with the foe. Their hearts and minds and all that.

Mali sucked her teeth, bit her lip, chewed on it. She had hoped to establish a strong base at the estate, use the mansion and the castle as defense against the northern forces, and just keep sending hunting parties everywhere in an attempt to sever the enemy's supply lines. That surely worked, and the invading army had noticed. Now, she could remain here and wait for a huge flood of relentless foreigners to sweep back and defeat her by sheer numbers. It would take no skill in the end.

Or she could abandon the comfort of a real bed and embark on a killing quest once more. Just like she had done against the Namsue. Except she had no idea what her enemy really wanted, she could not understand it, and it was about a hundred times stronger than her own force.

Well, she had volunteered for this.

Mali wished she could wait a month longer so that the soldiers could bring in whatever crops the fields yielded. She wished she could spend another year rebuilding the estate, digging trenches and dikes and moats, building towers and walls. She wished someone in the south of Eracia would bother sending some kind of message back so she knew they were perhaps still alive and in control of the realm, that Lord Karsten was still in charge of the people, that the army existed and had its reserves and the chain of command and leftovers from the last harvest so they would not starve in the winter. She wished she had more troops and that she could coordinate the defense of the realm more effectively. Most of all, she wished she knew what was happening.

Her wishing didn't make any of it better. No message from Somar or Paroth or Ubalar yet. Or anywhere else. For a moment, Mali wondered if this body of men and women was the last huddle of humanity left in the realms. Them against an entire world of foreign people.

All the while, unarmed women and children kept coming in their strange convoys across the fields and plains of the country, traveling south. Her troops intercepted them, rounded them up, and sent them back. No one ever really fought back, not in earnest. She still had her gaggle of friendly prisoners, who did not seem to object to being held captive by a foreign army or seeing their kin herded back the way they had come.

Madness.

I miss the border skirmishes, she thought. There was logic in that time. Even Adam's head chopping seemed like a lucid, logical idea compared to this.

"Eventually, we'll get fucked," Alexa said, echoing her thoughts.

Mali sighed. "So we leave a token force and march bravely forward?"

Alexa was tugging at her breastplate clasps, but they slipped in her sweaty fingers. "You should consult with Finley and Alan. They might take it personally if you do all the thinking for them. Let them feel as if they came up with the plan in the first place."

"What if we just run? Head south? Or retreat far north, let this storm pass?"

Alexa grimaced sourly, her opinion plain across her face.

Mali nodded. "Right, we cannot."

"The longer we stay here and delay the enemy, the better. Gives the rest of the nations more time to prepare. Gives us a sense of duty." Mali wasn't sure if her friend was not being slightly cynical. "But now, we need to change tactics. We can't stay put any longer. Static warfare favors large armies, and as long as we have the advantage of speed, we can dictate the time and place of the battles. From what we've seen so far, they are not using any horses, so we can move twice as fast as they."

"Forward it is," Mali said, going back to her earlier plan. Simple, straightforward, suicidal. But less deadly than waiting for a giant army to walk over at leisure and swallow them whole.

She would miss a proper bed.

"You probably want to rest," she told Alexa, feeling apologetic. "But I need you with me."

Legs rubbery from her frolicking earlier, she walked through the arched gateway of the mansion's low, mostly decorative wall and headed toward the castle. In order to create some semblance of order and reduce the chance of fighting and molestation, the two male commanders had their troops stationed in the keep and around it, while the girls enjoyed the mansion. It was not a fair arrangement, but there were far more men than women, and they couldn't all fit into Lord Karsten's bedrooms.

The soldiers were busy repairing the stonework day and night, strengthening the walls, making the fortifications that much sturdier and more perilous for attackers. In between rows of tents and large patches of ground covered in carts, boxes, and barrels of supplies, thick rows of sharpened stakes faced outward, making an approach risky. People had to weave left and right to get to the castle.

Bored sentries stood everywhere, broiling in the summer heat. Most had taken off their helmets, but that was as much nudity as Alan would let them have. Builders and workers, on the other hand, were wearing only short breeches. You could not scale a scaffolding wrapped in steel and leather.

The air smelled of tar, a sticky, sharp stench that made your head hurt. Men were smearing the black substance over the wooden gates and the tower structures to try to make them fireproof. Higher up, she could see carpenters braving the height, patching old roofs and building platforms for archers. It looked like a well-coordinated effort. The castle would stand not just mock siege engagements but also some real ones. The sorry Eracian army was coming together well. She should be proud. Alan and Finley, too. Now, though, she was going to ask the other two officers to mostly abandon the repairs and march on a suicidal journey against the northerners.

Soldiers saluted, but she was too tired to return the gesture. She walked on, silent, mind swimming with thoughts. The sun disappeared as she stepped under the portcullis and into the low, vaulted passage burrowing through four paces of rock and mortar, then the second gate. As she walked, the cadence of her feet turned hollow inside the gateway. Black murder holes glared at her. The yard inside was beaten and scarred from thousands of feet and hooves going about. Everything was covered in a well-hammered patina of horseshit.

There were crossbowmen on the walls and walkways, lounging on large, rough steps leading onto the parapet and around workshops, on balconies and inside windows of the inner buildings. Mali estimated five thousand people could withstand a force ten times their size for a few months, provided the cellars had enough stores and the wells did not get poisoned. Luckily, Barrin was blessed with streams of fresh water and ripe fields everywhere.

She found the commander of the Third Division in one of the small, austere offices, which had probably once been used by some clerk to keep notes of how the keep was running. The small, slitted window was good for firing arrows without exposing the shooter, but it let in insufficient light. Finley was almost perching in the wedge of sunlight, squinting at his own reports. Behind his back, through the wavy, cheap glass, she could see the divisions drilling, large worms made of shiny metallic colors, twisting, curling, mating.

"You have heard of the incoming force," he said.

Mali waved the commander's assistant away. "Where is Alan?"

Finley grimaced. "I believe he's taking a private moment. Bad food."

She nodded. Well, if she could conclude the order of battle without the other man, that suited her just fine. She was not in the mood to fight or argue. "I think we should leave the estate. We cannot fight this enemy holed up in here. That would be self-destruction. Token force to maintain the castle, some logistic units. We take the rest and ride east." The plan was forming inside her mind even as she spoke it.

Finley put one of his reports down. "East?"

Mali felt a tiny fly land on her earlobe and swatted it away. "That will take us out of harm's way. Then, we cut due south and strike at our enemy's flank. Strike, retreat, regroup, circle around them, strike again. We can probably maintain this strategy indefinitely."

He nodded. "A similar idea has crossed my mind. Once I heard of this new force, I began to wonder what the next wave would bring. After we defeat two thousand men, perhaps they will send twenty?"

"Piecemeal victory sounds good enough for me." But it would not last. The foe would realize that and send a huge, unstoppable force. When that happened, she did not want to find herself in an old, musty castle, counting her rations.

"Alan is not really in favor of marching," Finley added.

Mali glanced at Alexa. "Well, he can remain here. We will need a garrison."

Finley grimaced. "Truth be told, I don't relish the march or the fighting either. But then, we have no choice really. Still, I can't help but wondering if we might not be utterly lost—or wrong. We haven't received any news from the realm in a long time. So much could have happened since."

Mali realized she could not keep standing any longer. She plopped into a chair, sighing loudly. She was glad other people shared her fears and doubts. But that also meant her interpretation of the reality was most likely accurate. A grim prospect.

"Let us defeat this army. Then we will regroup and move out."

Finley put his hands on the edge of the desk. "Sounds like a plan."

Mali stared at her own hands. "I want to take the northern people with us, though." She had other ideas. She wanted to send a small force into Athesia to try to establish some kind of a pact with whoever ruled there. Sending letters was fine, but they were easily ignored.

"They are the enemy," the other commander objected.

Mali smiled. "Exactly. One day, if we figure out their language, we might begin to understand what this crazy northern nation wants from us. We might actually be able to talk to them. That is always better than outright slaughter, especially if your foe outnumbers you." And Bjaras would be coming with her.

Finley rubbed his neck. "I am not optimistic. If they wanted to talk, they would have done that already."

"It's a slim chance, but I will not squander it."

They talked for a little while longer, making a rough outline of their battle formation for the upcoming engagement. The enemy force was expected to arrive by midday tomorrow and would probably pass within ten miles from their position, if not strike directly for the estate. The terrain did not provide any great advantage for ambushes, but the three of them carefully examined the maps to make sure they didn't miss anything.

Then, they discussed the actual march, the strength of the different units, the readiness of the troops, the supplies. Not the proudest or most skilled army in the world, to be sure, but they had quite a bit of experience. That should count in their favor.

Alan would remain behind with three or five thousand men, depending on how ardently he argued when they presented him with the plan. The rest would move as a homogenous body toward Pain Mave, hoping to evade the bulk of the enemy force and nip at their exposed sides. Perhaps she could meet up with her son and his mixed Athesian army. She missed James.

Well, it was a well-planned idea.

Or a well-planned suicide.

"May I invite you for dinner?" Finley said when they concluded the talk of sacrifice and heroism.

Mali pursed her lips. "Why not." She looked at Alexa. Her friend nodded.

Finley gave her a small smile. "In two hours then."

Walking through the damp, musty corridors, Mali let her mind unravel. She wondered how Gordon would react when she told him about Bjaras. He had to know; she owed him that much. Or the fact they would be taking their prisoners along. She wondered if she wasn't being just a silly old whore trying to escape commitment, like she had done most of her life. Or maybe she was just a huge coward.

Well, we all might die tomorrow. Dreams of the future are for the naïve. But somehow, she did not believe her own conscience. She shouldn't be feeling any guilt. She shouldn't fret over what men might think about her actions. Only now that she was doing as she pleased, there was a pang of something else in her belly.

Gordon is a decent man, she figured. *So why am I doting over some curly enemy carpenter?* Madness. Then again, nothing in the past year made any sense. Enjoying sex was probably the only sane thing she had done in a long while. And now, her mind was going to rob her of even that. The only thing awaiting her was a brutal march followed by a hopeless war.

For a moment, she thought about Adam. That man had chosen the right moment to die, for sure. He had spared himself all the pain and fretting she was enduring right now. Because of him. All because of him.

She went to the mansion to prepare for dinner, black ideas swirling through her head.

CHAPTER 22

Sergei reclined in a large, heavy chair, staring at the table in front of him. An ancient monstrosity of oak fireproofed against insects and time, it had a map of Roalas and its vicinity spread over it, the details painstakingly outlined, every little crease and village known to the city's cartographers.

His obsession.

What interested him most was the budding mold around Keron. An insider enemy, for all he was concerned, accountable to its own truths and reasoning. Well, things were not that awful. Since his visit at that holy farm, Gavril's men had started cooperating with his tax collectors and soldiers, trying to appease him and reduce his suspicion.

Then, quite recently, they had started marching north.

Even now, if he bothered walking out onto a balcony and glancing over the cascade of rooftops, chimneys, washing lines, and the city's walls, he could see a long line of men clogging the road, a tail of dust wagging behind them. They walked slowly and in disarray, no two quite the same, with more ash-colored donkeys and thin-ribbed mules than real horses, with more soldiers of the faith barefoot than clad in boots. Still, the pilgrim force was impressive in its own right, and only a fool would have dismissed the sheer number of spears and swords in that snaky, never-ending column.

They were going north to fight an ancient legend. Incredible.

But it was worrying, nevertheless.

Sergei could ignore an occasional lunatic preaching his own crazed notion of the truth. He could not as easily disregard tens of thousands of people united in their cause, no matter what it was. You had to be a genius to sway so many hearts and minds with just empty, idle talk, and Gavril did not strike him as the brightest politician of the century. Which meant he was lounging in the court room, fireplaces mercifully cold now that his sister was away, and wasting time rather than preparing for this fateful war.

He sipped wine. It was a bit acidic but acceptable overall. The sour taste fit his mood.

"Your Highness, Duke Yuri has arrived," Giorgi announced, standing near the hall doors.

Sergei shifted his weight and smiled. Finally. After so many months being robbed of his army, ruling the city with goodwill and scant troops, he had finally received his reinforcements, and he would have them for the coming year. The relief he felt was enormous.

It wasn't just the threat of this imaginary northern foe; it was his disillusion with Sasha and her Red Caps, the lack of victory against Amalia, the fragile peace he had to maintain in the countryside with an ever-dwindling presence of force. Most of his sister's units were in the north, and he was waiting for the Caytoreans and Eracians and maybe even the nomads to test his resolve. With the arrival of Yuri's levies, and those of Count Pavel, reported just days away with the Sevorod contingent, he could bring the sorry affair of Adam's legacy to a conclusion.

Only he would let Amalia choose first. Peace, and he'd let her live.

Sometimes, before sleep, he wondered why he didn't lust for revenge against that girl so much anymore. It must be Vlad's death. Or maybe the fact he had destroyed Athesia and through that liberated his own soul. Killing wasn't as satisfying as he had imagined it to be, and the responsibility he had for these people under his reign now blunted his desire for vengeance even further. In fact, it felt like a burden, bitter, boring, will sapping.

Sergei rose and spread his arms in greeting. Yuri stepped into the hall, still filthy from travel. He was tailed by a handful of knights of his house, and they all trailed road dust after them.

"Your Highness," the duke said, bowing. The men behind him went down on one knee, tapping their chests in salute.

"Yuri, I am glad to see you. I wish we could have met in Sigurd for the Autumn Festival banquet. Alas, we must remain here in this cursed land." He knew he did not sound as aloof and regal as he should, but he just couldn't care anymore.

"My troops are ready for war," the duke announced. Some of his old-time conviction was back, the memory of his last year's failure washed away. Sergei hoped all his lords would arrive clothed in fresh morale. They had let him down during the Siege of Roalas, and in turn, he had abandoned them. Now, they all had a chance to redeem themselves.

"Please join me. Now, I'm afraid I have summoned you to help me make peace." Sergei pointed toward a chair.

The duke waited until Sergei sat down. Then he took his own place. He beat his gloves against the edge of the table, then tossed them onto the map. Matvey came over to pour wine.

"Peace?"

"I am going to offer Empress Amalia peace. If she swears loyalty to me, she will be pardoned, and all her men will be spared. Athesia will integrate into the realm, fully."

Yuri sloshed the wine in his mouth, buying himself time until he could think it through. "Your Highness, that is a bold decision." If he were disappointed, furious, or even slightly apprehensive, he tried to hide it behind the patina of brown chalk on his whiskered cheeks.

"If she refuses," Sergei said, leaning over the table, pushing a painted lead weight that marked Amalia's presence near Ecol, "then we will be having a war. This time, I will not be merciful."

Yuri pointed his chin east, past the glazed windows and paintings. "Your Highness, I have noticed quite a bit of traffic on the road ever since we passed Keron. Are those Athesian refugees returning home?"

Can I tell him about the meeting with Gavril? No, I cannot. Not everything. "The clergy has established a strong presence near the town. They are now marching north. Apparently, the priests believe there will be a conflict with some unknown force coming from outside the realms." Nonsense. Myth. Then, he could not forget the sight of those bodies returning home, or those pigs, slashed and pierced and butchered, and their wounds never quite so round and clean. He could not forget the look on Vasiliy's face as he tried to grasp the shame and failure of the royal house.

Yuri nodded. "Faith in this land is a good thing."

A safe, neutral statement. Sergei ignored the pious chit-chat. "What is the news from back home?"

"Intriguing, Your Highness," the duke said. "There is peace at the borders, but…" He paused. "The Batha'n people have suspended trade with us recently, for an unknown reason.

Likewise, the Badanese convoys will not travel north of Sigurd. From what I've heard, there are dozens of their ships moored in the city's harbor. They say they are waiting for the storm to pass."

Sergei frowned. Once, he had been a very religious man, and he would have felt a tingle of respectful fear down his spine whenever he heard an ominous snippet of news. Recently, he had grown to dislike rumors and gossip that professed the divine. He believed they were just tools of manipulation, created by the patriarchs and well honed to popular use. Now, as if the world was testing his resolve, he was being taunted by omens everywhere.

Gavril, now my own dukes are telling me bedtime horrors. "Intriguing," he agreed.

The duke nodded. "Other than that, the realm is prosperous. The harvests will be bountiful, and the banditry is at an all-time low. Even the Red Desert tribes are quite docile recently. I can hardly remember the last time I had to hang a brigand."

Sergei looked at his trusted scribe. Genrik was there, inconspicuous, like an ancient decoration, sitting outside of plain view and yet seeing and hearing everything, his hand deftly scratching ink lines over expensive paper, writing history. One day, Sergei knew, he would be measured by those pages. But would they tell just the boring facts, or maybe, would they also present his reasoning, his fears, his doubts, his courage? Probably not. Otherwise, how would future generations make the same mistakes as him, if not through ignorance of the lessons of the past?

I wish I could have sat with Pyotr to hear him think. Or the Eracian hero Vergil. Even Emperor Adam. He would have loved to have been there, to try to understand how their minds worked and how they had made themselves immortal.

"What is your strength?"

Yuri put the cup down. "Seventeen hundred heavy horse from my own household, plus about two thousand light cavalry, scouts, and some auxiliary units. About eighteen thousand footmen and men-at-arms, as well as three thousand crossbowmen and archers. I have brought basic supplies, food, and tools for approximately two months' worth of campaigning."

Reports mentioned almost twenty thousand men walking and riding behind Pavel. Within days, he would triple the strength of his army in Roalas. "I will need you to relinquish about one thousand spearmen for the city regiment, and another thousand for the tax duties and the Gasua garrison. You will take the rest north, toward Ecol, where you will join my sister's forces."

Duke Yuri looked down at the map. "Empress Amalia?" he asked.

Sergei tapped the mining city, maybe a little too forcefully. "She is holding Ecol and all the territories north from there. So far, she's withstood several attacks and avoided getting besieged. However, her troops are exhausted and severely depleted. She is roughly matched with the Red Caps, but you will sway the odds in our favor. Should there be more killing." Peace. He would offer peace first.

"Your Highness," Yuri spoke in polite, inevitable agreement.

"Peace or death, those are her only options," Sergei said, maybe trying to convince himself.

Yuri snapped his fingers, motioning for Matvey to refill his cup. "Do you have any idea what really happened with Adam's daughter, Your Highness? I heard Empress Amalia remained hidden in her brother's camp for several months. Then, one day she revealed herself, and he embraced her. Then, she had the bastard murdered."

Sergei snorted, slightly annoyed. He remembered Sasha's letter and the incredible story of Amalia posing as a commoner before being discovered and miraculously pardoned. He still did not really believe that.

"Emperor James was killed in battle, most likely. I am not aware how the two siblings made peace among them, and it makes no difference. We embarked on this war with Empress Amalia leading her nation. We will end it facing Amalia. Whether she has the courage to make another bold choice, it's entirely up to her."

The duke raised his brows. "As you command, Your Highness."

Sergei gestured, a generous wave of his hand. "You have had a long travel. Please report to the city's warehouse sergeant for resupply and repairs. Your troops must be ready to march in three days. You are welcome to lodge at the palace."

"I am honored, Your Highness," Yuri said. He realized he was being dismissed. He rose, bowed curtly, and marched out, his men following.

Sergei felt warmth on his left cheek. He turned his head and saw Genrik looking at him. "Yes?"

Genrik offered a thin smile. "I am pleased to see you like this, Your Highness. There is pain in your heart, but you are the leader of our nation once again. Parus needs a strong king."

"Perhaps it does. Perhaps it does."

Later, he summoned Lady Lisa. She arrived into the court room shadowed by two Red Caps. Sergei wondered what motivated her now. Fear? Hope? Did she believe Amalia could somehow prevail and regain the throne? Did she dread reliving the experience of her child dying again? The cold weight in his chest was a reminder of his own loss, and he would not wish it on anyone, even his enemies. *I regret to inform you that your son has been killed.*

No.

He dismissed everyone, including the high scribe. He wanted no one else to hear this.

She was watching him with a patient, passive expression on her face. He had to admire her courage. After all she had been through, he could never detect rancor in her eyes, nor any evil in her words and acts. She bore her captivity well, unafraid, resolved, at peace with her decisions. He envied her.

"You have called for me, Your Highness?"

Any other day, he would have loved to debate the future of Athesia with her, to hear her perspective on the recent developments in Eracia, to talk about Amalia or the High Council, to figure out what he should do with the clergy, but other things troubled him. The fact that Badanese ships would not sail north. Gavril's story. Stupid, silly omens.

"Do you recall the day your husband defeated my father's army?"

"Yes, I do."

His heart was fluttering, he realized. "What happened? What truly happened?"

She made a small, ladylike shrug. "My husband defeated the Parusite forces, Your Highness."

Sergei leaned forward. "I want details."

The former empress-mother waited until he reclined, as if he was some unruly boy. "I do not have much to tell. It was a quick, brutal battle, veiled in morning mist and rain. I watched from the city battlements, and all I saw was the Parusite cavalry ranks being mowed down. Adam won."

He inhaled sharply through his nostrils. From the first time since he'd met her, he felt like she was lying to him. Explicitly lying. "I find that rather improbable. Something else happened."

Lady Lisa was silent again, thinking. The corner of her lip twitched. "You must have heard the stories."

"I have," Sergei responded, trying to keep his budding anger down. "But I do not want rumors and bards' follies and soldiers' secondhand gossip. I want to know what happened that day. How was my father's army defeated so quickly?"

"I do not know the full extent of the truth, Your Highness." That twitch again. "It was a confusing day, full of terror and excitement and wonder. Many people would swear they witnessed a miracle that day, but as time passed, you could not tell truth from fiction. Now, all that remains is the legend. The question is, do you want to believe that? Is that the answer you sought these past twenty years?"

"I want the truth," he insisted, not quite sure if he really wanted to hear.

"The truth can be difficult to comprehend sometimes." A long, long pause. "Do you believe in magic, Your Highness?"

Do you believe in magic, Your Highness…

There it was. Just as he had feared. *So what now?* "I will ask you something else instead, my lady. A priest named Gavril is massing his congregation not far from Keron. You must have heard. He's asked me to lead my troops north to face an ancient enemy coming to destroy the realms." Amalia's mother was looking at him without blinking. "He's also asked me to make *peace*. What would you advise me?"

"You know my stance on the matter, Your Highness. You can continue waging war against your opponents"—her voice faltered slightly at the last word—"or you can focus on doing something meaningful. Giving people hope. Creating a legacy that will outlast you."

"Either way, I will be remembered." He pursed his lips. "Some will name their children in my honor. Others will swear I was the greatest hero to have ever lived. Many others will probably curse my late mother."

She shook her head, unconvinced. *And what about Vlad?* The unspoken thought floated between them. *How will you justify his death? You cannot. Your only salvation is peace, a courageous peace with your foes. Just like Emperor Adam did.*

"Everyone wants me to make peace. For one reason or another. I understand your motives. But I am not sure I can trust this man Gavril. So what would you have me do?" He didn't want it to sound like a request, but his tone was sharp. *A plea, a polite, respectful plea.*

Lady Lisa squirmed, took a deep breath. Sergei wished he could know what she was thinking, how her mind worked. He craved to understand how this magnificent woman operated.

"Ancient enemy, coming to destroy the realms?" she repeated.

He waited.

"You must not disregard that possibility," she said at last. A tingle crept down his spine. The patriarchs would probably condemn him for heresy, but he was beginning to suspect something he had seen a long time ago but never really bothered to acknowledge, blinded by the fear of his sire, the relief over his death, and countless generations of stern Parusite upbringing that left no room for doubt. He was beginning to understand there was more to the realms than just the plight of greedy humans fighting over land and rivers. It wasn't about belief either. Something else, and in the recent weeks, a strange feeling nagged at him, made him uneasy. But it had been elusive, at the corner of his eye, teasing, slippery, misty.

Meeting with Gavril had upset him. Seeing those pilgrims head north worried him. Now, talking to this woman, who did not presume to speak for gods or armies, it all fell into place. He was no longer just entertaining suspicion. He was certain. Magic was not just a fragment of ancient tales. And if magic could exist, why not old, ancient enemies from faraway lands?

Sergei didn't have all the details, and he wasn't really sure he would comprehend the whole story, but he was beginning to realize that his reign would not end in ruling over Athesians and flirting with the High Council and whoever called himself the monarch in Somar now. There was something else to consider now. Something bigger than his vendetta, his mistrust of his lords and the clergy.

Emperor Adam, you bastard.

Make peace with Amalia? Well, he could do it for himself. Or the people of the realms. Or maybe to prevent the realms from being obliterated by an ancient myth. The last bit made it easier. He almost felt relief against the backdrop of the terror rising in his soul.

Do you believe in magic, Your Highness? I do now, he thought. "Thank you, my lady, as always, it's been a pleasure. I am most grateful for your advice. You may leave if you wish."

She inclined her head. "Good luck, Sergei," she said, omitting his title, surprising him. "You will need it." Her feet shuffling on the marble, she left.

He remained in the seat, trying to grasp the enormity of the world's secrets and silently cursing the Eracian man who had started all this mess twenty years ago.

CHAPTER 23

Into the city, the soldiers went, walking on their two feet, armed and ready, frightened yet eager, spears gripped in callused hands, shields carried overhead to protect from arrows and stones. Out of the city, the soldiers came, limping, dragging themselves, many of those borne on stretchers.

It had been a month since the ill-fated attempt to infiltrate Somar. The night mission into the market area had failed miserably. To add insult to injury, the Kataji chieftain had then lured the Eracians into another trap, opening the gates for them, making them believe all was well.

Throughout the dun night and a bleak dawn, Bart had listened with utmost dismay to the shrieks coming from the city, the screams of death and agony as his soldiers were forced into narrow streets, pinned down with a heavy barrage of arrows, and then made to burn and suffocate in the deliberate fires set by the nomads. In the morning, he had watched the decimated battalions retreat, defeated in spirit and body.

The fighting had continued unabated ever since.

The Eracians were trying to force their way into Somar day and night. Fresh troops were streaming into the killing zone, all too aware most of them would not come out unscathed. Yesterday's forces would then return, for a brief sleep and some cold gruel, before going back into the slaughterhouse. The siege walls looked like an old tapestry, eaten by worms. Entire sections had been reduced to rubble by the trebuchet bombardment. Other parts had been sapped by Major Kilian's engineers. Still, the bulk of it stood, and it swarmed with rotting bodies and bled black blood down its pocked sides.

His army was holding a small section near the gate, finally captured after a week of deadly engagements against the tribesmen. For the past three weeks, the soldiers had been trying to break through the nomad lines to gain a new foothold deeper in the city. But every inch of ground was contested to the death. There was just no point surrendering or taking captives.

The Eracians were fighting the nomads door to door, in cellars, in gutters, in narrow alleys between burned-down buildings, anywhere a man could stand and swing a blade, standing on top of wounded comrades, right in that hot, squelchy, wet red mess if need be. When the swords became too blunted to cut through leather and flesh, when the spear shafts snapped, men fought with their bare hands, clawing and spitting and punching, wrestling with the nomads, trying to kill them with shards of stone or street cobbles or pieces of rusted drains. Anything that would make the other side bleed and hurt.

Inside well-barricaded houses, they found dead women and children, or they found starved women and children, and sometimes, the Eracian mothers and daughters joined them in the fight against the nomads. Smoke stung their eyes and made the air oily and hard to breathe. Roofs would collapse, burying men alive, and the other squad members would have to stop fighting and dig them out. Horses shied away from the narrow, packed streets, shied away from the screams and the blood and the flames. Even humans had difficulty moving through the ruins.

But the destruction in Somar was only a part of Bart's problems.

Every hour that passed, he wondered what was happening to the Eracian women, what might have happened to his wife. Was Sonya still alive? Or had the Kataji chieftain executed her out of spite? The longer the battle continued, the more desperate the situation would become. Worst of all, Bart knew he could not stop now. The killing would go on until one party was totally defeated.

Below the observation post, a fresh unit was marching to its death. Close to a hundred men, he reckoned, their uniforms clean, their weapons sharp and unbloodied. The men walked hunched, stiff, faces slack with abject terror, eyes glazed and staring nowhere, their gait that of the condemned before the gallows. Their captain was leading boldly, trying to cheer them up with hoarse battle cries and too much spit. All he got in return were pasty, dull rictuses of cold fear. Elation and courage were absent in the company's collective spirit. The banner rippled in the wind, rattling everyone's nerves.

With every step, they came face-to-face with more death. The endless stream of injured was not helping to make them bold and ready for the mayhem ahead. Normally in battle, soldiers got killed by sword or arrow, sometimes trampled by iron hooves. But they still looked human. Coming out of the city were all sorts of shapes, men burned to a crisp, with their skin like a sheet of wet scabbing, men mashed to a pulp by rubble. It sure did not inspire the new units.

Bart was standing alone on the high platform, because he did not want to interfere with his officers. He had exercised enough military leadership by sending his men to their deaths. Twice. Once when he had ordered the infiltration mission, the second time when he'd hurled them toward the city's open gates and into a deathly trap. He did not feel like contributing more misery. Faas, Ulrich, and Velten could cope well on their own.

Fifty paces away, inside a post much like his own, the three men were watching the progress of the fighting, giving orders to their adjutants, who then relayed them to the signalers. In turn, these men waved tiny red and yellow flags on top of large poles. In distant parts of the siege camp, units reacted to the command.

Ideally, the three men would be sharing three different posts all around the city, coordinating an attack from all directions. But all of the fighting was focused on the west bank of the Kerabon.

There was *another* of Bart's problems.

He had almost fifteen thousand men sitting in trenches and improvised forts north and east of the city, facing away from the fighting, awaiting the arrival of some foreign invader bent on destruction. So far, it had not arrived, but he was forced to keep a huge chunk of his army prepared instead of committing all able bodies to the liberation of Somar.

He had called this new enemy the North Death. There was no better way to describe it, it seemed.

The camp around Somar was rather quiet and empty apart from the men gritting their teeth, waiting to be sent to die freeing the capital. Women, traders, and thousands of refugees from the Barrin estate had all been sent away to the southern cities. Not having them around helped immensely. Their despair had been contagious, affecting morale. Sending them away had also reduced the chance of spies and saboteurs sneaking behind his lines, using the mess and confusion to gain easy entry. There was less opportunity for disease to flourish, especially with the wet season coming. And he had more food for his soldiers.

Boys and men had been conscripted, and some of them were training now; others stood watch against the North Death; others yet were readying to walk into Somar. An odd soldier of fortune or a thin-ribbed prostitute would wander into the camp now and then, but they found quiet, gloomy customers for their services.

Still, he had *more* problems. Constance. His uncle. They wouldn't let him be.

His mistress and her small horde of midwives and ladies-in-waiting were the only noncombatants left in the camp. He had considered getting rid of them, too, but he was still too much of a coward to lose sight of Constance. He could not begin to imagine what she might do if left to her own devices.

He heard laughter. One of the trebuchet crews, enjoying a game of dice. Since the attacks had begun, they were more or less unemployed and counted themselves lucky for not having to be in the thick of it all. Yes, they were lucky.

One month, and no success so far. Was the Eracian force that lousy, or were the nomads really that good in holding the city? He wondered how his nation had held its borders all these centuries, how they had managed so well in the border skirmishes. Maybe it was just a matter of fortune, and now their share had run out.

Emperor Adam took the last few grains with him, he thought.

At least his uncle had not lied to him about the foreign invaders. Ulrich's light horse did report an enemy presence, but mostly to the east. However, they did not seem poised on marching south. It would appear they were massing toward Athesia. In a way, it did not surprise him. When it came to Adam's legacy, he only expected mad, miraculous things and events. Perhaps this North Death was a challenger to the tale of his legend. The story of his victory may have traveled half

across the endless world, stunning everyone with its ruthless-
ness, daring them to try him, and now these northerners had
finally come to contest him. But it was ridiculous, he knew.

Bart looked across the field and, to his dismay, saw Lord
Karsten propelling himself forward in his direction. Gravel and
grass did not stop him. He pumped with his stringy, powerful
hands. His attaché, Tobin, walked behind him, hands folded.
His assigned guards trailed in a half circle, kicking their boots
in lazy strides.

"Bartholomew, Bartholomew!" the old fart was shouting.

What does he want now? Bart wondered with a tinge of despair. While his crippled uncle and his mother counted as noncombatants, he had not really managed to get them whisked
away to Ubalar either. They insisted they had a responsibility
toward Eracia and would not walk away from peril. Well, his
mother had mostly smiled.

In a way, it was a good thing, because he could imagine the
city mayor of Ubalar blanching at the thought of having Lord
Karsten take over the governance of the business and trade.
Then again, it meant he had to suffer them.

"Bartholomew!" his uncle repeated. He had wheeled himself into the shadow of the tower.

Delaying deliberately, Bart peered over the wooden rail.
His uncle was at the base, looking small and fierce. "Yes,
Uncle?"

"Well, are you going to stand there and humiliate me? I
cannot climb the stairs even if I want to."

Bart pushed his tongue between his upper lip and gums,
pressing until it hurt. "You wish me to come down there, then?"

"Before the Autumn Festival," Lord Karsten said.

Keeping his nerves calm, he climbed down the heavy
switchback staircase. A handful of his clerks and bodyguards

were waiting there, augmented by the unmistakable presence of the cripple and his somewhat embarrassed retinue. "Yes, Uncle?"

"How long is this folly going to take?"

Bart arched his brows. "Which one?" *Your tantrums?*

"The city attack is going nowhere. You keep sending those boys to die, and for what? That northern enemy will arrive any day now and destroy everything. Why are you even bothering? Somar is a lost place. Recuperate your losses and retreat. We can still get safely south and regroup in the Safe Territories."

Bart sighed, feeling tired. "Uncle, I will not tell you again. Keep out of the war business. If you mention this topic once again, I will have you sent away. You will certainly find the inns in Paroth or Ubalar more comfortable than our camp here."

Lord Karsten opened his mouth and closed it with a plop. "Your disrespect will not win you victories. You ought to listen to the people around you. They often mean well. And you are forgetting yourself. You might be the viceroy, and you lead this army, but I am still your uncle, and you will show proper manners.

"Why haven't you committed your mercenaries yet?" the cripple asked.

Bart looked toward the city, but it looked different from ground level. More sort of a shattered turtle shell, picked apart by vultures, than a city wrapped in smoke and death. The wall ruins gaped like an old woman's grin, with a handful of yellowing, rotten teeth.

He had kept Junner's olifaunts out of the battle, because he wasn't really sure how they would behave in that maze of fiery destruction. The animals had not been trained to trample through back alleys, and Junner was worried about sending them in with so many Eracian footmen. They might end up trampling the wrong crowd.

Deep down, perversely, Bart considered Junner his one real ally in this mess. His countrymen all had their patriotic motives, but they saw him as a stepladder for their success. With the Borei, it was the simple matter of money, nothing more. The mercenaries had been with him while he was the lowliest member of the Privy Council, and they were with him now that he ruled Eracia. Their attitude had not changed, and that gave him peace of mind.

He could not bet on the petty aspirations, grudges, and avarice of this or that noble or officer. But he could always count on the Borei to want to earn money from their employer…s. Luckily, no one could outbid him. He hoped.

"They are a strategic reserve," he explained.

Lord Karsten bahed and waved his hand dismissively.

Another host of soldiers was moving toward the city. The Second Regiment of the Fifth Division, Bart guessed from the device on their flag. They were passing in between the two towers. Colonel Maurice cheered them on from his platform. The major saluted, his motions wooden, and moved on. Unlike the earlier group, these men had seen the fighting already and were going for another attempt. They did not look scared because they were seeing burned men with no limbs coming out on stretchers. They were terrified because they had already been inside Somar once, and now, they were doing it again. Men could be only so lucky, and the odds were against them now.

They were all wet, doused with water so that flames would not stick to their clothes. Bart stopped arguing with his uncle and watched them go. Most men were too morose to notice. *They must be reliving the earlier fights,* he reasoned.

He had fifteen thousand fresh troops, and he could not commit them. It was maddening. With their strength, he might have taken the city already.

He could hear drums, and feet stomping in cadence with the dull beat. He could hear a shrill pipe, and the chorus of grunts and growls coming from the city like a wind. He could hear the noise of swords and fires, crackling. Farther away, a wagon was lumbering, loaded with a dozen wounded. Well, those soldiers were lucky enough, because they could sit on a hard bench and wait for an old mule to lug them back into the camp.

How much longer would the killing continue? Velten claimed they had lost four thousand men in the last week alone. There were more than ten thousand wounded. The hospitals had too few beds, so they slept in the same tents as the ordinary troops, a constant and vivid reminder of what awaited them all. He sorely lacked surgeons and healers, and even just ordinary men with a steady hand so they could pull and stitch pig-gut thread through gaping injuries. At the moment, he wished he could just buy barbers and physicians.

The perilous decision about asking the Parusite king for assistance still hovered in the dark confines of his conscience, beckoning, sweet and soft and promising. But that would probably mean giving up Eracian independence. Yet another problem.

"A horseman approaching," Corporal Rickey announced.

Everyone turned, one of the soldiers cranking his crossbow. Dashing across the mangled, grassy expanse was a lone rider. Not a strange phenomenon in the camp. Messengers often used fast hobbies to move quickly between divisions. Past the front lines, too, so it was probably not an assassin Abyssbent on his mission.

But there was something about the silhouette, about the urgency of the animal's trot that alarmed him. He was glad for Rickey's sharp eye. There was another man who deserved a promotion.

The rider was moving toward the two towers. It made sense if he wanted to bring a missive to the army commanders. He weaved elegantly around abandoned gear and refuse, past old spots of beaten ground that had housed the camp followers until just recently.

"Slow down!" Lanford shouted, raising his hand in warning.

The horseman pulled on the reins and brought his dappled little horse to a halt. "Where's Lord Karsten? I bear a message for him!"

Bart saw the old man grin and push forward, nudging men out of his way. "I am here."

Lanford stepped closer and grabbed the reins. "Dismount, lad. Easy."

"I'm not a lad, sir," the rider said, taking his helmet off. There was a girl underneath. Bony, and not very pretty, and with hair cropped short, but still unmistakably female. Bart frowned. What? He did not have many female troops around. None in the cavalry that he could remember. In fact, ever since Adam's revolution, the all-female units had been disbanded.

"Your name and unit, soldier," Bart said, ignoring the sharp look from his uncle.

The girl handed a horn tube to Lanford, who released the reins and brought the message to *him*. He flashed a grin back at his uncle.

"Beatrice, sir. Third Independent Batallion."

Bart ignored the lack of honorifics. She couldn't know who he was. *Third Independent?*

"I must insist, the message is for Lord Karsten, sir." She glanced quickly at the man in his wheelchair, but it didn't look like she knew who he really was. Well, most soldiers had never met his uncle. Lucky bastards.

"That is fine," Bart said. "I am Count Bartholomew of Barrin, the viceroy of the realm. Any message for Lord Karsten can be safely delivered to me. If it pertains to military matters, that is. It is about the state of our nation and country, yes?"

The soldier looked confused, so she fired off a quick salute. "Yes, sir." She coughed. "From Commander Mali, sir. And Colonels Finley and Alan."

Bart looked around him. Commander Mali. He could not recall that name.

"She was sent north by Commander Velten to defeat a Namsue detachment," his uncle offered, keeping his voice flat. "I personally sent Colonel Alan to assist in the effort. We have not received any news from either unit ever since. They were presumed lost, or gone too far north to communicate with us in a timely manner. With the arrival of the northern army, well…" He shrugged, an odd gesture for a man with his lower body all paralyzed.

"Oh yes, the northern detachment." So they were not dead after all. Or traitors. *But…good news or terrible news?* Bart wondered. He opened the tube. He read the message carefully. The northern army was right there, and it was shadowed by a tiny force of Eracians. The three officers called on all sides to unite and prepare for an all-out war.

The rider squirmed, looking uncomfortable. Then, with simple, practical precision, she opened a saddlebag, fished out a small canteen, and drank.

Bart knew he had to consult with his staff. This was monumental. There was an Eracian combat force that had made contact with the North Death, defeated some of their units, detained others. Valuable information. Critical information. Only the consequences were unknown. What was he going to do now? Here he had another reminder what doom faced Eracia.

Somar still remained in the nomad hands.

"You will have to ride back to your commander," he told the girl. Her boyish face contorted with dismay. "But not today. You have earned rest. Please report to the barracks. You will be given food and a bed, and if you want, you may wash yourself."

"Yes sir, my lord, Your Majesty, thank you." She smarted another salute.

Bart nodded at Lanford. "Please escort Beatrice to the local garrison. The fourth."

Around him, nothing had changed. The fighting in Somar continued unabated, the fields around it were filthy with human refuse, and a pall of chaos hung above the siege, with birds wheeling on hot currents from the fires in the city, waiting to pounce on fresh corpses.

Only he felt different. Resolved. *We will all die,* he figured. *My little feud is irrelevant. Constance is irrelevant. Sonya is irrelevant.* He didn't fully understand this foreign enemy, but he grasped its enormity, its finality. So perhaps he could relax and not worry about the implications and outcome of what he was doing. It didn't matter. *When faced with death only, any option you choose is good enough,* he thought.

"Summon the command staff. We need to discuss the next phase of this war," he ordered and left the shadow of the observation post, walking away from the city. He ignored everyone, especially his uncle. He walked toward the house where

Constance was raising his bastard. He was going to name his son today. He didn't want the boy to die without a name. That would be just pointless. Well, pointless either way, but he wanted it to be pointless *his* way.

CHAPTER 24

There were fourteen women and two babies in the room, thirteen women and two babies too many. Sonya hated the fact she was forced to share her lavish chambers with all those whores.

But Pacmad was doing everything he could to spite her. To foil her plans.

Small-dicked mongrel.

Since the Eracian attack, Somar had become a battlefield. No one was allowed out of their houses or their workplaces. Women were laboring round the clock, baking bread, hammering new swords and shields for the Kataji warriors, sewing wounds. Those who did not have a valuable profession had been forced into their homes and locked in, forced to endure the fighting in silent waiting.

If she looked through the window, she could see the deserted streets of the inner city, with only an odd soldier moving, patrolling, making sure the citizens did not try to plot anything against them. Stray dogs loped between buildings, scavenging the refuse. Dried leaves fluttered across cobbles, joining old piles of trash and neglect. The savages cared nothing for beauty, and the city had become one giant heap of midden and discarded rubbish.

Some distance away, the situation was very much different. Rooftops were on fire, old tiles cracking and bursting from the heat, shooting shrapnel high into the air like roasted corn. A thick press of Kataji veterans was hulking behind their barricades, keeping the Eracians at bay. For weeks now, the stalemate had reigned supreme, the only thing changing being the mass of dead bodies on both sides, although the carnage on the Eracian side looked much worse.

She had a great view of some of the battles, unimpeded by oaks and villas and tall buildings. She had seen the deadly engagements, raging in every little side lane, in parks, anywhere. She had seen the Eracians worm through shattered doors and windows into houses, fighting against the nomads hiding inside. She had seen the brave sons of her nation descend into dark cellars, where sharpened blades waited for them. Men had run through whipping flames, skittered down streets slick with blood and spilled sewage, crawled across steep roofs and fallen to their deaths on the hard stone below. The Kataji would throw fire bombs at the attackers, then retreat. Sometimes, the Eracians would burn their opponents inside houses, and sometimes, they found themselves trapped within an oven.

Pacmad had his warriors raze rows of buildings to prevent the fires from spreading. His device had more or less worked, because the destruction was limited to just where he wanted it to be. Those passageways running through neighborhoods also let his troops move with impunity, whereas the Eracians had to fight around every deadly obstacle. Even now, she could see a horde of Kataji goat-hopping through a lane of fresh rubble, trying to sneak up on an Eracian pocket. Sonya wished she could shout and warn them, but they were just too far away. And it would be dangerous for her.

She had no solid information, but she had heard of a few women putting up spontaneous resistance in a few districts, without much success. The organized insurrection had never happened, stifled before it had even started. Pacmad had simply severed her strings, quartered the city into small combat zones, made it impossible for her women to get together and act against the invader. Maybe he had planned it all along, and he had known nothing of her scheme. Or maybe he had discovered her treachery and let it be, tormenting her and leading her to a magnificent failure.

Sonya had no idea how long the fighting would continue and how it would end. The way it was going, the entire city would be destroyed, and pretty much everyone would die. If the Kataji began losing, they would probably kill all the citizens out of pure spite.

Shortage of food and growing disease would become threats all too soon. With so much death and filth lying about in the streets, rats and pigeons would soon start spreading the poison. There was no regular supply between districts, and Sonya feared most women had to do with what little provisions they had stored away. The only thing that gladdened her was that the nomads were also suffering from their imposed curfew.

Her nose was almost touching the thick glass, and her breath misted the pane, making the details blurry. It was stifling hot inside the monarchical chamber, but she did not want to crack open the window, because the stench outside was horrendous.

Outside the city, she could see the outline of siege machines and tall towers, and tiny people standing on those platforms, watching the battle unravel, a mirror image of her own impotent fury. She wondered if her brave husband was there, if he might not be watching the carnage unfold before his eyes just like she did. Did he ever think about her? Did he base his decisions on her fate, her safety? How far was he going with this siege and this killing?

She turned back toward the room, waiting until her eyes adjusted, a purple glare fading away. The women really had nothing to do, so they just sat around, talked, dozed. That slut Richelle was breastfeeding her little shite. How much milk could one little toddler slurp? It should be suckling and shitting at the same time, Sonya reasoned. Verina was talking to Lady Zoya, and Sonya did not like that. The viscountess was worrying her. Zoya was rather meaningless, and still…

Once, she had thought Richelle would be her greatest rival, but now, she was beginning to suspect Verina might be the chief one. Difficult situations really brought out the best and worst in people. This war was a perfect rite of passage for all of them, a test of personality, courage, and perseverance. Of all the women sharing her chamber, Verina stood out as an elegant, brave lady. Bitch.

Aileen was not there, of course. Not her.

Pacmad was keeping that whore to himself. He had locked up all the rest of them like animals and no longer bothered visiting. Maybe he was too busy. Fighting or rutting.

Sonya's privileges were gone now, her illusion of mastering the general fast eroding. She could no longer indulge in food and expensive clothing, and she no longer had her own maid. Her hair was a ruin, and her toenails were beginning to snag the carpet when she walked barefoot. She had begged the lone servant lady that brought them food and drinks every day for a soft file, but the peasant had just stuttered a silly apology and left.

They could not walk outside. They could not bathe. At least after Leopold's death, she had been imprisoned all alone, without all these sows and harlots to pollute her breathing space. Not getting raped and beaten had its perks, but in a way, this was worse. She was being robbed of her manipulative power, of her intellect, of her ability to withstand danger and pain. It was being mellowed by this fat, ugly assembly of Eracia's surviving ladies.

Whatever Pacmad had planned, he had done it well. The guild mistresses were locked up elsewhere. Merchant ladies, in yet another room. The Father of the Bear had separated them so they could not plot, could not discuss the war effort. Those with knowledge did not sleep in the same room as those with power and initiative.

Sonya considered trying to rally these sluts to her cause. But she could not really trust them. They would always be scheming, trying to best her, so when the war ended, they would be ahead of her. Besides, she was beginning to panic. It was a slow, silent scream building up at the back of her throat, a grain of dust that chafed. She did not really know how she might react if the Kataji won the battle for Somar. What if Bart failed to liberate the city? What if the Eracians were defeated and no salvation came to her?

Now that she could finally feel hope, the fear of losing it was maddening. She wasn't certain she could endure another month or year being locked in here with all these women, wrapped in uncertainty and constant danger, denied pleasure and power, and bereft of any real influence and wealth. What if Pacmad decided to give her to his soldiers? Or just keep her hostage forever?

No, she must never lose hope. She was the queen. It was her duty.

In a way, these women looked up to her. She was their leader. She gave them strength. They expected her to be confident and self-assured, to soothe their minds, to wash away their fears. She had to look after her subjects. It would be easier if they weren't all such conniving bitches.

Sonya noticed Richelle was looking at her, a faint smile on her lips. Then, the baroness plucked her girl from her teat and handed the child to Lady Charissa, a blobby, ungraceful woman. Sonya just hated how her thin black hair curled and how she had pale sideburns down the sides of her thick jowls.

That smile still on her lips, Richelle rose from the floor, dusting herself, smoothing the wrinkles in her skirt, and walked over toward Sonya. The other women glanced about, then continued their idle, worried chatter.

"May I have a word with you?" the slut said. Well, she had finally pried her daughter off the teat. It was as if she were there all the time, almost like a leech.

The intimacy of their time together had made most women drop titles when talking to other hostages, Sonya noted. At the moment, she did not mind too much. She pointed toward the corner of the chamber, the closest thing to privacy they would get in this prison.

"Please." Ever since Sonya had stepped in to keep Pacmad from beating her, Richelle was being nice to her, very timid, very respectful.

"I need to ask you something," the baroness said, her voice brittle.

Immediately, Sonya did not like this. "Yes?" Her voice was too sharp, too loud. One of the hens raised her head, looked behind. Sonya frowned at her, and she snapped her stupid head back toward the crowd.

"I know…Bart is leading the nation now," the whore whispered.

Easy, easy, do not panic. Sonya realized she was holding her breath. Carefully, she expelled it, took another one, expanded her chest, let herself think. This must be some kind of a plot. Maybe Pacmad was trying to fuddle her mind, make her confess things. Maybe the baroness was acting alone. Either way, Sonya must not let show her fear, must not looked worried or even concerned.

But how did Richelle know? Who had betrayed her? Was it Janice? Bibi? Some other clerk?

"Bart is the viceroy," the whore insisted.

Sonya was still thinking, knowing her silence was not helping. What should she do now? Feign ignorance? Shock? Surprise? Play along? This bitch certainly wanted something. Otherwise she would not have broached the subject.

"Bartholomew of Barrin?" Sonya said at length.

Richelle nodded, that smile so annoying. "Yes, *the count.*"

Sonya imagined pulling out her hairpin and stabbing the girl in her jugular. That should do it. But then, she would have a hard time explaining the woman's death to Pacmad, and her situation was perilous as it was.

Now, if Richelle knew, who else might?

All of a sudden, all those ugly faces around her looked even more suspicious.

She realized her heart was thumping hard. She could almost see the tight fabric of her dress fluttering with the bursts of her blood. "That is fortunate."

"I am really grateful for what you did that night," Richelle spoke, "which is why I have not told the general about the identity of the Eracian leader. I think it would be prudent of you, once the war is over, to favor those who helped and supported you during your captivity. Reward those who showed *loyalty* to Your Majesty."

Sonya liked the ring of it. If only she could bask in it. Alas, she was choking with terror, a black veil pressing on her nose and lips, making it impossible to gulp air, like that thing she had once done with Lord Elton. That smug, soft smile on Richelle's lips was making her livid. *Am I being threatened? Blackmailed!* She was furious, furious. Mostly because she had never expected Richelle to turn against her. *I should have let Pacmad beat her bloody. I should have never interfered. This is my payment for being merciful.*

"Most certainly," Sonya said. Lying was easy. Promises were just words, empty words, ethereal, meaningless. They meant nothing. In fact, Richelle was just being a stupid whore, presuming she could coerce her into obedience. How silly of her. Did she not understand all her threats would become insignificant the moment Bart retook Somar? Did she not realize that?

"I will be honored if certain lands and titles could pass on to my family. Nothing much. Just the repossessed assets of the traitors and the deceased, my lady. A small, humble share."

"Most certainly," Sonya repeated, trying to mimic that smile. This sow was beyond stupid. She was being suicidal. Did she not realize how fragile her position was? She should be trying her best to make Sonya like her. Instead, she was openly telling her plan.

There had to be something else. So what else did the slut know?

"You will not mind writing and signing a document affirming our little...agreement?"

Documents were just paper. They could burn. Water would wash off the ink. They got lost, torn away. New documents could easily be written, forged, stamped with any manner of seals and names.

"Richelle, darling, is all this necessary?"

"I just want a happy future for my baby," the baroness admitted, her composure cracking a little.

Sonya touched her shoulder. "Of course, she will be taken care of." Oh yes. All Kataji bastards would be taken care of. *You need years and years of practice before you can attempt to subdue someone like me, bitch.*

Richelle nodded. "Thank you, my lady."

Improper. Sonya withdrew her hand. She almost felt relief. She had expected the little whore to concoct a masterful scheme that would leave Sonya indebted till her death. Not this pitiful begging. She was almost disappointed.

Then, she saw the woman's face change. There was fresh smugness there. Sonya realized it wasn't quite over yet.

"My lady, if the faithful and loyal subjects do not get their reward after the war is concluded, there might be some difficulties."

Oh, there it was; there it was, the clout.

"Certain other truths might get exposed."

Sonya wondered what it could be. What? Deaths she had plotted? Affairs with other nobles and rich merchants? What else?

It looked as if Richelle could read her mind. Her eyes dropped down to Sonya's belly, then up again. Sonya tried not to swallow. How could she know? She could not. The baroness was just bluffing. Hinting. Sonya made a perplexed face, hoping it looked genuine enough.

"There is no reason for that to happen."

Richelle reached up with her own hand and touched a cold finger to Sonya's cheek, a brazen, disrespectful gesture. "My lady." She walked back to her bastard child as if nothing had happened.

Sonya remained standing, realized she was not acting naturally, making other women notice her, so she stepped back toward the windows and stared out at the destruction and smoke.

She had underestimated these whores. Women were usually frightful and insecure, but they were not stupid. They paid attention to little details, saw the gaps and inconsistency in truths and facts, figured out the missing parts on their own. Sometimes, their emotions took them down wild, stray paths, but not when it came to basic feminine affairs. Then, they could be sharper than a well-honed sword.

For the past year and a half, she had copulated with Pacmad. No one could doubt the potency of his seed, because he had managed to sire dozens of little bastards in that time. Meanwhile, Sonya's belly remained flat, except for the lazy fat of her captivity she just couldn't get rid of. It did not take a master of coin to figure out the problem. Pacmad's tiny cock worked, all right. Sonya's womb did not.

In her defense, she could claim rape usually didn't get the best results, and many women mistreated that way did not conceive. In the palace, most of the captives were younger women, and slowly, Pacmad was making them pregnant with his nomad bastards. However, there wasn't any lady her age without a child.

The general had no care for older, ugly women, so he had mostly left them alone. In a way, their ugliness had spared them and their children, leaving only the virile and beautiful to suffer the humiliation, the beatings, the rapes. Them—and Sonya.

In Caytor, it was quite customary for rich women to pursue their careers rather than motherhood. But in Eracia, they all still believed women should whelp babies to strengthen families and secure the wealth. Her own lack of offspring had been a constant rumor at court for many years now, but then, she had always had Bart. People would snigger behind both their backs but blame him. Now, there was no more doubt left. Men might ignore it. Not the ladies, though.

I'm not old, but I am definitely not young anymore, she thought, bitterness nipping at her tongue. She glanced at the roomful of whores. She was older than everyone present. She was the only married woman without a child in this lot, excluding Pacmad's bastards, the only one who had run out of excuses for not being a proud mother still.

Not evidence, but enough to start a powerful, lethal rumor.

She glanced back. Richelle was holding her girl, unconcerned, silent, smug. Bitch. Sonya almost admired her audacity, but the time for mercy and pleasantries was over. She would not make the same mistake again. Ever.

Well, she had always feared Pacmad would find out about her. Now, she had much bigger worries. What would happen if the court learned she was barren? Bart could legally disown her then. She could be robbed of her status as the queen. That would be a disaster. After all she had done for her nation.

Smile, you bitch, smile. You will get what you deserve. A large share, even.

She looked out of the window again, waiting for her husband to free her.

CHAPTER 25

Peace. It was right there in front of her.

Amalia sat on a palfrey, adorned with silver trappings. Her would-be court flanked her left and right, all of them on foot to emphasize her status. Master Hector was there, leathery, chewy, but clean and with a new uniform. Jarman and Lucas. She was glad for the blue-faced wizard. He was an impressive addition to her retinue. Xavier was standing right next to her. All of the Athesian legions' commanders shared her side.

There were more soldiers behind her, including three bannermen, half a dozen officers, and Agatha, who had insisted on standing with her empress, a brave but painful sacrifice on her behalf. If all went well, her maid would give birth about a month after the Autumn Festival.

On the opposite side of the field, the Parusite delegation waited. No horses there. Princess Sasha was wearing a maroon leather uniform, trousers, sword, and all, and she stood on her own feet, like her small, humble retinue of fighters.

Victors did not need pedestals, it seemed.

"Everything is in order," Toby, her new head of the imperial guard, said.

"Then there's no point waiting any longer. Proceed." She spurred the palfrey forward.

The Parusites took the hint and moved, too. Halfway between the two parties, there was an awning, stretched between four stout poles, with a single large table placed in the shadow of the canvas. Half a dozen clerks were waiting with ledgers and drinks. A circle of soldiers of both nationalities guarded the perimeter.

Amalia did not dare look behind her. Ecol was there, with its thousands of people, soldiers and refugees. The northernmost town of her shrinking empire. The last town really ever since Bassac had been evacuated.

The White Witch and his vast army had finally arrived.

The threat of their attack was immense. So huge that few people could really comprehend it. Even she did not dare contemplate the facts too deeply, lest they shatter her resolve utterly. A host of hundreds of thousands was gathering just a week away, getting bigger by the day, with an endless stream of new troops arriving every sunset. The Athesian scouts had watched from a safe distance, lips moving until they lost count, confused, dazed. No one really understood what would happen now.

Ecol had become her final bastion, a blister of defiance on the map of her failures. She could keep fighting and losing, or she could do the sensible thing: throw away her honor and bend knee. Make peace.

At least I have not been completely defeated this time, she thought. Her fight against the Red Caps had ended in a bloody draw. She had managed that much at least, enough to save face. Or rather, her half brother had. She could not claim James's Last Stand as her own victory.

Free Athesia, the parts still under her control were coming apart, savaged like a lamb attacked by a pack of wolves. Bands of brigands were prowling the countryside, preying on travelers and convoys and the displaced small folk. But any man sent to fight the local insurgence meant one less soldier to face the Naum threat.

She just had to choose.

Amalia noticed the princess was limping, and yet she had chosen to walk. So the rumors about her injury were true. She had to admire the king's sister. She was everything Amalia was not. Tough, brave, a real fighter. She would not cry when someone intruded in her bedroom; she would try to kill the trespasser.

This meeting was just a necessary formality, she knew, a ceremony that had to be seen and remembered. The officials had spent the last few days drafting the final agreement, with its little details. There would be no persecution of the Athesian defenders, no retribution. In return, Amalia would swear fealty to King Sergei and ask him to protect her and her subjects. Athesia would become a vassal state. Religion and taxes, those were the two things the Parusites would not compromise on. Other than that, they were surprisingly benign with their terms.

Finally, Amalia would lose her title. She would become just the governess of Athesia.

Amalia wasn't really sure why a man whose father had been killed by *her* father would be so kind.

The presence of that massive Naum force must be the reason, she figured.

She did not know what Lucas and Jarman had done with their magic, but they might have also sneaked into the Parusite camp and talked to Princess Sasha. They may have tried to convince her with the same stories they had used with James and her. Perhaps it had worked. Amalia could not think of any other reason why King Sergei would accept peace.

Maybe he is a bigger man than I thought, she wondered. *Maybe he is not obsessed with respect.* A true king would sacrifice everything for his nation. So would an empress. Only no one had taught her that lesson in Roalas, two years back. Well, they had tried, and she had been blind.

The Athesian delegation arrived first. Amalia dismounted, extremely self-conscious about gliding off the saddle elegantly. If she tripped and fell, she would embarrass her entire nation. Servants rushed forward to offer her drinks. One of the ladies was holding a brush to dust her skirt. Amalia waved them away. She took a deep breath and focused on the Parusite princess.

Sasha hobbled under the awning a few moments later, face hard, serious, battle worn. This woman had seen death and never once cried, Amalia knew. This woman was her superior.

"Empress Amalia of Athesia," Major Gabe of the Fourth Legion announced. He had been chosen to lead the proceedings because of his impressive voice and since he had a passing knowledge of law and commerce. His father had been a notable trader. "Princess Sasha, the commander of the Red Caps, sister to His Royal Highness King Sergei of Parus, speaking in his name."

No fancy titles on either side, Amalia noted.

"Please be seated," the major said, pointing at the two chairs on the opposite ends of the table.

Sasha sat down first, grimacing at her injury. Amalia waited, as protocol dictated, and then followed suit, feeling clumsy in her dress. She wished she could wear snug trousers like the princess. She wished she could fight with a sword. She wished the tomcat's edge of her ruined ear did not show under her hair.

Gabe placed two leather-bound books on the table and flipped them open. Written inside was the declaration of surrender and its terms. Some would call it peace, but it was surrender. Amalia was going to admit defeat and let King Sergei rule her people. She would officially smother her father's dream. Class and religion would return to Athesia.

But it was better than death. Had to be.

The officers stood around the two women, like a flock of fidgety geese, peering down but not really looking, trying to appear stately and calm. Amalia was not sure what they all thought, but she was certain the warlord did not like this. It went against his ambitions.

Jarman was pleased. But that only meant he had more people willing to die fighting Calemore together. It wasn't as if a bright future of cooperation and trust awaited them all. Still, it was the only way, he swore. The only way the realms stood any chance of surviving.

One day, our sons will rise against the Parusite yoke, she thought. *One day, Athesia will be free again.*

But she didn't dare think about children. To bear them, she needed a husband first. Someone to love and trust. Someone like Gerald. Certainly not a monster like Xavier. But Jarman had promised to protect her if she gave him peace.

She scanned through the neat, tight writing of a practiced scribe's hand. The details were meaningless now. It was all about the symbol of her signature. Keeping her hand steady, she signed her name and sealed the fate of her realm.

"You have done a great thing," Jarman praised.

It was later that day, and the world remained unchanged. Ecol still burst with people it could not feed, farmers and refugees and traders still demanded to petition her, to tell her about the roaming bands of thieves and killers in the countryside. She still didn't have any friends, or loyalty from her mixed lot of soldiers. It all held together almost by magic, one woven of coincidence, sheer luck, habit, and bittersweet torment.

"The future will tell," she said, trying to sound calm, to keep acid from her voice.

"Only today, you had just ten thousand men capable of fighting against the Naum menace. Now, you have twenty thousand Red Caps at your side. And still more are under way. The king is sending fresh troops north, and soon, we will have fifty thousand soldiers."

She shrugged. "And my patrols report the enemy has more than ten times that number."

Jarman pursed his lips. "We must not despair. This is a monumental event for the people of the realms. After so many years of war, there is finally peace between the nations. It is a fragile thing, like the pink skin on an old burn, but we must hold it together at all costs. And I will help you."

Amalia remembered something. "What about James's widow?" *She will not accept this peace.*

Jarman looked toward the celebration. "This is a great strategic victory for Parus. They have leverage against Caytor, and they sorely need it. Now, the High Council must have intended to use Lady Rheanna against you, but you have completely foiled their plan. Their ambitions are meaningless now. So they will be forced to accept a grudging peace like they did in your father's time."

Amalia sighed. "What will my Caytorean troops do now?"

He pointed north. "If they are wise, they will remain loyal. No one can doubt the threat of the Naum invasion anymore. Regardless, Lucas and I will handle that, if needed. I promise you."

She recalled Master Hector's warning. He had called Jarman's rumor a blessing. Maybe it was. Maybe she could finally put her fear of betrayal at rest. With the White Witch poised to strike into the heart of the realms any day now, there was no more time for strife in the realms.

Just a stone's throw away, the Parusites and Athesians and the odd Caytorean were mingling, honoring the peace agreement with loud music, drinking, joking, and feasting, seemingly oblivious to the death awaiting them. The celebration was taking place under the evening sky, because there were just too many people to cram into Ecol's small establishments. It was almost like the upcoming Autumn Festival, happening a few weeks too early.

While the officers chattered, and gulped wine, the soldiers were having no rest. Companies of Red Caps were marching into the Athesian camp to mingle and meet with their former adversaries and take defensive positions against Calemore's army. After months of killing one another, the two factions were coming together. There was a vibrant buzz of excitement among her soldiers, hardly any fear, resentment, or mistrust. The men were eager to meet so many foreign women, no matter that they had tried to hack them to pieces just weeks earlier.

Despite an orderly procession, there had been incidents all afternoon. Even though Hector and Xavier had ordered quartermasters to confiscate all bows from the sentries, a few stubborn men had smuggled their weapons to their posts and fired an odd arrow against the marching mass of women. The temptation had been too great.

Then, a few men had forgotten to say please before groping a teat and had their fingers and noses broken. Half a dozen men had been beaten for attempted rape, and another twenty awaited morning judgment, which would decide if they would hang. Still, it was a peaceful and friendly surrender overall.

Amalia looked at the cohort of revelers. *Amazing. Must be survival instincts,* she thought. Female officers and her own commanders were talking freely, discussing their worldly differences. Not a bad word about the assaults against Ecol. Princess Sasha stood apart, like herself, with a priest woman at her shoulder.

The most entertaining person in the lot was Captain Speinbate of the Borei. The mercenary had gold-capped teeth, and when he laughed, he shone. His olifaunts had been left far outside the main garrison to avoid panic. But his men moved in the crowd, and they had all the traits of professional swindlers about them. Amalia did not like mercenaries, but then she realized her own army was half paid for its loyalty. And these Borei had a certain friendly charm about them.

A dangerous lot, certainly.

She decided to drift closer. She had to be brave. She had to participate, show her strength. She could not abandon her people right now. This surrender did not absolve her of her responsibility. On the contrary, it only bound her harder. Everything that happened now to Athesia would be her fault. Everything.

The Borei captain was talking to Xavier. She saw tears of mirth in the warlord's eyes, a surprising phenomenon. Master Hector was nibbling a celery shoot, grinning broadly at the mercenary's story.

"...and the last one to hold wins!"

The old sergeant laughed hard. Xavier threw his head back and roared. Some of the drunken people nearby joined in. "I must see that, Captain."

Amalia stepped next to them. They sobered, but only a little. "Captain Speinbate, I presume?"

He looked her up and down quickly, not just a man sizing up a woman, an expert trader evaluating new merchandise. "At your service, Your Highness," he said. *For a price,* his eyes added.

"May I know what is so entertaining?" she asked, feeling silly and awkward. But what else could a defeated empress do? Go back to her inn, sulk, and cry?

Their mirth fled them. Xavier grimaced sourly. Master Hector clamped his mouth on the celery rib, and he looked like some rodent. The Borei tried to smile, and ended up looking like he was picking his teeth. "Hmm, not sure if you should. But if you insist."

"Please," she said.

"Well, we have this game," the mercenary explained. "You take several volunteers, and you make them drink oil from these beans we grow in the south." He held his thumb and forefinger up, half an inch apart. "Brown with black dots. We call it *kesset.* So they drink a cup each, and it makes their bowels go loose." He clapped enthusiastically. "Now, the competition is, they stand naked on a white sheet, you see, and the man who holds the longest without soiling himself wins."

He's just told an empress about a shitting competition, Amalia thought. *What a man.* "Thank you," she murmured, feeling stupid for intruding. She moved deeper into the crowd. Inevitably, her feet led her to her new ruler, or rather, his sister.

"Your Highness," Amalia said, feeling strange.

"Your Excellence." The princess returned the greeting.

Amalia thought about something smart to say. Discuss war? No, not now. She could pretend her life was normal and simple for one evening, one night. "Will you move into Ecol now?"

Sasha shook her head. "No. I prefer to lodge with my troops. Gives me purpose and awareness. A commander that sleeps away from her troops is a bad example for all."

Amalia nodded. Was this a jibe at her soft imperial upbringing? Or just simple, practical truth? But she was glad the princess did not want to sleep in Ecol. That meant she could still hold Brotherly Unity and pretend to own something.

Officially, Princess Sasha would rule Athesia, she knew, but Amalia would be allowed back to Roalas, where she would govern the princedom. It would be like before, only the money would go to Sigurd. Provided they defeated Calemore, that was.

The priestess at her side gently tapped Sasha's forearm. The princess turned, scowled, and saw the sun was gently setting, coloring the evening clouds orange and pink.

"It is time for the evening prayer," she announced.

Prayer?

A horn note rose into the air some distance off, but it had a mellow, relaxed tone to it. Not a cry to arms, not a warning against an enemy army, a summons of a sort.

The priestess raised her hands and began chanting, her voice too low to discern the words. But Princess Sasha knelt, closed her eyes, and prayed. All around, the Red Caps officers did the same. Then, Amalia did the same.

She closed her eyes and kept her mouth silent, but she knew this was expected of her. Halfway through the ceremony, she peeled one lid open and stared. Everyone was at half their height, kneeling in the grass, all except the Borei, who were watching the prayer with an amused look on their scheming faces. The Athesians looked shocked, probably as much as she was.

Humiliation is nothing, Amalia thought. *I am here to protect my people.*

Soon, it ended, and the celebration continued just like before. Amalia moved woodenly through the crowd, trying to salvage what little dignity she had left, but the festivity moved past her eyes in a sad blur.

In the morning, a duck-waddling Agatha woke her. For a moment, Amalia thought it was just another day, and she had dreamed the humiliation yesterday. She would go into the common room of the inn and talk to her advisers and officers, who would be assembled and waiting. They might begin discussing war, provisions, and banditry even without her, as they often did.

But Agatha looked worried.

Still drowsy, Amalia thought something awful had happened while she slept, so she rushed to the window and squinted against the bright sunlight. Soon, her eyes adjusted, and she saw a peaceful Ecol wake to another day, oblivious to the threat looming to the north. The fields were littered with the leftovers of the previous night's celebration, shattering any last shred of hope that she may have just dreamed her downfall. Life was ignorance, rolling down a hill until it hit something and stopped, she thought.

I am no longer am empress, she figured. That much wasn't a dream.

"Amalia," Agatha said. She sounded very tense.

"What is it?"

"This is different, Amalia. They are waiting for you. The Sirtai wizard wanted to come up here, but I would not let him."

Amalia looked at her maid and did not request any clarification. Mind swirling with gloomy ideas, she dressed quickly, squished an apricot open and tossed the pip back into the bowl, bit into the soft orange flesh and found it too sweet for her taste, and then went downstairs.

Whatever happens, I will face the consequences bravely, she promised herself.

In the common room of the inn, all of her staff was assembled, plus several Red Caps. They stood around a single stranger who looked like a traveler, a man of precise yet nondescript looks and age, dirt on his clothes the only sign of imperfection. He looked well at ease with all the soldiers glaring at him. Behind them, hidden by the shoulders and heads of her officers, several more travelers waited.

Jarman stood right next to the man, looking quite cheerful. The contrast in his mood was just as startling and alarming as the presence of this stranger. There was something about him that made her feel worried. She just could not explain it.

But it was like that night when Calemore had stolen the bloodstaff and the book.

"Good morning, Your Highness," he said, his voice a pure song. "My name is Gavril, and I bring thirty thousand souls to assist you in your war against evil."

Then, one of the Parusite women stepped sideways. Not deliberately. It was just too crowded, and standing idly was boring, tiring. Everyone was fidgeting ever so slightly, and there was nothing wrong about that. But as she moved, Amalia could see behind her.

There was a taciturn man with a long moustache there, a big, fat boy that looked frightened, and another, skinny lad with ancient eyes, radiating the same timeless ease as Gavril. He looked even more modest than the other man, except for the object he was holding in his right hand.

A perfect glass rod, topped with claws.

Her bloodstaff.

CHAPTER 26

"You need blood," Tanid said. "Fresh blood."

Ewan looked around him. All he could see was wet grass.

On the far side of the valley, a few miles south of Bassac, a large, muscled arm of the enemy army was milling. One might almost think an early snow had fallen and clad the hillslopes in soft powder. But the illusion went away the moment the large patch of white moved and shifted and spread tentacles.

Tanid's eyes were glazed with grim determination. "We need a corpse then."

Only they did not have a corpse. Tanid's eternal eyes spoke, *We will have to create one.*

Ewan stared at the god who called himself Gavril, and did not like him very much right then. If this war was only about him, Ewan would have left him to his own devices and random twists of luck. But it was more than just that. It was about the people of the realms, and for some strange reason, Ewan felt a need to be their champion. The same people who had shunned and feared him.

Human sacrifice sounded wrong, no matter what, even if it meant providing munition for the bloodstaff. The sleek rod was empty. Ewan still had not fully figured out how its magic worked, but the blood part was rather simple. You needed regular supplies of warm red, or it would not fire. The fields around the town were littered with old, bloated, and half-eaten carcasses of both livestock and refugees, but they were not *fresh enough*, it seemed.

A tiny part of him was excited to see the ancient weapon in action. He wanted to see how it behaved, what kind of damage it could render, what range it had. He was imagining it spewing wild bursts of crimson fire; he imagined it shaking violently in his arms, straining his muscles. He imagined the sound of thunder, great, splitting peals, and a whoosh of air flattening the grass stalks around him and raising a ring of dust. He imagined its red arrows fleeting in a shallow arc halfway across the battlefield and mowing down enemy troops with indiscriminate lack of emotion.

But until he fired it, he would not really know.

"We need a corpse," Tanid repeated. He looked behind him, below the crest of the hill, where his two constant companions were waiting, the surly ax wielder and the big, shy boy, who seemed to be another Special Child, much like himself.

Scouting missions normally fell on the shoulders of the common troops, hardly the leaders and their hive of trusted guards. But Tanid had wanted to glimpse the movement of the Naum army himself and goad Ewan into using the bloodstaff against the enemy.

Apparently, witnessing the bane of the realms in the flesh made people go beyond logic and healthy precaution. The two Sirtai wizards were there, too, trying to keep their odd islander excitement at bay. The blue-faced man was not trying that hard; the mask of old ink hid his emotions well.

In just a few short weeks, Ewan had turned from a lonely orphan, traveling the dusty trails of the realms, into a god's

companion, cohorting with Adam's daughter, with the sister
of the Parusite king, with a horde of experienced warriors and
killers from all corners of the world. Oh, he had missed quite
a lot of real life while locked away in the Abyss, and still more
searching for answers about himself, dragging Doris and Constance across the realms, going to the Oth Danesh land on a
flimsy promise of redemption.

He still was not quite sure what to feel about this latest
turn of his fate. He had gone from being a feared tyrant to
a grubby pilgrim, and yet, he was at the center of attention
once again. He found the interest in him strangely comforting.
No more of the blind terror he had suffered in Kamar Doue,
just pure, keen fascination with his abilities, and mostly his
weapon.

Ewan was slowly trying to piece together the power dynamics between Empress Amalia, Princess Sasha, Jarman, and
Lucas. The younger Sirtai wizard was almost giddy with joy
over his arrival, as if the bloodstaff signified the solution to
all their problems, and Ewan—as the one holding it—along
with it. Lucas was more reserved, more cautious, and so was
the Parusite Red Caps leader, who did not seem that interested in magical weapons, but she could appreciate the human
reinforcements.

Amalia's regard was the most intriguing of all. She seemed
frightened of him, and she hated him at the same time, and
he did not know why. Then again, she looked up to him as
if he was the one person who could redeem her, who could
wash away the last two years of her failure as the Athesian
leader. All the while she eyed the bloodstaff with a curious
mix of wonder, coveting, and fear. It left him uneasy, and he
believed she knew more about this magical weapon than all
the others.

Or so he guessed. It was hard to tell with politics so tightly woven into every word spoken, with fragments of ancient truths invading into the modern reality, with his own identity still remaining a painful mystery.

Tanid was too busy, too divine to devote himself to just one man. Ewan was, after all, just a tool.

"Ludevit," the god called. His voice was slightly muted, as if he feared his voice might carry a whole league away. It was impossible, with the wind slapping the trees senseless and whistling through cracks in the rocks, but the size of the Naum contingent had a humbling effect on everyone, including the deity. "Find a volunteer." Tanid turned toward Ewan. "Strange. If we were back in our camp, we could just go to the infirmary, ask the warden for someone who is terminally ill and might not live past the Autumn Festival, and bring them over here." The season would turn in less than a week.

The man with the moustache nodded and struck back down the goat trail, toward the small base in the foothills. It was a small mobile force, with light mounts and supplies for just a few days, enough to see them safely back in Ecol.

When Tanid had asked Ewan to accompany him north on an expedition, the two Sirtai had almost shouted they would be joining the perilous ride. The young man had insisted on seeing the bloodstaff being used. It was a strange combination, his academic passion and genuine lust for violence blended into a passive, rational demeanor. Then, stranger still, the empress had asked to come along and had to be convinced to remain behind, should things turn ugly.

Eventually, Princess Sasha had ordered her vassal to stay in Ecol and help administer the war preparations. Food, discipline, army detail, they needed a lot of attention and trust, and Amalia's familiar face helped. Red Caps were taking position in the same trenches with the Athesians, and from what Ewan had heard, they had fought each other bitterly only months earlier. Now, they would be defending their land, entrusting their lives to one another.

Beefing up their strength was the Army of the One God, as Tanid called it, which kept on assembling, with the newly arrived forces spreading around Amalia's town. The pilgrims were an unruly, colorful lot, with an obvious lack of military training, but they shone with zeal and fearless dedication, and that made up for the chaos and squalor they brought with them.

The god shrugged almost apologetically, and Ewan forgot about his daydreaming. "Now, we will need someone to sacrifice themselves."

Ewan swallowed. Was he going to allow Tanid to murder someone? So he could feed the bloodstaff?

After all, he had come to stop Calemore. He understood the burden and the price. He knew what it would take and that he would be killing people, thousands of them. Why did he feel a sudden flood of disgust at Tanid's notion?

Maybe because whoever had to die didn't really have a choice.

"This is wrong," he said.

The shy boy looked up, his face constricted with guilt. Gavril noticed that, but his expression remained unchanged. "Ewan, we are fighting a war of survival. Everything we do will be wrong to some degree. Our moral compass is steering us through the deep, dark waters of sin and regret. But out of this necessity, a hope will be born. A hope of the realms, for all of mankind."

"So to survive, we must become...them?" He pointed toward the white enemy.

Tanid smiled, an entire age compressed into a single press of lips. "You understand the threat the White Witch poses. His army will bear us no mercy, will grant no quarter or consideration. True, that does not make our own decisions any easier. But it makes our responsibility greater."

Ewan stepped off the large, wind-blasted rock and walked toward a scree of stunted trees. At least he would not be able to see the enemy screening force, would not deliberate their deaths every moment while they waited for Bad Luck Ludevit to return.

The part that really saddened Ewan was the intimate knowledge that this was something he had to do. The inevitable sensation of grief throbbed in every fiber of his being, in tune with the ancient instincts and alien knowledge that imbued him. His stomach muscles were taut with premonition, except the outcome was obvious. It was just delayed by time, waiting for the future to arrive.

Calemore would not share his doubt, he knew. Damian's son would not be bothered about human losses. After all, they were meant to be. Mortal creatures were expendable, and in the worst case, you sped up their short lives by a few quick decades. The White Witch had planned the destruction of the gods and their followers for countless centuries. Now, he was bringing the old war to a conclusion.

Ewan just happened to be the unlucky champion of humanity.

The size of the Naum force was truly staggering. The white blotch across the valley was just a tiny finger, milling, probing, exploring the defenses of its foe, coming closer. The nations of the realms were still trying to understand why they were being attacked by some strange people no one had known existed.

Ludevit was coming back from the small camp, a soldier of the holy army trailing after him. Ewan swallowed. He focused on the camouflaged tents, on the muffles covering the horses' shanks, on the silence and the lack of fire rings, on the erratic lament of the wind. The huddle of scouts was standing, looking up toward the crest, their faces indiscernible, just pale blobs swathed in leather. Ewan wondered what they were thinking. Adulation for being given the chance to sacrifice themselves for Gavril? Something else?

The two Sirtai joined the ax wielder as he climbed to the top of the hill.

"This is Javor," Ludevit said, short of breath. "He will do it."

A young man with a broad, sun-blasted face stood near the moustached warrior, looking bright, eager, and completely unconcerned. Ewan wondered if he knew he was giving up his life. Did he understand what they asked of him?

Tanid smiled and laid a gentle hand on the soldier's shoulder. "Thank you. The gods and goddesses will bless you."

The young man had tears in the corners of his eyes. "Tell me what to do, Father."

The god did not hesitate. "Lie down here. There. Just lie on the ground. It will not hurt."

Ewan glanced at Jarman. The Sirtai did not look comfortable, but he did not look like he intended to interfere with or stop this madness. "You will give away your life willingly?" he asked.

Javor had lowered himself onto the wet grass. "Yes, sir. If my selfless act can save others, why not? And I will be loved by the gods." His voice trembled at the last word.

Tanid rallied. "We ask soldiers to give their lives in the names of many causes and virtues. We ask them to stand in a line with their comrades and raise spears against the rushing tide of cavalry. Or to slice deep into flesh of other men. To fire arrows against strangers two hundred paces away. How is this any different? Or less noble?"

Ewan looked toward the white enemy. "Are you asking this man to die in order to save the realms or because you want to see how this works?" He hefted the crystal rod.

Jarman looked away. Shame, at least, Ewan thought. But still, not enough, not enough by far.

Tanid stepped closer to the scout and gently caressed his hair. Javor turned his head into the stroke, eyes closed, face ecstatic. The power of religion held him in a warm, beautiful sway, and nothing would change his mind. Once upon a time, Ewan might have invested his soul in prayer, in the love of gods and goddesses, but now he knew different. He had spent eighteen years locked in the Abyss, sharing their thoughts, their fears, their ambitions.

Their greed, their lies, their schemes—they were just like those of ordinary men.

A higher cause or a selfish cause? Ewan wondered, staring at Tanid. Perhaps there was no distinction for the one remaining god, and all he had was raw survival. Even so, it was wrong.

"This is not about you, lad," the blue-tattooed wizard said. "Not about your morality."

Ewan was taken aback. But he recovered quickly. "Is it about yours?"

The Sirtai did not answer.

Javor stretched back like he was resting and closed his eyes, eerily serene. Ludevit hovered nearby, watching the crowd carefully. Then, he laid his gimlet eyes on Ewan. The rest followed suit, waiting for him. It was up to him to act now, and bear the guilt, too.

Take one human life so I can take many more? he wondered. His immediate desire was to curse them all and just leave, but he knew it could not be like that. He could disregard petty human motives, but he could not ignore his legacy. He had stopped Damian twice. He had killed him. He had swum to the bottom of that lake on purpose, gripped the ancient weapon, and now carried it with him, because the world had a role in store for him. He would be deluding himself if he thought it would be anything but brutal and grim. This *was* his legacy, after all.

Ewan toted the crystal staff. "What do I do now? Just press it against the body? For how long?"

Tanid pointed. "Any visible part of the skin will do. The bloodstaff will suck as long as you keep contact. The level of blood will determine how much munition you will have at your disposal against the enemy."

On the ground, Javor was listening, and his eyelids fluttered once or twice, but otherwise, he was unperturbed. Jarman was carefully watching him, judging, weighing, waiting.

My legacy. Ewan sighed. He looked at the soldier one last time, but there was only blind devotion painted there, too painful to watch. "Are you certain, Javor?" He ignored the nervous, hungry crowd around him.

"Yes, sir. Please."

Insane.

Corpse, Tanid had mentioned a corpse. But the soldier still lived. So what now? Ewan was going to kill him? Or maybe he could save this fool from his own destruction.

"Must he die?" Ewan grabbed at the last shred of decency still left at the hilltop.

Tanid's brows shot up. "Well, no. If you're careful, you can draw only a small amount of blood. But the enemy force is too large. We will need all of it. Javor will give his life for the gods and goddesses, for all of us."

Why not kill the man first, Ewan wondered. But he knew. They all wanted to witness this magical weapon in action, all of its secrets.

"Please," Javor insisted.

"Please," Tanid added, oozing pure, golden compassion.

You have killed before, Ewan's conscience purred. *You have taken life. For no other reason than selfish gratification. You called it survival and justice, but it was your own power, your invincibility exerting its superiority over the world.*

He was too tired to be the moral scale for the whole of humanity. It was too much of a task. Deep down, he knew his friend Ayrton would have told all these butchers to go bugger themselves, but then, what good would it do when the white army swept the lands and murdered everyone? They sure had proven their intent in Bassac.

My legacy, he thought, the taste in his mouth bitter, the pain in his chest a surprising token of what little humanity he still had left.

"So be it." Ewan carefully pressed the butt end against Javor's upturned palm. The soldier jerked suddenly and gasped, his eyes going wide. A rush of syrupy red filled the rod, climbing fast. Ewan gaped, fascinated; then he realized the scout was still alive, bleeding to death. He yanked the bloodstaff away. Ghostly pale, Javor crumbled into a ball, moaning. Still alive.

"He will live," Ewan whispered, hopeful. Perhaps you did not need a corpse.

"He will die. You have taken too much," Tanid told him. "He cannot recover from the loss of so much blood. You should at least use all of it now." The god pointed toward the almost-unconscious soldier. "Please. Have mercy."

Ewan tried to control his outrage. "No. Enough."

The god calling himself Gavril nodded at Ludevit. The man removed his ax from his belt and swung deftly. The half-moon blade chopped into the soldier's neck, almost severing it. There was no squirting, no sputters, just a lazy leak of red that colored the grass. The moaning and the spasms ceased.

"Now, please, take the rest of the blood, while it's warm."

Ewan wanted to hate Tanid, but it would be pointless. The god had his own measure of right and wrong, and they went beyond anything Ewan could imagine. Almost in a trance, an oily bubble of disgust wrapping his emotions, Ewan pressed the bloodstaff against the neck wound, and the tendrils of crimson snaked into the staff, filling it up. Soon enough, Javor's corpse was a wizened husk, dry and the color of old bone.

He looked at the weapon, hating himself a tad more. *I am a monster.* He looked imploringly at Tanid.

"Level it against the Naum forces. And squeeze the rod in the middle, there." Tanid stepped back, and everyone else followed suit. Ewan realized he was holding an ancient artifact of magic in his hands, and it could do untold damage.

Ewan turned toward the Naum force. It had advanced half the distance across the valley, and it was probably about a mile and a half away. You still could not tell individual soldiers apart, but their menace was that much bigger, more palpable.

He spread his legs for better leverage and braced himself. Thunder and fire. He pressed. Silence. Deathly silence. A streak of red pellets, almost too fast to see, sped across the gorge and soon became just a shimmering dazzle of crimson dust. The torrent of magical hail crashed into the hillside, halfway to the target, upsetting stone and dirt. But still, there was no sound, no violence.

"Too far, they are too far," the young Sirtai wizard observed, standing near him, craning forward. "You need to elevate the weapon. Higher."

Ewan frowned. Like an archer, then. He pointed the bloodstaff toward the cloudy sky.

"Less. About seventeen degrees," Lucas said, angling his arm in a mock salute.

Ewan closed his fingers on the rod again. More red death sped away at an incredible speed, and then, he noticed the front ranks of the enemy van crumpling, dissolving. You could see a great cloud of debris rising, masking the distant, silent carnage.

"More," Tanid insisted. "Aim wider."

Ewan held the weapon at the slight elevation and moved it left and right, spraying magical death against the enemy congregation, watching it diminish, watching it become a still carpet of white on the wet slopes of the nearby hill. Several stragglers were fleeing, beating back toward their encampment, clambering away. He could only imagine the chaos and terror amid their ranks. But from this great distance, with nothing but the wind whistling in his ears, it felt surreal, clean and simple. Quite merciful in a way. Elegant. Noble. The way death ought to be.

"The weapon works," Jarman said in a reverent whisper.

"It is magnificent," Gavril intoned. "We will save the realms."

But not my soul, Ewan thought. Why had he done this? Why? To stop Calemore? He understood the significance of his act; he understood the importance, the necessity. He recalled the lament of murdered gods in the Abyss; he remembered Damian. This was justice. But that did not mean he would ever like being the instrument of delivery. Never that. Once you got used to the killing, you lost your humanity. That was what Ayrton, his dear friend, would have said.

Once, people who had killed in the name of various causes could go to the Safe Territories and ask for forgiveness, ask someone else to embrace their guilt and remorse, to cleanse their souls. He knew better than that. For him, there would be no one to share the burden. Weeks ago, he had felt relief at meeting the one remaining god. Now he realized that deities never quite shared human emotions. On the contrary, they had created men so they could unload their own onto their creations. Cowardice in its perfect form. And he was an accomplice.

Perhaps one day, he would figure out why he had been made this way, why life had steered him toward loneliness and pain. Perhaps one day he would figure out a way to undo his legacy and regain a normal, simple life. Until then, he was a monster, and ignoring that would be to lie to himself. He would never forget that.

Disgusted, disillusioned, he went down the slope toward the camp, ignoring the religious and scientific celebration taking place behind him.

CHAPTER 27

"Higher. Go higher. Careful. Now, shake the branch."

The thin boy was scrambling through the crown of the apple tree like a little monkey, his feet deft on the slender branches. They bent and creaked, but did not break. The last fruit of autumn was always the sweetest. A few big, succulent apples would always remain near the top, defying wind, rain, birds, and the inexorable pull of the ground. Not today.

There was a nervous rustle as the lad tilted the branches left and right, swaying them like a banner. The big apples swayed, refusing to come down. But then the stems broke, and they plummeted onto a stretched-out blanket held by three other youths.

Calemore approached and scooped up one of the red fruits, wiped a season of dust against his shirt, and bit into the shiny, unblemished skin. Delicious. Divine.

He could have used magic to get the last apples. But that would have been sacrilege. Using magic to somehow alter the natural growth of an apple tree. Crazy. If he had to do that, he might as well destroy the world altogether, because there was no point to its quirks, imperfections, its randomness, and mostly its complete disregard for those who trod upon it.

Soon, the human monkey was done, and he clambered back deftly, fearless. He dusted himself off, bowed to his master, and ran back to the camp. The three other boys lowered the blanket, collected the apples into a silk-lined basket, and carried it away.

In their eagerness to prepare for the autumn and winter, some of his soldiers had cut down half the grove for firewood. Any other time, Calemore would have punished the morons for their transgression, for using fruit-bearing trees as kindling. He would have ordered the woodcutters tied to the back of a wagon and dragged until their guts left a slimy trail down the road, like slugs. Now, though, he had just asked the commanders to exact their own judgment over the ruin of an orchard, as it should have been left intact for after the conquest. Next year, once the war was complete, the nation would need food.

The taste for killing had left him. Nigella had bewitched him.

Only now, he had a new reason to try to regain his love for violence.

Someone had used a bloodstaff to kill his men.

Someone had found the second example.

He had thought it lost in the war somewhere, buried under hundreds of thousands of tons of molten rock and earth. He had thought no one would ever remember that it had existed, let alone figure out where it might have last been used before the defeat of Damian's and his forces. Even he had forgotten all about it, until now.

Apparently, though, the one surviving god was much more resourceful and cunning than he had imagined.

That scared him. Genuinely scared him.

The bloodstaff could not kill him, but it could utterly decimate his troops. That would render his eternal plan useless, undo the generations of careful preparations. Well, if his stupid father had not tried to double-cross him, he could have been a god by now, and this forceful invasion would never have taken place. Too late for that now. Brute force should have decided the battle, and his enemy had just undone the element of surprise and numerical advantage that he had. His success was no longer certain. The victory of the Naum forces was not a foregone conclusion. Far from it.

Real, stark fear, exhilarating, breathtaking, gut clenching, ecstatic, bloodcurdling, terrifying.

Everything he had ever wanted was at stake now. He might not become a god.

The realization almost made him scream in fury.

It wasn't the challenge that galled him. It was not the uncertainty. It was the understanding he could no longer rely on his immortality, on his magic, on his power to win this war. He had just become as insignificant as his opponent.

Almost human.

Flawed.

Calemore walked into the ghost town of Bassac, its buildings mostly intact, the streets empty and quiet, apart from an odd team of engineers inspecting the damage, searching for traps, examining the livability of the place. The defenders had fled, leaving most of their belongings behind, apart from the crucial bits like food and tools. Bassac might house people, but the winter would scourge it clean unless his craftsmen could make it hospitable for the coming wave of Naum families.

A small procession was coming toward him, three wagons teamed up with mules, plodding slowly over old, worn cobbles. The wind stirred, and a whiff of death tickled his nostrils. Munching the apple, savoring the tart juices, he walked toward the deathly convoy and looked into the back of one of the carts.

A neat pile of bodies was gently festering in the sun of the last summer days. The people of the realms would welcome the autumn in one of the evenings, boost the strength of the surviving god with their stupid prayer. His foe was just getting stronger, more confident, and he was becoming insecure, frightened. He had to visit Nigella, the risks be damned. He must have her prophecies.

The bodies looked just like he expected, serene and clean. Some had tiny punctures in their armor and bodies, almost too small to notice; others had their limbs severed cleanly, as if by a giant cleaver. They looked all too peaceful, nothing like the chop of a typical battle, when these stupid humans rushed against one another with hammer and sword. This was death in its higher form, beautiful and precise.

The only problem was, the dead belonged to him, not the other way around.

He had not planned for his enemy to gain the second bloodstaff. That made him wary, hesitant, maybe even confused. It ruined all his planning. He had intended to use the entire strength of Naum in one unstoppable wedge, drive south down the spine of these realms, and then split west and east and finish the survivors. Now, the massive throng just meant his forces posed an easy, large target for the wielder of the second weapon. Compressed together, for a quick slaughter.

So what should he do now? Abandon centuries of preparations? No. That was inconceivable.

He would just have to risk going against the surviving god in person.

He had intended to remain behind the scenes, guiding his troops to a leisurely victory, to let them sap religion from the land, to slowly weaken the god until he withered and died. Or maybe wait until the god was killed in an errant battle.

Now, this ugly development in the war meant he had to get personally involved. He still must not murder the deity, but he could assassinate his most trusted followers and army leaders, kill his champions, cripple his organization. A great risk, but one he must undertake. He must.

But what if the survivor was wielding the bloodstaff himself? What would he do then?

That scared him.

He had no answers. But he expected his bespectacled, homely prophet to provide them. She would unravel the future for him, tell him what he must do. She would help him best his enemy. Besides, he missed her, no matter how much he hated admitting it.

Nothing was quite working out as he wanted. His troops were suffering significant losses in the northeast, and it could not be just the weather, the terrain, or bad luck. Not anymore. There must be a ghost army shadowing his own force, trying to hamstring his supply lines. That suggested a very keen, resourceful, and agile enemy. The unification of the two bodies was taking still much longer than he had foreseen, with delays and loss of transport. In the south, the enemy was gathering in larger numbers, still a fleck compared to his own might, but then, they no longer needed the numbers.

Humanity had its share of dirty tricks, and it did its best to thwart him by the simple virtue of being unpredictable. The humans' greatest, deadliest weapon.

He found the elders in one of the abandoned inns, and they didn't have anything good to report. The usual share of confusion, road wear, illness, ineptitude, withering food supplies, slow convoys getting lost, and the horse training hobbling along like a cripple.

"We have almost three hundred fast animals," the elder of Tirri reported. "We will have our first unit of scouts ready in a few weeks. We should be able to match the locals then. They will no longer have the ability to outmaneuver us."

"I want ten thousand," Calemore said. They did not argue.

He had considered extending a friendly hand to the mercenaries and scum of these realms, offering a boon to their greed, but the language was a great barrier. His troops did not speak the Continental tongue, and no one could piece together the Naum one around here. Large sacks of gold would work, but it would just add more confusion. After all, he had come here to destroy the people of this land.

Use them now, then discard them later? he wondered. That might be a sensible idea. But that was how corruption started. Soon enough, he would be fielding an army of sellswords, and the purity of the conquest would be tarnished by the grayness of their morality. He must not let the two sides mingle. He must not let humanity takes its vile, unpredictable course. He owned the souls of the Naum people, but not their collective human spirit, not their curiosity and their desperate need for empathy. The enemy must remain a blurred, nameless identity.

Which meant his troops would lack good cavalry for much longer, and the winter rain and snow would only make everything more difficult. But it did not matter. Time was irrelevant. Even if this war took another decade, or another century, he would prevail. He would destroy the realms. He would make sure the surviving god died, and that he became one. That was the only thing that really mattered.

Only, with the bloodstaff in the enemy's hands, everything had changed. Everything.

Making two weapons had been a great mistake, he realized. He should have forged only a single, unique item for himself.

But he had grown desperate toward the end of the war, so he had yielded to foolishness and unleashed another bloodstaff into the world. Now, it was back, to be used against him. That served him right.

Calemore had once read a book, titled *Immortality Is Death*, written by some ancient wizard before the great war. The man had claimed the inflexibility of eternal life made those blessed by it rigid and slow and vulnerable, trapped by their own greatness, their own disregard for time and its quirks, aloof and too self-centered to adapt to changes. Once, long ago, he had considered the wizard's work to be a beautiful binding of bollocks, stupidity in prosaic form. Now, he fully understood the implications behind the book's conceited message.

A bucktoothed woman had finally helped him grasp the message.

And her son, Sheldon. The boy showed extraordinary promise.

Through them, he could realize what his own perfection would not let him.

He still did not know what he would do once the war ended, and victory was the only thing he could imagine, because defeat was unthinkable. He still wondered about Nigella, about her affection, her ability to understand him, to respect him, to cherish him. Did he want blind obedience from her? No, he had that in endless amounts, and it left him empty. Terror did not excite him anymore. Total submission was boring. But if not terror, what then? What could she offer that would make him feel grand and whole once again?

This pursuit was becoming more and more of a hardship, emotional, mental. The fear over learning his enemy had the second bloodstaff was the best thing that had happened to him in a long time. Made him feel alive again. But that would end one day, and what then? He would become a god. What then?

What then, indeed?

Oh, how he envied the silly humans and their insignificant existence.

The short, fierce struggle with a known defeat in the end. And still they fought, bitterly, even with dignity, with laughter and joy, with a sense of completeness that mystified him. If he had ever wondered what Damian had tried to achieve with mankind, it must have been this.

So what would he do with Nigella? What could she offer him after he became a god and made complete his ancient vow? What would her humble, average existence offer him that could scale against the greatness of creation?

Everything, it seemed.

But that would mean what? Make her his equal? She could not be his equal. Make her into a slave? A servant? Was there anything that could make his sense of futility go away? He still did not know. But the answer was there, in that tiny cabin near Marlheim.

I have figured out how to become a god, but I can't figure out one woman, he thought. Stupid. Just like Damian. The knowledge was there, a jester cackling, only he was powerless to stop it.

First, I will make sure the bloodstaff is safe, he swore. *Then I will try to piece my future into a meaningful mosaic. But easy tasks first.*

He left the elders and their boring reports behind and struck south.

CHAPTER 28

The throne room burst with activity. Round the table, Archduke Bogomir and Dukes Oleg and Rolan sat and shared the view of the map showing Athesia and the outline of the neighboring realms. The north of the land, facing toward Natasha's father, was covered in a large piece of white cloth. No one really knew the disposition and the exact numbers of this Naum force, but everyone agreed that it was huge. Huge beyond reckoning.

A letter from one Commander Mali of the Third Independent Battalion of Eracia urged him to accept the dire facts.

Earlier that morning, a weary rider had reached Roalas bearing a message for whoever held the city. An impudent challenge, by all means, and maybe even an insult to his authority, but not since he had met with Gavril and seen his tens of thousands of followers marching to fight this incredible enemy. Now, he treated any sort of rumor, bad news, and oddities with prudence. The fact someone had sent a letter with no clear recipient in mind did not mean they had worded it as a slight; it probably meant the sender was deeply out of touch with current affairs, or the letter had been sent from a great distance, and the information could be quite significant. And so it was. The isolated Eracian contingent shadowing the enemy army was the best source of knowledge he had on the Naum invaders since first hearing about it. He valued the message dearly and had quickly summoned his lords for a discussion. Those still in Roalas, that was.

They want me to make peace, he thought. *Well, I am.*

Amalia had accepted his generous offer and bent her knee. Officially, Athesia was now Parusite territory, subject to his law. Adam's empire was no more. Twenty years after being forged in blood, it had ended in a quiet, somber defeat.

He had probably been too generous, he thought. He allowed the blasphemous name to remain, and he would grant it the same treatment as his other duchies. Amalia would be his vassal, and she would make sure that people prayed and paid money to the crown. He would do his best to forget all the bad things in the past two years. Vlad's death was no longer meaningless, was it?

Sergei stared at the map.

Well, Athesia was his, for now. Soon, it might not be.

Sasha's own letter strengthened the view held by the Eracian officer, gave color and flesh to Gavril's omens. The enemy was there, a giant sprawl of people, aligned halfway across the Barrin estate in Eracia all the way to Pain Mave. They didn't want to negotiate. They did not care about making contact with the people of the realms. Their only intent was destruction. Unstoppable, even with all of the might of Parus arrayed against it.

Then why had the enemy halted its advance?

Waiting for the nations of the realms to gather? So it could crush them more easily? Baiting? Teasing? Gloating? Something else, much more sinister?

Normally, his lords would be quick to make suggestions. They all had decent military experience, and they loved nothing better than to move colored pieces of wood and tin on a stretch of canvas, making monumental decisions of life and death with crude miniatures. Today, though, they just stared, bored their eyes into the layout of the terrain, wondering.

"Maybe we should try to flank the enemy?" Duke Rolan said at last. He was the father of Vlad's widow, and he had not yet reconciled the loss of his son-in-law. His arrival was a surprise, because the Parusite law exempted him from sending troops. Still, he had marched north with half his household, under the impression he would be given a chance to avenge his family and honor.

He would be denied that opportunity, but at least he had a new foe to contend with.

"That will not be advisable," Sergei remarked. "If we march west, we cross into Eracia, and they will surely not like our troops trampling through what little land they still have left, in between this Naum invasion and the Kataji menace. Moreover, I did promise not to interfere, so any transgression would be a breach of my word as well as a clear declaration of war. If we march east, we must cross half of Caytor, and we do not know what to expect there. The High Council will not love me for making peace with Amalia, and they will love our troops on their soil even less. Not after the Oth Danesh fiasco."

Duke Rolan was tapping his upper lip fervently, thinking hard. He was a very temperamental person, and he did not like dallying, apologizing, or compromising. "Then, we just head north?"

That seemed to be the only real course of action. "North."

"Head-to-head with an enemy that outnumbers us three or four to one?" Duke Oleg retorted. "But we have the faith on our side, and gods and goddesses will surely guide us to victory."

Sergei looked at his vassal wearily. *No pious blathering, please,* he thought. He could not understand how anyone could still maintain their belief after hearing all these stories about ancient enemies and magical weapons. It went against everything the patriarchs and matriarchs had taught the nation for generations, and it all had turned out to be untrue.

Archduke Bogomir was silent, probably cautious ever since departing Athesia in disgrace last year. Well, if some humility would make his war counsel smarter, Sergei did not object to a moody, protracted silence.

If one stared hard at the land's drawing before him, Sergei mused, one might not notice the crowd of advisers, adjutants, and clerks hovering nearby. Whatever he and his lords decided today would transpire into battle orders.

I may have bought myself a favorable chapter in the history books by forging peace with Amalia, he thought, *but the future generations will judge me harshly if I make a poor work of this northern menace.* He looked up from the map. *Or rather, not at all.* That was a relief. If he lost to this White Witch, there would be no history books to exonerate him or blame him.

Sometime later, once the war was over, there would be time to contemplate magic and ancient tales, he knew. Now, he must focus on being a fierce army leader as much as a king. Rather like the man who had left him this sorry inheritance.

"Brute force, yes," he admitted at last. "But cunning, too. We should focus the bulk of our units as far north as we can, which would be the town of Ecol. This will convince our enemy that we are focused on a direct confrontation. However, we need to find a way to get some behind the enemy lines, like Colonels Finley"—he consulted the letter again—"and Alan and this Commander Mali."

Now, he needed a female's touch. Lady Lisa. Maybe even his sister. Women were good at thinking obliquely, even when they held the upper hand. He was wondering what the best way of defeating a superior enemy really was, and all his ideas and tactics came up bloody all too quickly. He was smart enough to acknowledge that much. Adam's widow would surely know. But he could not invite her here.

She was still his hostage, maybe even more so than before. Amalia would regain her rule of the city and the region, in his name, but that did not mean he could just free her mother. Lady Lisa would remain his honored guest for years to come, until he could build some trust with his new vassal. He did not doubt Amalia's surrender was one of dire necessity, maybe propelled by the Naum threat. But if they won, she might begin nourishing resentment and bitterness all of a sudden. He did not expect Adam's offspring to just forgive and forget.

Strange how the human mind worked. When faced with this colossal threat, it was almost too easy to disregard all other affairs, to neglect the future, to focus solely on the enemy and fight it to the bitter end. And on the same note, the brain kept scheming and plotting, twining and threading scenarios and ideas that whorled decades ahead into uncertainty. So maybe Amalia was preoccupied with the white armies at her northern border, but given a chance, she would start thinking all about her honor, her survival, and her vengeance.

He needed Lady Lisa to balance the sorrow in his heart. He needed her perspective on reign and power and the price one might have to pay to gain those. But he could not have her in the same chamber as his lords, because they would not understand.

He could tell some of them were displeased with his meek treatment of the foe, with his seemingly dishonorable resolution of the war. But they didn't dare say anything, because they carried a heavy burden of their own. So they somewhat trusted him, and they feared him, and he would have to work hard to justify his decision. Parusite kings never settled for anything, and he seemed to have been the first.

Or they had and then had their smart scribes write it down the way people liked. He glanced at Genrik.

"Gennadiy." He called his third squire. "Summon Sergeant Daria."

Sasha had left the woman in charge of her Red Caps garrison. She was a capable and experienced officer, and she might have some suggestions. Because he could not see a stealthy way past the white wall of the ancient myth threatening the realms.

One of the aides murmured something in Bogomir's ear. The archduke nodded. On the other side of the room, the crowd stirred, nervous, restless. All of these men wanted their chance to prove their worth in waging war, at least over a beautifully drawn map, but no one dared interrupt him. The Siege of Roalas had scarred their lips shut.

In a way, it was a good thing. But even the king needed advice sometimes.

"Your Highness," someone interrupted.

Sergei raised his eyes. Bisected by a shaft of daylight streaming from a side window so that his legs were bathed in autumn silver and his torso left in a mute shadow, one of his court aides stood near the throne hall doors, looking hesitant.

"What is it, Ruslan?" The man was a very distant cousin, Sergei remembered.

"Head Talker Svetlana kindly requests your presence at the dungeons, Your Highness."

A low murmur spread through the lordly lot. Bogomir shot an angry glance at the aide, challenging his intrusion.

Sergei scratched his head. After the death of his son, he had been too distraught to worry about the minute details of his rule, like who ran his questioners. Very practically, Sasha had appointed one of her own officers. Administration must never cease, the king's pain notwithstanding.

"That urgent?" he grumbled. "Anything else you wish to tell me before I delay my war preparations?" The head talker believed she could order everyone into submission.

Ruslan hesitated. Then he shook his head. "No, Your Highness. But it is quite urgent."

Sergei looked at Giorgi. "What have you planned for me?"

The adjutant smiled dryly. "Your Highness, Under-Patriarch Evgeny wishes to discuss this year's preparations for the Autumn Festival. He believes the blessing of Vlad's Temple should coincide with the celebrations. He also wants to talk about the comba—"

"Yes, yes," Sergei said impatiently. He had done enough for the clergy already. And he would not open that temple until every last detail was perfect. He glanced at his frightened distant cousin. The lad looked rather uncomfortable for an unimaginative aide. Perhaps Sveta did not want his nobles to overhear the message. Very well. Sergei rose. His dukes quickly followed. "We will resume this meeting in an hour. Borya, with me."

Stretching his legs, Sergei led out of the hall, his lieutenant of the guard and four other soldiers in tow, their armor polished, their capes twirling. It was an impressive sight for all those who needed impressing, he knew.

"Your Highness," Ruslan spoke, stepping with him but keeping back out of deference, "apparently, the head talker has information about the death of your son."

Sergei halted abruptly. One of the guards almost collided into him. He spun wildly, and the aide cringed. "Vlad's death?" A storm of emotions swept him, and he wasn't sure where to put his hands. They itched with anxiety.

Ruslan swallowed. "Your Highness, she asked me to tell you this when you were on your own. But only she has all the details. I apologize."

Sergei glanced back toward the hall. His court was standing like a gaggle of bored housewives, trying to interpret his gestures and motions, now that he was outside their hearing. He was glad the clerk had not mentioned anything earlier. He was not sure how he would have reacted. Then again, Sveta was a very meticulous woman, and she must have instructed Ruslan about his message very carefully. Entice the king; make no scene.

He did not quite remember the route through the palace, only that he found himself in a small, damp room with Sveta, several talkers, and a cheerful, whiskered man who seemed all too happy about his predicament. Most people under the scrutiny of the talkers usually spent their last moments murmuring prayers, talking nonsense, and smelling of feces. Not this fellow.

"Your Highness," Sveta said, bowing, "I am sorry to intrude on your time. But I have vital information about the death of your son. I felt it was important enough to ask you to see me here."

Sergei tried to focus his thundering mind. "Please." His voice sounded thin.

Sveta pointed at the prisoner. "This man was apprehended in Gasua five weeks back. He was a member of a small rebel cell working in the city, trying to spread fear and dissidence. Apparently, they were not content with just shouting slogans against you; they tried to recruit people into their band, they assassinated those who cooperated with the Crown, and they even did a fair share of looting, rape, and roadside banditry to finance their mission. Our forces finally put an end to their activity recently. Most of these rebels were killed, but some surrendered. We thought they ought to be hanged publicly, and we got the ropes soaped, when this vermin here said he knows who ordered the death of the prince heir." She coughed. "Your Highness."

Sergei was staring intently at the whiskered man, but he was just leering, glaring back, totally unafraid. Either he was totally mad or he knew something that could save his miserable life. Well, his gamble had worked so far. They had spared him the noose and shipped him here, whole and without any bruises. That could change at any moment.

"You know who killed my son?"

The man nodded, clicking his tongue.

Sergei took a deep breath to steady his nerves. "Tell me."

The prisoner licked his lips, then casually flicked a roll of spit toward Sergei.

Sveta nodded at her talkers. One of them grabbed the prisoner in a headlock, and soon, the man was purple and wheezing into a hairy forearm choking his scrawny neck, a quivering thread of spit hanging from his lips. A second man gently removed a spiked hammer from his belt.

"Thank you, Sveta." Sergei stopped the maiming before it happened. The head talker had done a commendable job so far. He did not want any confession under torture. He wanted this man to tell him the truth. "What is your name?"

"Alice," the man croaked, then coughed loudly.

"That's a girl's name." Sergei pointed toward a chair, and the third talker slid it over. He sat down.

"No lies, swear. Alice is me name. Me mom wanted a daughter," the man gargled. He tried to sound cocky, but Sergei could sense his fear.

"Release him," Sveta ordered.

Sergei clasped his hands. They were steady. Strange. "Now, tell me."

Alice was massaging his neck. "Swear, Your Lordship. I'm telling the truth, honest."

"People in your position tend to be inventive if it saves them from the gallows. Your luck has just run out. You'd better confess now, or things will just get worse for you."

"Promise you'll let me go free, Your Lordship," Alice rasped.

Sergei leaned against the crude backrest. He was totally unprepared for this. He had never expected anyone to come forward and claim any knowledge about his son's death. He had assumed Vlad had been killed in the confusion of the battle, or maybe as retribution, but he had reconciled the idea he would never learn the truth.

And now this.

Only a madman would embrace his wrath. Or a condemned fool who had nothing to lose.

Sergei sighed, feeling tired, defeated. "Please, I really do not have patience for this."

Their eyes locked. The cockiness that had colored the man's silvered cheeks was gone now. Almost humbly, the prisoner nodded, still rubbing his neck.

"I understand, Your Lordship."

"Good. You will tell me everything you know. If what you tell turns out to be true, you will be released. You will swear an oath to the Crown, and you will become a loyal citizen of

Athesia. However, if this turns out to be a ruse, your death will be a slow one."

Alice swallowed audibly, a wet, slimy sound. He frowned, uncertain, eyes flickering toward Sveta and back. "So I tell you the truth, you let me go?"

Sergei sighed. "Yes."

The prisoner cocked his head. "So all me sins are pardoned, eh? Your word as a king?"

Sveta was waiting for a cue to bludgeon this fool, but Sergei would not allow it. "Now, tell me who killed my son."

Alice tried that cheerful expression from earlier but realized it would not do. "I don't know who killed your son as it was, Your Lordship. No, wait, wait, wait! I know who ordered it. I know who ordered it." He was holding his hands above his head, the spiked hammer just inches away.

Sergei felt his stomach roil. "Tell me."

He burst into the Garden of Joy, trampling flowers, kicking dirt. Lady Lisa watched him with a passive, resolved look on her face. There was no fear there, or surprise.

"Your Highness," she greeted, rising. "The flowers will die in the autumn anyway, no need to kill them early."

He huffed, barely able to control his wrath, his disgust, his sense of betrayal. "Did you order my son killed the day I took Roalas?"

She was silent for a moment, watching him intently. "Yes, I did."

Sergei closed his eyes. He could hear Borya unsheathing his sword. "Put it away," he hissed.

How could she have done that? And then greet him so coolly, so regally in the throne room? All those talks he had with her, all those noble, compassionate ideas? Was it all posturing?

Was all that one giant lie? Had she played him all along? Was he such a lousy judge of character?

Sasha had been right all along. This woman was the enemy.

"Why?" he asked, trying to keep tears at bay.

"Your Highness, you know why. You were given terms. You broke them. You paid the price."

It's my fault, he thought maniacally. *I killed Vlad by storming the city. They warned me. They did just what they had said they would do.* He had known that from the beginning, and he had deliberately condemned his firstborn. Because the realm was above any one man, including the prince heir.

The pain in his chest did not lessen.

"You killed my son!" He wailed.

Lady Lisa was adamant. She was Adam's widow after all. What else should he expect?

"No, I did not. But I sent soldiers to kill him, because you set out to destroy what my dear husband had spent eighteen years building. You decided family honor was more important to you than the lives of your family. It was your choice. It had always been your choice, Your Highness."

Sergei realized his palms were bleeding, his nails gouging deep. He had allowed Amalia to live, as his vassal. He had given her peace. Had he known this before, he would never have accepted this miserable peace idea. He had been duped. Sasha was right, like always. *Sorry, Sister, I failed you.*

He was done being the weak, silly king.

He was done being the fool. He was done being nice and compassionate.

Adam had taken everything from him. His father, his son. No more. He would sort this out the old Parus way, blood for blood. He would honor the fool's peace, because he was an honorable king, but he had no obligation toward this evil woman. His mercy had just run out.

He wiped tears away. "Lady Lisa, for the murder of Prince Heir Vlad of Parus, I condemn you to death. You will be executed on the first day of autumn. You may pray if you wish. Borya, escort the prisoner to her chambers."

CHAPTER 29

Nothing would spoil the ceremony now. Not the smoke, not the moans from the wounded, the grumbles from bored, inebriated, and frightened soldiers, not the distant screams of battle, not even the bad music from a traveling band that just happened to stumble into their camp.

Bart would see the heroes of Eracia honored properly.

Last night, everyone had drunk their share to the changing of the season, knowing all too well what the coming of the autumn meant. Shorter days, colder mornings, more rain, more disease. And still, the Kataji held Somar.

Bart had spent time equally shared between his officers and the regular troops and a quick gamble with the Borei. Junner had assured him they had a surprise for him this morning, so he was somewhat eagerly and apprehensively looking forward to that. He had played the majestic and benevolent part of the nation's ruler in absence of another ruler, ingraining the very real possibility that once the war ended, he might be the best candidate to become the monarch. It was a very vain, self-indulgent thought, but to stop now would mean throwing away all he had achieved so far, making each and every death meaningless, both the assassinations he had bought as well as the glorious, courageous sacrifice of the Eracian troops in the city's ruined districts.

Now, he was doing something even more meaningful: decorating distinguished fighters for their valor and outstanding performance in the field of battle. Not many men, and those carefully handpicked by their officers.

There was Maks, born in a border village near the Territories, to a Parusite mother and an Eracian father, who was extremely good at sneaking behind enemy soldiers and slicing their throats open. Smiling Maks, his comrades called him, and he claimed seventeen Kataji dead. Rusty was the best crossbowman in the force, with a steady hand and great accuracy. According to various reports, Rusty had killed dozens of nomads with a heavy bolt through their eyes. Jochen was nowhere near as lethal as his friends, but he had saved three women from a burning house. That was just as important as slaughtering the tribesmen, Bart knew, because he needed brave men to dash inside burning buildings and search for Eracians.

Others were there, too, each with his own shred of heroics, and Bart was wondering if these men should be forbidden from taking any more action, because their image had become more precious than their combat skills. Unfortunately, his officers insisted they should continue fighting, because they could not spare any warriors, great or otherwise.

The least Bart could do was lavish them with praise and money in front of their units.

His entire staff was arranged behind him in a proud semicircle, trying their best to look presentable, although some looked positively ill from too much wine last night. Uncle Karsten was there, not to be bested, and even Constance.

She had become quite cheerful in the last few weeks, ever since Bart had taken more interest in his son, ever since he had decided to name the boy. It gave her hope that maybe, maybe Bart would learn to love the child and that she might gain her rightful place at his side.

He had named his son Adam. He loved the irony.

Constance was standing at the end of the line, shoulder to shoulder with one of her she-devils and a pair of bodyguards. Young Adam was perched on her chest, moving his tiny hands. Constance had brought him out so he would *soak up* some of the majesty. Bart was still convinced that children couldn't really see, hear, or understand anything in their first year of life, but he had indulged his mistress.

"For your valiant service and selfless acts of courage in the face of certain death, you are each awarded a gift of one hundred gold coins, as decreed by His Majesty Lord Bartholomew of Barrin, the Viceroy of the Realm," Velten's aide announced. There was an appreciative sigh in the crowd behind him, coming from the common soldiers. This was a small fortune, but Bart did not doubt it would soon be wasted on drinks and whores. Such was the life of a soldier.

He stood a little to the side so he could watch both the heroes and his officers, and behind them, more importantly, a bevy of his lords and ladies. Both Countesses Anniken and Ernsta were there. While they had mostly kept out of his way ever since the attack on Somar had started, Bart did not doubt they kept scheming quietly behind his back, doing their best to make sure he was removed from power once the war was ended. There were others there, some who openly supported, others who covertly hated him. Margravine Diora seemed to have mellowed her opposition, but that meant nothing.

Well, Bart had new, secret weapons he intended to use.

He had unleashed his mother against them.

And he intended to have a quiet word with Lady Melicent, Sonya's mother and his mother-in-law.

Shit and gold attracts all kinds of insects, Bart mused, and sometimes, it was really hard to know the difference. They buzzed and buzzed, and their touch often left you feeling filthy.

He had no particular reason to hate the mother of his wife, except that she had birthed and educated her daughter, and he could not really let that slide. Unlike Sonya, she was far more delicate about her goals and ambitions and usually tried polite, shy charm first. Getting her daughter married to Bart had diminished her need to fight for wealth, so she had mostly spent the years at her family's small estate in the southwest. Now, though, she clearly understood the peril, both of losing Sonya and—once Sonya was safely rescued from Somar and the war ended in an overwhelming Eracian victory—of not having Bart leading the nation.

That was probably the best motivator for Lady Melicent of Leighmoors to behave like innocence incarnate.

She stood near the other harpies, smiling softly, her eyes trained on him. Bart stared through her, pretending to scan the crowd. Commanders Faas and Velten were walking down the line of heroes, shaking their hands, asking silly questions, patting them on the shoulder or back—and handing them large, heavy purses of coin. The soldiers looked all too humbled by the attention, the demons of their experience hiding behind the tense lines round their mouths and eyes.

"I am honored to lead such brave men," he blurbed into the expectant silence.

Applause exploded through the audience. Some of the soldiers hooted and whistled right into the ears of the nobles arrayed before them. Bart was pleased.

The ceremony ended, and the gloomy autumn morning descended once again. Not far away, Somar burned. The Eracians were holding almost half the city, having paid the price in seven thousand more dead. Fingers of black smoke rose from at least ten different locations inside the capital, and Bart knew the fighting would be fiercest there. Just like last night, just like two weeks back, the Kataji were fighting with mad ferocity, not giving up one inch of the occupied soil.

The bleak scene of troops marching to their deaths had become a routine. No one really paid it attention anymore. Most of the soldiers had toughened up, losing their humanity before they lost their senses. It made for a camp of brutal, cold, dispassionate warriors. If Bart had wondered about Eracia's military before, he no longer did. He had secured the next generation of killers. Whoever survived the horror of Somar would be an excellent soldier of the realm for years to come.

Not all had the strength to shut their minds to the terrors. Every now and then, a blubbering idiot or a stone-faced man would be led away from the camp, to join the slow procession of cripples going to Ubalar, with a letter of early discharge and a tiny retirement bag, mostly loaded with coppers.

Still, the attacks continued, day and night, relentlessly.

Not stopping until Somar was freed.

Bart waited until the audience dispersed. He noticed some of his noble friends and foes trying to get near him, but he had instructed Major Paul to keep them away. He would meet them when he felt like it. What he really wanted to do was see Junner about his surprise.

Sloshing through old, regurgitated mud, Bart walked toward Junner's garrison. It was well marked by a fence, with every third post flying a flag or some odd ornament, usually an animal head. The Borei made sure their privacy was respected,

even if they took every pain to disregard everyone else's. Even
from a distance, the size of those gray animals took Bart's breath
away. Every time. He could imagine them plowing through
Somar's lanes, leaving human pulp behind, some Kataji, some
Eracian. Not what he desired, but he was beginning to wonder
if he ought to get his mercenaries busy. Even if just for the sake
of appearances.

Junner had more than proven his worth in the past, and
Bart was indebted to him. Without the mahout, he would
not be the viceroy now, maybe not even the lowliest member
of the exiled Privy Council. Somar would most likely still be
fast held by the nomads, and the Eracian pride would be in
the gutters.

The mahout was standing near the entrance to their enclosure, talking to two other Borei. One of them was idly flicking
his olifaunt switch against the post. Soon enough, Junner saw
him approaching and grinned. "Lord Count!"

Bart kept his own grin away. "You promised me a surprise," he said.

Junner turned serious for a moment. "Ah yes. Indeed." He
looked past Bart, at his small retinue of guards. "Alone."

"Lads, make sure you do not lose any money," he told his
soldiers and stepped into the crazy world of the Borei. It was
as if an invisible veil was lifted, to reveal charms, wonders, and
smells. The color, the thickly studded mess, the absolute lack of
any semblance of order assailed his senses. "How do you manage to run your camp this way?"

Junner clicked his tongue. "Ah, Lord Count. It is a disguise. Keeps thieves busy. What's the point of sorting out everything neatly so your enemies will find it all easily?"

There was a mad logic to it, Bart had to admit. He realized the mahout was taking him toward a tent that had more

patches than original cloth, with a goat head bolted to one of its masts. There was an unusually large gathering of the Borei in front of the tent, and they seemed to be arguing. One man was holding a small notebook and writing feverishly in it; another was collecting money from the rest. A bet of some sort? Most likely.

"Come inside, Lord Count." Junner beckoned with all the charm of an expert storyteller.

Bart entered and had to blink a few times until his daylight blindness evaporated. He had expected to find the tent crammed with loot and junk. Instead, it was empty save for a single chair and a table with breakfast leftovers on it. In the chair, though, there was a man, hands bound behind his back, legs tied to the chair legs, and weighted with a chain, his head covered with a black bag.

"Remember two years ago, during the Balance, how that Athesian empress kidnapped the Parusite heir right under his nose? That was brilliant, you have to admit. Well, we thought we ought to try something similar. So there you go, Lord Count, a present for you." He approached the bound man and removed the head bag with a flourish.

Bart frowned. He did not recognize this…prisoner. It was a fairly nondescript face, made even plainer by a solid dose of beating. The man's nose seemed to have been broken, and he had livid spots under his eyes. *Well, he could be a Kataji soldier,* Bart thought. *Who then?*

Junner chuckled, reading his confusion and anticipation. "We couldn't find the Kataji general. No, that was too much of a task. But we managed to nab the chieftain of the Lomyedi tribe. Their clan is closely allied with the Kataji. This is their leader, Semgad."

Bart remained standing near the entrance, his head spinning. "Your men sneaked into Somar? You managed to capture this man alive, amid all that chaos and killing?"

Junner nodded. "Chaos is our friend." He chuckled again.

"And now?" Bart asked. He was talking to a Borei. Nothing was free. The frenetic chatter outside only strengthened his suspicion.

"A gift for you, Lord Count. We heard how your lords and ladies grumble about us being useless, so we thought to prove our worth. For you. For free."

Bart smiled. "Nothing is free, my friend."

Junner hissed. "Very good, Lord Count. You are learning."

Bart realized something else. He pointed behind him. "That bet. It has to do with this prisoner."

The mahout clapped his hands. "In a year's time, you could become a Borei. Honest, Lord Count, you are such a quick learner. So…what do you want to do with the captive?"

They must be betting what my next action will be, he thought. *Sneaky bastards.* "You have interrogated him, I am certain?"

A nod.

"And you have gleaned all of the valuable information this man could offer you."

Nod.

"So now you want to see what I'm going to do."

Junner was waiting, his mouth open.

What now? Do I ransom this man back? Kill him? Torture him?

Bart stepped closer. "Are you Semgad, the chieftain of… the Lomyedi tribe?"

The tied man worked his jaw and gobbed a wad of red spit. It landed impotently between his feet. "Fuck yourself," he lisped, his lips torn and swollen.

"On my honor, Lord Count, he is," Junner supplied. "We have captured four of his men, too, and killed half a dozen during our risky endeavor. So what are you going to do now?"

Bart looked at his Borei friend. "I assume you have a suggestion."

Junner closed his eyes and let out a small chirp of victory. "I knew I could count on you, Lord Count." He approached the trussed nomad and yanked him to his feet, holding him by his right elbow. Then, he pushed him out of the tent, the large chain dragging. The prisoner seemed to be in a great deal of pain, and he limped stiffly.

Outside, the crowd of mercenaries went silent in an instant, all eyes on Junner, his captive, and Bart, who was wondering how much money this little game was going to cost him. But he would indulge the Borei. After all, it was his one genuinely fun moment this morning.

He was already contemplating the consequences of Junner's raid. The nomads might get spooked, realizing their enemy could get into the city and abduct their officers and chieftains with impunity. In turn, this could trigger panic and a quick defeat, or make them do something rash, unpredictable, and extremely costly for the Eracians.

For instance, they might decide to finish off their hostages.

But it was too late for any regret. Bart was not going to stop. Even with half his army destroyed, he intended to keep on fighting until Somar was freed or every Eracian warrior died trying. Negotiations were out of the question. Anything less than a total defeat of the nomad menace was simply not acceptable.

So he knew what he had to do. He would not trade Semgad back. He had no interest in keeping him as a prisoner. At this point in the war, the Lomyedi chieftain was just another soon-to-be corpse.

"Comrades, Lord Count has chosen to hear *my* idea," Junner announced, to the obvious dismay of the other warriors. A handful of bags quickly switched hands. Bart realized he had just secured the payment for the previous night's escapade. Junner looked at him. "We have this game. We play it with respectable enemies once they fall into our hands while still alive. Do you consider these nomads to be a respectable foe?"

Bart wondered what he felt toward the Kataji and the other clans. Resentment? Hatred? A definite dose of respect for their tenacious bravery and cunning. He had to admit that much. "Yes."

Junner raised a hand and pointed at the man with the ledger. He mumbled something in his tongue, but it obviously meant more money for the mahout. "The game is called the Cinnamon Challenge," the Borei said in Continental. All around, deft hands began producing all sorts of items, a tiny bag with a powerful smell of the expensive spice, a small water clock, a wooden spoon. "If the player can swallow an entire spoon of the spice powder before the water runs out, and survive it, we let him go. Simple, no? We play, Lord Count? Do you wanna bet?"

Bart glanced at the battered Lomyedi. He did not seem so defiant right now. "Continue."

The mercenaries pushed the man to his knees and spread a white napkin before him. Then, carefully, they laid out a large, brimming wooden spoon of the copper-colored spice. It was worth its weight in gold, Bart knew, and to use it this way meant either genuine regard for the player—or utmost derision. He was not really sure what the Borei had in mind. Still, he was not really sure what was so dangerous or enticing about this game.

"What happens when one eats the powder?"

Junner snapped his fingers. "The powder is very, very fine. So even the tiniest amount of breathing gets it in your nose. And then you begin to sneeze and cough and retch, and then it gets into your lungs, and they bleed. Quite entertaining to watch."

I see, he thought. "Go ahead."

Semgad was looking genuinely afraid now. "I do this, you let me go?"

Bart ignored the shoving and pushing around him, the mercenaries placing their last bets. "Yes."

Junner said something in the Borei, and one of the soldiers removed a pin stoppering a metal bowl floating in a somewhat larger pan. Immediately, the bowl began filling, threatening to sink. The nomad prisoner exhaled carefully, a shuddering breath of kicked-in ribs, and with a trembling hand reached for the spoon.

"If you spill, we add more," Junner warned.

Later, Bart found time to entertain his court, discussing the future of the realm with people who wanted to see him removed. He let them enjoy their false sense of superiority, and then, he gently set Sonya's mother on them.

He found more time for his uncle and told him nothing of the grisly execution he had watched earlier, with the nomad vomiting blood until even his muscles grew too tired to spasm, and he choked on his own bile. Junner offered him a large bag of gold and silver, his share of the game, but he refused. He wasn't sure if he felt disgusted by the ordeal, but it just did not feel right.

Finally, he tumbled Adam on his knees, making stupid faces that children supposedly loved, although the baby did not respond that much. His fault, Constance claimed, because children took time bonding with their parents. He did his fatherly part in the confines of her cabin so no one would witness his humiliation. Still, his mistress was pleased, and he got an autumn present from her, too, after so many months of solitude. He was becoming the monarch of the realm, he realized. Slowly, carefully, he was building the reality for after the war. It still wasn't won, but somehow, he knew, Eracia would win. The realm might get obliterated by this northern army, but he would free Somar, and he would free Sonya.

Just days ago, he had dreaded the moment. But no longer. He had decided what he must do.

CHAPTER 30

Disappointment. That was how Jarman summarized his time in the realms. He had expected Adam's children to bring salvation to the land, to defeat the White Witch. Instead, they had both failed him. James had died, and Amalia turned out to be a frightened, confused young woman, not quite sure how to handle defeat.

He most certainly had not predicted a thin, unassuming lad would arrive one day in Ecol, carrying a bloodstaff. That was beyond even his dreams. He still wondered where Ewan fit in the bigger scheme of things, and the notion frightened him. After years spent at the temple, where all things had precise logic, the uncertainty of this war worried him. He was not quite sure how to interpret the recent events, and he was loath to make any decision, because it might turn out to be a grave mistake. Apparently, revenge was a double-edged blade.

In a situation like this, there was only one way to proceed.

Using the razor-sharp methodologies hammered out by Armin Wan'Der Markssin.

There is always a motive, his father would say. *And every motive stems from a need. If you can figure out the need, you will figure out the crime.*

That was easier said than done, but he was trying his best. He realized he would not solve the puzzle of Adam's offspring by focusing on the emperor's death, nor the rash decision of his daughter to challenge all the realms. Her loss of the bloodstaff was intriguing, but not peculiar. Calemore would surely want his magical weapon back. How it had gotten into Adam's hands in the first place...that was too much.

So the White Witch had upset the balance of power in the realms and brought about the defeat of the young empress. Then, the Caytorean councillors had found and sponsored Adam's bastard as leverage against her aggressive diplomacy. Their plot had almost worked, but it was hard to beat the randomness of stray arrows in battle. Lords and peasants died as equals.

Now, there was the boy Ewan, and he was a great piece of confusion. Unrelated somehow, it seemed. And yet, he held the key to the victory of the people of the realms against Naum. Which made Jarman's plan of a great unity among the continental nations redundant. He did not like that. If this awful war was a tree, then Ewan had just pruned a giant branch off the crown. Or created his own sapling.

Jarman kept staring at his drawing, a piece of coal pressed between his fingers. No, Ewan came much later. So did Gavril. There were older, unresolved mysteries. He knew his father would never neglect any detail. Armin called it cause and effect.

When Lucas and he had first met James, the emperor had reacted with too much familiarity to their claim of magic. And then, when they had asked him to believe their story of an impeding doom, that dandy Caytorean Rob had intervened and helped convince him to listen to them.

There it was. Why would Calemore want Rob dead?

Amalia had met the witch, but not James. And yet, he had been rather receptive to the notion of an ancient enemy threatening the realms. Far too receptive, now that Jarman had hindsight of the situation.

Months later, the Eybalen investor got assassinated with the bloodstaff.

Not James or Amalia. A seemingly unimportant adviser to the emperor. Why?

Jarman realized once he solved this piece, he would know the whole truth. But his best investigative skills had only left his fingers smudged in soot. Frustrated, he tore yet another piece of thin paper off the clerk's notebook and tossed it away. There was a small heap of intellectual failures lying crumpled behind him.

It all comes together, he thought. *But I lack the reasons. I lack the motive.*

His father would probably have figured it out long ago. Jarman's Anada education had left him well versed in spells, but he was a lousy explorer of the truth.

Jarman wished he had Lucas's pragmatic approach to life. The old, experienced wizard did not worry too much about all these uncertainties. He knew he could not control them, so he focused on the elements that he could. At the moment, he only worried that the protective shield around Amalia held, and that it would alert against human intruders, too. And there was the small matter of defeating the gigantic Naum army, which was still sitting maddeningly idle.

Was Calemore waiting for all the nations of the realms to consolidate their might before he attacked? Would that make his conquest swifter? After all, the larger the defender's forces, the easier they were to track down and destroy. Jarman was all too aware the witch had the second bloodstaff. He had used it once already.

His thoughts strayed to the Eybalen investor. Why had the witch murdered a wealthy member of the High Council? What did he matter? *Why* did he matter?

If Calemore had not bothered targeting either Amalia or James, it meant he considered them meaningless. True enough, James had died, and Adam's daughter was now a puppet in the hands of the Parusite ruler. For some reason, Jarman felt the witch would not bother with King Sergei either. For some reason, he felt the scrawny youth named Ewan was the champion of the realms.

That meant his mission was a complete failure.

Jarman wondered what would have happened if he hadn't bothered sailing for Caytor. Thinking more deeply, he was fairly certain he had breached the first rule of investigation. He had let his emotions steer him. He had lost objectivity. Now, events were unfolding in some bastardly manner, because of his meddling. In fact, he might be responsible for Rob's death. He had pushed James toward difficult truths, he had prodded him about magic and ancient weapons, and it was the councillor helping James along. What had Rob known to warrant his death?

There. That was the key to the victory against Calemore, he knew. But he had destroyed that possibility. Now, he had Ewan, and he was frightened to push the young man, because he might precipitate an untold disaster that he could not control.

Jarman rose, smoothed the wrinkles of his robes, and left the inn. He found Lucas in the backyard, talking to Ewan. The holy man, Gavril, was not there.

"Only human blood," the blue-faced wizard said.

Ewan nodded. "Yes." He pushed a bucket with his foot. It joined half a dozen other pails, each brimming with a syrupy maroon liquid that had the unmistakable texture of slowly congealing blood. "Cow, horse, sheep, goat, dog, cat, pigeon, pig." He shrugged.

"Jarman," Lucas said, turning.

The young man nodded in solemn greeting. Jarman had a feeling Ewan did not like him very much, not since the butchery of those Naum soldiers near Bassac.

"We were trying different types of blood to see if any could substitute for human sacrifice," Lucas explained. "It seems not."

Jarman leaned against a large barrel. It probably held winter cabbage. He glanced at the boy and his weapon of destruction. No story had ever had such an unlikely hero, he thought sourly. Jarman was almost too afraid to contemplate dissecting this young man's past. He was troubled by his eyes, troubled by what he might discover. Ewan had the countenance of someone just coming to terms with his body and voice, but he had the behavior of an old, tormented being who had witnessed too much pain and suffering.

Perhaps this war was too big for him. Maybe he should just listen to Lucas. They could pack and leave, head back to Sirtai, leave the crazy people of the realms to their gods and wars, let them resolve their ancient feuds on their own. Sirtai would survive anyway, he figured. Just like it had in the first war so long ago.

"Are you planning an attack against the Naum forces?" he asked.

Ewan looked at him coolly, almost derisively. "We are defending ourselves, are we not? So we will defend ourselves."

Jarman wanted to urge the boy to commit himself. But it was so easy goading someone else to do the killing when you didn't have to do it yourself. He kept his mouth shut. He might have mastered the basics of communication that passed for civic behavior among these people, he knew, but he still could not comprehend their sense of honor and guilt. The continental nations didn't believe in right or wrong, he realized. They believed in justice, no matter how they defined it.

No, he must not push this lad. That would truly kill his investigation.

Lucas realized Jarman wanted to talk to him. "Thank you for your time," he said to the youth.

Ewan nodded at the older wizard and walked around the back stall of the stable. Once alone, Jarman finally spoke his mind. "How do you measure a man's worth? Is it his word?"

Lucas's face was unreadable, as usual. He beckoned Jarman to follow him and led out of the backyard, the same way Ewan had gone. They greeted the handful of sentries casually and wove their way out of the busy square and into a side alley. The sky above was racing them, as if someone was pulling on a carpet of puffy white and lead and pale blue.

Ecol was so crowded, it was impossible to breathe. With all of the refugee population of northern Athesia converging on the town, with the addition of Gavril's pilgrims, Sasha's troops, and the Parusite reinforcements trickling from the south, Ecol was bursting. Any stretch of dry land of flat cobbles was good enough to pitch a tent. There were grubby, naked children everywhere, playing in the gutters, chasing rats.

Lucas led, his massive, forbidding presence clearing the path better than a file of shock cavalry. Jarman trailed, all too aware his question remained unanswered.

It wasn't long before they left the town's center, and it became easier to inhale. Still, the fields around Ecol were just as busy, but at least you did not have the buildings hugging you, smothering you. The old manor house was almost finished, and hopefully, Lucas's and his assistance would be valued enough to relocate them from the greasy inn. On the surface, everyone behaved as if the world was just lazily inching toward rain and wind. No one seemed to care it might all end in a massive surge of Naum forces.

Soldiers had little to do except to gamble and associate, men on one side, women on the other, a gulf of curiosity and old animosity yawning between them. The Borei were there, and all the wild-eyed pilgrims, and the elite troops of the Parusite nobility, drawn over from their secluded camp by simple human curiosity. The strained relations between different factions had thawed a little since the Autumn Festival. The end of the world had color and style, for sure.

Lucas kept walking, his stride long and efficient. He did not look back. Jarman got distracted by the figure of a fairly busty servant woman returning to her camp, but there was no time for that. He followed his friend and mentor.

Finally, the tattooed wizard stopped near the mining camp. The din was impressive. A thousand smithies growled and rang and hissed. The air stank of burnt metal and wood. You could hear men cursing as they mauled iron against anvil; you could hear the miners gasping in relief as they left the dark, hot pits and brought a fresh load of ore to the brisk autumn midday.

"You think supporting Amalia is a mistake," Lucas said, insightful, candid, brutal.

"I promised to help her. I convinced her to give up her father's empire...for what? So all these people can die by an ancient weapon they cannot see or hear?"

Lucas was silent for another long moment. "You made the best decision given the facts and knowledge you had at that time."

"Did I?" Jarman really wondered. Had he been blinded by his desire to avenge his third mother? "We are protecting

Amalia with our magic. Soon enough, we will start killing people using our skill. To what end?"

"This war will not be won by the bloodstaff. The fact the
nations of the realms fight together is more important. It is
how it should be. You know that."

That gave him a pause. "Is it?"

Lucas made a slow, deliberate nod. "Yes, it is."

Jarman sighed. "How can you be so certain, friend?"

"I share the same doubts as you. However, I choose to respond in a different manner. You asked me how you measure a
person's worth. This is how you measure it."

Jarman wondered if he deserved his first tattoo. Lucas had
not mentioned anything yet. "I wish I had your courage."

Lucas started walking again. "What is courage? Stick with
your decisions, no matter what? Ignore reality? Adapt? Choose
the best or the worst alternative once you realize your plan is
not panning out as you expected? Keep your promises?"

"I don't know," Jarman admitted.

"Courage is being willing to live with the consequences
of whatever you decide. So tell me, Jarman, are you willing to
accept the outcome of this war, whatever it may be? We have
come here to avenge your third mother. The same reason I was
bonded as your life slave all those years ago. You are following your instincts, your experience, your desire maybe. Perhaps
Amalia is not the brave leader you wish her to be. Neither was
her dead half brother. This peace is not the teary-eyed union
between respected rivals, but a bitter necessity among old enemies, none of which know the full extent of the truth. So
your courage, Jarman, is to understand you do not control the
situation. Are you still willing to keep on fighting? This goes
against everything the Anada have taught you. What are you
going to do now?"

Jarman stopped walking. His friend moved on awhile longer; then he turned and faced him, his blue face radiating brutal honesty. Did he want to be a part of this ugly reality? No. Was he going to give up? No. If he left now, he could not live with himself.

Lack of courage is also courage, no? he mused.

"We are staying," he announced. "What now?"

Lucas approached him. "We minimize the elements we cannot control."

Jarman looked around him. He had to examine the situation from the perspective of their foe, not his own. Calemore considered the humans insignificant, it seemed. He was not worried about kings and emperors. But he had come forth to assassinate a young Caytorean.

Then, there was that half Sirtai in Amalia's camp.

"Why would the White Witch kill Rob?" he spoke loudly.

Lucas shrugged. "I do not know. Let's find out."

They walked back into the chaos.

CHAPTER 31

"Why have we stopped?" Stephan complained.

"Wait here, sir," Bader said and stepped out of the carriage into a world painted golden, russet, and dying green.

Stephan slumped against the padded seat. Best silk, best feathers, but after so many weeks warming his backside against the soft, supple fabric, the texture chafed like a leper's cheek. He had traveled halfway across Caytor, and with every mile, the journey got uglier. Oh, the nature turned pretty with the shortening of the days, but the news coming from the northwest was grim.

On his last travel through the realm, he had rested in one of Goden's fairly cozy lodges. Not this time. The little place had become a ghost town, with all its inns closed. Too little trade, the townsfolk complained, which meant he had been forced to evict half a dozen families to lodge his considerable entourage. He had paid the villagers, and they had been glad to accept the coin, but their faces had been sour and full of rancor as they herded their children into a barn.

Then, the village of Pasey had offered equally lukewarm hospitality. The freight station outside the village stood abandoned. No known reason, no sign of a plague or banditry, no fires. They found the stables empty, without even a single bale of hay. Strange, because the High Council paid for those so that couriers and messengers could have a place to spend the night or change their horses. The phenomenon worried Stephan because it had occurred less than a day away from Pain Daye. Did it mean something bad had befallen the mansion and its inhabitants? Or had Sebastian lost all power and control of the area?

Bader returned, looking cryptic with his one healthy eye. "Refugees clogging the road, sir."

Refugees? Stephan thought. He stepped out, ants tingling in his arse.

His small private army was waiting for the surge of humans to step off the gravel and let them pass, but there were just too many people, and they were milling. Stephan shielded his eyes against the silver glare of a clouded afternoon, the sun hiding somewhere to the west.

Entire families were migrating away from Pain Daye, carrying what little possessions they had on their shoulders, dragging filthy children behind. Most of the boys and girls had a rope round their waists so they wouldn't get lost. A few thin-ribbed dogs were slinking round the group.

"What do you wanna do, sir?" Bader asked. Some of the riders were getting impatient, their horses frisky, neighing, stomping their hooves. One of the men was donning his iron-padded gloves, as if he expected to get his hands bloody.

"Ask questions," Stephan said. He reached out and grabbed the sleeve of an old man walking nearby. "What is going on?"

The fellow touched his straw hat in a respectable greeting. "Fleein' the war, milord."

"What war?" Stephan asked, but the grubby tide swept the man away.

"Ask questions. No violence," he told Bader. The mercenary melted into the mass.

Stephan waited, and the flow just would not end. Bader returned soon thereafter, shrugging. "Just nonsense, sir. Some army got their villages burned. They don't know who."

This won't work, Stephan figured. He stuck his head through the carriage window. His clerk, Nudd looked up. "Get a bag of coppers, quickly. And get out."

Confused, the clerk stepped out.

"Get up there, onto the roof."

Frowning, Nudd obeyed.

Once his aide was standing on the carriage, in plain view of all the refugees, Stephan clapped his hands. "A copper and free bread for those who answer questions!"

Soon enough, he was under siege, and his men had to draw weapons to keep the hungry, almost riotous crowd at bay. Mouths started gibbering and shouting, answering questions that had not even been asked. But Nudd somehow managed, pointing, and Bader and his men flicked coins and some of the hard bread they had in their baggage. They would reach Pain Daye soon anyway, and they could get fresh food there.

I hope, Stephan thought.

When some of the refugees got too pushy, they got slapped or shoved away, and when a grown man tried to pry a loaf from a screaming girl's hands, Bader waded into the seething mass and broke his nose. No one tried to steal bread or coin after that.

Soon enough, they were out of currency and pastry, and the refugee train moved down the road, but Stephan had heard enough to feel worried. Lord Sebastian, as they called him, would not permit them to stay. He had even expelled some of the last of Amalia's folk, which gave him some credulity, and instilled a sense of fairness among them, they said. There was a huge army coming from the north, burning, pillaging, killing everyone. War was at their doorstep, and they had to flee to save their souls. It was the end of the world.

A purple evening greeted them at the doorstep to the highly protected manor house. The many walls hugged the path left and right, with torches burning in alcoves at head height so they illuminated anyone approaching the well-armed guards on the parapets and in the sentry towers above. Stephan could see their silhouettes against the canvas of darkening colors, and he felt there were just too many guards and patrols present.

Guild Master Sebastian and a respectable regiment of help was waiting for them in the front yard. The servants carried lamps, and their faces looked lurid. Still more soldiers with crossbows and wickedly sharp spears stood everywhere around.

"A pleasant, if unannounced, surprise," Sebastian greeted.

Stephan shook hands with the man, wondering how much he should disclose right away. He chose nothing. "It's been a long and hard journey," he offered in return. "I hope you can accommodate my retinue."

Sebastian pretended to look over his shoulder and appraise the train of horses, wagons, and armed men. "We will manage."

Several hours later, he was having dinner with the guild master. The two of them sat alone behind a table. Stephan thought the décor to be too somber, and it was too dark. But the food was quite pleasant, especially after the last few days of cold scarcity.

"Refugees, in central Caytor?" Stephan remarked. Not the best way to start a conversation, he figured, but probably the safest. He needed to hear more from the guild master before he prodded him about Lady Rheanna.

However, the other man did not seem interested in easing up the talk. "The cities of Marlheim, Faldset, and Keybough seem to have been lost. The entire north of our realm is under invasion by some terrible, inconceivable army coming from beyond our borders." He pointed dramatically. "From farther north."

"I thought there was only an endless stretch of grassland there," Stephan said almost childishly.

Sebastian grimaced. "Well, apparently, there is an end to the prairie, and it is home to many hundreds of thousands of people." His face dropped its sarcastic mask, and he leaned closer, looking worried. "Stephan, the common people like to exaggerate. At first, I thought this was some ploy, maybe by Amalia, to destabilize the realm. Then, I thought these people had lost their homes in a natural disaster, and were maybe hoping the council would offer them help and protection, so they tried to paint their plight in some way we could sympathize. But dear councillor, I have had credible reports from army scouts. There's some huge force moving against us, and it's only days away. If you'd arrived a few days later, you might have found the mansion abandoned."

Days away? Stephan swallowed.

This changed everything.

"You are certain?" he said.

Sebastian drank from his cup, maybe too eagerly. "I only have bad news for you, Councillor."

Stephan forced himself to cut into the thin, bleeding slice of veal, to chew on the delicious meat. He nibbled on roasted asparagus, pretending this was just a polite evening meeting between two affluent business partners.

"Empress Amalia has made peace with the Parusites," the guild master added almost casually.

Stephan coughed into his wine. What? The one thing he had tried to prevent had happened. He was too late. All his plans had been spoiled. Ruined.

Now *that* changed everything.

Sebastian was watching him carefully, his eyes slightly glazed in the weak light. "She has accepted the rule of King Sergei. Athesia is now officially a vassal state of the Parusite realm, under its protection. Amalia will be restored to her rule as a governess—or something." He waved his hand.

That silly, stubborn girl had signed peace with her enemy? After having held half the Eracian court and half the High Council captive for so many months? After destroying eighteen years of quiet in the realms? After losing Roalas to the Parusite forces? Now she would bend knee?

Incredible.

Sebastian continued, "As you can imagine, I am no longer really needed. I still need to figure out what I ought to do. It was young James who spared my life from the likes of you, and now the boy is dead, so that leaves me without my employer and savior. I owe nothing to Amalia. Especially not now that she's buried her tongue between Sergei's butt cheeks."

The guild master poured himself more wine. The red brimmed over and spilled. "But then, I was never one to betray my business partners, never one to back out of a contract, unlike most of you fellows. So what am I going to do? Become a traitor to Caytor by following this girl? Half the forces left at the mansion have already deserted, gone back to being private armies in the big cities, or who knows what. Well, Amalia is not going to like me now that I have sent her the rest of her folk, but now there's peace in Athesia, and they can go back to their homes. No need to toll the Caytorean economy over some refugees who are no longer refugees. And we have enough of our own. Too many. I wouldn't let them stay, you know. If this army comes here, I don't want to be the one to condemn thousands of innocents to their deaths."

Stephan listened, his mood darkening. Son of a bitch. Everything that could go wrong had gone wrong. Not just wrong. It had knifed the humiliated, battered good and left it bleeding to death by the side of the road.

"Well, I guess the question of your loyalty is not that difficult to answer," he said.

"What do you mean, Councillor?"

Stephan tried to force a smile onto his lips. "You have committed yourself to Emperor James. And now that he is dead, to his widow, Lady Rheanna."

Sebastian did not speak for a while, but Stephan could hear him drinking, the soft gurgle of his throat bobbing with gulps. "That is an interesting assumption. I wonder why you said that."

"I do not blame you," Stephan added, maybe a bit too quickly. "I believe we share the same goal. We are both Caytorean patriots. We want the best for our realm, for our people. We want to uphold the promise of thriving commerce and great cooperation between ourselves and Athesia."

The guild master snorted. "King Sergei can offer us all that, easily."

Stephan rubbed his smooth, freshly shaved cheeks. "In that case, make ourselves rich. Well, richer." He put his own cup down with a loud thud. "Now, tell me the truth. Where is Lady Rheanna? And where do you stand in this mess?"

Stephan was tired. He wanted nothing more than to sleep in a soft, large bed. Well, maybe have his privates fondled by a red-haired girl with big, pearly teeth. But he was riding a horse, jostling his kidneys, Bader and Sebastian at his side, four more cowled, armed men behind them, two of them his.

I heard Sebastian was taken to an empty field in similar circumstances. Otis and Melville expected James to get him killed. Instead, he pardoned the fool, spoiled their plans. Now, he is taking me somewhere, and I might find myself on my knees, bound and begging for my life.

That was unlikely, he reasoned. First, he had two soldiers to protect him. Second, Lord Malcolm would not send him on a suicide mission. Which meant Rheanna was probably somewhere in the vicinity of the mansion, whole and safe and scheming. Sebastian was an ally, most likely.

Autumn's bite was still weak, and the wind was only refreshing rather than chilling. The narrow path they followed was overgrown with weeds, and the thorny bushes snagged at their horses' shanks. The animals did not like it, and soon, they slowed down. They were forced to continue on foot.

The moon showed its face only now and then between the clouds, but it gave off enough light to see the world. Stephan guessed they were approaching an old farmstead. He heard a lone frog gargle, there was the sound of running water, a piss trickle really, and then, only the wind, humming in a dozen voices.

"I knew I could not act publicly," Sebastian spoke, his tone hushed. People tended to respect the night for some reason. "Once I received word from Warlord Xavier about James's death, I was faced with a very difficult choice. Rebel? How could I?" He spread his hands. "I was surrounded by his men, and they were loyal to him. If I had tried to uphold my own belief, I would have probably ended up dead. So I greeted Lady Rheanna with a smile, I had her locked up, and then told her of my plan. She was mistrustful at first, but then she got convinced it was not a plot to get her heroically killed."

"What did she promise you?" Stephan pressed.

It was too dark to see the man's face. "Control of all the guilds in Eybalen."

Fair enough. A decent price to test one's loyalty. "Why not Amalia?"

Sebastian crunched weeds with his boots. "There's something about that girl I do not like. No backbone. No integrity. And I was right. Took her just one or two pitched battles against the Parusites to tuck her tail and yield. You can imagine what happened at the estate once the soldiers heard about that. I almost had bloodshed on my hands. Separated the Athesians and Caytoreans quickly, tried to pacify them with gold and mostly empty promises."

Not bad, Stephan thought. The guild master had been busy, and quite successfully. Well, his little provisional rule of Pain Daye was coming apart, but what with the threat of this invading army, and the alliance between Amalia and Sergei, it did not really matter. They both understood. They had to focus on helping Lady Rheanna.

"I have notified her of your arrival," Sebastian said. "She agreed to meet with you. Alone."

Stephan nodded. He waited patiently while one of the guild master's cronies patted him up and down, searching for hidden knives. "Watch my berries," he snapped as the man's gloved hand came too close.

"Clean," the mercenary growled.

"Good luck, Steph," Sebastian hissed.

Holding a small lamp that dripped light like honey, he tiptoed over uneven earth and pushed the door to a low shed. Inside, a small group of armed men was waiting for him, several crossbows aimed at his head. The men had woolen masks concealing their faces so he would not know who they were. Clever.

One of them, wearing a simple black tunic, jabbed his finger toward another door. Stephan nodded and walked over. The door did not open. He waited until he heard a bolt slide back in its groove, and the door creaked to expose a black, narrow passage. There was an odd smell coming from inside, sort of female perfume and mold.

He found Lady Rheanna seated on a comfortable sofa, reading a book under the light of several expensive silver lamps. There was a black curtain hiding a small window behind her. A servant was pouring a second glass of wine, for him, he presumed, and another masked guard waited in the corner of the chamber, his sword drawn.

"Welcome, Councillor," she greeted.

"Good evening, my lady," he said in return. Or was it early morning now?

She stood up, and he was instantly reminded of her luscious appeal. The upheaval of recent months had not marred her beauty in any way. Lady Rheanna looked well fed and rested, serene, composed, in charge of the situation.

"I hope you will not begrudge my hospitality," she said, sounding rather amused. "Sit down."

There was a simple chair for him. He sat down, all too aware of the soldier with the unsheathed blade standing just behind him. The servant handed him the glass of wine. He had drunk too much already, he figured, so he sipped politely, not expecting to be poisoned. Hoping.

"Thank you for your time," he began.

"My father notified me of your pending arrival," she said. "This is the only reason why you are here. Tell me, *why* are you here?"

Stephan put the glass down. "Well, I am not so sure anymore. When I left Eybalen, I came here to try to help you assert your legitimate place as the empress of Athesia, foil any attempt by Amalia to make peace with Parus, and work toward a bright, prosperous future for Caytor, as promised by your late husband. Now, things have changed."

She nodded. "Yes, they have. So, I will ask again, why are you here?"

"I presume your claim to the Athesian throne is no longer relevant? And that we ought to focus on fighting this new threat in the north?" He was waiting for some kind of response from her, but her face betrayed no emotion.

"Wrong on both accounts, Councillor Stephan. My claim will remain as long as it can serve a purpose in any future negotiations with Parus. The only question is, will the High Council offer its full, unreserved backing? Then, regarding this army invading our realm, I am not a military strategist. There is little I can do about it."

He was taken aback. Well, it had been a long time since he had talked to Rheanna. He had forgotten how sharp she could be. *I should have kept that in mind after meeting her father.* Well, she needed him. She needed allies at the council.

"I would like to offer my help," he chirped miserably.

"Why do you think I need any help, including yours?"

"I have dealt with Empress Amalia before," he suggested.

"Amalia is irrelevant now. We must focus on King Sergei." Lady Rheanna almost looked disappointed in him. He did not dare raise any other, more delicate topic. Fuck, he was tired, he wanted to sleep, he had had too much wine, and he had been given no chance to ponder over all these ugly developments infecting his realm. But to back down now would mean admitting defeat.

I need a miracle, he thought.

But his mind would not offer any.

"Is that all, Councillor? You came all the way from Eybalen for this?"

"Please." She was hiding in some smelly barn, and yet, it was he who felt miserable. *You are doing it wrong,* he thought inanely and, in his head, pictured two young male dogs trying to outhump one another.

Lady Rheanna waited. If she were bluffing, she concealed her desperation perfectly. Then, almost too casually, she picked up her book. Stephan tried not to stare at her breasts, molded under that tight dress. He tried to fire up wisdom inside his brain, tried to think of some business brilliance that would save him an embarrassing failure and a long ride home.

Start at the end, he reasoned desperately. *What do I want? How do I get it? What gets me the best advantage in this situation? What has changed in the last years and worked? What hasn't?*

He had always known the answer, really. In the past two decades, Caytor had seen itself humiliated by the Feorans, then by Adam, then more recently by the Oth Danesh, and now finally by Parus proper. Trade had always been the lifeblood of the council, and it had striven to maximize its profits. That was all that mattered, and the rest was just politics. His own position and influence had not changed much in that time, not before, not during, and not even after his captivity. His ascent was impervious to the mundane events, it seemed, and it didn't care much for human kings and emperors, for their rise and fall. He had earned a few coins betting with his friends, but not much more than that.

All of that was just the usual share of Caytorean economy.

Now, there was a new, unexpected element, and it was the army from the north.

"I presume a large number of councillors has fled from the razed northern cities?"

Rheanna flicked her delicate wrists. "Dozens. Master Sebastian is entertaining them in the mansion."

Stephan rose from his miserable chair. "They will have left all of their assets behind, save maybe some personal belongings. But if they have any large funds, they must be kept in banks, like yours, so they will be at the mercy of their creditors and people like…your father. I presume these men and women will need strong financing to get back on their feet. They will need willing sponsors who will take the risk of supporting destitute councillors, left without their businesses, their farms and workshops, and their manpower."

Lady Rheanna smacked her lips softly. "I see."

"This is a great opportunity for those who seek to improve their standing with the council. I believe my journey to Pain Daye has not been in vain, my lady. With your money and my charm and wit, we could change the landscape of Caytor in the coming years. We will leave the matter of combat to those who understand it, of course."

"Then it's just the matter of influence to you, Councillor?"

Stephan inclined his head. He had everything, really. There was little else he could want. "My initial plans were somewhat different." He stepped closer, and he could smell her. She wafted a pleasant scent, as if she did not spend her days inside a tiny barn. Maybe she did take morning strolls, pretending to be a farm maid.

Rheanna seemed slightly uncomfortable with him looming above her, so she stood up, her lithe body emanating warm energy that enticed his libido. "If I grasp your plan correctly, I will have gone from being the prospective empress to a merciless leech, doing my best to make a handful of councillors left without a home become forever indebted to you. In turn, you will do your best to make me popular with the High Council."

"More or less," he agreed. *I had bigger plans, but Amalia and some unstoppable army have spoiled it for me. Still, I'm not one to weep over sour milk.* "Meanwhile, we will ask King Sergei for military assistance. From what little I have heard, our private armies cannot stand up to this threat. We will ask him for help, and you will kindly drop any claim to Athesia. We might iron out a few favorable trade deals."

I will be the architect of future peace and economy for Caytor, he thought, mind hopping into the distant future like a wild rabbit. *We might not be a society of one ruler, but there's no reason why the council ought not to favor one man more than all the others.*

Not what he had intended, not at all. Not in the least. A total disaster. And yet, this might be the best opportunity for his realm in a long time. For the moment, he did not want to think what might happen when the northern force swept farther south. They would have to flee Pain Daye with the rest of them, but the road to Eybalen was long. Hopefully long enough to forge lucrative business deals that his destitute partners would not be able to refuse.

"I believe you can come out of your hiding, my lady," he said. "The council is split on what it should do, but the latest developments will convince them of our common goal. You are a valuable asset, and you will help me restore peace and honor to our land."

She smiled. "Your delusion is quite commendable, Councillor, but it is about the best thing we have right now."

"So you agree?" Stephan probed gingerly.

Rheanna extended her hand. "Yes, Councillor." Her composure cracked a tiny bit. She might not be desperate, but she was close. "I will accept your offer."

He wanted to know what kind of thoughts whirled inside her pretty head, but it did not matter now. He clasped her soft fingers, savoring the touch. *I must be mad,* he figured. *There is some giant fucking army coming to destroy the realm, and I relish fine talk and the dreams of humiliating bankrupted partners even more. Ah, the small delights in life.*

When he left the barn, it was dawn already. He felt mildly nauseated, as if he had drowned in cheap wine. But it did not matter. He had a lot of work to do. Make sure Lady Rheanna was escorted safely back to the capital. Bring all those other councillors along and start enslaving their souls. For the first time in so many years, he had a vision, a clear vision of unity in the council. The realm was in much greater peril than ever before, but this was the precise moment to prove he could succeed where so many others had failed. To restore Caytorean pride.

Admittedly, it would begin with a few lows. He was going to beg the Parusite king for help. He was not really sure there would be any Caytor left come the next autumn. But it did not really matter. He had found Lady Rheanna when so many others had failed. He had secured her cooperation. As a woman who had tamed Adam's son, she was a great catch. One day, he might even get her into his bed. There would be time for that.

Going back to see Guild Master Sebastian, he started formulating the letter for King Sergei, telling him that the idea of a new empress in Athesia had died earlier that night. He hoped the man would be smart enough to grasp the hint.

CHAPTER 32

S he could see the Eracian flags just underneath her window. Kogan's Park teemed with her fellow countrymen, moving in tight ranks. Most of the trees had been cut down or burnt. Still the sight brought a tear to her eye. It was so touching, so beautiful.

Sonya would stand for hours watching the battle unfold. Every day, it ended with the Kataji still holding the palace. But every day, Bart's men got that much closer. Inch by inch, they retook the lost alleys and houses. Sometimes they razed them to the ground, sometimes they torched them, but they would not let the nomad scum hold them.

A fresh battalion of Eracians was marching toward the Alley of Kings. On the scorched rooftop of Lothar's Theater, a handful of archers was goat footing from one end of the building to the other, trying to get within range so they could rain death on the tribesmen still holding the far end of the large palace square. It was almost impossible to see the stonework underneath the thick layer of dead bodies, broken carts, and just random debris.

Farther away, Eracian engineers were busy trying to rebuild a bridge over the Kerabon so they could cross to the still-unconquered part of the city. There was a strong pocket in the northeastern sector, and it prevented the brave soldiers of the realm from converging on the palace and freeing her. She could see tiny boats floating on the slow-moving arm of the river, and what looked like water lilies, but she knew those were bloated corpses of horses and men. Then, a gust of wind would shift the columns of black smoke from the fires, and it would block her view.

Bart, my love, I am waiting for you, she thought. She had been waiting for days now. Her husband's troops had advanced less than a quarter of a mile in the last week. At their current pace, it could take them many more weeks before they finally gained a foothold inside the palace. The waiting was agony. And now, after so long, she was starting to lose her composure.

Arrows filled the air, were loaded again, then more arrows. She did not know where the shooters were, but the hail never stopped. Muffled screams and curses floated up to her chamber and vibrated through the shit-stained windowpanes.

In the Street of Heroes, angry Eracians were hacking at the foundation of a large, respectable house, trying to bring it down. Must have been a horde of those filthy nomads lurked inside. But the ax blows did not seem to do much damage. Near the palace, most of the buildings had thick stone walls, and they did not burn or collapse that easily.

There, she saw one of Pacmad's men dash out of a window and hurl something down. A rock maybe. The attackers—no, defenders, these brave men were defending the realm—fired at him, but the shafts just bounced off the walls. On the nearby rooftop, which had gaping holes from trebuchet hits, several more Eracians were trying to get closer, but the other establishment was a whole story higher, and they did not have ladders or grapnel hooks.

That house must go down, Sonya goaded. She imagined its yellow bricks crashing down in a cloud of dust, choking the street corner. She willed it to collapse and bury those nomads alive.

One of the rooftop fighters slipped, slithered down the uneven tiles, kicked a few down on his comrades below. He managed to stop his deadly slide with his boots in the rain funnel. His fellows tossed him a rope, dragged him back up. They crawled forward. Tried to loop their rope round the chimney of the nomad-infested corner house. Missed. And kept missing. Each time, Sonya gritted her teeth, clenched her fists, urged them on.

They succeeded finally. By now, Sonya was sweating, exhausted, sharing their pain and danger. Tottering with armor on their bodies, the Eracians crossed over, a whole squad. Then, they just stood there, undecided. At the ground level, someone was gesturing wildly. Through the window? Get in there through the window? She wasn't sure, and neither were the soldiers.

Mercifully, it wasn't raining, so at least they could count on dry, sure footing. She took each death personally. It was her duty as the nation's queen.

The soldiers started peeling the roof tiles off, exposing the grid of old wooden rafters. They might get in there by cutting a hole in the ceiling of the upper floor, then sneaking inside and killing the barricaded mongrels. A few paces below, the Eracians aimed their crossbows at the windows, making sure the nomads could not fire at them. It was going to be a slow, costly take-over, she reasoned. If only the defenders could collapse that building somehow.

Something changed. The men on the roof stopped peeling the tiles. The men in the street began waving their hands. Back, back. Get back. She frowned. Why, after all that risk? Yes, she could see the anger in the posture of those soldiers. Grudgingly, they obeyed and aped back down the rope to the other house. She noticed they were no longer paying attention to the nomad shelter. They were watching in the direction of the Street of Heroes, following its curve.

A large body of Eracians was coming over. She frowned again. Their uniforms did not match. They looked too colorful, almost like the nomads.

Then, she saw it.

A huge gray thing, twice the height of a horse, with a flopping nose, like a snake, huge bleached teeth, and tattered ears that flapped nervously. There was a man seated on the massive round bulk of that monster, and she gaped stupidly at the sheer weight of its body, at its fat legs that stood thicker than a common man.

What was that? *Bart, darling, what kind of wild, wonderful tricks did you bring along?*

"My goodness," Fidelma gasped, plastering her ugly face against the window. Other women joined her, and soon, a whole roomful of whores was doing its best to look and sound shocked, surprised, and delighted. Stupid bitches.

"That is an unholy thing," Richelle said, not to be bested by her peers.

Unholy, Sonya thought. The whore wouldn't be able to tell a temple even if she was being raped inside one.

Whatever the gray beast was, the Eracians did not seem afraid of it. On the contrary, a ragged cheer exploded through their ranks. She burned to know more, but she was satisfied with what she saw. The nation's fathers and sons had that lumbering monster to their aid.

The beast shimmered. No, it was armor. *That thing is wearing armor!* she realized. Now that it was somewhat closer, she could clearly see large pads of steel on its head, the sides of its body, the front of its forelegs.

Ignoring the sluts around her, she watched. Several men brought a long length of chain and snaked it through the bottom-floor window and out of the nearby doorframe. She believed she saw one of the soldiers tie the other end to the huge gray animal. Yes, the monster edged backward, and the chain went taut. Like a crowd of ants, the Eracians skittered away.

She watched with elation as the yellow bricks began to crumble and fall, and the whole section of a wall crashed down. The door and the window were no more. Those nomads were frantic now, trying to fire at the monster, but the Eracians kept them pinned down. With a shield above their heads, several fighters dashed forward and tied the chain again. The monster pulled. More rubble toppled.

And then, the entire house groaned and fell forward. It slammed into the opposite side of the street, and a belch of thick dust rose in swirly billows, obscuring her view. She could hear the masonry wailing in agony, and the Eracians shouting, cheering.

"Amazing," Verina supplied, giving words to everyone's feelings. "We are victorious."

We are still here, slut, and you'd better keep your mouth shut, Sonya snarled.

The street was blocked now, but that monster quickly cleared the mess. Soon enough, the Eracians streamed through, joining their comrades for a bitter fight in the park. The remaining trees offered only glimpses of the combat, teasing, annoying.

The war was not over yet, Sonya thought. She had to keep her hopes down, be patient. She had to endure this madness for a little while longer. No matter that the Kataji had not

bothered to bring any food in the last two days, no matter that
the slop buckets were overflowing. The women were all filthy
and haggard and smelled like shit, but it was a small price to
pay for freedom. Luckily for all of them, Sonya had ordered
them to keep some of the daily rations aside well in advance,
knowing a situation like this might arise, and they all had a tiny
cup of water to wet their throats and some hard bread to settle
their stomachs, but no one bothered to thank her. No, they
took it all for granted, stupid whores.

Sonya would have lashed out at them, but she remembered Richelle's threat. No reason drawing attention to herself.
Not now. Besides, her throat was sore from too little drinking,
and she did not want to waste her strength on trifles. Standing
by the window was costly enough on her waning reserves, but
it was worth it. She had to witness the glory of her realm. It
was her duty.

The door to their chamber banged open with a kick. The
bitches startled. Sonya maintained her composure and just
turned around slowly, trying to wet her cracked lips.

One of the Kataji tribesmen was standing there, sweaty,
dirty, a drawn sword in his hand.

The end? Sonya wondered, feeling sad.

He tossed a water bag inside, and it sloshed noisily onto
the carpet, but luckily, it did not open and spill. "Drink quickly. And then get out here. Now."

No, not the end yet, she reasoned. You did not feed your victims before gutting them. As befitting her station, she walked
over, ignoring the click in her little toe, and lifted the skin. It
was quite heavy, and her arms trembled. She needed more than
old bread rinds to keep in shape, it seemed.

With selflessness that would have disgusted her only a
year back, she handed the bag around and drank last. By then,

the skin smelled of spit and unwashed mouths, but she drank eagerly, feeling a wisp of strength coursing back through her veins. Much better. One of the babies started crying. *Must be Richelle's,* she thought, swallowing the lukewarm water.

"Now, out. Get out here." The soldier waved them into the corridor.

Hesitantly, the women flocked out of the chamber. There was cold, pasty fear on their faces. All but Sonya. She was calm, composed, regal.

"What is happening?" one of the sluts blurted.

Sonya was convinced the Kataji would not bother responding, but he did. "General Pacmad is moving you out of this shit palace," the warrior growled.

Hesitantly, the women filed out of the smelly chamber into the corridor. They were all afraid, not quite sure what would happen now. Pacmad might decide to kill them all, because he was losing the city, and this could be his one last act of defiance. But Sonya did not share their sentiment. She still held the waterskin in her hands, a token of hope. And anguish. She realized her captivity was not over yet. She would have to endure this agony for some time longer. It was as if the chieftain was doing this on purpose to torment her.

They must be taking us north, into that last pocket of solid Kataji defense, Sonya wondered. They would probably exit the palace from the east, sneak around the park, and then head into the neighborhoods under enemy control. Bart's men were probably going to free the throne later that day. After seeing the gray monsters in action, she had no doubts.

"Faster," the nomad snapped. "Or I will smash your fuckin' teeth!" He led on without looking back. The women followed, because they were too terrified to do anything else.

Sonya found herself at the end of the column, with Baroness Richelle just ahead. Surprisingly, it was not her daughter making all that noise. The woman was glancing back now and then, as if she expected Sonya to radiate encouragement at her.

Just to imagine that whore had the nerve to threaten her, she thought. *Just look at her, frightened to her bones, all scared shitless now, but in a quiet corner of a room, she had no problem plotting and spitting poison.*

There were torches burning in the corridors, giving off foul smoke. Some of the women coughed too dramatically. Most of the nomad rubbish had been cleared away, probably to give more fighting space for the warriors. But apart from their little snotty line, there was no one else around. Sonya imagined she heard boots thudding against cold stone, the shuffle of leather, the groan of wood and the jangle of armor, men cursing in Kataji and Continental, the unmistakable clatter of violence. No screaming, though. Or maybe it was the chaos from before, still echoing in her temples.

The warrior led, not looking back. He did not walk too fast, but the women were just too scared, and they seemed lost. The familiar turns and twists of their prison suddenly looked alien, dark, and menacing, as if they hid death at every corner. Sonya was too annoyed, especially since she had to stare at Richelle's rump and that ugly girl bobbing her pasty-white head over the baroness's shoulder.

Wait…

This panicked retreat is an opportunity, she realized. The queen must be prepared to step in and defend her realm at all times. Every moment was a ripe chance for her to prove herself, to show her subjects that she cared for them. It was her duty. Now, as ever.

It did not matter that some armed soldier was leading them from one peril to another, taking them into more captivity, more pain, hunger, and suffering, and looming above all the others, a pointless, shameful death. Sonya had to transcend past her fear. She had to act, in the name of her people, for her people.

The gap between the front of the column and the rear was widening. Good. A deep stairwell to her right, leading toward the servants' area, a handsome flight of big, rough steps, more than a score of them fading into the murk of the unlit floor below. Good.

Sonya stumbled. "Oh, my foot," she wailed.

Richelle turned around. She flicked a quick glance toward the rest of the group, and the last woman was a good dozen paces away. The sound of a baby's crying drifted down the corridor, getting weaker and less annoying. "What is it?"

Sonya glanced up at the baroness. The woman had every right to be concerned. Unlike the other women, she stood to gain quite a lot once the war ended with the Eracian victory. But that would only happen if Sonya survived. So she had to show sympathy and care. Farther down the hallway, the other women just kept walking, not looking back, too selfish or just too terrified to pay attention. Good.

"My toe. Pacmad broke my toe, and it hurts now," Sonya whispered.

Richelle bent lower to inspect her leg. That stupid baby swiveled its giant head and stabbed a cold blue stare at Sonya.

"We need to go," the baroness said, sounding anxious, glancing toward the receding silhouettes of the other others.

Sonya put her foot down, straightened. Richelle was standing right in front of her, facing the other way, toward the deep stairwell. "Yes, we do," Sonya said and shoved with all her might, no longer faking her pain.

Wordlessly, the baroness tumbled. Just as Sonya had expected, her motherly instinct took over, and she cradled her child rather than tried to break her fall. She slammed into the edge of a step with a spectacular crunch, her head bouncing. Then her arse rose and tried to overtake the upper body, and soon, she was tumbling, all limbs flying, scraping against the rough wall mortar, thudding wetly as she rolled lower and lower, utterly without control.

Soon, she reached the bottom of the stairwell, and all was still. No one cried, not the mother, nor the baby. Sonya glanced into the murk. It was a little hard to tell, but she had seen enough dead bodies to know a wrong angle for a human neck. Baroness Richelle was dead. The baby, a lump of soft meat lying next to its mother, was also very still, but it did not really matter.

Sonya waited another moment. Then she screamed at the top of her lungs.

CHAPTER 33

Javor's death still haunted him.

Ewan had not recovered from the massacre, even though he knew it had saved countless lives. Without him, the combined force of Parus, Athesia, Borei, and the pilgrims would have had to fight the enemy hand to hand, with sword and spear. But the logic could not sweeten the bitter feeling in his throat.

Tanid tried to convince him that his use of the bloodstaff had checked the entire Naum army. The enemy camp was in panic and disarray, confused, frightened, too stunned to move. And every day they earned was a blessing. It gave them more time to prepare, to dig fresh trenches and hammer fresh stakes in front of them, train more recruits, stockpile their winter reserves.

Calemore's troops had it worse. The army was just too huge to support itself, so their food levels must be running low. With the rain and cold coming in, the Naum forces would find resupply all the more difficult. They did not have horses, and their movement would be excruciatingly slow. Winter would favor them, though. Naum was a cold place, and snow was the natural habitat for these soldiers. While Amalia's and Sasha's men would curse chilblains and black toes and numb ears and noses, the Naum warriors would wade merrily through the drift, impervious to the harsh bite of winter.

Which meant they had to somehow win the war before the blizzards.

Tanid also claimed Ewan's attack would ferret Calemore out of his hiding, make him rash and prone to mistakes. He might expose himself and get himself killed. The god was confident Ewan would destroy him with the bloodstaff just as he had slaughtered all those men. A simple task with only a tiny amount of emotional scarring.

Several days back, Ewan had really gotten irritated by being treated like an expensive tool. He found a moment when Gavril was without his followers and confronted him. "When do your divine powers come into play?"

"I am saving my strength for when it matters. When the White Witch finally moves against us, I will tamper with the weather to foil his troops' movement. I will use fog and rain to cause confusion and slow their progress. And I will shield the rest of you from Calemore's own magic."

Somehow, Ewan did not believe him. He did not doubt the god would use his powers to weaken the enemy, but he did not really believe Tanid would risk his own life too much. He would hurl his pilgrims forth, and he would cower behind Ludevit and Pasha—and Ewan. His own sacrifice would be the very last.

Ewan understood the importance of leaders. Generals ordered men to their deaths and held back, watching the toll rise from a safe distance. That was how it worked, and it should not be any different for gods leading their own armies, he figured. Still, there was something about Tanid that rang beyond pure selfishness and calculated cowardice. It was a skewed sense of personal worth that clashed with all that was human.

The two Sirtai also seemed quite eager to stake their claim in the war. They did not relish fighting, but Ewan could see the subtle, egomaniacal desire to be the ones who defeated the son of a god, a legendary relic from an ancient time. He could not guess the reasons, but the need for glory was there. The bloodstaff did not just leech blood from its victims. It leeched humanity, too.

And he was still lonely. The massive human company around him did not lessen his feeling of being all alone. He longed for friendship and intimacy, but no one in the camp had enough to share. Everyone was preoccupied with their thoughts of war and personal loss.

Amalia was the only one to pay him any special heed, but her attention was quite the opposite. She haunted him.

She was obsessed with the weapon, he knew. She burned to touch it, to hold it, and he knew he must not surrender it to anyone. The bloodstaff was his, and he alone would use it when needed, at the expense of his own guilt.

Tanid was standing a short distance away from him, in front of a fresh ditch, staring north. His two odd henchmen were lurking nearby; Ludevit looked focused, Pasha bored and timid, like he always was. Those two must be Special Children. There was no other reason why the god would keep them around otherwise.

Their presence made him feel that much less of a monster, but it was a tiny spark against the overwhelming void of his loneliness.

"What?" Ludevit barked suddenly, startling him. Then, Ewan heard a sound, like a giant rock shattering. Then, another. Another. A quick cascade of them, getting closer. It was—

Pain.

Sharp, blinding, beautiful pain.

After so long, physical pain, white-hot, searing.

He saw the earth in front of the axman explode, large wet chunks of upturned earth and old tree roots flying in all directions. Then, Ludevit exploded. Unceremoniously, he burst open into a pale red flower.

Ewan stood, paralyzed by the treacly agony of burning pain in his left arm, staring stupidly. He had not even blinked. Pasha looked sideways, and then his left arm detached, ripped off like a bit of cloth from an old doll. More earth ruptured.

Ewan realized what was happening.

Someone was firing bloodstaff pellets at them.

Silent, deathly destruction, like the one he had rained on the enemy just weeks back.

Still standing like an idiot, he glanced at his left hand and saw a couple of his fingers missing. The small one and the one next to it were gone, sliced off. Blood dripped onto the ground below. More wet earth showered him.

He jumped into the ditch behind him. Wet, muddy rain sprayed on his shoulders and hair. The pain was debilitating. It pulsed through his body, almost blinding him with its intensity, but he had to focus. He had to fight back.

"Gavril!" he shouted.

"Save me," Tanid whimpered, huddling in the trench not far away. Lumps of meat covered the back of his tunic, but he did not seem to notice.

Ewan realized he was still clutching the bloodstaff in his right hand. He lumbered up, shaking, and looked up over the mound. People were running everywhere, ordinary soldiers trying to figure out what was happening. But they milled mindlessly, unaware of the threat that had just shredded several of their comrades.

One of the wagons had been punched through. A Red Caps soldier was lying against one of its shattered wheels, eyes wide open in shock. Ewan saw that both her legs were missing. Another body lay in the wet grass not far away, the signs of its mutilation hidden.

Pain. He cherished its return. But the sensation threatened to choke his mind.

"Mom…Mom…" someone moaned.

Ewan saw it was the boy Pasha. He was lying on his back, weeping. "Don't move." Oh, he was getting nauseated from the throbbing sizzle in his left arm.

"Forget him! Fight back!" Tanid rasped. "Fire that thing! Destroy Calemore!"

"Use your magic," Ewan snapped. "Heal my hand!" He showed the ruined fist to the god.

Tanid stared at the bleeding limb with a dazed look, then shook his head. "No, no. It is no good."

Ewan sagged against the trench wall. He was dizzy. He had to take care of his wound. Those sounds again, rocks shattering.

He cowered inside the ditch, hoping the pile of dugout earth was thick enough to stop the pellets. A flurry of screams rippled through the camp above. Several soldiers jumped into the trench by his side, looking terrified. Some were bleeding from small scratches caused by flying splinters and shards of stone, but they looked immensely relieved to lurk there.

"Use the bloodstaff!" Gavril foamed.

A nearby hit blasted a massive chunk of land away. For a moment, Ewan was blinded by the debris. Behind him, soldiers wailed, trying to wipe their eyes. Another blast, and Pasha's body slid down the mound and into the narrow furrow. The boy was still alive.

"Mom…" he wept.

Ewan lowered the bloodstaff by his feet. He tore a strip from his shirt and gingerly pressed the cloth to his left hand. He gasped breathlessly, almost fainting. The surprise was just as sharp as the real physical sensation. He had thought himself invincible, immune to damage.

Apparently not.

His whole body shaking, he wrapped the cloth round the wound. But it was so hard doing it with one hand. "You," he called to the nearby soldier. "Bind my hand. Now. And you, take a look at this boy. See if you can stop his bleeding."

Glad to be given commands, the Athesians moved quickly. The second one slid past Ewan, his thigh accidentally rubbing against his fist. Tarry blackness stabbed at Ewan's eyes, and he bit off a curse and tasted blood in his mouth.

"Fight him!" Tanid was shrieking.

"He's dead, sir," the soldier mumbled. "The boy's gone."

"My hand," Ewan whimpered.

Tanid was crawling on all fours, pushing past Ewan and his shivering medic. He laid his divine hands on the bloodstaff. With a last drop of consciousness, Ewan noticed and pushed his foot hard against the crystal rod, burying it in the wet ground. He would not let the god use the rod.

He almost fainted again as the soldier tied a clumsy knot against his palm. It was a ridiculous tourniquet, but it would have to do. The cloth was turning red quickly. The pain was like a hot furnace, but Ewan was almost getting used to it. Swallowing back vomit, he shoved his right shoulder against the trench and slid up again.

Calemore was still firing the weapon against the camp. But it was not an incessant torrent of pellets, more of a calculated destruction, probably aimed at crippling Tanid's most valuable assets. Pasha. Ludevit. Himself. Special Children.

A cart burst, slivers flying with an ululating, whirring noise. Pieces of wood landed all around Ewan. Soldiers of the realm were running away now, leaving the injured and dead behind. They still did not understand what was happening, but they knew they had to get away as quickly as they could.

I am vulnerable to this thing, like anyone else, Ewan thought, feeling human again. It was such a strange, perverse elation. He tried to see a pattern in the mayhem, to try to figure out where the witch might be firing from. But it was so hard to tell. Those pellets could be coming from a mile away.

A hundred paces all around him, there was not a single thing left intact. Calemore had destroyed everything. If not for the safety of the trench, they would all have been dead. And that was still a viable option, it seemed.

More pellets, and they slammed into the ground to their left, leaving deep gouges, showering huge chunks of debris into the ditch, choking it closed. Another salvo, and the trench was blocked on the right side, too. The White Witch had cleared the killing zone of any obstacles and hideouts that Ewan and the rest could use. If they wanted to escape, they had to dash across a naked clearing.

He knows we are here. He is waiting for us.

Ewan aimed in the general direction of the highest knoll to the north of his position and fired. A soundless torrent of rubies sped away. He was not really sure if his aim was good, but it did not matter really.

Not good at all. Calemore responded with his own deluge. Ewan flattened himself at the bottom of the ditch. Pellets hammered into the ground all around him, almost burying him alive in dirt. The other soldiers were doing the same thing, trying to keep low and still, even as death flailed maybe two feet above their prostrate bodies.

I have just given away our position, Ewan figured.

"You must stop him!" Tanid shrieked.

He wants you, Ewan knew. It was all about this god right here. The pain had become a dull ache up his entire left arm. He could not move the healthy remaining fingers. He could not flex his wrist or bend his elbow. That whole thing was a dead, hot weight.

The silent thunderstorm ceased suddenly.

"Ewan! Ewan!" someone was shouting. "Ewan!" Jarman.

"We are here," he hissed. His mouth tasted like clay and blood.

Just behind the god, the Sirtai hopped into the trench. He was filthy and sweaty. "Are you hurt?"

Ewan flopped onto his back so he could breathe more easily. He let go of the bloodstaff once more and gingerly lifted his left hand by the shred of a sleeve. "Lost my fingers. Ludevit and Pasha are dead."

Jarman nodded gravely. "Lucas has raised a defensive shield around us. We will be safe for now."

Soon, dozens of soldiers were there, trying to get the survivors out of the trench. Ewan tried to stand, but he sagged, and they lifted him on a stretcher, the bloodstaff pressed close to his body. Apart from some mud on his clothes, Tanid was unhurt, and he stepped out on his own.

"Let me take a look," Jarman spoke, coming closer. "Lower him."

Ewan winced as the Sirtai wizard probed his hand. He was growing weaker by the moment. The feeling of vulnerability was strangely uplifting. *Human again,* he thought. *At least some parts of me.*

"I can stop the bleeding and seal the wounds, but your fingers are lost forever," Jarman said.

Ewan nodded dumbly.

"Do you know the exact details of what happened?"

Ewan inhaled deeply through his nostrils, trying to stave off bile at the back of his throat. "Calemore attacked us all of a sudden. Without warning. Killed Ludevit right away. Got Pasha, and the lad bled to death. Got me." Blackness clouded his vision, and he blinked. "I got up to see what was happening, must have shown my face to the witch. He cut us off, started blasting the ground."

"Brace yourself," Jarman warned.

It was too much. A white rod of anguish stabbed him through the shoulder, up his neck, and under his jaw. He could not find any breath to gasp, so he just moaned mutely into a chasm of black despair that gripped his face. But then, the agony eased.

"You still need urgent medical attention," the Sirtai confessed. The stretcher jostled, and Ewan was in the air, feeling light and disembodied. "What? Speak up."

Ewan realized the words he was telling had only happened inside his head. He was confessing about his supernatural strength, his immunity to fire and cold and sword blows, and how it had all changed just moments ago. He wanted to share his revelation with the wizard. He would certainly know more. The young man hailed from the same land as that famous investigator that had taken him to the Broken Isles. The Sirtai were wise people…

"Ewan, try to stay awake," Jarman urged.

"If you hadn't showed up," Ewan mumbled. From the corner of his teary eye, and through the silver woolly mist descending on the world, he could see the remnants of the ditch now, far more shallow than it had been earlier that morning, all that mound chewed up, earth blown apart by the magical pellets. With a little more time, Calemore would have cratered out enough land to hit the men hiding at the bottom. *And I have helped him pinpoint the digging. Fool.*

The sky opened up. It began to rain. Ewan was glad for each drop on his seething skin. Today, he had tasted his own death. After so long, he was so much more human than he had been in a long time. Maybe coming here was the answer to his legacy.

He passed out.

CHAPTER 34

The situation in Ecol was grim.

Ever since Calemore's attack against Gavril and Ewan, there was a deep sense of helplessness among the soldiers and citizens alike. The common troops realized they could die any moment, anywhere, without prior warning. They could be going back to their barracks and suddenly find themselves missing an arm or a leg, or maybe dead in a red, hot puddle. That was no dignified way for men and women of the sword to die.

For Amalia, the personal hurt was even greater. Every night, she dreamed of Calemore coming to her, taking the bloodstaff away, ruining Athesia. She sometimes saw Adelbert watching her pee, smirking. She would wake up covered in sweat, stiff and tired, choking on despair.

Then, she would go out, to try to shake out the phantoms of gloom, and she would see that scrawny lad Ewan gripping the bloodstaff. And her hopes would return, focused down to a glowing obsession. She would stare at the glass rod until her eyes watered.

If she got hold of that weapon, she could defeat the northern army.

If she had the bloodstaff, she could destroy Princess Sasha and King Sergei and restore pride to her realm.

If she could somehow get her hands on the beautiful artifact of magic, she would be unstoppable.

Alas, even with his left hand maimed and wrapped in a mushroom of linen, the boy would not let go off the staff. He would cradle it, never relaxing his grip.

Amalia knew she had to be close to him, without raising too much suspicion. But her duties kept her away. She was too important, too precious to send on scouting missions, too valuable to squander on simple tasks. Jarman, Lucas, and Sasha would just not let her get close enough to the bloodstaff.

Ewan might die one day, just like he almost had nine days earlier. What then? Who would take the weapon then? Who would be its new owner?

Her thoughts drifted to her half brother and his Caytorean friend Rob, who had also perished in a haze of blood and muscle, like so many soldiers last week. She hoped Jarman's magical shield still protected her against Calemore, and that he had enough strength to defend her both against the White Witch and human threats. Now, it seemed, he would have to extend his protection to Ewan and maybe Gavril, and she did not feel confident about it at all. After all, Calemore had almost killed James and her that snowy day. He might try again, and he would not miss this time. If only she could hold the Bloodstaff…

My name is Calemore. I'm also known as the White Witch of Naum.

She was deeply suspicious of Gavril. There was something wrong about him. Then, where had Ewan found the bloodstaff? A *second* example no less. What did that mean? Maybe that the same Lord Erik who had given the weapon and the book to her father had also known Ewan? But how could that be? Ewan was just a boy.

She felt confused, worried.

For the thousandth time, she wished she had read *The Book of Lost Words*.

The one weak, jaundiced light of happiness was the birth of Agatha's son. Her maid was still recovering from the ordeal. She had a fever, but Jarman promised she would be all right soon. Amalia had begged the wizard to use his magic to stave off any infection, and the Sirtai had grudgingly agreed. Oblivious to the hazards of childbirth, Pete was strutting through the camp, chin raised, a silly grin on his lips. The man had changed completely, from a barely restrained brute to a responsible husband. Amalia was truly happy for Agatha. At least one of them had managed to get her life sorted out.

Pete's joy also helped others cope. Captain Speinbate had given the young father a small present, a fertility idol of some sort, shaped like a tiny man with a gigantic phallus. Amalia guessed it was yet another crass Borei joke. Then, the gold-toothed mercenary had also begged Pete not to name his child in the first year, because it was bad luck.

Amalia had secured a small satchel of silver for her maid. She did not know when her funds would run out, and she wanted to make sure that Agatha was well-off, at least. The future flow of Caytorean money was uncertain now that Parus had taken over Athesia, and Amalia was not sure if Princess Sasha would be forthcoming with any help, at least not until the war ended and Amalia took her place in Roalas as her vassal.

If they won the war, that was.

With the bloodstaff, she could solve so many problems all at once. But it was no longer hers.

Amalia wondered how much she really knew about the history of the realms. She wondered how much her father had known and tried to tell her. All his teachings, all his warnings, they must have steered her toward this, only she had been too proud, too stupid to heed his advice. Now she had to fight on her own, unaware of so many crucial details and developments. What was Calemore really trying to achieve? What did Jarman know? Who was this Ewan? Or Gavril? Then she remembered Adelbert lurking in her chamber, and a shiver ran up her spine. She was just a silly girl who had once thought she could rein in the world to her liking.

She stared at Ewan.

The boy carried with a fresh dose of vulnerability she had not seen before. His calm, almost-timeless composure had cracked, and he no longer bore with that sad, frightening look of apathy on his young face. If anything, he seemed invigorated by losing two fingers. But maybe it was just shock. Or the effect of magic the bloodstaff had on its surviving victims. No one could really know how the weapon affected people.

The bloodstaff caught the weak light and threw it back at her in a flash, teasing her. She could see the gleam of wine-like blood trapped inside the crystal rod, the menacing wink of the claws at the top end. No matter where it was used, the weapon remained clean, unblemished, without scratches or spots.

She had to stop fantasizing about holding it. She had to focus on mundane things.

She was no longer the empress, no longer the owner of that thing. She had lost her privilege to decide the fate of the world.

What she had to do was make sure she survived her latest humiliation. Maybe the Parusites were willing to give her a second chance, but she was not so sure about her own people, about Xavier and the rest of the Caytorean soldiers.

Her surrender was probably a blow to their ambitions and expectations. The warlord must have expected to marry an empress, and maybe he would be content with a governess, but she couldn't really tell what he wanted. He was a man of violence, and he demanded power and fear. With Princess Sasha leading the realm now, his position was in jeopardy. And that made him extra dangerous.

Warlord Xavier had to die.

Amalia really wondered what would happen to his men—to James's men. His plan of taking over Athesia and making a strong, powerful alliance was dead, much like the plan's creator. Caytor would not gain anything from her surrender. Rheanna's ambitions, even if they still existed, were just an idle threat to the might of the Parusite conquest. Amalia was not sure if she could trust any one of them, Master Hector, Sebastian, all the others. They were Caytoreans, and they had their own agenda.

She suspected whatever they decided to do, the swine-faced Xavier would lead them. She had to get rid of him, and that would probably cripple the rest. Just enough to make them acknowledge her and focus on the northern threat. That alone should be enough to unite all the nations.

Amalia planned to ask Jarman to make good on his promise any day now.

But what if the remaining Caytoreans rebelled, or tried to assassinate her? What if they just deserted? Or refused to fight? Her purge had left Xavier with the troops utterly loyal to him and his goals, so she was not sure how they might react to his death. But she had to be brave. She had to do something. Leaving things as they were would not help her.

Forget about politics, she thought. *It's no longer your domain. King Sergei will decide how to treat the High Council and what kind of demands to make.* Maybe offer them favorable trade deals if they forgot the Oth Danesh incident? Maybe ask them to send more troops to help fight the Naum forces?

He might decide to disband her legions and send the Caytoreans home. She would hate to leave loose ends. She wanted to have closure. To figure out what Guild Master Sebastian might try. To put an end to Rheanna's claim. Then again, she might be reduced to a mere spectator, watching others more skilled in the art of diplomacy and intimidation make all the important moves.

What did that leave her? Just a bit of personal spite.

At least she could exterminate Xavier.

Amalia saw Jarman walking toward her, with Captain Speinbate in tow. She frowned. That was a surprise.

For a moment, she thought something was wrong. She glanced around. Her new home, the restored manor house, was a small fortress, bristling with soldiers. A hundred craftsmen were going about making daily checks of the fortifications, trying to reassure everyone, including themselves, that sharp lumps of wood, rope, metal, and stone would stand up to the northern tide and the all-too-vivid rumor of a magical weapon that could punch through rock and steel with ease.

The Athesian contingent, mixed with Gavril's people, would hold the city, the nearby mines, the several small forts. Princess Sasha wanted space for her own troops, so they would deploy on the flanks, where they enjoyed better discipline and hygiene. The Borei also required room to use their olifaunts, and Amalia was glad those monsters would be elsewhere when panic and fear stabbed through the ranks.

Everyone was busy, or seemed busy, but it was mostly a desperate need to keep themselves occupied so they did not have to ponder too much about the impending defeat. The wait was agonizing. No one knew what the White Witch really intended, or why he still held back, but his surprise assault a few days back meant they could not relax.

Gavril and Jarman were fairly certain the witch would attack them head on, because he wanted to utterly destroy the people of the realms, and he would not miss an opportunity to kill off such large prey. Surely not after Ewan had decimated one of his armies with the bloodstaff. She had no doubt the previous week's attack was revenge, and the fact Ewan still lived was nothing short of a miracle.

"Amalia," the Sirtai wizard called, his red robes stained with mud and water. The mercenary was looking around playfully, as if he were inspecting the work around the manor house.

"What is it?" she said, maybe too harshly. Xavier was standing a stone's throw away, talking to several officers, pointing left. Just behind him, Master Hector was eating something, probably an egg. Amalia had not forgotten the talk with the old, leathery sergeant. He would favor Caytorean interests first.

"I believe Captain Speinbate may have a solution to your problem."

She narrowed her eyes. "What problem?"

Jarman inclined his head ever so slightly. "*Your* problem."

Amalia tried to wipe emotion from her face. "Oh, my problem."

The gold-toothed man stepped closer. "For a small fee, if you do not mind. True, the Parusite king has retained our services, but they only cover all-out war efforts."

Amalia felt suspicious. Was this some kind of a trick? Or was Jarman trying to keep his hands clean and still keep up his promise? "Well, what did you have in mind?"

"Something discreet, quiet," Speinbate whispered.

She sniffed. "I have heard of Pum'be assassins." Her voice almost faltered; a ghost of a pain skittered up her skull. "But I have never heard of Borei assassins." All around, life went on as usual, strained and full of military activity. No one was paying them much attention.

"My lady, you do know we are experts in breaking sieges?" He waited until she nodded. "Good. Now, you do realize sieges are extremely costly affairs? All that waiting, bad food, disease, not to mention the storming of the walls themselves. Sieges are not very profitable when played by the rules. But if you can get the key participants convinced to end their war game a little earlier, you save a lot of time and money and countless lives. Well, we have developed our own methods of making sieges end faster."

Amalia liked his theatrical ways, but she was still unconvinced. "Go on."

The captain smiled, flashing her with gold. "Besides, you do know how the Pum'be nation was created, right? A Borei warrior shagged a goat, and they had a child." He did not wait for her to acknowledge the joke. He guffawed loudly.

"They can help," Jarman insisted.

"What will be the price?" she asked.

The Borei shrugged. "I am already the governor of the princedom," he said, not without cold emphasis. "So something else perhaps?" The gleam in his eyes matched his teeth.

"Master Jarman will pay you," she suggested, trying to sound mildly disinterested. She had already paid the wizard with her surrender. The nations of the realms were coming united, just as he wanted, and he had promised his help in return. Let him make true on his word.

Jarman pursed his lips. After a while, he nodded. "Yes, indeed."

Captain Speinbate smiled. "In that case, I will be glad to offer my services."

"Good day," Amalia stuttered. Suddenly, she was feeling uncomfortable. Wearing a waxy smile of her own, she retreated, taking a random path around builders and engineers and soldiers. Eyes followed her, some friendly, some openly hostile, others full of sorrow or disdain. She wondered what her Athesians thought of her now. After all, she had destroyed her father's creation, robbed them of their independence. They were now subjects of King Sergei, and that meant prayer at dawn and dusk, something that hadn't been seen in Athesia in two decades.

"Your Excellency," someone called, a female voice. She halted. One of the Red Caps, a burly woman with short hair that matched her bleached leathers. "Commander Sasha wishes to speak to you. Please follow me."

Her old imperial instincts kicked in. She wanted to feel annoyed at being summoned by an ordinary soldier. She wanted to glance past her shoulder, but she knew there was no one behind her right now. She was just a high-ranking clerk, serving Parusite interests.

The Red Cap woman led east, just past the congregation of Gavril's followers. The holy man was talking to Ewan. The boy had a sick, pale expression on his face, but his grip was firm on the bloodstaff. Oh, if only she could grasp it for a few moments, she could wipe away all her mistakes and regrets.

Almost all of them. The bloodstaff would not bring the dead back. She swallowed a lump.

The religious army did not inspire in their military abilities. They were dressed and armed poorly, and their camp looked filthy and disorganized. They had more livestock and dogs than horses worth riding into battle. But they counted for something. Their zeal would see them through the worst of autumn and winter and the imminent carnage.

By contrast, the Parusite garrison was spotless. Neat rows of barracks and tents, well marked, with wide paths to allow soldiers to assemble and move through. Rows of trenches cut through the camp, the shallow ones made to carry away sewage, the deep ones studded with stakes designed to stop enemy attacks and hobble horses, not that the Naum army had any. For now.

Only several months back, the Parusite and Athesian forces had fought here. Her brother had died near the mining camp. Now, this same ground hosted King Sergei's troops, as if the old carnage had never happened. She could see old pieces of rusty metal embedded deep in the loam, a testimony to the bitter fighting. Things not worth stealing, she figured.

Princess Sasha did not believe in fanfare. Her own shack was identical to so many others shared by her subordinates. Then again, it also made her that much more difficult to track and kill for enemy spies and assassins. Clever. The only nod at protocol was the beefed-up security around her shed.

"Do you carry any weapons, Your Excellence?" her Red Cap escort asked.

I wish I did. It would mean I knew how to use them, she thought, bitterness gripping her chest. "No."

The soldier looked her down and up. "Please enter, then."

Amalia took a deep breath and pushed the plank door inward. It creaked on fat iron hinges.

Most maps Amalia had seen in her life had either lain on tabletops or been hung from walls as tapestry. She had never seen one strung like a cowhide left to dry. But the layout of the nearby terrain, etched in colored charcoal on a stretch of brown skin, bisected the small cabin. On the far side, she could see several silhouettes, moving, talking in hushed tones. It looked like an insect, with too many arms and legs, coming to life behind a thin cocoon.

"Around," the escort suggested.

Amalia edged past the map. The king's sister was talking to three other women in uniform. There were no servants, no guards around. The only other person was a priestess wearing ocher-colored robes, sitting at a small desk, writing.

"Your Excellence," Sasha greeted, not really looking at her.

Amalia curtsied. "Your Highness."

The princess nodded. "I want to commend you on your behavior in the past weeks. I had not believed you would be able to see past your petty misfortune. But apparently, I was mistaken. The conduct of the Athesian soldiers is reasonable, and there have been very few incidents. You are not happy with your predicament." She paused, and now her royal eyes bore into Amalia, weighing her. "But you have proved your worth. Ecol is as ready for war as it will ever be."

By ready, you mean a town crammed with refugees and beggars, with people forced to share their houses, the streets stalked by prostitutes, thieves, and opportunists, and the countryside whispering with robbery and panic? In that case, I have done superbly. Athesia is the prime example of a failed little empire, reduced to a shameful mockery of its proud past. And it only took me less than a year to ruin everything.

"Thank you, Your Highness," she muttered.

"Now I must ask you to leave the battle lines," the princess said.

Amalia felt her gut clench. "I do not understand, Your Highness."

Sasha looked at her. "I think you've done what you could. I will need you in Roalas. Your presence will help restore order in the provincial capital. That will allow my brother to march north under full strength. The king has no business governing a city. He needs to lead his nation."

Amalia swallowed. No. No. She was useless, she knew, but not this. "Please, Your Highness. I must remain here. There are still too many problems that I must oversee. The loyalty of the Caytorean troops. The claim of my brother's widow." She would not let her voice tremble. No. "Besides, I have intimate knowledge with the artifacts of magic, and I have met the White Witch before. My experience should be valuable in the coming weeks. With all due respect, I must ask you to reconsider, Your Highness."

Amalia realized the cabin had gone quiet. All the officers were silent, watching her. Princess Sasha was holding a small, sharpened piece of red charcoal, hand poised over the Weeping Boughs. That ought to be a good location to keep a small reserve of light troops, or maybe launch ambushes.

Amalia held her breath. She wanted to mention Jarman, but that would make her sound silly and desperate. The Parusites had no obligation toward the Sirtai. They did not care for magic. Sasha had probably left things as they were to maintain order among her various ranks, but she might dismiss Jarman and Lucas from her camp, too. What would they do then? What would that man Gavril do? Or Ewan?

The priestess in the back of the cabin looked up and nodded at the princess. Amalia tried to decipher that look. What was that? Not just advice from a trusted aide. There was something else there.

Sasha put the crude pencil down, dusted her fingers. "So you would challenge my decision?"

Amalia bowed her head in deference. "Your Highness, I have willingly surrendered Athesia to King Sergei, and I will abide by that agreement. However, like you, my duty is to the people of this land first. If I were to tuck my tail and flee south, it would be construed as a defeat. I am certain that the legions would fall apart. The Caytoreans will defect. The Athesians might rebel."

The princess stepped closer. The woman was lithe, formidable. Not a lady. A fighter. "Your duty, as the king's vassal, is to obey your ruler. I represent the king, and I believe that you will best serve the Parusite interests away from Ecol. You have done your share."

Amalia realized she had been dismissed. Her body turned around and led her out of the cabin. Outside, nothing had changed, but the world looked gray and dreary. A pointless place to be in. After all she had done, all the fighting, all the scheming, all her begging, she had finally rendered herself surplus. No one needed an inexperienced girl who had lost all her battles. She didn't inspire anyone, she held no sway over anyone, she was indebted to killers and wizards, and she had even misspent her father's wisdom. She was a total failure.

I will not cry, she promised, gritting her teeth until the joints of her jaw hurt. *I will not cry.*

As she stepped past the last line of stakes, she saw that man Adelbert going about his business. He glanced at her once. He, too, owned a piece of her soul. But she had nothing left anymore. So what did it matter if she pledged some more? Nothing stayed nothing.

In that moment, a strange, raw sensation engulfed her.

Fuck everything, she thought. *They want me gone? Well, I will fight to the death. I will show them.* It was an empty promise, she knew, but it didn't matter anymore. She was Adam's daughter, and she would die fighting.

Suddenly, she laughed, tears pouring down her cheeks. She barked at the sky, mad, ignoring the strange looks from the soldiers and pilgrims around her. She did not care anymore. The ball of emptiness in her stomach melted away, replaced by giddy elation. Amalia was almost too glad for having asked the Borei to murder Warlord Xavier. It was almost funny.

Jarman, Lucas, Hector, Adelbert, all of them, may they all burn. She was tired of their scheming, their selfish plans, their stupid ambitions. Who were they? How dare they? She would show them. She was Adam's daughter. She would show them. They thought they could extort her? They thought they could use her?

She would let them. She would give them everything they wanted. Because you couldn't defeat nothing; you couldn't halve it or deplete it. She would set the bastards against one another and let them drown in their greed. *Fuck war. Fuck peace. Fuck everyone.*

When you have nothing to lose, everything is a gain, she figured.

Laughing and weeping at the same time, she retreated toward the manor house.

CHAPTER 35

Nigella flinched as the lightning struck the earth somewhere nearby. The cabin lit up with brilliant white; an eyeblink later, a painful peal snapped through her skull as the ground beneath her feet shook. Sheldon was entirely unperturbed, playing with his lead figurines. All he could think of was soldiers and war nowadays.

She let the din in her ears subside, then squinted back at the pages of the book. She was determined to complete reading it soon, no matter what. The lamp oil and candles provided by the Naum men were quite good, and her little home was illuminated brighter than ever before. But she definitely needed new spectacles for her eyes. Only all the glassblowers in Marlheim had been killed, and no one could polish a pair of new lenses for her. Calemore's troops were not familiar with glasses. The way she knew her lover, he probably would not let short-sighted people live in his distant kingdom.

He still had not visited her. She was feeling lonely. She missed his companionship, no matter how abrupt and terrifying it was. She longed for his touch, for his sharp intellect, for his humor and even his merciless remarks. She longed for his wild passion, when he let it show.

Every day, she sipped her tea, and she never added laser-wort these days. She still believed that Calemore and she could be together one day.

Despite everything she read in *The Book of Lost Words*.

"Mom," Sheldon called, distracting her.

Nigella sighed. "Yes, Shel?"

The boy squirmed onto the bed. "I'm done playing with my army. I want to do something else."

She looked about the cabin with some small measure of frustration. Her home was never meant to be a child's domain. Sheldon had been supposed to grow up in the city, as an apprentice, far from her witchcraft, her customers, her disappointments.

The Naum invasion had come almost too suddenly, and she didn't have enough toys and things that would entertain a nine-year-old boy. All his things had burned in Marlheim. But he was a smart lad, and he liked to keep his mind occupied.

"I can show you how to make a pie later," she suggested.

"I don't wanna do that," he said, almost whining. Outside, the rain hissed against the timber.

Nigella pushed her chair back. "Son, please. There's nothing much to do. But you must be patient. Hopefully, tomorrow, the torrent will end, and you can go play in the hills." Not that she relished seeing him drag mud into the shack, and worse, those Naum soldiers following him, trying to talk to him in their foreign language.

Unfortunately for Sheldon—fortunately for her—it did not seem like the rain was going to abate anytime soon. It had been pouring almost the entire week. The seams between the timbers of her house had started to leak, and the floor was damp. But just earlier that morning, despite the wind and cold and whipping downpour, several Naum men had worked on the wood, trying to daub the leaks.

The boy huffed. "I really wanna do something else."

Could she blame him? He had been locked in there with her for so long, without any other children to play with. He was just a boy, after all, and she was probably too morose to make him happy like he needed. Well, what Sheldon really needed was a father figure.

Someone like...

No, that would be too much. But then, what did she expect? If someone like Calemore ended up loving her, what would happen to Sheldon? He would be a part of their intimacy for a long while, until she could find another trade for him. Somehow, she doubted the Naum people would be tolerant toward the strange child in their midst. They would hate him, and because of Calemore, they would fear him. He would be different; he would be an outcast. Just like she had been.

More thunder, but it was drifting away, and the clouds remained dark.

"Mom, can I read your book?"

Nigella gripped the edge of the table to steady the tremor in her left hand. Gently, with the other, she pushed the book away. It was open, its oily, perfect text almost shimmering on the fine paper, inviting the eyes to pore over it, to get lost in its ancient, convoluted secrets.

"No, you cannot," she whispered.

"But Mom, I don't have anything else to do. You always told me I must read books."

Yes, read books, become smart and educated, gain advantage over the privileged Caytoreans. He had to do it, because he would have no slack in his life. She could not give him anything apart from her own bitter experience. James had at least secured a future for Shel, until Calemore had come and destroyed it all. Not that it lessened her disdain for James in any way.

For a fleeting moment, she wondered how he was doing. Then, she hoped he was dead, too, like Rob. Maybe she couldn't bring herself to ask Calemore to murder him, but she wouldn't shed a tear if she heard of his early demise.

I can't let him read this thing, she thought, her heart beating rapidly. She was suddenly scared. She understood the implications of the book, of its secrets. It was no ordinary thing. It was a powerful tome of magic, and its truths were dangerous and dark.

But then, Sheldon wasn't an ordinary child either.

He had magic in his veins. All Sirtai did to some degree, and he carried that bloodline. He had lived in her shadow, behind her magic, her divinations. He had met the White Witch. And the boy understood the words of this Naum nation. So maybe he deserved a glimpse of the magical book.

What am I doing? she wondered. *Have I gone mad? What will Calemore do if he learns I let Sheldon read from the book? What will it do to his mind? Can he even grasp the truths written inside?*

"Come here," she said.

Sheldon hopped over and sidled up into the second chair. He was still a small boy, and his legs dangled. He raised his chin, looking down his nose at the heavy volume.

"It's called *The Book of Lost Words*," she heard herself say. "This book must not be copied. You may remember what is written in its pages, but you must never write even a single word anywhere else. Never. Do you understand that, Shel? It is very important."

Sheldon seemed unfazed. "Why would a press master make only a single book?"

Nigella smiled softly. "I do not think this book was made in a press."

Her son looked keen. "It was written entirely by hand?"

She did not really know. "Maybe."

His small fingers probed. She moved the book closer. He touched the pages, ruffled them gently, traced a finger along the thick, perfect cover. His hand hovered above the text, and his face took on the look of a young, eager apprentice, trying to mimic the gestures of his superiors, trying to soak in their candor and professional appreciation for the fine art and details of the work before him. He looked so adorable, and it would have been an idyllic moment if that book hadn't been Calemore's.

"Is it very old?" he asked.

"Yes, it is."

Sheldon scrunched his nose. "So I may not copy its words, Mom?"

Nigella almost panicked. "No, you cannot. You must promise me, Son. You must never do that."

He nodded vaguely, but she knew he would obey. "Who wrote this book, Mom? Was it Uncle Calemore?"

She sniffed. "I told you not to call him that. Calemore is not your uncle."

Sheldon ignored her. His eyes were watery in the lamplight, locked on the perfect binding, on the smooth flow of text in a lovely tilted manuscript. "What is this book about, Mom?"

The future. Nigella hesitated. "Old stories. Myths. Legends. But they are all written in a special way so that the reader must interpret the message for themselves. It's not very interesting." She tried to dissuade him.

But that only got him keener. His small head was almost hovering above the book, and he was trying to push himself up against the table. Such focus, such childish wonder, it was mesmerizing.

"So can I read, Mom, please?"

Nigella flipped the page. She had not read the next one. She had no idea what words hid there. And she wasn't certain she would like to know. Recently, the images of possible truths coalescing inside her head were more sinister than before, and they left a cold, metallic tinge in her soul, in her nose and her mouth. Whatever the book was trying to tell her, it was grim. But she still could not separate her own life from Calemore's. The twin destinies snaked round one another, confusing her. She was trying to read for herself, to unravel her future, but it was impure, tainted with glimpses from another life.

In a way, she was desperate.

Calemore would return to her shanty one day, and he would demand answers, truths. What if she could not provide them?

Then, her son could speak the Naum language. The *how* of it still haunted her, but maybe she was too much of a coward to try to learn the reasons. Maybe she should not be afraid of using her son's gift. Maybe he would be able to tell her truths that she could not see. She might be blinded by her upbringing, her emotional scarring, her inhibitions and fears. He was still unfettered by the world's ugliness.

But she promised herself, she would never jeopardize his life. Never.

Reading a little from a magical book could not hurt. Could it?

"All right, you may read now. But do not read out loud. Do not repeat the words. Just read to yourself." She was ready to yank the book away if he tried so much as utter a single syllable.

Sheldon picked up on her mood, and his face turned somber. Face slack with concentration, he started reading. Nigella watched him intently, watched his eyes scan left and right, left and right, moving down the page. His lips were pressed tight, silent. His skin was soft, relaxed. Whatever he was reading was probably boring. He might decide playing with toy soldiers was more fun. She hoped it would be like that.

Suddenly, he burst out laughing.

Nigella almost yelped, clawing at the book, closing it with a thump. She was trembling, her whole body fluttery. "What it is, Shel?"

Why am I doing this? she wondered. *The Book of Lost Words* was not a child's book. She was making a big mistake. Calemore had entrusted *her* with the tome, not the boy. She was doing a very dangerous thing here.

The boy was still wearing a big grin on his face, one of his teeth still missing. Nothing on his young face indicated any worry. Whatever he had read seemed rather funny. Unlike her own visions and interpretations.

"What is it?" she repeated.

"Mom, the book says I'm going to be a prince. That I'm going to have ten wives! Pffff."

Nigella blinked, trying to keep tears away. Joy? Relief? Terror? She was not really sure. *I'm a fool.* Oh, she hated herself. But what could she do? Sheldon was penned up in this miserable little hovel, and he was a child. He could not understand war.

Prince? Trying to calm her nerves, she opened the book again. This time, she read the same passage.

Nothing of that sort.

Her mind filled with different images. The garbage of words misted into a field. Old shrubbery, stripped of leaves, it seemed. No. Wooden stakes, all angled in one direction, facing toward a dark black stain on the horizon. She frowned. There were no people there, just a sense of great loss, a black hole of pain and sorrow, yawning, sucking on the coldness of a dreary day.

Her son, a prince. And she a queen. She remembered Calemore's words all too clearly. *Nigella, I would make you into a queen. Would you like that? I only want to look after my son. He will be a prince then. I don't know what I want.*

She still did not know. A queen, what did that mean for her? What would she be a queen of? What people? Did she really want that? She kept imagining the future for herself, with Calemore at her side, and quite often, warmth suffused her at the thought of that. Then, at other times, there was only pure despair waiting for her in the knotted folds of time. It would be charming to be a queen, to have servants, to have people bow to her. But that was just a silly, sweet, perverted thought, so sweet her jaws went numb with hurt. It wasn't for her. She was not destined to be a queen. She was ugly and shy, and she belonged at the side of some man, if she were lucky. Maybe it was Calemore.

She wasn't so sure anymore.

"Sheldon, go play with your soldiers," she blurted.

The boy frowned. "Mom, I wanna read more."

Nigella closed the book. "No. Enough. Go play on the bed."

He wasn't very manipulative, her Shel, but he still tried to pout and make her resolve crack. When he realized it wouldn't work, and she was adamant, he retreated to the bed and started fiddling with his old toys.

Nigella took a deep breath and closed her eyes. *The Book of Lost Words* was definitely a magical thing. And it revealed whatever it wanted to its reader. For Sheldon, his dream of princedom. For her, a dark, despondent future. What did that mean?

She would not separate from her son. She wouldn't let anyone take him away.

She would not let anyone corrupt his pristine soul. Not even Calemore.

But maybe it was just a metaphor. The book might be lying, revealing a childish illusion of some greater truth in a way that a nine-year-old could understand. Maybe her son was destined for greatness, and the only way he could perceive that was through princely deeds. Sheldon was a smart lad, and she did not doubt he could achieve greatness one day if properly guided.

Only, looking outside the window, she could see that Caytor no longer belonged to its people. There were no people left. Just these Naum strangers. Sheldon might be a prince, but it would be of a nation that spoke a different language, abode by a different culture.

Maybe Sirtai? Yes, that could be it. Her son might succeed in her homeland? Perhaps the future was bright and happy, but she still had not deciphered all the pieces, and she was drowning in the gruesome parts. Perhaps Calemore would lose in his war. What then? What did it mean for her? Or for Sheldon? And what if he won?

What if he won?

She looked at her son. He was everything she had. Nothing else mattered.

"Shel."

The boy raised his head from the impromptu battlefield. "Yes, Mom?" He was bored, but he did not look sad or angry.

"You know I love you, Son, more than anything in the world?"

Sheldon nodded. "I know, Mom."

Suddenly, she had an urge to hug him. She rose and walked over, knelt by the mattress. Her hands crushed him to her chest, and he protested. Sheldon did not like to be hugged. No man did, as far as she knew.

"I won't let anything hurt you."

"Can I be a prince, Mom?" he whispered against her bosom.

Nigella stroked his head before he yanked himself away, slowly but persistently. What could she tell him? A prince of what? But he deserved it. After all the hard life he'd had, all the abandonment, he deserved greatness.

"Maybe."

He pushed his soldiers away. "Are you crying, Mom?"

Almost guiltily, she removed her spectacles and swiped a lone tear away. "No. It's too dark, and my eyes are tired."

"I want to read more," Sheldon insisted.

"That book is not good for you. It's a book for adults," she tried to reason.

"But I like it. I want to know what happens next." He squirmed.

Nigella raked her hair. "No. But you know what? When the rains end, I will ask the soldiers to try to salvage books from the library in Marlheim, if there are any left. You will like that, won't you?"

"Can I go with them?" His face lit up.

A gust of panic slammed her, even as the torrent outside lashed against the cabin walls on all sides, trying to bring it down. "No, Son. Those men are soldiers. Their profession is dangerous. You must stay with me, here." Then she remembered his strange ability to understand their tongue. *One day, I will have enough courage to try to unravel that.* "You will tell me if they ask you to do anything."

Sheldon nodded again, silent.

Nigella remained on the floor, her knees cold and itching. Her son, a prince. Who would believe that? It sounded nice, almost story-like, a poor boy rising to greatness and glory, but then, if she glanced at the burned-out husks of the nearby town, if she stared at the convoys of hard-eyed foreigners leaving for a war of extinction in the south, the sweet illusion evaporated.

Whatever Calemore was planning, it could not be good.

Now, her son might be involved. She would die before she let harm touch him.

When it came to her boy, there was nothing in this world that could stop her. Not even a pale-eyed witch whom she thought she might be in love with.

I'll die first, she swore. *Die or kill.*

CHAPTER 36

*W*hat *kind of enemy does not respond to your baits?* Mali wondered. *One that is too stupid to comprehend the situation or one too powerful to care?*

So far, the foreign army had not bothered halting its advance just because they had a thorn in their backside. Oh, they would send a sizable body of troops to engage the pest now and then, but the vast legion would just plow on south.

Mali hated being wrong. And with this white foe, everything she decided turned out badly.

She had thought severing its supply route would cripple it, or at least slow it down, make it distracted and weak. She had thought attacking from behind would give the enemy pause, force it to reconsider its plan, make it veer off its course. Perhaps she had contributed to the defense of the realms somehow, but it would take a brilliant strategist to explain it to her, because she could not see it.

They were somewhere in Caytor now. Or maybe Athesia, her son's realm. She wasn't certain. Without any people around to tell her whose taxes they tried to avoid once or twice a year, it was hard telling where the borders touched. Any stream, hill, or large village could be a landmark. Without any folks left, everything looked the same. Wild, eerie, grim.

"What do you think?" she rasped.

Alexa was licking her lower lip industriously, concentrating. They had one old map, but it depicted a world full of people. Still, they thought they were somewhere in northern Athesia, about five days from Bassac. The road they followed was supposed to be the Traders' Stretch, and it supposedly went all the way to Pain Daye, and that was where James might be. Only days back, they had passed a large intersection where the road forked south toward Ecol, Gasua, and eventually Roalas.

Some Eracians called this artery the Road of Old Memories, because it had barely been traveled for centuries, until Emperor Adam restored the commerce between Caytor and her land. Well, perhaps it was that. Because she could not really be certain.

The river bisecting the horizon was definitely the Hebane, and it was fat with rain and mud. The banks were overflowing, licking at the willows and twenty-foot cattails growing on the marshy banks. A long bridge ran across, and half a dozen livestock barges thudded gently against one another in the shallows on the western side.

Getting ready to step onto the rafts was the tail of the northern enemy.

It was such a perfect ambush location, and she knew it, and she knew the enemy also knew. Finley and she had been nipping at their heels for weeks now, taunting, teasing, raiding, killing them. A few times, the monster had reared and roared and fought back, but always kept on moving south, almost fanatically.

So the northerners must be aware of the few Eracians trying to be heroes just behind them. Why would they not take more precaution then? Why leave their baggage train almost unprotected? Why bother loading the barges when the bridge could also be used?

Mali suspected it was damaged. Some of the pillars stood at funny angles, and maybe the floods and the strain had made sections partially collapse or bend. She wondered if the entire army had crossed the river just there or followed the near bank south to another, more favorable location. But the torrents had washed away the prints, making scouting that much trickier.

"I sure do not like it," Alexa admitted at last, and spat.

"It's such a succulent prize," Mali whispered. If she ordered an attack, it would be a slaughter. The enemy would be pinned against the riverside, unable to maneuver, with no cavalry to counterattack. Their precious cargo would be lost. So why did she fear this?

Ever since leaving the Barrin estate, they had enjoyed great success in combat. A couple of large, even tense skirmishes, a dozen smaller ones, countless interceptions of patrol units and small supply caravans, with few losses. She should feel confident and emboldened. Instead, she was chewing on fear.

"I really don't like it," Alexa insisted.

Mali nodded. She was still trying to figure out the terrain. But the plains and small, modest hills all looked the same. The heart of the realms was mostly flat, a bad place to get lost in. You had no way of knowing where you really were.

Theresa wiped her runny nose on her sleeve. The woman was sick, but she refused to relinquish her duty even for a few days. "If we defeat them, that means, what, five or six thousand fewer of these bastards to worry about? And we gain control of the river crossing. So if the enemy needs to get back, they either travel north, all the way to Elfast, or go south to Ecol. With the winter closing in, the Hebane is not going to get any slower or less deep, so it's a strategic win for us."

"Unless it's a trap." Mali voiced her suspicion for the tenth time that day.

"I don't think we should engage them," Nolene added. "After all, we've long left Eracia. It's no longer our war. We should go back home."

Mali looked at her youngest major. The woman was right, in a way. Fighting this war of sacrifice sometimes felt pointless. Who were they defending really? Their own realm? Their monarch? Who was their monarch?

"For the time being, the enemy wants to hurry south, but I have a feeling they will circle back to Eracia once they finish whatever they are looking for." Alexa knelt down. "They have ravaged half our realm already. So it's coincidence or luck that took them away from Somar, but this isn't an army to leave an unfinished affair behind them."

Like us, Mali thought. She had other reasons to press south. She wanted to get closer to her son. She wanted to meet James. She wanted to help him. And the enemy force was marching south, into his empire, and it would probably not stop until it saw the shores of the Velvet Sea.

"We haven't come here just to admire their organizational skills," Finley chimed in. Mali had almost forgotten the colonel was there. But he and his staff mostly listened, deferring to her.

"We do our best," Mali murmured. *Or die trying.* She had never liked that idiom.

Alexa grimaced. "This is bad. The earth is wet. Progress will be slow and tiring."

"Our food reserves are low," Mali reminded her. A lithe, fast army could pack only so much salted beef and old cheese. They had a big advantage over the northern enemy, but that also meant the land was nude of anything edible by the time they got there. The abandonment, the rot, the bad weather, and the enemy hunger did their work quite thoroughly. "Those carts look heavy."

"A mouse got caught in a trap," Alexa singsonged.

Mali sighed. "We need to cross the river. We need to get to Ecol. If the town is empty, I want to salvage whatever we can before the snow. And if there are any Athesians left there, I want them to join our side so we can fight together."

Her eyes scanned the crowd around her, seeking doubt and opposition. They lingered on Gordon a moment too long. He had not said anything about her affair with Bjaras, but he knew. If he were hurt or just vexed, he never showed it. He pretended things were as usual, but he lacked his usual gusto, his passion. Perhaps she was a coward, and she had ruined everything, yet again.

The fight would be a good distraction from her self-loathing, she figured.

Less than an hour later, the Third Battalion and the Third Division moved forward, side by side, Finley's heavier body on the east flank. Mali sat on a horse, in the center of her force, surrounded by a small guard. They just plowed on, toward the Hebane.

The enemy stirred, and soon enough, shrill pipes moaned against the overcast sky. The two fishing villages hugging the bridge came alive. The convoy became a confused centipede, trying to untangle its many legs, but it could hardly move in time before the Eracian contingent slammed into it.

White-clad soldiers started forming a weak, disarrayed picket line, but it looked pathetic. Hardly professional, with too-wide gaps, a bending front too near the sloping riverbank. Mali did not object to easy victories. They were preferable to hard ones, and to losses.

Halfway to the enemy lines, she noticed Finley was lagging. That annoyed her. After so much time together, she expected more from her male colleagues. They were supposed to be able to march in discipline, and definitely maintain a unified spearhead.

"What is he doing?" she remarked loudly, but mostly to herself.

Alexa shielded her eyes. It was a dreary gray day, but the cloud cover was still quite brilliant, and patches of it shone like white gold, hiding the sun behind them. "Fuck."

Mali reined her horse. It fidgeted, displeased to halt in a stream of soldiers. The line parted and flowed around her, girls with grim faces, concentrating on counting their steps and watching their comrades on the left and right.

Then she saw it, too, and she understood why Finley was lagging.

No road dust, but she could see a blot of white-clad troops approaching from the north, converging toward Finley's division. The enemy wedge was huge, and it probably counted just as many souls as the supply train near the river. The odds had just doubled against her.

But that wasn't all. The wedge was moving too fast for infantry.

The enemy had horses, thousands of them, and it seemed to have learned how to ride.

"Shit," she heard herself say. *Stay calm, composed. You must remain confident.* "Keep moving." Finley would have to fight his own war now. If she stopped, she would just create a choke point, making it impossible for all the troops in the rear to maneuver. Her own battalion might have fewer troops, but with its several detachments, it was a powerful, experienced force, and it could probably defeat the riverside contingent, especially since she had the advantage of terrain and movement.

Not for long, it seemed.

The marshy banks burst. But instead of ducks and other angry birds, a flock of enemy troops poured out, dashing onto the dry ground, joining the convoy troops, merging, edging the sharp ends of their spears forward. In unison, they closed ranks and advanced. The haphazardly arranged wagons became excellent defense points.

"It is an ambush, all right," Mali admitted.

Alexa nodded once, slowly. There was nothing they could do now. They had to win the battle and cross the river. At least the far bank looked empty. There did not seem to be any enemy units there, but some might be hiding in the tall grass, or in the small village that dipped its fingers in the murky water.

Arrows took flight from behind the loaded carts. Early shots, gauging the distance.

"Spread about! Shields up!" Mali cursed under her breath as she uncinched her large oval wooden shield from the side of the saddle. Holding that thing while riding was a challenge.

Still more troops, all clad in shades of white and light gray, were coming out of their hiding places, by the river, from behind small clumps of low, sagging trees, the seemingly abandoned fishing communities, everywhere. A squad here and there, a gang of spearmen joining the press, but it grew like an avalanche, collecting debris, growing fatter and more menacing with each second.

Groans and screams rippled through her ranks. A few women sagged or knelt down, weighted down by the iron rain, pierced through shoulder or calf. Walking under an arrow shower was a chilling affair. She had always hated it. There was nothing you could do but silently count and thank your luck.

With bad visibility, she could not see the whole front line. The bridge was there, still looking intact and yet somehow brittle and wounded. Maybe it could not be crossed. Maybe she would have to fight for the barges, but how could she hope to load her girls onto those fidgety rafts under fire?

She had wondered about the enemy. Well, it had responded finally. With force, precision, and determination. All her illusions were gone.

Then she remembered something.

"Major Donal!" she shouted, pushing sideways through the thick press. Arrows clattered all around her.

The Elfast officer was leading his own regiment on the right flank. He slowed down. His aide raised a small red flag, and the snail behind him bunched and halted.

"Commander!" His voice came shrill, crisp with terror.

"Please send a company back. I want them to bring the northerner called Bjaras here. Shield him well. But get him here quick."

He saluted, and a handful of his light riders detached and headed back, away from the killing. The noncombat troops, the supply units, and her prisoners waited less than half a mile behind the main force, with their own small protection. Now that she thought about it, the enemy might even try to strike from a third direction, but that was unlikely. Mali had scouts patrolling the area for several miles north and west. They would have warned her.

Taking a deep breath, she headed back into the mayhem. The arrows kept raining, coming like hail in quick, deadly waves. They didn't kill many, but they did not need to. It was enough to cause morale to plummet and make everyone's guts tighten into a hard, cold knot. Soon enough, the line was wavering just as the two nations collided.

She tried to direct the combat as best as she could, but the fifty paces of distance between her and the bloodshed was like an infinite chasm. Her throat was sore, and she was shouting and waving, but the battle just took its own random course. It was now up to the training and instincts of her subordinates.

Now and then, she flicked her eyes left, trying to see how Finley was coping. But it was too hard to see. Damn, she had fallen into this trap like an amateur. The enemy had waited for so long before retaliating. Well, they could afford all their losses, it seemed, so they didn't need to fight back when she wanted them to.

The Eracians seemed to be doing well, because she found herself nudging her horse over a sprawl of bodies, the human carpet red and muddy. The enemy wagons were right there, bristling with arrows, caked in blood, decorated with unmoving human dolls.

The soft ground sucked on the hooves and feet, making people and animals struggle. The din was unbearable, one long cough of metal and meat and squishy wetness that was part autumn, part pure, sweaty pain.

"We need to get to the bridge!" she swore.

Soldiers pressed against her, keeping her safe, and she crabbed forward, into the enemy mass. The white men fought well, and whatever they lacked in skill, they compensated for in numbers.

Like Dwick again, she thought. But back then, they had all been green or rusty, or both. Now, she was fighting for her life when she could have just admired the enemy efforts from afar, timing her attack more carefully. Desperation and cockiness would do that to you.

I won't get to see my son, she lamented, ducking as splinters of hacked wood flew above her head. Mali was suddenly panicking. Why was she fighting this war? To defend Eracia? Well, she had left her realm long behind. She had defeated the Namsue. Why keep killing? Maybe because she missed this sorry thing called war. Maybe because that was what she was meant to do, rather than waste her life pretending to be a scribe in some shithole, keeping her regrets and mistakes well hidden. This was better. Right?

A snarling male face stepped into her view. She took a splinter of a second figuring out who it belonged to. Not one of her troops, or Finley's. She slashed, and the face split in two.

The fighting wouldn't end. Now and then, Mali looked up and tried to figure out where the sun might be. It was still behind a gray blanket, but she knew it was afternoon already. Not a good time to still be fighting a desperate battle.

But her troops held formation and pushed and pushed, slicing into the enemy ranks with efficiency, and the enemy was yielding. All those months of fighting the nomads were paying off, it seemed. She was tired, but there was still fire in her muscles, and she could still swing the blade. The northern force edged away, melting along the riverbank, but not across the span of wooden road laid above the Hebane.

Air. It was cold and refreshing, and suddenly, there was so much of it. Mali found herself staring at the leaden river surface. From afar, it had looked like a sheet of beaten glass, but up close, it was oily, with silt and vegetation bobbing on the surface. The scattering of dead men drifting south did little to improve the sight. The fighting had killed all the cattails, and the earth was pocked with thousands of footprints. An old willow was watching the battle, swaying, bodies heaped around it as if resting in the shade.

The bridge was maybe a stone's throw away. Silent, free of any souls.

One of the barges had lost its mooring and was drifting away. A handful of soldiers were standing on it, still fighting. The wiser ones jumped into the Hebane and swam back to the shore. Others just kept trying to kill one another, and soon their grunts and shrieks were lost.

"Commander! Commander!"

Mali spun around. Dolan's aide was waving a small light-blue flag. It meant soldiers returning from a mission. She liked the man's methods. Half a dozen riders pushed through the weary lot of panting men and women and joined her side. Bjaras was holding dearly to one of the armored horsemen, his eyes wide.

She slid off her saddle. Her troops helped the curly carpenter dismount. He was hunched low, and he looked afraid. He kept looking around him, trying to figure out what was happening.

"Bjaras! You need to help me. You need to understand me!"

Of course he did not. He was still a silly, handsome enemy man, and she did not know what lurked inside his head. But she needed his perspective on the combat. She needed to hope he might be able to tell her something, anything.

"Bjaras, if you see something important, tell me." She saw Alexa approaching, two junior officers in tow behind her.

A messenger trotted over, kicking mud. So young, she was barely a woman. "Sir, Corpsman Lydia wants to know if it's safe to retrieve the wounded."

Mali was annoyed by the distraction. "Does it look safe? No. We ought to cross the river. We should." *Should we?* "Bjaras, talk to me. Why aren't your countrymen fleeing there?" Too easy. It was too easy. She held the west bank now, and it seemed most of her battalion and its auxiliaries were there, intact. Her enemy had lost maybe half its troops, and the rest were beating a slow retreat into the soggy fields.

Way too easy.

The girl nodded and dashed away. Alexa rushed to replace her. "Well, it seems like we've beaten this lot. We help Finley now?"

The Third Division was still fighting the enemy cavalry some distance to the north. Smartly, the colonel had deployed some of his units to the rear so the bridge contingent could not circle behind him. His main body held good formation, and it did not seem in distress, but it seemed like he would be busy for a while. The evening was gently creeping in, and she did not want to be fighting—or worse, crossing the bridge—at nightfall.

Mali looked back at the bridge, to the other side. *Why didn't the northerners flee over? It makes sense. They could hold the other side with a token force.* No sign of enemy troops there yet. But maybe she was due some luck after all. Maybe the enemy had not timed all its moves perfectly, and maybe a third force had been delayed, and she had the crossing.

Or maybe they were smarter than she believed.

"Get some engineers to inspect the bridge. I want to make sure it's safe to cross!"

"What about Finley!" Alexa pressed.

Mali blew snot on the ground, inhaled sharply. "No. We go across, and he follows. Relay the order. We disengage, and if needs be, we will fight the enemy cavalry on the *other* side, with our spears lowered at the bridge, not the other way around."

Alexa pointed. "You know what will happen if another force turns out to be there!"

Mali pushed a thumb into her jaw joint, trying to ease the thumping of blood in her ears. "Yes, I know. But I suspect if we stay here, they will soon turn up and block the crossing, and then we will be really buggered. Get Finley to begin his retreat toward the bridge. Order Gordon to move the supplies here. Now."

She could not describe the frustration she felt for leaving the Third Division to fight its own battle, but there was no other way. Her girls had to be ready to dash to the far side of the Hebane if they spotted any sign of another ambush force.

Sappers streamed past and stepped onto the bridge. Like little monkeys, they spread, some going forward, some lowering themselves on ropes to inspect the columns and supports. A small body of crossbowmen hurried forward. Nothing happened, and they crossed to the far side safely.

One of the engineers whistled and waved. "Get a cart over. We need to test the weight," their lieutenant translated. He was a short, stocky man, with a huge chunk of hair missing from the side of his skull.

"What about all these carts?" Alexa asked, still winded.

Mali sighed. "We leave them here. We have our own wagons." Shame, but she had not calculated this battle that well.

Lumbering like a sloth, the rear guard was inching toward the battlefield. Gordon's men guarded the flanks, weapons drawn. It was such a slow, agonizing procession. The horses and wheels got bogged down, and men had to help free them. Lydia's women rushed ahead, bearing stretchers, and they started rescuing wounded soldiers from the miry fields, loading them onto the already heavy, bulging carts.

"It will take them at least an hour to get here, another hour to cross," Alexa estimated.

"As long as it takes," Mali hissed. At her side, Bjaras was frowning toward the bridge, mouthing silent words in his own, foreign tongue. Her skin pricked. "What do you see, handsome?"

A horn sounded. Finley was starting to retreat. Then, three short notes.

Enemy sighted.

She could see the crossbowmen on the far side waving urgently. She did her best to see what was happening. The willows obscured the view somewhat, but the fields of Athesia and the road to Bassac looked empty. Still deserted.

Bjaras muttered something loudly and moved forward. One of the soldiers tried to stop him, but he shrugged her off and loped toward the bridge. The engineers were still busy checking the massive construction and had reached the second half. From the north, the first companies of Finley's Third started arriving, clogging the wet, busy crossing ever more. They looked tired and bloody, and they dragged limping brothers-in-arms behind them.

"Where the fuck is that new enemy?"

Then, just as she had expected, she saw movement on the far bank. No white uniforms this time. Gray and muddy uniforms, as men started rising from their hiding places up and down the riverside. They had spent the better part of the day half submerged in the cold muck, obscured by the wild green growth.

Mali raked her hair. What now? She needed her soldiers on the other side. If she stayed here, she'd never cross. But if she waited for Finley to fully regroup, the enemy would fortify its positions on the east side, and it would be dark. Bjaras was walking up the bridge, waving his hands urgently. The Eracian sappers were watching him with distrust, some hanging from their ropes over the sides.

The rear convoy was still a good half hour away. Damn. She had no options.

"Lieutenant Cody, what do your men say?"

The engineer whistled sharply, making her skull tingle. The sappers waved back. "Safe to cross. No more than five hundred at any one time. No more than twenty carts."

She took a few deep breaths to steady her nerves. "Girls, get ready. We are crossing over."

Alexa spat again. "That's not a smart idea."

"Do you have a better suggestion? Meagan, take your riders first. Go!"

"Yes, sir!" The noblewoman spurred her mount, and the cavalry rushed onto the narrow span, the iron-shod hooves hammering against the planks in a hollow, painful cadence. The engineers moved to the side to let them pass. One of the men lost his footing, slipped, and fell into the river. He began a slow swim downstream.

Bjaras was standing in the middle of the road, waving. Mali's blood curdled. What was he trying to warn them against? What did he know? Too late now. On the east bank, the muddy northerners were hunched over, spears raised, waiting for Meagan. Mali almost looked away as the two sides clashed. She thought she could hear the piercing screams of women and horses even this far.

With panic pushed deep down into the belly, her companies started crossing. A light jog, four abreast, eyes scanning everywhere for new dangers, for a sudden volley of arrows. Nothing like being pinned down by a barrage in the middle of a bridge.

She was getting worried about the northerners on her own side, the ones that had retreated. Would they regroup now and strike again? But no one reported any new fighting. In the confusion of the battle, Finley's men merged with her girls, and the bridge became very narrow and tight.

It was her turn to join the mayhem. An engineer signaled for the next batch. She climbed into the wet saddle with a groan and moved forward. Gordon's men were getting closer. She saw her captain, and he gave her a short wave. She waved back and nudged the beast onto the groaning timber boards.

The noise intensified all of a sudden. She could hear the wind moaning around the old, moldy ropes. She could hear the river belching lazily. The screams from the far side, the hush of a thousand sore throats from Finley's men approaching the river. A rippling banner marked the colonel's unit, and he was nearing the crossing. Arrows still whizzed, almost like an afterthought, and there was a thunderstorm of screams coming from all directions.

The bridge felt fragile and narrow, and it swayed. It bucked. It groaned. Bjaras was waiting for her, and he was still panicking in his voice. She did not understand. No one did. The sappers were still watching the supports, inspecting the cracks and the ropes, and while concerned, their faces did not contort with immediate danger.

Her troops were spilling onto the far bank, directly into the cauldron of killing. The pace slowed, and she was getting really nervous. But so far, the Eracians were moving forward. Good, good. It meant her girls had gained a solid foothold on the far bank, and there was still hope.

Bjaras put a hand on her reins. He was almost yammering in panic. But she could not tell a bloody word of what he meant. It didn't sound good. It could not be good. He was pointing back toward the west shore. Urgently.

I am ignoring my own instincts, she realized. *I brought him here to tell me something. He* is *telling me something. Why didn't those northerners flee across the bridge?*

Fuck.

"Theresa! Theresa!" she shouted as best as she could.

The major halted, turned around. "Sir?"

Mali shook her head. "We are going back. Get everyone to turn around, and we march west. We'll figure out how to cross the river later, elsewhere. This is bad." Mali raised her arm and made a circle motion above her. "Turn around. Back. Back! Relay the order. Finley, hold at all costs!"

The shuffling was impossible, but no one fell. The bridge protested with a low, deep moan. One of the ropes thrummed. Going back was easier. It was faster. There was no one waiting to poke you with a sword, for a change.

I'm stupid, stupid. What was I thinking?

Gordon's men were waiting in the mud, looking confused. Frightened drays were whining, adding to the chaos. Mali waited until the press of footmen around her eased a bit. Bjaras was following. He was still talking, but he looked relieved.

"Thank you, my northe—"

There was a sudden noise, and the bridge opened below her feet.

CHAPTER 37

What a glorious morning, Bart thought, the cold rain notwithstanding.

"Your signature here, please," Commander Velten said, pointing with a gloved hand.

Margravine-Soon-to-Be-Duchess Diora hesitated for a moment, but then she added her name to the long list of signatories. Her aide heated a pencil of wax over a candle, pressed it against the bottom of the page, and the lady knuckled her ring into the red blob.

There, it was done.

Bart had just become the monarch of Eracia.

Frankly, he had thought his struggle would be harder, longer, messier, bloodier.

Instead, he had achieved the title of the nation's ruler with just a tiny bit of intimidation, some careful plotting by Sonya's mother, and a whole lot of bribes and promotions. People had not really opposed him, it seemed. They had just wanted their share.

Everyone was there. Army commanders, Countesses Ernsta and Anniken, the spiteful master of coin, other leeches, worms, parasites, and sycophants, everyone who thought they could profit from this change. Well, Eracia was a proud realm once again.

Somar would be fully liberated in a matter of hours. His troops were conducting a mopping action against the last isolated pockets of nomads, mostly those cut off from their main units, so they did not know about the retreat or plain refused to budge from their defensive positions, and now, they simply awaited their deaths. A steady stream of Kataji and other tribesmen was fleeing west under the watchful eye of the Eracian forces.

A leaden sheet of icy rain made the world dark and blurred, but it had also put out the fires. You would never know a heavy pall of smoke had hung above the city until only yesterday, stalking the rooftops and streets. For the past few days, the Kataji had held in the northern quarters, burning all they could, trying to stop the inevitable defeat. But Bart's army was invincible, it seemed, and he felt like he could do anything.

He would do anything, in fact.

Those around him felt it, too, and quickly tucked away their morality for better, less gloomy days. Being rich and noble was better than bleeding your freshly cut throat into a gutter. There might be people with scruples and principles in the camp around Somar, but not too many and not with too large reserves of scruples and principles. Ultimately, being pragmatic was a defining characteristic in a member of the court. Besides, gold had its own spiritual value.

Bart knew he could have lashed out at his old foes and rivals. But spite was a poor quality for the victor. He had to be benevolent; he had to be optimistic. His actions would shape the future of Eracia, and it was best if they all started with reconciliation and national unity. They might have had their differences once, but it was only because they all cared about the realm in their own special ways. An act of loyalty, really.

"Well done, congratulations, Your Majesty," Countess Anniken offered, her thin lips stretched into a big smile. She bowed respectfully.

Following her lead, the rest did the same. Men stepped forward, and Bart shook their hands. He could well afford to be magnanimous.

Not to be bested by anyone, Lord Karsten wheeled himself forward, rolling the rims of his wheelchair over unsuspecting toes. But he was like a hammer-driven wedge, and no one could halt his persistent approach.

"Nephew, I am so glad," he beamed. Then, in a hushed voice, "I am so proud of you, Bart. This is a glorious day for all of us."

Bart mounted a soft smirk onto his face. "Thank you, Uncle." Then he remembered his other duties, no less important. "You will all excuse me, ladies and gentlemen. Please await the last confirmation from the army that it is safe to enter Somar."

Their eyes, slightly glazed with greed, followed him out of the command lodge. Four soldiers held a large oiled tarp above him so the rain would not touch him. It was so wide, even the wild splash of drops in the mud couldn't reach his leather boots.

His monarchical retinue followed. Alke and Edgar were now royal servants, and they looked like they could climb walls on pride alone. His small band of soldiers would become an honor guard, hopping up the ladder of promotions like a band of cheerful monkeys. At the moment, they still lacked in gilt and velvet, and their rusty armor and wet uniforms had taken a beating in the furious rain, but nothing could spoil their moment of glory.

He led toward the cabin where Constance resided, a short dash through the storm. It was surrounded by more men, Borei and Eracians alike. Just as he had planned.

Greetings, smiles, messengers. One of the notes caught Bart's attention. "Colonel."

Paul frowned, not expecting to be singled out among the audience.

Bart handed him a square of oiled paper. "Paul, your wife and son are fine. They are in Ubalar, well taken care of. Once we complete our victory, you have my leave to visit them."

The man was still frowning furiously, trying to keep the slap of rain away, but his relief was obvious. His brows drooped; the etched lines round his eyes softened. "Thank you, Your Majesty. I am truly grateful."

Bart patted the man's shoulder. "And so am I." He stepped into the small shack.

His mistress was sitting in a chair, hands folded in her lap, her eyes red from too much crying. In the left far corner, near the window, Junner stood, holding Adam. They were watching the rivulets of water sliding down the pane. The boy looked delighted. So maybe babies could see after all.

Occasional silent lightning lit up the sky, turning it silver. But you could not hear the thunder anywhere, just the rush of water gnawing at the timber, lapping against glass, plinking against tin and slate.

"Lord Count," the Borei greeted. Adam turned and waved erratically.

Bart smiled. He was beginning to develop a liking for his son.

Constance bobbed in her chair, trying to rise, but she remained seated. "Bart," she said weakly.

He nodded at her. "Have you considered my proposal?" he asked.

She bit her lip, and fresh tears coursed down her cheeks. "You know I cannot—"

Bart lifted a finger. "Now. No. Please, no more crying. You must decide. Right now."

Constance swallowed. It took her a few moments before she found courage to speak again. "Yes. I will do it."

He clapped his hands lightly. "Excellent. Then all is well. We sorted that out."

"You are taking my son away from me," she whispered, without malevolence or anger in her tone, just pure sadness.

"He is my son. He is a young prince now. He cannot be a bastard. He cannot be the child of a Caytorean girl fleeing from her home." Bart shrugged. "He belongs at court, where he will be loved and raised properly."

Constance was staring at nothing. "You are a monster."

Bart refused to let dark thoughts cloud his mind. "Adam is my son. I will love him and take care of him. He will never want for anything. In a way, you will be there, too. I cannot forget you, Constance, and I will not forget you. Dear, you shaped my life in your own special way. But your goals and desires go against everything I have tried to build in the past several months. Eracia is more important than your personal ambitions. This sacrifice must be made."

"You are all the same," she murmured.

Bart leaned forward. "What?"

She gritted her teeth. "You are all the same. But when it comes to responsibility, you always blame the woman. You are filthy animals, all of you!" Her hands bunched into small fists over the small curve of her belly.

"Do not be so bitter." He ignored her remark. It was a shadow of her past, and he was no longer interested. "You are an attractive, smart young woman. You will find yourself a husband who will cherish and respect you. But I cannot be that man. I am sorry."

"I hope you die," she spat.

He inclined his head. "Does that mean you do not want my gold?"

She hesitated, sucked her breath in. Maybe he was humiliating her on purpose, but he had offered her a fairly lucrative deal. He knew losing one's child could never compare to money, but she would get a huge sum of gold and a letter of credit to start fresh. She would have to leave Eracia, but she would go back to Caytor pretending to be a young Somar girl, and Bart's document would vouch for her family ties. If she had a dark past back home, she would not need to struggle with it ever again. He was being rather fair.

Or, she could refuse. In which case, she would leave the camp empty-handed. He knew she knew that, but he had to let her make her own choice. Still, he had never expected her to refuse his money.

"I hate you," she said weakly and started crying again. "I hate you."

Bart pursed his lips. "I understand. But you will realize this has to be done. Imagine what would happen if someone learned I had sired a bastard to a Caytorean woman? What would happen then? Would there be a war between our realms? Would people try to assassinate you? Did you really think you could become my wife? You are not an Eracian! You can pretend as much as you like, but you would never have become a lady of the court in Somar. As to our predicament, well, you

came to me, remember? You sought me out among all those
other men. You betrayed that lad Ewan. You let me *fuck* you,
and you let that child grow inside you. You chose to have him,
and I am glad for it. But it is all you, Constance. All you."

He realized he was getting flustered.

She sighed. "It is all my fault. Of course. Silly me."

He was not certain if she was being sarcastic. But it did not
matter anymore.

Constance brushed her hair away. "Can I hug him one
last time?"

Bart shook his head. "No, I'm sorry." He waved at Junner, and the mercenary walked over. Bart extended his hands,
and the boy sidled over, pumping with his little feet against his
coat. Despite his tiny size, he fretted with a great deal of force.

"Who will be his mother now?" she asked, her eyes moist
again.

Bart blinked rapidly. "It is not important. He will be well
taken care of." He paused. "Good-bye, Constance. You must
leave today. You will have an armed guard whichever direction
you choose to go. It's war everywhere, so I would suggest you
head to Parus, and maybe cross over into Athesia via Bridgen,
and then find your way to one of the coastal cities."

Constance did not see him. Her eyes were locked on
Adam. "I love you, Son."

Bart felt his chest tighten. It wasn't easy for him. He turned
around so the baby would not make any sudden gestures toward his mother. There was no need to make matters worse.

"Lord Count, a little hat for the young prince!" Junner
said cheerfully, handing over a thick woolen sock. He reached
over the boy's overlarge head.

"Wait, let me do it," Bart said. Gently, he pushed the
hat over Adam's fuzz and covered his ears. Then, without a

backward glance, he stepped out of the cabin and left his crying mistress behind for good.

It was midday, and the rain had respectfully stopped so the victors could march into the liberated city gallantly, chins raised high. Commander Faas reported no more enemy troops in the city. The tail of the defeated Kataji beast was being harried by the auxiliary units over the western plains, fleeing the battlefield.

One year and a half after taking Somar, the nomads had been defeated. It had cost Bart sixteen thousand souls, but he had won. He had restored pride to his nation. For the first time in centuries, Eracia had something to boast of.

I would not call myself Vergil, Bart reasoned. *I will let others decide that.*

He was mildly surprised by the success of his campaign. He had not really believed he would be able to unite the nation under his banner and make the southern and northern armies cooperate. He had not believed he would have the charisma and audacity to rein in the aristocrats and keep them focused on freeing the city rather than fighting their own personal wars of greed. And truth to be told, the casualties were rather low.

He had lost a huge chunk of his troops, and many more spent their days and nights freezing in wet trenches, still awaiting the arrival of that strange, horrible invader, which never came. But the nomads had lost more, and finally decided to retreat once they realized they would all get killed if they remained in Somar. Once his commanders had figured how to make the best use of their soldiers, and how to fight inside the narrow, littered streets, the favors had turned. The Borei olifaunts had also come in quite handy. He could hear the songs in the army ranks, and the wonder of those gray beasts would be remembered for generations.

"Are you ready, friend?" Junner asked.

Bart looked at the mercenary. "No, not really."

Junner slapped him on the back, not too gently. "Don't tell me a man like you is afraid of a woman!"

"Not just any woman. She is my wife. Don't laugh."

"You are too lenient with your women," Junner chided in between snorts of laughter.

"Perhaps," Bart agreed, his heart thumping a steady, excited beat in his chest.

"Ah, never mind me, Lord Count. You are doing fine."

Bart gazed toward the city gates. Hardly half a mile away. Behind him, the army had arrayed itself in long columns, displaying its colors. Well, the wind was too strong, so the banners were furled for now.

"What if she's dead? What if she's alive?"

"You know what to do," Junner encouraged him. "We discussed this before. Lord Count, it's like a game of cards, or any other game."

Bart gazed at the mahout. "And what will you do now? The war is over."

Junner wagged his finger. "Lord Count, war is *never* over. I hear you plan to chase those nomads all the way to their tribes. Extend Vergil's Conquest. Then there's the northern army we must heed. War is human nature, friend. It cannot end. When it ends, we all end."

Bart could not resist the man's charm any longer. He smiled, some of the tension in his muscles melting. "You're either a bloody genius or a complete fool."

The Borei shrugged humbly. "I am a man of profit, that's all."

Bart rubbed his eye. "What about the rest of your forces? The ones still retained by King Sergei?"

Junner pointed northeast, in the rough direction of that huge foreign army. "We are all friends now. We will fight together. It does not matter who pays for our services, does it?"

"Well, I will be very glad to have you around. I still need to figure out how to beat you in a game of cards, or any other game, you cheating bastard."

Junner slapped him again, almost making him fall from the saddle. "Now, there's the Lord Count I know."

Bart enjoyed it for a while. Then his mirth slipped away, and he turned serious. "Well, this is becoming embarrassing." All those thousands of men, waiting for his signal.

"You are the monarch, Lord Count. They wait as long as you wish."

"You know, I am no longer a count. My official title now is different. Your Majesty. That's how you address me."

Junner snorted. "For me, you will always be Lord Count."

Bart shrugged. Deep down, that was still how he felt. But he would learn how to be the nation's ruler. He would. Like he had learned so many other things in these past several years. Well, he had embarked on a mission of peace. He had finally brought peace. Most of the Eracian dignitaries taken hostage in Roalas were still alive. And he had forged a sort of a peace with the ruler in Athesia. It was no longer Empress Amalia, but it did not matter. King Sergei had loaned him his troops, and in a way, he was indebted to him. Which meant Eracia would be very favorable toward Parus in the years to come. All in all, he had done exactly as he had promised Leopold.

"How's Adam?" he asked.

"Safe and warm with those baby women," Junner told him.

Prunella and Irma had found it in their hearts to love gold, too, it seemed. While they might never really like him, they would keep their old mouths shut and take the best care of his son. Bart was glad he could resolve everything so easily, so *peacefully*.

Now, Sonya, the one part still left unresolved. The one part he dreaded.

It surely would not be resolved if he stayed standing in the wet field outside the city.

Fuck it, he yelled in the frightened confines of his soul and waved for the army to march forth.

CHAPTER 38

A loud crash startled her. Sonya woke from her fitful sleep, hungry, filthy, exhausted. Her little chamber was dark and smelled of mold, but at least she was on her own, without any other women to intrude on her peace, as little as she had these days.

She stood up, her head almost touching the ceiling. At her feet, her chamber pot was full to the brimming. There were no servant ladies in this place.

Another crash. She winced involuntarily. It was closer this time. Footsteps were creaking on the old wooden floor outside, but she had no idea who it was. No sounds of fighting, no screams, just frenetic steps of urgency.

Sonya wished she could leave her tiny prison, but the door was locked on the outside.

Almost a month back, Pacmad had taken them all out of the palace and led them, just as she had suspected, into the northern quarter. There, he had corralled them inside an abandoned orphanage, where its plenty of small rooms made for an excellent prison. She had been separated from the rest of the noblewomen. Once in a while, a soldier would bring her some food and water, but she had not seen any real sunlight or bathed since.

The situation was dire. She knew it by the fact the general had not even bothered to investigate Richelle's death. Sonya had not seen him for a long while now. She was not even sure he was alive or what he might do with the rest of them. The defeat of the Kataji invaders was imminent, but every moment stretched into an eternity. With nothing else to do, she spent her time thinking, talking to herself, trying to keep her sanity, trying to reason out the end of her captivity. What would happen once Somar was fully liberated? Would Pacmad take one last joy raping and then killing them all?

The door to her chamber crashed open, splinters and dust flying. She yelped and sat down on her small wooden bed, cowering. A block of bright light assailed her almost-naked, shivering form, and she suddenly felt exposed, vulnerable.

There was a Kataji warrior standing in the doorway, gripping a sledge in his muscled arms. "Out."

Her body was too weak from the lack of activity and bad food. She gingerly stepped into the hallway, a long, narrow corridor with dozens of cells on each side and small windows, buried near the ceiling, all along its length. Confused female ghosts were leaving their own chambers, looking just as disoriented and feeble as she felt. She recognized them as her peers, and her hatred flared, but it died away all too soon. She was too worried about her own self-preservation to care about these whores.

Silently, the soldier led them away, just like one month back. Sonya glanced at her forearms, at the tiny, livid incisions she had left there with her nails, counting them again, the old ones pale and barely visible. Yes. Thirty days, more or less, she figured. Thirty cold meals, just one cycle of menstrual pain, and her belly was cramping again, so it could not be more than that. But she had read how women in captivity sometimes lost too much weight and stopped bleeding altogether, and her pain might be mere hunger. Well, she still had some dignity on her hips and chest, still looked like a woman. She still had her best weapons.

She had to step over the body of a dead tribesman. He looked familiar. Yes, that was the man who had fed her the past several weeks. His face was caked with old black blood, and his arms looked broken. An empty key chain lay by his mangled fingers. What had happened there?

The mess hall of the orphanage already had a whole bunch of other women in there. Strangely, the Kataji were feeding them, bowls of some hot gruel and wedges of rye bread. Most had musty, itchy blankets covering their shoulders.

Sonya frowned. What did this mean? Did Pacmad intend to give them false hope? Or did he plan something more sinister? And if he had time to feed his prisoners amid all this chaos, maybe the nomads were still not losing this war. The thought terrified her.

Where was he?

She found herself in a rough chair, staring at a bowl of oatmeal. Oh, she was hungry.

Almost too casually, Pacmad strolled into the hall from a side entrance, shadowed by three soldiers, their swords drawn. The chieftain looked tired and dirty, like everyone else, but his face was calm, and he was in control of things, like he always was. He flicked his fingers. One of the warriors approached, and the general whispered in his ear. The man nodded and went into the kitchen.

Sonya saw him and forgot all about the food. She pushed the chair back and stood up, leaning against the table until she was strong enough to stand.

"Pacmad," she called. On the far side of the bench, Verina stabbed her with a gaze of deep consternation.

The Father of the Bear noticed her. His eyes clouded with disdain. "What do you want?"

Sonya tried to bear herself regally. "I must talk to you, please."

Pacmad did not speak for a while. He waited until the soldier returned from the kitchen and handed him a wooden bowl brimming with the same gruel. "Talk." He began spooning the breakfast dutifully.

"Alone, please," she pleaded.

He waved her over. The three bodyguards stepped back. She shuffled close, and her broken toe clicked once, just to annoy her.

"You should eat," he chided.

Sonya nodded weakly. Yes, the sensible thing would be to gobble her own ration as soon as she could, because she could not be certain there would be more food anytime soon. But she just could not eat, not just yet. She had to know first.

"What will happen to us?" It was barely a whisper. And she braced for a punch or a backhand.

Instead, he kept on chewing the white flakes, some of them sticking to his stubble. "Nothing. You will soon be freed by your countrymen."

Sonya reeled. She could not believe her ears. Why was he tormenting her still? Was he just trying to be mean and cruel and to derail her mind? To make her elated, and then see her cry hysterically? To flare her hopes up and then smother them in a vicious grip?

But his face was as serious as she had ever seen. He was still the mongrel with his blue eyes, but he did not seem to be jesting. "Yes, you go free," he repeated, his voice emotionless.

Someone pushed past her. She almost fell. In that moment, she realized how pitiful she was. The old granite floor beneath her bare feet was icy cold, and the air in the hall was quite frigid, too, despite the kitchen heat and the press of bodies. She only had a simple dress on her body, and she had long forgotten what it felt like to be warm and comfortable. Her muscles were cramped and stiff from the cold, and she carried with a hunch that made the grumble in her stomach and the bite of the oncoming winter against her shoulders and legs somewhat easier to bear.

"Why?" she asked, madness gripping her.

"Your monarch saved you all. I get to leave the city unscathed, and you get to keep your miserable lives." He pointed with his greasy hand. One of the Kataji warriors came close and draped a blanket round her arms. "Noble captives are always useful. You should eat. I promised you'd all be healthy. And I keep my promises."

Sonya pulled on the quilt, and it chafed against her skin. But soon enough, a fuzzy breath of warmth spread through her chest, and she almost wept. In a way, she felt disappointed. She had never really managed to break him. Pacmad had turned out to be too sly, too intelligent, even for her. The realization irritated her.

Now, of all things, he would just leave, granted safe passage for sparing the lives of his captives. It was infuriating. After all the evil he had done, he would go home to his clan as a man who had killed the Eracian monarch and held its capital for so long. Somar was now in ruins, and thousands had died trying to free it. Pacmad would surely be sung a hero by his tribesmen. That was simply not fair.

Sonya wished she had fury in her heart, she wished she could just lash out at him, until her voice turned hoarse, but all she felt was a cold, numb emptiness, a sense of defeat.

Another form stepped into the hall. A woman, young, beautiful, dressed in an expensive gown, and with a mantle of white fur round her shoulders. Aileen.

What was she doing there?

"Hello, Sonya," she greeted cheerfully. Her delicate hand reached and touched Pacmad's neck, playing with his filthy locks.

Sonya swallowed bile. What was happening?

Pacmad looked over his shoulder and grunted appreciatively. He swallowed the last of the oatmeal and belched, then wiped his cheeks clean. "Don't mind her."

Sonya wasn't sure who the last sentence was meant for, her or the whore. Aileen was smiling as if there was nothing wrong in the world, blissfully ignoring the crowd of terrified women in front of her, not seeing the carnage and destruction outside the sooty windowpanes.

"When are we leaving, honey?" Aileen purred.

"Very soon," the chieftain responded, cupping her chin with his greasy hand.

"Where are you going?" Sonya blurted.

Pacmad grinned wickedly, his eyes shining. "She is coming with me, back to my clan. She will be my new wife. Maybe my first wife."

What? Sonya thought. What! This little bitch? Sonya remembered how she used to drivel when Pacmad raped her, remembered all the crying and whining and fear. Now, she acted as if she had won herself the most dashing prince in all of the realms. Impossible. She would not let herself be one-upped by the likes of Aileen. Never.

"Take me with you," she whispered. She would show Pacmad that she could be just as beautiful and irresistible as Aileen if only he gave her a chance. She would edge the little bitch out until she was despised by everyone in the clan and not even the donkey keepers would fuck her. She would show them both that she was the most talented, most desirable woman in the world if she put her heart and mind to it. No more games.

"Please, take me with you," she repeated, and her voice sounded whiny. She could not be crying. That couldn't be happening. And what was she doing on her knees?

The general stared down at her for a moment as if she was mad. "No."

Sonya gripped his leg, holding tightly. "Please."

He kicked, and she fell. "Get off me, you crazy woman."

Aileen giggled behind her hand. "So pitiful."

Pacmad sneered. "Yes, she is. Don't worry. I don't want her."

Sonya wiped the tears in her eyes away. "Why? Why?"

He leaned over her, and fresh fear poured over her. She had not felt his wrath for a very long time, and it sobered her. "You can't bear any children. You're useless! Aileen will birth many sons for me. Now, eat your fucking food." With that, he left the hall, the young whore trailing at his heels. His bodyguards fell in line, and the hall went back to its business.

Sonya slumped. There it was. The one battle she could never win.

She rose to her feet, pretending not to see and hear the derision and hushed gossip around her, and went to eat her oatmeal.

Some time later, Eracians entered the orphanage and greeted the women with brittle voices full of emotion. She was recognized and led away from the others. Sonya watched in a trance as the soldiers led her to back to the palace, through streets choked with rubbish, debris, and decomposing, bloated bodies. She wasn't really sure she was in Somar still. When she stumbled, too weak to walk, the soldiers carried her, keeping her warm and shielded from the rain.

At the palace, a host of servants awaited her, and they took care of her. She was given good food and wine and was bathed twice. A freckled girl spent time brushing her hair and clipping her nails. Then she was robed in a silk dress. Finally, they led her back to the throne hall and asked her to wait there. No one else was in the large chamber within.

With her belly full, and her skin cleansed of filth and her soul of some of the humiliation, her mind started racing once again. She began to wonder what would happen next. But after all she had lived through during her captivity, what could possibly be worse?

She did not have to wait for long. Soon enough, a man stepped into the hall. Feet clacking against the red-veined marble, he walked forward, between the slender columns. There were no furnishings, no coats of armor, flags, paintings, or statues of past monarchs, but at least her countrymen had cleared the nomad refuse away. Sonya remembered copulating with Leopold in the private chambers behind the dais. The thought caught in her throat when she realized who the man approaching her was.

Bart, her brave, loving husband.

He had come to her.

Then she saw another figure near the entrance. An older woman holding a bundle in her arms. She stayed back, though, allowing Sonya to soak in the visage of her savior in full.

He had changed. He looked pretty much the same, except for his beard, which made him look older and wiser, but he carried with newfound pride she had never seen before. His gait was sure, his shoulders pulled back, his back straight. In the past, he would always seem troubled, preoccupied, weighted with the responsibility of his position at court, always worrying, an unbecoming, an unfashionable burden for someone like her. No more.

He was watching her carefully. But he did not smile or say anything.

"I missed you," she said. She was being honest. She really was.

Bart just pursed his lips. "I have been nominated the new monarch of Eracia. From this day on, the royal bloodline will be Barrin. You are the queen of our nation. Congratulations, Sonya, you've got even more power than you ever wanted. The highest title in the realms."

Sonya tried her best to keep her composure. "You…did that?"

Bart smiled. "Yes, I did." He turned around. The woman holding the bundle moved forward. "And there's more."

Sonya watched with expectation as the woman shuffled closer, and then her elation at being the queen coalesced into terror. The woman was dressed like a midwife, and she was carrying a baby in her arms. Without a word, she handed the child over.

"Take him," Bart goaded. "Careful."

"No," Sonya whispered.

"You must. This is *your* son," Bart insisted.

Her knees almost buckled. What was happening? She had almost fainted. Bart was holding her upper arm, pinching hard.

"Listen to me, Sonya. Listen to me. This is Adam. He is *our* son. *Your* son. You gave birth to him in the city sometime after I left for Athesia. I have sworn witnesses who will testify that you are his mother."

"But I—" she moaned.

"I have spoken to your mother. It's all right. He is your child."

"He is my child?" she repeated stupidly.

"Take him, please."

Sonya extended her arms. The boy looked curious and was trying to figure out her face. Bart's hands hovered nearby to make sure she had a steady grip on the child. Once the midwife relinquished Adam, she bowed and left without a backward glance.

She stared at the thing in her arms. The one thing she could never produce. The one thing she had never desired really. But now, if she dared, she could be a mother. Did it matter who gave birth to this boy? Bart said he belonged to her, and she would not argue with her husband. Never again.

"But the ladies of the court—"

"They will make sure to bring back some forgotten memories, or else," Bart explained with such brutal calmness, she fell in love with him. She never had before, not the day they were married, not since. But now, there was joy and warmth in her heart. She was happy. What could a woman possibly want more?

"From this day on, Adam is the heir to the throne," Bart continued. "You will raise him to be a strong son, and you will love him more than your own soul. From this day on, if you ever cheat on me with another man, or do anything that would besmirch my honor or jeopardize that boy, you will find yourself wishing the Kataji still held you captive. Do you understand me, Sonya?"

"I will do as you say," she promised. She meant it. Why would she not? She loved her husband.

Bart softened a little. He stepped close and laid a gentle hand on her cheek. She thought it trembled, but that could not be. "In time, I will forgive you all these past years. I think it will be all right."

She started crying, unable to dam her feelings. "Yes, it will. I love you, Bart."

He grinned. "Excellent. I must admit I missed you, darling."

Sonya let out a little sob of joy at hearing him call her that. Oh, how she craved his flattery, his approval. It would be all right, indeed. She would make sure he loved her back. She would fight for his attention and forgiveness. She would pay him back for the eleven years of misery she had given him. And she would raise his son to be the proudest prince the realm had ever seen.

"That is settled then. You must have been through a lot. But you must stand at my side at the liberation ceremony tomorrow. Do you think you will be able to do that?"

For you, my love, anything. "Yes, Your Majesty."

He waited a few moments, fighting some inner conflict. "Were you mistreated in your captivity?"

Sonya would not tell him all she had been through. He should not know that. "Some. But I'm fine. Did you really let the Kataji go?"

"I just wanted to make sure you would not be harmed." Only Bart would be man enough to sacrifice the sweetness of victory to ensure her own safety. That was how much he loved her and cared for her. "But that's a mere act. Soon enough, our forces will march northwest and conquer all of the nomad lands. This time, though, there will be no mercy. I will slaughter them to the last soul."

Aileen, don't forget to kill that one, too, she thought, but kept her mouth shut.

"There's a threat of another war looming. I will need all the political help I can get. The nation is in ruins, and rebuilding Somar will take years. I think you would be best suited to lead that effort so I can focus on military affairs. Do you think you can do that?"

"Yes, Your Majesty. For you, anything."

He believed her this time. He leaned over and kissed her cheek. "Just like a younger couple." He chuckled.

She was feeling rather aroused, she realized. Later that night, she would fuck her husband with all the ferocity of eleven years of miserable marriage. It would be like their wedding night, only with true love and excitement. For a moment, she felt like a silly maid, about to lose her virginity. The sensation was exquisite.

Soon, she was laughing, loudly, freely, basking in the strength of her loving husband.

Even little Adam joined in with tiny, gooey noises. For Sonya, it was the best moment of her life.

CHAPTER 39

I
t was the longest retreat in the history of mankind, Calemore mused.

For the past several weeks, the enemy had been steadily marching south, with the Naum army nipping at their heels. After just a few short days of intense battle, they had fled Ecol, and now, the surviving god and his mongrel pack of Caytoreans, Athesians, and Parusites were nearing Gasua. Once the town fell, the road would be open to the holy places in the Territories.

Such a temptation.

The rains had slowed down everything. Cold torrents had washed over the land day and night, making streams overflow, flooding villages and uprooting trees. The earth had become a brown soup, and even men could hardly walk through the knee-deep muck, let alone draft animals pulling carts. His supply train—what was left of it—was bogged down maybe a hundred miles up the road.

The people of the Old Land had an advantage over him. They counted fewer numbers, so they could move faster. They were also more accustomed to wet weather. The Naum folk had no experience with rain, only ice and snow, and they struggled with all this water. Soon, very soon, the favor would swing back. The incessant downpour had given the enemy a few days of respite. But no matter. Nothing could stop the Naum force.

Calemore was standing at a crossroads—what used to be a crossroads, the old sign pointing south and east floating in a shit-colored rain puddle. Huddling at his side were five miserable elders, their drenched furs sagging heavy on their shoulders. He did not care about the slap of icy drops in his face. He was too focused on what had to be done.

Originally, he had planned to drive south until he clove the realms in two. But now, there were so many succulent prizes around him, within his reach, just days away. At his right, he had the Eracian border forts, half a dozen of them, hiding behind the next crinkle of soil and stunted trees. Farther south, the road snaked through a hill pass, leading toward Talmath. And while he knew the old haven of the gods was a home to ordinary settlers now, he longed to send his troops there to destroy every last trace of faith from the land. But that would mean diverting some of his efforts away from the main campaign.

Then he had the Hebane and the Telore. If he could somehow master their winding courses, he could ferry tens of thousands of troops south, ahead of his foe, cutting them off, encircling them, preventing any further escape. His forces could then take Roalas and float all the way to the seashore and maybe even capture some of the coastal cities in Caytor. Then he could handle the rest at his leisure.

But did he dare send tens of thousands of people who couldn't swim down raging, overflowing rivers? It wasn't the human sacrifice that galled him so much; it was the risk.

His eastern army had finally overcome its difficulties and was moving to join him. They were plowing across central Caytor, trying to salvage the last of the crops and livestock left by the fleeing population. The winter would not be pleasant, but if there was one thing the Naum soldiers did well, it was to embrace the snow and blizzards. The army would converge on the other side of the Telore, so they could make even better use of the river to speed their travel. Again, he wasn't certain if he dared risk the bulk of his troops to drowning.

He really should visit Nigella.

"Take your coats off," he ordered the elders.

Without reluctance, they obeyed, tossing them over to their warriors. Good. He wanted them to embrace the rain, to learn how to cope with it. This land would become their new home, and they had to master the elements.

"The rain has crippled our progress," Calemore stated. "But I want you to devise a plan how to move the troops forward regardless. The enemy expects us to remain dug in until the storms pass. I want to surprise them."

His mind strayed back to the last few days, the skirmishes, the exchange of magical power.

Well, his assassination attempt on the second bloodstaff wielder had failed.

Just as he was about to pulverize that man, enemy wizards had raised a powerful defensive shield that prevented him from reaching them. It was his fault. He should have noticed their presence earlier, when he had murdered Nigella's former lover. He should have realized they had magic back then, and focused his efforts on defeating them first.

But the knowledge there was another bloodstaff out there had dulled his wit, made him reckless. So he may have turned a few Special Children into red mush, but there would be no more opportunity for a surprise attack like that. Not anymore. Not easily. The wizards kept guard day and night, and all he could do was direct the magical pellets against the human army, but then, they fought back with their crafty, powerful spells.

He had not expected the people of the Wild Islands to be involved.

It meant his campaign would have to last awhile longer. Once he conquered the realms, he would deal with the island people. *Ah, they call themselves Sirtai nowadays.*

In fact, his attack against that scrawny-looking man and the rest of the god's servants was a big mistake. Only in retrospect did he realize the foolishness of his deed. He could have accidentally killed the surviving deity and thus unmade all his efforts in becoming one himself. There was no real way of knowing what plain identity the god might have assumed, and he was probably using his own magic to make himself even less visible.

At least he had killed a few of them. And now, they could no longer use the bloodstaff. They were afraid, and they knew he would fire back viciously whenever they tried to use it. Likewise, the Sirtai wizards would try to kill him with their own magic if he used the weapon. So no one used it, but he had bigger numbers, and that meant victory for him.

Calemore realized he should focus on trying to devise a plan to dispose of the wizards. Or at least render their powers useless, allowing him to use the bloodstaff without any worry. Once the islanders were incapacitated, the god would be helpless. The humans were insignificant.

No, they are not, a hidden corner of his brain whispered urgently. *Do not underestimate them. Do not dismiss their urgent need to stay alive and fight off death at all costs. They will try anything to outwit you, and they will not be burdened by the cockiness of immortality.*

Maybe he should have killed that girl Amalia when he had the chance. He should have killed all the other rulers, crippled the nations, caused chaos in their ranks. But it was so unnatural for him to reason war in that manner. How could any one human be so different from the rest? Or more valuable?

Then he remembered his bespectacled lover, and his doubts soared.

He had to make sure the Special Children were ineffective, that the god remained confused and isolated, and that human leaders could not make any decisions. He had to make sure the wizards did not kill him with their alien magic and that the enemy could not use the bloodstaff. That was all. His troops would do the rest. If he used them wisely.

Logic, passion, which one to choose?

The events of the last few days decided it for him. He would push south, and the people of Eracia and the Safe Territories would consider themselves lucky for being spared. For now.

"Elder Buan, I want your men ready for a night attack."

The clan head bowed, but there was doubt in his eyes. Calemore had never expected that. But these men were exhausted, starved, maybe even afraid, and the rain was sapping their resolve.

Well, the killing would toughen them up.

The clan spent the entire evening getting ready. They had no dinner, because there was no food left with the front units. Then, Elder Buan moved his eighty thousand men south through fields that looked more like a lake with clumps of grass than a field of green soaked in rain. Of course, the torrents never stopped hissing. The landscape looked like it was a boiling pan of oil.

Through the night, the Buan marched using their snow-shoes. They didn't work quite as well as on a powdery white carpet, but at least the men managed to drag their feet forward instead of sinking to their knees. Close to dawn, the army reached the god's position, the slowest of the units to flee the wrath of Naum.

Calemore stood some distance from his troops. He knew the defenders might hurl magic back, and he did not want to be near the carnage. He wanted a clear field of vision so he could direct his powers back at the Sirtai and maybe destroy them. He also had to look for the deity and his own tricks to make sure he did not accidentally kill him. Then, there were those gifted freaks, but he believed he had killed most of them.

As always, his eyes scanned the land without seeing, trying to sense the second bloodstaff. It was there, but its presence was muffled by the stifling choke of the beating hearts of the weak, dirty mixed lot of Athesians, Parusites, and other nations of the realm.

There were no fires in the enemy camp, and everything looked still. Only tents, brown like the mud they were slowly sinking in, with a rare animal coughing its sick neigh or bray into the wet morning rustle. Gasua was somewhere out there, behind the screen of rain and autumn chill, and he thought he could see the faintest outline of Bakler Hills just beyond.

Calemore put aside all his problems and doubts now. No more idle thoughts about Nigella quivering beneath him, no more thoughts about the scarcity of tools and food and horses, no more regrets about past blunders, useless questions about his enemy, no more considerations of the weather, the readiness of his clans, the delay in progress, the complications, the involvement of magic in his campaign.

He emptied his mind and prepared for the battle.

Silently, the Buan squelched forward. Never was there a slower charge, Calemore thought bitterly. Almost like cretins on stilts, the Naum soldiers moved against the people of the realms, the rain hiding away the grunts and curses. The enemy woke up and tried to raise an alarm, but it sounded like the yawn of a dying man.

He felt the tingle of magic before he could see it. From a different camp, not the one he was assailing, a solid ball of compressed power rose in an arc and landed square in the van of his force, scattering men aside. He smiled, even as his guts recoiled at the foreign feel of the wild islander magic.

They were so desperate they risked his wrath again.

It was almost an unspoken rule, but he leveled the blood-staff against the distant target and let loose a steady stream of pellets. A few moments later, another clump of magic sped in his direction, this one landing in the pond of muck not far from him. His troops kept surging on, closing the gap in their midst, flowing over the rent like ants.

Calemore responded again. A boring duel, all in all, he figured. His enemy could not see the destruction, and he couldn't see the torn corpses caused by the blood pellets either. They lobbed their magic across the battlefield, more a statement of intentions and abilities than any real contribution to the death toll. But Calemore's troops did not need help. They had numbers to compensate for the hunger, the lack of gear and cohesion, the foul weather.

They tried their luck again, and the magical clout came almost near enough to worry him. He raised a shield around him and watched the debris fly and hammer against an invisible pane. Trees, mud, rock, almost like there was a raging windstorm out there. He fired back, emptying the weapon. Then, casually, he waded through the mire until he reached the corpse of one of the Naum soldiers killed by the wizards. He bent down, touched a finger to a white cheek. Still warm, freshly dead. He drained the hot blood and filled the rod.

The enemy attacks had stopped. They must have figured out they couldn't win this way. Or they might have drained their magical strength. Calemore felt slightly worked out himself, but he had plenty more left to challenge the enemy if they tried playing unfairly. The only thing he worried about, really, was the bloodstaff. Men drained of magic eventually, but that weapon could fire as long as there was death about. But it would seem that its wielder was a coward and did not dare use it.

His troops were now pushing into the enemy camp. As always, the foe would fight for a while, try to stall, but the other, more distant camps were already trying to pack and get away. They would retreat another few lethargic miles in this foul weather and hope that the Naum forces would lag behind for a few more hours. Well, true, he could not mount a serious, crippling attack without several days of careful preparations, and he wished the bloody rain would stop soon, but he could wear them down, even if it cost him five times more casualties.

Calemore had not studied the enemy culture much, but he thought the rabble trying to stave off the Buan were Parusites. They were usually more organized than the rest. And they were staunch believers, so their death was even more valuable.

He realized there would be no more magical fighting today. He started west, where the sky was still bruised and sulky with the livid gray of a retreating night. He walked into the rain, climbed a knoll with half its trees lying down and rotting. Not much scenery, but at least he could see the flow of troops. The Naum bulge, the bucking sickle of the Parusite camp, the retreat of the troops farther south. But they seemed to have divided their forces. Maybe they were trying to confuse him? Should he pursue south, after the larger contingent, or handle those fleeing toward Gasua?

It could be a diversion, but then he remembered the Eracian army that used to prick his backside for so long. Well, if he let them be, they would straddle the roads once his army rumbled past, and they would endanger the supplies and families following after.

Calemore raised his hand. Lavea dropped from the sky and landed on his forearm. Tough bird, and it didn't tire when its wings got wet. Rain or snow, it laughed at the puny humans dragging their feet below.

He magicked a message for the Tirri and Nishose elders. It might take them a day to get moving, but he wanted them to besiege Gasua. Meanwhile, the rest of the force would keep pursuing the god's army. As they had been doing for the last several weeks. Day after day, he would keep attacking, and they would keep retreating farther south, until they eventually ran out of land. Then, they would all die.

He spread his arms wide, and the tough flier took off.

The details of the landscape around him were scant, but he relished what he could see. Mayhem and desperation so real you could cup them in your palm. Even as a painter, his eyes struggled to grasp the full color and emotion of the battle unfolding before him.

Shrill notes rose into the sky. The enemy was trying to communicate, sounding its call of panic and misery. The Buan were in bad shape, too, but he had dozens of other clans, and another elder would prepare his forces for the march the next day. Their challenge might be different. They might have to fight for a river crossing, or just plod through mud until they dropped from exhaustion, or maybe they would storm another encampment. It did not matter. Nothing would stop him.

Every day, he was nearing his victory. The people of the realms were dying, and their god was getting weaker. He wished he could observe the dynamics between the leaders of these nations, taste their terror, see how they made decisions given their limited knowledge, power, and experience. He wanted to know if he could somehow corrupt their magic wielders, to know if there were any more Special Children left around. Sometimes he wondered if the enemy might not be springing a trap of its own, just as elaborate as his plans. But it could not be. No man was that astute.

Even a blind beggar could see the outcome.

Within a few weeks or months, or maybe years, the Naum army would win by the simple grace of attrition. Which brought him closer to the questions he couldn't answer just yet. What would he do once he became a god, and what about Nigella?

He was also thinking more about Sheldon. Still a child, but with a sharp mind, and his mother's blood. If properly raised, he could do wonders. Rarely did Calemore spend much thought to what role humans around him could fulfill. Normally, they were just fodder. If not for slaughter, then for some other mundane task. Sometimes he needed them to sow crops, sometimes to clean latrines, and sometimes to fear him.

But that concept was wearing off fast. He no longer relished fear and blind obedience. Boring, even disheartening. Only he was not really certain the Naum civilization could elect a free, unafraid mind from its midst. Its culture was lodged deep in reverence and unquestionable loyalty to his image. For countless generations, the nation had lived isolated behind the Veil, in the snow and the cold, and the only thing it had was its immortal leader. They worshipped him and, in that, blunted their souls.

Not that he expected them to rebel, but even a small change of heart would take centuries. How could he steer them away from the very ideal he had created? With more force? That could not work. They had to figure it out on their own. But to rule them yet again as mindless drones, that would be torture.

Oh, how Nigella had poisoned his mind. Once he would have been content with just killing the remaining deity. Now, it was just inertia. A habit. He didn't really care for that any longer. So there had to be something else. Something beyond revenge. Something that would motivate him once he won this war.

All his brilliant mind could summon was Nigella and her son.

Sheldon might be the answer to his problems.

He still had time before fighting *that* battle. So, he pushed the thought back into the black recesses of his soul and focused on simpler things, like exterminating the people of the realms.

CHAPTER 40

Amalia had burned to return to Roalas.
Well now she was, but not how she had imagined.
She wasn't leading; she was fleeing.

For a month now, the enemy had been pushing south relentlessly. A seething mass of men and steel, slow and ungainly, rolling like an avalanche, like a collapsing mountain. There was never any grace or great order in Calemore's tactics, never any deep planning. The White Witch was sacrificing his troops without regard to numbers, restraint, or finesse. He just marched forward, and there was nothing they could do to stop him.

Amalia had hoped Ewan would use the bloodstaff to kill the northerners. Only, when you had *two* such weapons, aimed at each other, it was best not to use them at all. Every time Ewan had hazarded firing the blood pellets at the enemy, Calemore would respond with his own magic, sowing death. Now, it seemed, the boy was simply afraid.

Princess Sasha had vehemently objected to the Sirtai using their own power, but after she lost almost half her forces, her resistance had melted away. She did not approve of magic, but the only sensible thing was to let the wizards be.

Gasua had fallen the previous week. Day and night, the northerners had sent their men to die, wave after wave, until the friendly lines had simply collapsed. Cold to the bone, without any food or sleep, the defenders had tottered away from the death, no longer caring. Many had deserted, and others just followed the big army, seeking hope and strength in numbers.

They were all exhausted. People counted themselves lucky if they could sleep four hours. That wasn't enough, not for the body or the mind, and their senses were dulled, their patience short. She could not trust her own judgment, let alone that of the men around her.

Amalia pulled on the reins. Her horse neighed but then halted, stomping nervously. As the king's vassal, she was entitled to a carriage, but she refused to ride inside a wooden box on wheels, deprived of any control. The saddle was a torture, but she kept her eye on the human animals around her, waited for her moment to strike back at her enemies. Lately, she had gained so many she could hardly count.

At the foot of the hill ridge running south, the small folk were winding through the canyon. They sounded much closer than they were. Amalia could hear the crunch of boots on gravel, the smack of hooves, the wet, racking coughs. Every now and then, a lone figure would veer away from the procession, walking like a drunk, and then simply fold down in the wet grass, never to rise again. No one bothered herding the strays back to the convoy. No one cared anymore. The strong would survive, and that was all that mattered.

Across the valley, a knot of bandits was watching the Athesians make their lethargic flight. Once the army and the refugees went away, they would scavenge the bodies, collect what was left behind. Animal carcasses, lost blankets and tack, a sack of rotten food, it was all good plunder for them. They did not complain. Princess Sasha kept her riders close and would not chase them away. She needed every soldier ready to fight the northerners.

The enemy was maybe two miles away, following at the same sickly pace. They were just as malnourished and weak as her own people, but they counted a hundred times more. Looking back, she thought she could see the swarm of troops climbing over a low wooded crest. Athesian stragglers were maybe a bow's shot ahead of the Naum army, already forgotten by their kin. To try to save them would mean more death, more losses. It would be madness.

Gavril was down there, among the men and women and children, preaching. He made sure they never forgot their gods and goddesses. Their bellies might be empty, their toes might be freezing, they might be shitting brown water, and the children might be dying of lung fever, but as long as they had faith in their hearts, they would live. So he promised them.

A goat bleated, a forlorn sound. They still had some livestock. But soon, they would have to start eating their own horses.

She nudged her small filly off the track so she would not impede the troops coming up behind her. Mostly footmen and footwomen, all insignias long worn-out. Everyone looked identical: pale, weak, dirty, muddy all over. Today, there was no rain after so many weeks of icy torrents, but the air was frigid, and breaths misted. There was no sun, either, to warm their skin, just a low, sullen cloud cover, and it licked at the higher hilltops, bleeding its fluff against naked treetops.

Amalia saw Jarman approaching. He was riding side by side with his blue-faced friend. The two Sirtai were miserable, but they still looked noble, dignified.

Well, we united everyone for the war against Calemore. It didn't do us any good, she wanted to say. But she was just too tired.

I am still here, still leading my nation, she tried to convince herself.

A barefoot soldier shuffled past her, face slack, eyes closed in fitful sleep. He marched on, following the rest of the army. There was no cohesion any more. Athesians and Parusites and Caytoreans mixed freely, truly united in their misery. Only the Borei still managed to keep apart somewhat.

"You must keep moving," Jarman chided weakly, joining her.

Amalia nodded. Her shoulders hurt fiercely. She had blisters on her backside. Her toenails were turning squishy white in her sodden socks. That could not be good.

"When does this end?"

The wizard inhaled slowly. "When we win," he grated stubbornly.

She considered opening her mouth, but what would be the point? She resumed her slow march.

Later that day, they were intercepted, even as a needle-thin drizzle started, cladding the world in a silky hiss. A friendly force of almost thirteen thousand Parusite troops, coming from the south, fresh, clean, full of hope, zeal, and illusions of a quick victory. They also brought food and herbs and new weapons. Thunderous cheers exploded through the ranks, and it was almost enough to lift everyone's spirits, even for just a moment. But they had seen this before, and so far, they were still fleeing the enemy, and their bellies were still empty.

Amalia had lost track of all the dukes and counts that King Sergei had sent north. Still, somehow, she had to admire his dedication to this lost cause. He could have just left and ridden home to his warm home country and carefully prepared for the war, instead of sacrificing his best troops for the sake of these nonbelievers and their questionable loyalty. That was a lesson for her in how to be a leader.

The army still kept to its higher vantage point. The civilians bogged the lower passes, pushing, shouting, cursing, or just staring ahead with glassy, uncaring eyes. There was a scuffle near one of the open field kitchens, and as usual, men shoved the women and their babies aside, gobbling all the rations. Rape, that was the dessert. But even Princess Sasha could not afford to kill the offenders.

Uphill, there was more discipline, but not by a great measure. Soldiers moved in tight groups, Red Caps apart, Xavier's men apart, her Athesians apart. There was little trust, and you could get knifed over a wrong look. If you stole bread, you could get killed. Some soldiers had whores, taken from the camp below. Women gave away their bodies in return for some gruel and protection. Amalia had found the Borei methods objectionable before, but now everyone practiced them without shame.

The filth stopped short of the higher-ranking officers, but it was always there, a stink you could not wash away. And even among the king's nobles, there was no greater comfort. Sometimes they ate food just as cold, and they could not afford to shave their beards or cut their hair short. Amalia had wine and fire every now and then, and a thick ring of bodyguards to protect her from her own troops.

She sat on an old crate, eating thin cabbage soup with a wooden spoon. The taste was bland, but the warmth in her guts was a blessing. Jarman was chewing on an onion like it was an apple. Lucas was standing, looking north at the enemy. He was probably using magic right that moment.

She saw the Caytorean warlord coming toward her, pushing through the crowd of her guards. His tabard had mold growing on it, but he did not seem to mind. "Your Excellence."

Amalia sniffed. "Yes?"

Xavier forced a weak smile onto his whiskered cheeks. "A private word with you?"

Jarman grimaced, but then he unfolded his weary limbs and shuffled a short distance away. He could probably overhear everything—or react, if the man turned out to be a threat.

Xavier knelt in the muddy grass at her feet, groaning. His sword pushed into his ribs, and he had to lean sideways to free the scabbard from the muck. "How much longer will I have to wait?" he whispered, his foul breath hot on her cheek.

She had expected no more, no less. "Once the war is concluded."

He shook his head, breathing through his nostrils. "No. That's not good enough." His gloved hand flopped onto her thigh.

Amalia froze. "You do realize if I scream that you will die?"

Xavier smacked his lips. "I'm no fool. But you think I'm some kind of a dog, don't you? I stayed with you through all this shit. I expect some fucking loyalty in return. You promised me something. So I don't get to be an emperor, fine. That Parusite bitch spoiled that, fine. But I still can be a proper noble, and your title sounds just right. Now, I've been waiting long enough." His pig eyes were shiny with fury.

Amalia put the bowl away, trying to keep her hand from trembling. Jarman cast a quick glance at her, wondering if he should interfere. No, she was done being a coward.

"Listen to me, swine. Your persistence is admirable, but you should admit defeat. It's over, warlord. If you want to leave, please do. This Naum enemy will be coming to Caytor all too soon. Your valuable experience will be needed there. Who knows, the High Council might grant you one of the titles you crave so badly."

"We had our agreement." He almost sounded offended.

"That was before...all this," she explained, trying to sound calm and unafraid.

"You fucking whore," he growled. His fingers squeezed harder. But then he let go, rose, and stormed away.

Amalia looked at Jarman. Captain Speinbate still had not killed this man. She was wondering what he was waiting for. Or maybe he was just too swamped with defeat and panic, like everyone else. Maybe the wizard had not paid him yet.

The evening was settling in. The drizzle stopped, and the cloud cover climbed higher, away from the quiet, dark camps. Amalia thought it was almost unnatural, because there was very little wind. But as soon as the clouds dissipated, a fierce cold settled in. The grass frosted over, became crunchy like glass. The air was sharp, like a blade, cutting invisibly at her cheeks, her throat, her fingers.

She huddled herself in a swath of musty blankets, alone in a tiny tent that was too low to stand in, her saddlebags a hard, painful pillow for her head and neck. Outside, soldiers walked in quick circles, trying to warm their limbs. Someone was crying. There was too much coughing. Horses snorted into the frigid night. Just as her mind began to roil, she wondered how Agatha was faring. Her maid was with Pete now all the time, with his troops, protected better than the princess herself.

The night came alive with the blare of a horn. First, a distant one, then one closer, and soon, the entire camp was alive with a screeching noise.

No, please, she begged. But there was no escaping it. The Naum troops were attacking again.

She reached for her boots. Her knees were cold and would not bend easily. But she managed to bundle herself quickly enough and wormed toward the slit of silvery gray that was the outside world.

Something big and hot bowled into her, toppling her back into the tent, crushing her, squeezing the breath between her ribs. Amalia wheezed and flopped, but the heavy thing would not move. In fact, it squirmed, just like her. Even in the charcoal murk, she could never mistake those piggish eyes.

Xavier.

"You can scream now," he said.

Her arms scrabbled, but he had her pinned down. He was much stronger. This was Roalas all over, but she was done crying and begging. Instead, she kept her mouth shut, kept what little air she had behind her teeth, and tried to wriggle herself free.

The warlord started tearing her clothes off. Luckily, she was plaited in several layers of good, stout wool, and the Caytorean struggled ripping them away. But then, there was the knife, and it cut, and it raked across her skin, and there was the smell of blood in the tiny tent.

Amalia began to whimper. *Must be the pain,* her mind confessed. So why was her vision blurred?

Her left hand flopped free, and almost instinctively, it jabbed at the swine's face, clawing, pushing into the soft socket of his eye. The mercenary began to howl, and he tried to swat her fingers away, but he had the knife in his hand, and he almost cut himself.

Her right hand was free now. It slithered out from below his bulk, swiped off the oily pool of blood on her stomach, and slapped into his neck. She didn't really know what to do, but the soft spots were there, neck, eyes, every man the same.

"Bitch, I'm gonna fuck you bloody," he rasped. The knife fell away, and he clouted her hard, once, twice. Tried to grab her chipped ear but missed, and she almost cackled with mad glee, even as her vision narrowed. Tears, darkness. Amalia flailed at his face, but her limbs were heavy now. Outside, the horns were howling.

She could hear him tearing more of her clothes. The icy earth kissed her back, her legs. She was naked now. And he was going to rape her. Best if she fainted, she figured. Best if she didn't witness this shame. But no one would say Amalia hadn't fought for her life. No one would say she just cowered there and wept like a little court girl. She was her father's daughter, and she would die before she surrendered. She would—

The warlord flew off her, like a puppet yanked by its strings. He swallowed a curse and vanished through the tent's narrow opening. Amalia rolled sideways, huffed, retched dryly. The knife was resting by her side. She hesitated for a second, grabbed the blade and her torn clothes, and rushed out.

Xavier was on his knees, gripping feebly at a chain round his neck, face purple and swollen. A Borei warrior was choking him, even as dozens of soldiers of all colors streamed past. Another mercenary was standing nearby, sword in hand, watching and grinning.

"Good work, Your Empress, you almost had us worried," the one doing the killing chirped.

The second one touted, shaking his head, "Yes, would cost me a fortune if he'd done you in."

The warlord was making gurgling noises, spit dribbling down the side of his mouth. His face was the color of a rotten plum now. His hands were touching his chin, as if feeling the whiskers there. Amalia was cold, terribly cold, but she didn't care right now. All she wanted was to plunge the knife into the swine's heart.

"Wanna do it, Empress?" the swordsman asked.

Amalia gathered her breath and lunged forward. She stabbed toward the chest, but the blade grazed sideways into his arm. The Caytorean hissed thinly. She aimed again. Belly. There, she couldn't miss it. She touched the injury below her own ribs, leaking blood into the freezing night. Stabbed, stabbed again. Her fingers were on fire, and she realized she had cut herself.

"That's enough." The second warrior stepped forward, dragging her away. He had a bandage ready and was wrapping it round her middle. "Goose lard so the wound don't stink up. Good work. I earned my coin back. I bet on you. Excellent."

Amalia nodded dumbly. "You're welcome." She collapsed into the mud, retched again, and it was as if someone had kicked her in the guts.

The Borei laughed. "It's fine. You will live, lass. Just a scratch there. Your fingers won't be as delicate as you might like for a few weeks, but that's what happens to all amateur knifers. Not your fault. You did well."

Someone put a musty blanket round her shoulders.

Just as quickly, the two mercenaries vanished in the chaos. The warlord's corpse remained there, strangled and stabbed through, already caked over with mud. No one paid him any heed. No one paid her any heed. The men and women were running to meet the enemy. But she knew what was going to happen. Soon, they would be retreating once more, fleeing the northern force. It couldn't be stopped.

Calemore was going to win.

The air was no longer black, she noticed. It was peppered white. Snow.

"Amalia!" She recognized that voice. The wizard. "Amalia!" He sounded like a frightened girl.

"What?" she bawled. He was standing above her, panting, looking worried.

"Oh no. Come here. Are you hurt? Lucas!"

Somehow, she stumbled up and let herself be dragged away. But then she realized she could walk. She was bruised and cold, but her legs obeyed, and the pull of pain round her abdomen was just a line of fire, nothing serious. She was stronger than that. Fuck them all. She wasn't going to be a coward anymore.

"I will heal you with magic. Show me your hand."

Amalia wanted to refuse his help, but what would be the point? She must use him, use all of them, and once she was done, she should discard them, abandon them, crush them pitilessly. They were all just tools, serving her.

She looked at the wizard, his hair dotted with silvery flakes.

Then, the world started spinning and went black.

She woke up in a carriage, a small lamp swaying above her head, painting the interior jaundiced. Agatha sat opposite her, face full of worry, her baby asleep in her lap. There was someone at her side. Jarman, wearing clean blue robes. He looked haggard, but his face lit up when he noticed her stir.

"Where are we?"

"Still fleeing the northern army, I'm afraid," he admitted.

Amalia glanced down at her body. Clean, warm, no trace of pain. She stared at her right palm. There were pink lines where she expected to see gashes, across the bridge of her hand, down the side of her thumb. The Sirtai was wearing a solemn expression on his face. Was it humble self-satisfaction?

She pushed herself off the plush seat and moved the velvet curtain aside, just an inch. She couldn't see much, just a gray swirl.

"We held as long as we could. But we were forced to begin retreating into the night. Luckily, the earth has frosted over, so the passage is much easier for us. Not so for the enemy, because they must tread in our mush. They are steadily falling behind. We could gain as much as a whole day if the weather continues like this."

Amalia wanted to hear more details, but at the moment, she felt content not knowing. The snug, hot safety of the carriage was good for her. She felt protected. At the back of her mind, a lone thought was floating, like a piece of driftwood, trying to remind her that she had stabbed a man. A monster, a butcher, but still a human being. She hadn't just ordered him hanged from the gallows or cut down with a sword; she had personally delivered the lethal blow. What did that make her?

She didn't want to know just yet.

Agatha was crying, she noticed. Silent, hard tears. Jarman's face wasn't humble, as she first thought. It looked pained.

Amalia frowned. "I'm all right," she whispered, reaching out toward her maid. "I'm fine."

Jarman swallowed loudly, his whole head bobbing. "Amalia…"

The safety fluttered away like a startled bird, and dread settled in, cold like the night outside. Her muscles tensed, her body went rigid, and phantoms of pain arced through her gut and arm. Something was very wrong. She worked her mouth to form words.

"What is it, Jarman?"

The wizard didn't speak for a while. "King Sergei found out your mother was behind his son's kidnapping and death. He...ordered Lady Lisa to be executed for treason. Amalia, your mother is dead. I'm truly sorry."

Amalia let her head slump against the cushion. She closed her eyes so she couldn't see her maid weeping. Numbness, there was nothing else in her soul. Her reasoning was telling her this was wrong. She should be sad. She should be furious. Something other than this stupor. But she couldn't bring herself to feel anything. Not this night.

I will get them all, she promised. *I will show them.*

CHAPTER 41

E wan lurched forward as the wet rope snapped in his hand. He fell onto his knees, and his crippled left arm sank into the brown slush. He rose, feeling no pain, no weariness, no cold. His brief reacquaintance with humanity was gone again, and his senses deprived him of any weakness.

He stared at his left hand. Two fingers gone. He had heard soldiers talking about ghost feelings in missing limbs, as if they were still there. Nothing of that sort in his case. All he had was a hand that wriggled funny.

"I need another rope," he declared loudly.

A teamster on his left reached into the back of his cart and tossed him a fresh coil. It was thin and frayed and eaten by weather and mites, so it would probably last only a few miles, like the last one, but it would have to do.

When Ewan was done tying the rope to the wagon, the other man and his ox were gone down the road, joining the slow, miserable exodus of the people of the realms.

He yanked on the rope to make sure his knot was sound, braced it over his shoulder, and started pulling again. The rope protested, the wagon protested, but then it groaned forward, freeing its wheels from the mire some would call snow. Well, maybe it had been snow, but not after tens of thousands of feet, hooves, and paws had churned it into a brown-stained butter.

Ahead of him, the road twisted, wriggled through an abandoned village, and then loped over a hilltop. Most of the Athesians and pilgrims had already gone to the other side, but there were still a few hundred people struggling. A half-size contingent of Parusite cavalry was trampling through the sodden fields, keeping rear guard, eyes turning around nervously, seeking the enemy. But the forested stretch of the hills to the north was empty.

Ewan kept marching, sinking deep, sliding, but not giving up. He was hauling two wagons of injured soldiers, tied together, with twenty-seven men loaded into the tiny space. Amalia's troops had even attached stretchers on the outside, strapped some wounded there, too, and then bundled them in blankets so they would not freeze.

The two oxen had been butchered for meat, so Ewan had volunteered to replace them. At the moment, no one was complaining about his superhuman strength. They were all glad there was someone moving them farther away from the Naum army.

He followed the half-frozen ruts, stepping around discarded gear. The bodies of those too weak to travel had been pushed away, some covered in snow and mud. The tail of the fleeing column consisted mostly of dwindling supplies and the wounded. Ewan had the moans of the dying and the caw of hungry birds for company.

The seven odd thatched houses that made the settlement in front of him should have been empty, he thought, frowning. But he saw pale smoke rising and a huddle of men standing at the roadside, not really bothered by the flow of dejected, demoralized countryfolk and soldiers streaming past.

The rope snapped again. He stumbled again, but did not lose his footing. He glanced around. There were no more wagons behind him. His was the last one. All the others were gone ahead, and he was certain they wouldn't bother stopping. There was a lone, limping soldier in a long coat making stubborn progress south, using his sword as a prop, a raven hopping behind him, mocking him. Ewan thought about calling the man over so he could ride in one of the wagons, but they were already too crowded and too heavy.

"I will return shortly," he told the delirious passengers and trotted toward the village, right hand holding the bloodstaff, tied over his back to keep it from wobbling. Several soldiers, it seemed, were warming their hands over a pitiful fire. Ewan thought he saw a child hiding behind someone's leg.

If he were like any other man, Ewan would try to be cautious. But he couldn't bother with that anymore. He didn't care about discipline or danger.

"Fellows, I need some help. Do you have a spare rope or maybe a chain?"

One, with a face swathed in filthy rags, looked up from the tiny fire. "What for?"

Ewan pointed behind him. "Need something to lug those wagons. I've got wounded people there."

"What's that on your back?" another ugly mien asked him.

"Never mind that. Will you help?"

"He wants help," a third mouth grunted derisively.

"Gotta pay us. That's right. This is a trading post now."

Ewan sighed. He did not want to point out to these half madmen, half deserters what would happen to their little business endeavor once Calemore's troops arrived. But he had no goodness left in his heart. He couldn't care about everyone. He could not save everyone.

Ignoring them, he poked his head into the nearest house. Small, dark, entirely empty. He realized he wouldn't find anything worth using in this hamlet. Maybe he could push the wagons? But no, that would be silly. They would steer wildly. He raked his hair, frosted with dirty ice. Abandon the wounded? Why shouldn't he? After all, everyone else had.

He heard a soft, mucky rattle, and a small, scruffy dog pattered over, but then it stopped halfway, wrinkled its nose, and fled. The scrawny child rushed from behind a tree of legs and chased after the animal. Ewan did not want to contemplate what a little girl was doing among these so-called traders. He had seen too much death in the past several months, and he just couldn't make himself care any further. It was impossible.

Ewan walked back to his two wagons, already anchored hard in the gelid mush. He didn't have a smart answer for the Athesians. Leave them now? Let them be killed by frost, hunger, or the northern warriors?

By now, the limping soldier had circled the village and was trying to climb the hill, the black bird still chasing him. On the other side, the land stretched into a ripple of fields all the way to Roalas. Apparently, King Sergei had arrayed all of his strength awaiting the invincible, mythical enemy. The remnants of the unified army of the realms, with its scattering of Gavril's followers, Sasha's Red Caps, Amalia's colorful bastard army, and the king's own legions. They had been so successful campaigning through Athesia the previous year; now, they were fleeing unceremoniously, ruined, exhausted, without hope.

Ewan wondered about his destiny. He had come north to stop Calemore. Only he hadn't really done that. Not at all.

The witch had almost killed him. That was such a sobering, humbling experience it had almost broken him. Ewan had meant to use the bloodstaff against the Naum force and check its advance. Maybe even destroy Calemore. But it didn't work. The witch knew when Ewan used the weapon, and always retaliated with precision and brutality. Now, Ewan was almost afraid to use the bloodstaff, because he knew it would not stem the Naum progress. At best, it would decimate a handful of enemy soldiers. At worst, it would get him killed.

He did not relish ending up dead just yet. His invincibility might be a sterile experience, but he still cherished what life he had, and he did not want to trade it in. He felt there was something else, something more he could do to redeem his soul. Something that would add meaning to his existence. Something that might sweeten the terrible pain of abandonment, of the time spent in the Abyss, the loneliness, the self-loathing.

I can't use the bloodstaff, he mused, *and that means Calemore wins. Just like that.*

It couldn't be all that was left for him. To witness defeat and destruction of all that he knew.

It couldn't be just that.

But he didn't even have a god to pray to anymore. No one to give him any hope, even a false one. Tanid was a coward.

Ewan still vividly remembered how the deity had hidden in the trench while the White Witch pummeled ruby death around them. He remembered a more recent attack by Calemore's men. He had found Gavril hiding in the cellar of an old house in yet another village, waiting for the storm of death to cease, while Jarman and Lucas risked their lives fighting against the witch. Their magic was strong and unique, it seemed, but alone, they couldn't stop the enemy tide. They could not stop Calemore on their own.

Anytime there was magic used against him, the witch would retaliate with the bloodstaff. He would fire back, killing hundreds, confident that Ewan could not kill him with his own copy. The weapon was useless against Calemore. Maybe Ewan had overheard that from the Sirtai wizards or the cowardly god, or maybe the knowledge had just erupted in his head after reading *The Pains of Memory*, or maybe it was a relic from some ancient time, lodged in his being. It didn't matter.

Ewan was useless.

But that was a sorry end to his misery. He refused to accept that.

There must be something more, the reason why I exist, the reason why I can't feel.

His disappointment made him bitter. So he had withdrawn from the rest of the humans, trying to do some little good with his muscles. He let the princess and the former empress and Jarman and that craven god sort out their own problems. He didn't want any part of that. He didn't want to be their tool. He did not want to be the outlet for their scheming.

The only person who seemed genuine in his actions and intentions was Jarman's silent blue-tattooed companion. But if he shared any sympathy with Ewan, he kept it to himself.

He stood in front of the wagon, staring at the soldiers, the handful of those still awake. They stared back, eyes wide and glazed with fear. He had nothing to offer them. This burden was just too much.

Then, he sensed a presence, even before the army scouts raised a cry.

You could hardly see the horizon line. It was blurred with mist, snow, and clouds the color of pure gloom.

Across the broken line of the land and through the dapple of trees, the enemy army began coalescing, tainting the landscape. Ewan knew the foe suffered just as much as they did, maybe even more. The Naum folk had to walk though the ruins and refuse left by the Athesians and Parusites. The enemy had even less food. But they didn't seem to mind the cold, and they had superior numbers to compensate for any tactical losses.

The patrols shouted and whistled and bugled their warnings, then turned about, heading away from the menace. The hilltop became a swarm of slipping hooves and cursing men. Soon enough, those supposed to defend the last knuckle of supply carts were mostly gone. No one cared about the stragglers anymore. It would be a waste of good, healthy lives. Whoever remained behind was meant to die, it seemed.

Ewan scanned the fields. Maybe a few walking dead there. His own two wagons, the fools in the village, but that was all. The filthy stretch of the tortured terrain was abandoned. The people of the realms were hurrying away, trying to save their hides.

What do I do now? he thought. Turn tail and run? He could sprint until he overtook Sasha's vanguard, and be in Roalas days before everyone else. He could leave all this madness. But the ghost of a memory of a dear friend echoed in his mind. Ayrton would never run.

Maybe he could just lug one of the carts, save half the wounded? His conscience growled with displeasure. Adjusting the bloodstaff strap, he reached for the broken cart trace and tried to pull on it. But it was slick with mud, and his fingers—those he had left—slipped. Well, there was no other option. He raised his fist up and punched through the wood. The trace splintered, and almost shattered, but its shape still remained intact. Pushing his hand into the hole, he hauled.

He fell and sprayed icy mud, but he made the two wagons move. The injured men started goading him, whispering encouragement. Teeth ground together, he made another step, and another, and he crossed the hamlet and started uphill. The little dog was barking at him from a very safe distance.

Ewan led the two wagons off-road, where the footing was more solid. Naked shrubbery tore at his clothes, snagged at the bloodstaff. The vegetation had no respect for the magical weapon. He slammed his boots into the gray crust, kicked his toes into the gravel and rock. And started slipping. No matter how hard he pummeled at the frozen earth, he just didn't have enough traction to move the human loads on those narrow, slick wheel rims up a wet snowbank.

Ewan looked across the valley, toward the enemy. It would take the Naum fighters several hours to reach his position, but at his undignified crawl, they would reach him eventually. He could not outpace them, not with the injured soldiers.

At the friendly hilltop, the last carts and horsemen were gathering, soon to vanish forever. Ewan realized he would just have to force them to help him. Either they would lug the wounded or they wouldn't travel at all. He let go of the trace.

"I will not abandon you. I will return."

Free of burden, he dashed like a snow cat, easily catching up with the Athesians and Parusites. They were watching him with a pained look, marveling at his tenacity and stupidity. And there was a healthy dose of fear there, too.

"You will help me with the wounded, right now," he snapped, breath deep and clear.

"Fuck yourself, cripple," one of the horsemen spat back and wheeled his horse south.

Before he knew it, Ewan was gripping the bloodstaff, aimed at the soldier. But he knew it would be foolish. Calemore couldn't spot him while he pretended to be just another miserable refugee. However, if he used the weapon, the magic would give him away.

"Help or die," Ewan warned.

"Those men are already dead, you fool. You'd kill us all for nothing!"

Ewan flicked a quick look down the slope. Maybe he was trying to save an ideal rather than human lives. Maybe. Giving up now meant giving up his last shred of humanity. No.

"They won't be left behind." He was tempted to press the button and pulverize them. That wouldn't save his twenty-seven injured, though. And he would add more death and grief to the land drenched with misery.

There was a wind of angry protest from the men around him. So what should he do? Kill one man, and the rest would obey? What if they did not?

"You will help him," a deep voice rumbled, silencing all argument.

Ewan saw Lucas standing some distance away, eyes locked on the huge tide lapping toward them.

No one argued. With almost enthusiastic urgency, a dozen riders rushed after Ewan. They tied their nervous hobs to the carts and began hauling. By the time they reached the flat ground, the Naum force was only a mile away. The air vibrated with the buzz of metal and leather and death.

"Keep going." The soldiers and the teamsters were taking the wounded out from the two wagons, moving them elsewhere. Dumping them unceremoniously alongside old gear and sacks of rotten barley, sliding them up into the saddle behind other men, tying them so they wouldn't fall off. Some might not make it, but no one cared right now. The Naum force was almost upon them.

Ewan was watching the enemy, trying to keep calm. But if he wanted to save these people, there would have to be bloodshed. He couldn't use the bloodstaff, so it would have to be personal. He would have to wade into that human mass and start killing people with his bare hands.

"It's never easy," Lucas preached in a calm voice, just nearby. "Ask yourself why you're doing this. Then, it might become *easier*."

"Thank you," Ewan mumbled.

"Thank you. For reminding me what we're all about."

Ewan glanced at the Anada wizard. "Will you fight?"

Lucas nodded once. "I will shield you and distract Calemore."

Ewan realized the Sirtai might know more about him than he should. But there was no time for questions. No time for making his heart flutter with hope. His journey of knowledge had ended long ago. He had all the pieces, but not the answer to his pain, or his legacy.

Behind him, the last of the refugee convoy was fleeing hurriedly away. The sky was alive with birds, cheering the bloodshed, welcoming a feast.

Ewan took a deep breath. He might die today. His magic might fail him. He never knew. Maybe Calemore would spot him and cut him down with his own bloodstaff. Maybe his agony would end today. But no matter the consequence, he would do his best to save those people.

Almost lazily, he stepped down the way he had come, knee-deep in old snow. The Naum force was churning forward, and he could see faces in that huge, quivering mass. Thin, gaunt, filthy, with huge eyes beaded with fear, just like those of the people of the realms.

What made one lot more valuable than the other? Nothing really. Just chance.

The enemy didn't really pay him any attention. He was just one scrawny lad, marching willingly toward death. Somewhere to his left, a column of earth exploded, and a rustle of screams shook the Naum ranks. Must be Lucas, engaging Calemore, baiting him.

Ewan didn't move as the enemy spearman tried to stab him. The leaf-shaped head stopped dead against his skin, then raked up and over his shoulder. The soldier gasped in astonishment before colliding with him. Ewan almost wept. But he had to do it.

He punched the man's face, caving it in.

More spears jabbed at him, and soon, he was surrounded in curses and growls and shouts in a foreign language, and everyone was doing their best to slay him. It was as if ants were crawling over his skin, and he couldn't really tell what they were doing. Swords, axes, spears, lashing, breaking, bending against his stonelike body. The Naum troops were hacking madly at him, at their own white fear. There was no retreat. These men could only march forward, or be trampled by those coming behind.

I am doing this to save the people of the realms, he told himself. He was red all over, red like a newborn baby, caked in hot human pulp, blinded by the blood dripping down his face. He punched left and right, killed people with a single blow, leaving a pile all around him. Before long, he had to wade through a mound of corpses to get away, to reach a new spot where he could do some more killing.

There was no end to the enemy force. Nor to his strength.

He kept on punching, tearing, hoping the madness would end soon.

One way or another.

CHAPTER 42

Keep an eye on her, Jarman told himself.

Amalia's reaction to her mother's death was strange. Reserved, almost emotionless. He could remember his own anguish when his third mother had died, and so he was worried about Amalia. Quite a bit.

"Keep an eye on her," he told Timothy, the young lieutenant who used to be James's squire. The boy had not lost his innocence, but he had been well fattened in battle hardship. A man was emerging from his youthful countenance, one with few words and many strong deeds. Someone useful to have around.

Timothy nodded. "Yes, sir." He understood what was at stake.

If Amalia decided to retaliate, the brittle alliance between the Parusites and Athesians would shatter. It wasn't enough that they all might die soon, trampled by the unstoppable Naum army; they did not need a bloody conflict among themselves a handful of miles from Roalas. It might be Sergei's rule now, but it was Amalia's city, her people.

This close to the capital of Athesia, news traveled much faster. They had ample reports about what was happening in the city. Sergei was beefing up the defenses. Any boy strong enough to hold a sword was given a uniform and asked to join the soldiers manning the walls. The streets had been cleared, the people sent south. No matter what the Athesians felt about their new ruler, he was taking his responsibility seriously. He was protecting his new subjects like he would his own nation, and he was sending convoys of women and children south to Parus.

Which was why the people of Roalas had not rebelled against him over Lady Lisa's execution. That, or the greater fear of the huge white army swarming across the land held them docile and obedient.

But that did not mean Amalia might not decide to take revenge. It might be a stupid act of defiance, one last suicidal attempt at righting wrongs that could not be remedied. She might choose to strike against the Parusites or just flee. Maybe try to kill the princess with her own hands. Either way, the fragile unity would break. That would mean more chaos, more dying.

Even without the former empress exacting her payback for her mother's death, the situation was lousy. Since Xavier's death, half the Caytorean troops had deserted, led by one Colonel Gilles. Master Hector had tried to stop him, and the scuffle had left more than eighty dead. A fair share of Athesians had also taken to other roads, away from the fighting. Even some of Gavril's men had abandoned the holy pilgrimage.

The people of Athesia tried to mingle with the troops and pilgrims, trying to secure protection or earn an odd coin for some hard work, but mostly, they were just a burden, slowing everyone down, draining the resources. Still, out of some odd sense of responsibility or maybe fear of mutiny among the local legions, the king's sister was marching them on, toward Roalas, toward some temporary safety.

Jarman laid a gentle hand on Timothy's shoulder. Months ago, he would have been appalled by his own gesture. Now, he had learned the importance of these friendly pats and handshakes. He couldn't let his temple education ruin his work. After all, he had come here to avenge his third mother.

Would that ever happen?

Most likely not.

So what should he do? Flee like that coward Gilles?

The lieutenant nodded and walked away from the makeshift command tent. He did not venture too far. A cook was burning small black sausages over a fire, and a long line of junior officers was waiting for its share. Several Red Caps and soldiers in the service of Duke Yuri were making sure there was no jostling or thievery.

Jarman spared the sorry day camp another quick glance before ducking back into the second tent, the one where Amalia and Lucas waited for him.

Adam's daughter was sitting in a simple canvas chair, staring at the red-hot brazier below her feet, eyes glazed with images only she could see. Her maid was feeding her daughter, a pale breast peeking out from under thick woolen blankets. His life slave and tutor and friend was standing, watching the entrance, face unreadable in the stifling murk.

Amalia couldn't see the princess anymore. Sasha had dismissed her, and for all she was concerned, Amalia was just traveling south with the rest of them before taking her role in Roalas. She didn't bother investigating the death of the warlord, or the rumors of an assassination attempt against Amalia. Sasha had one objective, and that was bringing as much of her army back to the capital. Everything else was secondary now.

For Amalia, that meant no closure for her mother's death. She could not confront the princess or maybe even discuss it with her. Who knew, perhaps that would actually help defuse the situation. Instead, left alone to her festering, Amalia was breeding her rancor, her guilt, and her desire for violence. Jarman was worried.

His plan had not only fallen apart, it threatened to transform into an ugly, dangerous monstrosity.

They were losing the war, and he might never get his own vengeance. Like Lucas had said, the war was not going to be won with the bloodstaff.

But how then?

Scouts reported Calemore almost two days behind. He was regrouping after a deadly fight. Apparently, that lad Ewan had magic.

He was a Special Child, then.

Jarman wanted to cling to that. Jarman wanted to hope. But nothing seemed to matter. Gavril was behaving like a frightened animal. The troops only followed orders because they feared being killed for disobedience. Every day, more and more Caytoreans fled to their realm.

Now, no one could predict what would happen when Amalia finally returned to Roalas.

"You should eat, Jarman," Agatha chided.

Jarman rubbed a hand down his cheek. He had grown thinner lately. He was using magic, and that bled his strength worse than the cold and a meager diet. He was straining his own life-force. He was constantly tired, constantly weak.

He smiled. His finger touched the platter of rye bread and a block of pig lard, studded with spruce seeds. Well, he was still considered important enough, it seemed.

"I want to talk to Amalia, please."

The once empress glanced up sharply, sniffed. The girl was recovering from a mild illness, on top of everything. Being wet and cold wasn't good for anyone's health. "Agatha stays. She is not going out there into the cold, into that chaos, with all those animals."

"Lucas will protect—" he began.

"She stays." Another sniff.

Jarman sat down opposite Adam's daughter, the warmth from the red coals in the rusty brazier seeping into his shins even through the layers of tweed. It was a pleasant sensation. He thought he should be somewhat apprehensive of Amalia's sickness, but the exposure to the filth of the realms had numbed him to his former strict insistence on hygiene.

"I am worried about you, Amalia," he admitted, trying to ignore the maid.

Amalia squared her jaw. "Are you? Well, use your magic and kill Sasha. That will make me better."

Jarman grimaced at the thin, wet wall of the tent. Just another stretch of fabric away, the princess was discussing war affairs with Sergei's dukes, Captain Speinbate, and the scattering of Athesian legion commanders still left with the army.

"You need to look at the broader picture," he said.

"You are a hypocrite," she accused, venom dripping from her voice, eyes blurred with tears.

He tried to keep his face straight, angry at her words. He had come to the realms to avenge a woman who wasn't even his own mother, twenty years after the deed. He had put aside his fury until the right moment, and wanted her to understand his motivation.

"My nation does not exist anymore. Athesia has been reduced to a sorry column of starving people, a handful of soldiers still deluded with the glory of my father's victories, and mercenaries who try to blackmail me at every turn, not that I exist anymore. Once you solve all these problems for me, Jarman, I will look at the broader picture."

"From what I heard, your mother did commission the death of the king's heir."

Amalia snarled at him. "I know what happened."

"But that does not mean—"

"Amalia," Lucas spoke, his voice deep.

Everyone turned to look at him. Even Agatha's girl stirred.

The blue-faced Anada was silent for a moment. "Nothing can change death. Nothing can change how you feel about it. How you feel about your nation. Princess Sasha may have dismissed you from her service, but you still have a duty toward your people, and titles make no difference."

Amalia wiped her nose with the back of her hand. "You may ignore reality, wizard, but I cannot."

Lucas didn't move or even blink. "Do you think your father would have given up now?"

Jarman saw the girl change. Her face turned hard, locked with emotion and deep thought. She opened her mouth, but then bit her response back. A frown crept onto her features, twisting her youthful, exhausted beauty.

"So what do you recommend, Lucas?" she asked in a hushed tone.

"If you think the royal house of Parus has done you an injustice, then you should seek your vengeance. But not now. Not today. Let us end this war first. Let us win against Calemore. For all your self-pity, you are still a leader of these people. They look up to you for support. You cannot abandon them now for your own little vendetta. If we somehow defeat the White Witch, you will have your chance for justice against the princess, or the king. Just remember it is your family that robbed King Sergei of both his father and his son."

Amalia leaned forward on her knees, staring into the fire again. She seemed to be on the verge of tears. "So what do I do now?"

"Talk to Master Guilliam. He claims to have devised a new weapon based on his earlier models. If we get to Roalas safely, he will be able to modify the existing siege machines to fire much more effective, more lethal loads. Master Hector is still loyal to you. Harness that to your advantage. Princess Sasha is the provisional ruler, but she is not liked by the common troops or by the people. Make sure you regain your old popularity, so that the king and his sister never think again of sidelining you, for the fear of rebellion."

Amalia was afraid, Jarman realized. "They might just decide to fight again, and I will be defeated. Again."

Lucas shook his head. "Not after this war. The Parusites have lost huge numbers. The king's lords will have to return to their own country within the next year. Athesia will be left with its own people, its own troops. Sergei will not be able to hold this new princedom without your help. So, it is you who must decide the future of Athesia. Will you ruin everything over the death of your mother? Did King Sergei ruin Athesia over the death of his son? Or did he give this land another chance? Gave *you* another chance? He rose above it. Is he a better person than you?"

Jarman realized his silent, formidable friend had been doing much more than hurling magic against the Naum troops. He had been studying politics, trying to predict the actions of the local rulers. Jarman wished he had done the same, feeling slightly ashamed. He had focused too hard on his frustration and the magical piece of this war, neglecting the people. Perhaps he needed many more years away from the Temple of Justice before he could handle the ordinary continental people.

The former empress sniffed again. "Thank you, Lucas."

The wizard nodded solemnly. "You will excuse us. Jarman and I must talk."

Jarman realized Lucas had just done all the hard work for him, and there was nothing else he could add. Feeling somewhat embarrassed, he edged out of the tent, back into the winter cold. Sasha's officers and Sergei's nobles were milling, their meeting ended.

The camp was seething with activity, mostly because it was too cold for men to be idle. He could see one of the olifaunts lumbering down a narrow lane dug between two rows of old, patched tents, its gray hide wrapped in blankets. Too many olifaunts had succumbed to the cold, but at least they had provided everyone with ample meat—for an appropriate payment to the owners, of course.

Fires were coming alive, almost like glowworms in a summer forest, a blessing after so many weeks of rain and storms and endless marches. Sergei was sending food, timber, healers, iron, trying to help the retreating army as much as he could. Wounded soldiers were being taken away in carts, civilians shuffled away so they wouldn't drain the resources or distract the troops. Even the whores were herded south, because they, too, were a burden and caused fighting and strife among the troops. King Sergei might have defeated Amalia, maybe even humiliated her into submission, but he was serious and committed about defending his new scrap of territory.

"How do we win this war, then?" Lucas asked suddenly.

Jarman stepped away from the noise.

"I do not know," he whispered, ashen-colored snow crunching under his boots. "Ewan?"

Lucas pointed with his head. The boy was standing in hip-high snow just past the last row of tents. He did not seem to mind the chill, his shoulders sagging with only a thin shirt speckled in old blood. The lad had not changed it since that day he'd waded into the enemy lot and butchered them with his bare hands. Bought them all a few days of respite. Maybe saved them all.

"We must not push him," Lucas warned, as if he knew what Jarman wanted to suggest.

Jarman bunched his fists, released them. His fingers tingled with cold, or maybe chagrin. Within hours, the scouts would probably report the enemy tide approaching again, and they would be forced to break camp and start their torturous journey once again, sleepless, hungry, hopeless.

Jarman almost wished it to end. He was miserable. He hated the uncertainty. He hated having to hear the bugles cry into the night, hated watching men limp through slush and slip on ice, with no one stepping up to help them, hated seeing horses butchered for meat, their red innards smoking in the winter mornings. He hated the crushing despair, the stink that not even the cold could smother, the borderline violence in every set of eyes.

"We must do our best to protect him," he said.

"Even if it means dropping our shield around Amalia?" Lucas countered.

Jarman hesitated, then nodded. If Calemore won, none of them would matter. "Y…es."

Lucas glanced at him. "Maybe you have learned something in this strange place after all."

"If we win the war, do we just…leave?"

Lucas stepped past a horseshoe of wagons forming some symbolic defense around a regiment's tent space. Several soldiers were shoveling fresh snowfall off the tarps; another was oiling the axles. More men huddled in the lee behind, gambling with strips of cured meat, an acrid gray smoke from a small ring of fire biting at their faces.

A couple of sentries walked past wearing wide-soled shoes. They had found those with the Naum soldiers, and apparently, they helped men move so much more easily over the soft drift.

Lucas waited until they were gone out of earshot.

"We cannot remedy everything. We can't make peace. We tried to help these people unite. It is up to them to make the best of it. If we win, the land will be torn, the people poor and miserable. The old rivalries and wounds will remain. But that's something King Sergei, Amalia, the High Council, and all the rest of them will have to resolve, just like they did before the northern threat emerged. The realms were always a place of strife and grief. Ever since the first war."

Jarman swallowed. His own throat was sore a little, and he hoped he wouldn't catch any nasty continental illness. "I still haven't figured out anything about the death of that Caytorean, Rob."

"What about our half-Sirtai friend?"

Jarman was taken aback. He had not spent any thought about that man. But he was always around, always seemed to pull through all the fighting and misery. He might be an asset, and his magic would be valuable. But Jarman hesitated approaching him. He did not know what he was doing here, and he didn't want to risk a confrontation until he knew more.

As if you have time for that, you fool.

"Do you find anything odd about Gavril?" Lucas pressed.

Jarman stopped walking, and instantly, the cold slithered round his ankles. "No."

Lucas motioned for him to keep moving. "Then I guess you are not yet ready for your first tattoo."

A dumpling of anger flared in the pit of his stomach. "Let us win this war. And go home."

The older wizard snorted. "Then I will ask you again. How do we do that?"

Jarman glanced around. Ewan was gone.

I am just a child playing a game of adults, he thought with a great sense of worthlessness, the words from his friend and tutor biting deep. *Maybe this revenge is not just about killing the criminal. Maybe it's about me becoming a better man, a better wizard.*

So what should he do? Try to engage Princess Sasha? Approach Ewan, demand he sacrifice his soul? Resolve the mystery of Rob's death? That would tell him a lot, he knew, but he just wasn't as good an investigator as his father. The moment he admitted that, the easier it would be for him.

He really hated the uncertainty. He hated the realms. Everything was so imperfect. There was no closure to anything, just the prolonged suffering, prolonged human selfishness and pettiness, even when faced with total destruction. Nothing seemed more important than private little feuds and the dark little desires in people's hearts.

With no brilliant answers coruscating in his mind, he kicked through the snow, walking farther away from the filth and stench and chaos, but he knew, no matter how far he went, he could not escape them. The war had him.

CHAPTER 43

Mali watched the squad of horsemen approaching her force, with deep suspicion. Not northerners, for sure. A blessing. But after so long without seeing a friendly soul outside her own troops, she felt alarmed.

Being alone in the world was a terrifying experience. Now, not being alone was equally stressful.

They were coming down the road, Somar at their back, all right. So it would seem they were Eracians. Her patrols reported the squad to be friendly, but they had not yet intercepted them, just followed them at a safe distance, crossbows and horsebows laid across the pommels of the swords, waiting.

Mali was standing in what used to be Ecol before the northern forces had scourged it clean. Most of the houses remained, but the furniture, tools, and weapons were gone. Her own troops were stripping rooftops and using the thatch and supports for kindling. At least they were warm.

Since the ambush at the river crossing, she judged any strange phenomenon with a heightened sense of paranoia.

Six men—riding almost leisurely down an iced, abandoned road, the leather-sleeved shins of their horses kicking snow, spears aimed at the puffy sky—were nothing to worry about.

On the contrary.

Her eyes glared south, at the former Athesian forts, now just empty husks, howling with the wind. Fields of discarded gear, tents, and tack, picket stakes poking through the white crust, their sharp edges blunted by heaps of the snow's woolen cover. A manor house that had seen better days, scaffolding creaking, swayed and squeaked whenever a gust picked up, an eerie and loud noise in the silent city. The mining camp gaped its broken teeth and eyes at her. She thought she could see human bodies, frozen leftovers and bones, scattered across the sheared rock and inside the pits, half covered by snowdrift.

Closer still, every building was an ambush point. Mali almost expected angry northerners to jump through dark windows, waving axes and swords at her. She expected to find beggars moaning at her, dogs and rats snarling when she passed by a narrow alley. But the absolute absence of life remained, making her edgy and frightened. Even the presence of what was left of her and Finley's troops did little to diminish the graveyard ambiance that infused Ecol.

How she had survived the bridge disaster was still rather unclear to her. One moment, she was standing on the groaning structure, another she was drowning in icy water, too dark to see, so cold it made her swallow involuntarily, made her chest spasm in agony, made her vomit even before she had air to heave.

Her troops had rescued her, but hundreds had died; hundreds more had caught lung fever and died in agony days later. As she knelt in the mud, hacking, spitting bile, Finley kept on fighting, and the enemy pressed its attack. Soon, she was forced to swallow her misery, ignore the tremors in her muscles, ignore the bluish tinge of her skin, and plunge toward death once more, killing, trying to avoid being killed.

They had won, in a way, with half the men and women dead. The bridge was gone, and they couldn't head across the river for another hundred miles. Hardly the outcome she had desired.

The northern army was long gone. By the time she and the remainder of her troops had recovered and reached Ecol, the enemy had probably gained a two-week lead on her, maybe more. She was probably not going to be able to find them again before the spring, let alone stop them or even mildly hamper their advance. The snow and the scarcity of food had put a halt to any enthusiasm with her soldiers, replacing it with stupor and weariness. No one wanted to march anymore. They were too tired.

She had been defeated.

It was her fault. She had grown too cocky in her early successes. She had underestimated her opponent. When commanders did that, men died aplenty, and sometimes they died too, taking their shame to the grave. Somehow, she had survived when so many others had not.

The foreign squad was coming closer. It had passed in the shadow of one of the empty forts.

Mali lowered the looking glass, wiped the extra grease from her brow and the bridge of her nose. She handed it to Meagan. It was the girl's personal tool, with an inscription, not a standard army trinket.

We wait, she told herself, nervous, fidgety.

Alexa shuffled over, her breastplate smeared in ash to keep from shining and to keep the frost away. Her girls were snow veterans since the previous year, and they had all learned the little tricks needed to survive.

"You look like shit," her friend whispered.

"Is it my hair?" Mali flicked her soggy, filthy growth.

"It's your attitude," Alexa admitted, pursing her lips.

Mali nodded. "I need time." She looked back toward the brown line slicing through the snow. The small squad had been stopped, and her women were disarming the riders. She heard a crunch of boots. Finley approached, his breath misting, a cup of something hot in his gloved hands.

"My men found a hidden cellar full of goodies. We'll have onions and turnips for another week or so. But we really need to decide what we should do, because we'll have to start rationing food even more strictly than before."

I have been defeated. The decision is obvious, Mali reasoned. "What do you say?"

Finley rubbed his ear. "I'm so bloody tired," he said in a low voice so no one could overhear him.

Mali shared his sentiment. Every day, it was harder getting up in the morning. The cold sapped all energy; the bleak, abandoned city sapped their spirit. And the bridge failure had made them all too aware of how small and weak and underequipped their little army was. Reminded them all of their insignificance. You could wrestle with the weather and squeeze fresh morale from the soul if you tried hard enough, but you couldn't fight your own worthlessness.

The six horsemen were coming on foot now, surrounded by two dozen wary women. They had their swords out, and their crossbows were aimed at legs and kidneys.

Mali sighed, steeled herself. Her own retinue spread in front of her and the other officers, forming a human shield. Mali flexed her fist a few times, streaming flesh blood into her fingers. But she didn't feel like drawing her sword even if they tried to kill her. Of course she would, she wanted to live, but the effort was unfathomable.

The lead rider stopped. "I am Lieutenant Holger of the Second Division, Second Army. I was sent to seek Commanders Mali and Finley. Do I have the honor?"

There was a wave of excited, hushed talk among the troops nearby, rumor spreading like wildfire. They had been isolated from the rest of the world for so long, seeing these six Eracians was almost a miracle.

But Mali couldn't let any emotion show.

"At your service," Finley chirped before she could say anything. So she just squirmed idly.

Holger reached under a layer of thick black fur and produced a sealed message tube. He extended his hand and waited for one of the privates to snatch it from him. Carefully, a girl soldier knelt, unwrapped the hide, and popped the lid, aimed toward the ground. Nothing sinister came out, just a rolled length of oiled paper.

The private handed it to Mali. She held the paper open, the edges curling annoyingly. Finley's face intruded in her vision. She could hear his breath, the one clogged nostril whistling away, and she could smell him, smoke, pig grease, months of bad hygiene.

So much had happened while she had labored north to Emorok and here. The world had gone by, briskly, without waiting for her return.

Apparently, there was a new monarch in Eracia. One Lord Bartholomew, formerly of Barrin.

He was calling them home, away from the madness and killing and the northern menace.

He was planning his own war, it seemed. In the spring, the Eracian army would march west, against the nomads, to exact vengeance for the desecration of Somar and the suffering of the people. In so many words, this was going to be another Vergil's Conquest, it seemed, and she had the privilege of taking part in slaughtering and raping the nomad tribes.

Wonderful.

Someone hawked and spat, adding glory to the event.

"So we won eventually," she said into the terse silence around her. At least something good had come out of this miserable affair. Half of Eracia had been spared the wrath of the northern army, and the capital city had been liberated. The land had a ruler once again. It had law. It had discipline. It had meaning. The sorry, ragtag army that had been raised to handle the catastrophe was now an experienced, well-honed body of troops, maybe even better than the ones she had led during the border skirmishes. Twenty-one years of shame, erased.

If she went to Somar now, she would be hailed as a hero. She would bask in glory and flattery and attention. Going home meant hot food, hot baths, proper shits, a normal life. For her, it would be a return to her old life, her crimes long gone and forgotten. She did not have to be a nobody in Windpoint. Well, that place probably didn't exist anymore. She could maybe retire, or lead the army training.

No, wait, she figured. *I will find myself in the nomad country, killing people once again.* It would be all the fun of the past year and a half, and then some.

But then, even that war would end one day. And the monarch would let them go home finally, take off the uniforms, and put the swords away. Only somehow, she envisioned the white horde of the northern army coming back after having ravaged and ruined all of the realms, coming back to settle that one last score, to destroy the one scrap of land they hadn't touched yet.

Mali would have to lead her girls once more and for the last time, fight this huge, invincible army, until she ran out of troops, luck, or both. Until she died.

Fuck.

At this point, all she wanted was to see her son. She missed James badly. And he was growing up without her, in the clutches of some expensive Caytorean lady. That couldn't be good for him. She had to see him before war tore them apart forever.

Maybe even now, he was leading his own forces against the northern menace somewhere in central Caytor. Maybe he was retreating, or pursuing the foe from behind, like she had been doing.

The near drowning at the bridge had shaken her. She was no longer a young woman. She was pushing her luck. She could die at any moment, and it would be a great pity if she died before seeing those she loved one last time.

"Thank you, Lieutenant. Major Nolene will see to your accommodation." That also meant a thorough investigation of all he knew. Mali didn't wait for anyone to respond or say anything else. Pretending to be busy, she pushed back through the crowd and went to wrestle with her own thoughts.

"I know what you're thinking," Alexa said, approaching.

Mali slid off the coal wagon, dusting her numb rear of snow. "Do you?"

Alexa stopped walking. "Yes, I do. And I am coming with you."

Mali smirked sadly. "Again?"

Her friend shrugged. "What the fuck am I supposed to do at my age? I've followed you for the past twenty-odd years. A few more won't make much difference. At least we'll be together, and I miss that boy as much as you do."

Mali scooped up some old snow, its wind-blasted texture sharp and unpleasant against her skin. "How are we going to justify our departure? We can't just vanish like the last time."

Alexa looked behind her. Four female soldiers were standing about fifty paces away, uncomfortable yet alert, watching their commander. Mali waited. "A reconnaissance mission."

Mali snorted. "One that requires a battalion commander and her deputy to leave the main body?"

The blond major inclined her head. "Does anything else make any sense in this bloody war?"

Mali left the mining gear behind and started walking toward her friend. The snow chattered under her soles, making guttural, incomprehensible accusations. "No, it does not."

"You can relinquish your command to Finley. You can appoint one of the girls to lead the Third while we're gone. And we should probably take your curly northerner with us in case we come across some of his fellow countrymen."

Mali dropped the snowball, her fingers tingling with pain. "We head for Pain Daye."

Alexa nodded. "That was the last place James wrote to us from. Let's hope he is still there."

Mali was about to respond when something tugged at the corner of her eye, a curious detail. Distracted, she veered away, toward the heap of old stone and broken timber blocking a mining shaft. There had been a major engagement here, sometime in the last year, she figured. Athesians fighting the northerners, maybe. Or some other army clashing with its foe. She had no idea. Lieutenant Holger might know something about it.

What drew her attention was a rib cage. It could have been a boar, only it was ten times the size, with huge spears rising like bent swords from the ground. Part of it was still buried, and she didn't want to stir the cover, didn't want to know what else she might find underneath. But those ivory spears frightened her ever so slightly. What kind of monster was this? Did those northerners use some strange beasts no one had ever seen? She had heard of the Borei using large siege animals, but she had never seen one. Besides, what would the Borei be doing this deep in the realms?

"Pain Daye," Mali repeated, reaching forward, but then she hesitated. She did not want to press her fingers against that bone.

Finley took her news with a great deal of surprise and suspicion. But living a whole life pretending to be someone else had taught Mali to become a decent liar, so her words came true and extremely reasonable, and the colonel found it hard to argue.

"You can send any number of your ordinary troops." He tried to resist.

"And then what? What if they meet with the Caytorean forces? What if they encounter some of the enemy? Who makes the right decision? I can't leave that responsibility to any of my girls or your men. If there's a mission I wouldn't volunteer for myself, then I have no right asking my own troops to risk their lives and do the same."

Finley looked around him. He didn't like the empty, haunted homes either. Their lodge was an inn, and she thought she had read "Brotherly Unity" on a faded billboard swaying above the entrance. "We cannot afford to lose you, Commander."

Mali smiled. "You won't lose me, Finley. I will return. Until today, we haven't seen a living soul in a year. We don't know anything that's happening in the world. The enemy force has gone south, so that leaves us time and space to maneuver, to prepare. I will not squander this opportunity to try and mobilize as much help and support as we can gather for the resistance against the white foe. Maybe Eracia and Caytor still bear a grudge, but I don't care. I will not let even the slimmest chance for survival slip because of stupid pride and ancient slights."

The colonel was still not fully convinced. "Mali, we are not politicians. From what this Holger fellow reports, the Parusites may have helped us win Somar back. So it means an alliance with their king. We cannot side with the Athesian rebels or the High Council."

Does that make my son a rebel, too? One fighting for a lost cause? But she said nothing on that matter. As far as the ugly world was concerned, Emperor James was Adam's son, not hers.

"I don't care about politics." Maybe a little. "This isn't about politics. This is about survival. You have seen the enemy, Finley. I will not rest until I'm certain everyone knows about the threat."

"We have sent messages," the colonel whispered.

"Can we afford to wait until they respond? I will not."

He hesitated for a long while. Then he doffed his gloves and extended a pale hand. "Good luck, Commander. I am sure you will need it."

That's sorted out, she thought.

"I am taking Bjaras with me," she said.

Gordon said nothing. He stared at her, eyes big and full of hurt.

"I know what I did was a mistake." She marched on, ignoring the emotional ambush. "And I am sorry. I never meant to hurt you. But you must remember we never promised each other anything beyond simple physical pleasure."

"Thank you for reminding me," he mumbled.

"I will return," she repeated, hoping it was not a lie. "And when I do, I think I will have courage for us to try again. Together. Committed. I just hope you will be willing to forgive me and to give me another chance."

The captain of the skirmishers tried to keep his face passive, but his cheeks twitched, and the corners of his lips curled. "You are going to Pain Daye?"

Mali sighed. "That's my plan. I will need Bjaras in case we encounter any of the northerners. Nothing more. But I must meet with the High Council, I must find Emperor James, and I must convince them all to join the war against the enemy."

"They might have already," he supplied in a thin, sad voice.

"We do not know that. But do you think this white foe will just vanish one day? They will march back north. I am certain. And we must find a way to stop them. This is my burden. But I must ask you to help Meagan keep the battalion intact. Avoid heavy battles. Keep safe. We will meet, if anything, in a few months." She leaned over, trying to kiss him, but also to silence anything else he might try to say. She feared she knew what he might utter, and she didn't want her chest hurting any more than it already was. Maybe she was a coward, but she was trying.

Gordon softened. He kissed her gently, chapped lips to chapped lips. He smelled like onions, and she didn't dare think what she smelled like. "So long, Captain. We'll meet again."

He touched a hand to her shoulder, then retrieved it. Was he crying? Men! But then her vision started to mist, so she blinked hard, spun around, and walked away with a purposeful stride. Gordon was a decent person. For an old, bitter female officer with more scars than common sense, he was actually quite a catch. She should keep that in mind.

Later that day, they did a quick exchange of command. With only a few hours of daylight left, she was heading east, with Alexa, Bjaras, a burly female guard named Suzy, four horses, and fives mules swaying silly with packed food, blankets, and weapons. Hopefully, that would be enough until she found civilization again. If she found it, she reminded herself.

"Son, I miss you," she whispered into the wind, marching away from Ecol.

CHAPTER 44

Usually, Stephan liked the way Eybalen looked in the winter. He liked the sight of the city seen from inland. The land dipped slightly, the creases of hilly terrain sweeping away, and the cove opened, revealing terraces, the farming villages, the hive of the city, the sprawl of the harbor, the choppy shimmer of the sea.

Not this time.

The hills were dappled in ice, glistening like a mirror, blinding, sharp. Winds from the harbor had polished the crust to a sheen like silver, and his head hurt from squinting, trying to keep the glare out of his eyes. But he wouldn't pull the curtains closed. He hated sitting and jolting in darkness. He could not hear the city yet, but the smoke from the chimneys and workshops, and the stillness in the port, told of a besieged place, waiting for winter to ease its grip.

What bothered him was not the smudge of chaos, the absence of white sails coming and going to Eybalen, or the howl of the wind bending the trees and shrubbery northward. It was the sight of two new large army camps on the slopes outside the town, expelling their own smoke and stench.

They looked like cow turds picked through by grubby fingers, as if someone had hoped to find nuggets of gold deep in the brown piles. There was no order, just concentric rings of greater or lesser shit sprawling any which way the land went, and not even the cover of snow could hide the ugliness.

In all his life as a councillor, he had never seen an army outside Eybalen. Not during the Feoran revolution, not in the war against the Eracians, not once during Adam's reign. Now, it seemed thousands of armed men hogged the road into the capital, one on each side. That could not be good. Not at all.

He was not bringing any good news either. Behind him, in the hundred-odd carriages, rode the displaced councillors, mayors, and investors from northern cities, now entirely without homes and at his mercy. Behind them farther still, endless convoys of refugees followed. He was bringing half the realm to its heart, and it could not be good either. But it was an opportunity.

The mythical army from the north turned out to be a real one, it seemed. Less than a week after arriving at Pain Daye, they had evacuated the mansion and gone back south, taking gold and food. A small, suicidal part of him wanted to see the enemy regiments, to see the myth stomp through Caytor, but he believed the words of so many scouts coming back slack faced with fear.

For several days, the enemy shadowed them, and there was a real fear they would be forced to engage in battle with a small cadre of inexperienced solders and thousands of refugees slowing them down. Then the foe veered west, going toward Athesia. A blessing, a curse, Stephan just did not know. When drunk, he suspected the enemy might be in league with Amalia, but sobriety brought back more logical thoughts to his mind. This northern army, whatever it was, brought doom to the realms. The rules of the game had changed. The game itself had changed.

Rheanna and he had done their best to consolidate their power among the destitute councillors. He had bedded his way through a number of less likely agreements with some of the female candidates, while James's widow had more subtly hinted at potential rewards in return for cooperation. They had indebted dozens of men and women in return for funds and hope, and Stephan could not wait to get back to the city. He would have powerful backing in any meeting with the rest of the High Council, and he could slowly work toward grabbing more power, more influence, and sidelining his opponents.

If only this northern threat would go away.

He was genuinely surprised by the presence of army camps outside Eybalen.

The carriage jolted to a halt, and the woman in his lap stirred but didn't wake. Hailey was a small honey merchant from Marlheim. Not that important in the greater scheme, but her vote still carried some small weight, and he'd liked her company during the long, boring days of travel.

Stephan pushed her off him, but she remained sound asleep. He craned his neck, stretching sore muscles, opened the door, and hopped out. Cold air slapped him.

Bader was sitting on a horse, looking alert, his always-filthy hair fluttering. His henchmen were spread all about, and hundreds followed around their caravan and in the fields. Some were private soldiers, others newly hired mercenaries, a handful of veterans from James's time, disillusioned of their earlier ideals.

The road ahead was blocked. Several carts, loaded with stones, were parked perpendicularly to the hard-packed gravel, forcing any wagon or carriage coming south to weave slowly past their lumbering bulk—or sidetrack into the deep snow. Going around the barrier was trickier, because large, sharp stakes broke through the white crust at least fifty paces on each side of the road.

Three soldiers with old-looking yet very sharp halberds stood in front of the barricade, seemingly bored. A fourth sat on top of one of the wagons, his legs covered in a checkered blanket, a crossbow resting in his lap. Behind him, the city flag fluttered on a pole.

That square of canvas was probably the chief reason why their convoy had not tried to break through past the obstacle. This affair was sponsored by the High Council.

Two men were coming up the road, approaching the barricade. They were on foot and did not look armed. Eyes watering from the sun's glare, it took Stephan a few moments to realize who the left figure was.

"Adrian?" he called, but the wind just washed his words back north.

His bodyguard turned, then looked back at the road.

Stephan waited, buttoning up his coat.

His friend was still somewhat fat, but he walked with a sure gait. It wasn't like him not to be drunk at midday. "Stephan, you swordfish. You're back."

"Adrian," Stephan offered more cautiously. What was his friend doing outside the cozy brothels and wine cellars?

The other councillor looked past him, at the convoy of animals and wheels and soldiers stretching north. "The patrols reported a large body of people coming our way, but I didn't expect this huge tail behind you."

Stephan embraced his friend and found his clean scent alarming. "And what are *you* doing here?"

Adrian shrugged, a sheepish grin on his face. "Well, you must have heard the rumors. Our nation is under attack. There's an army coming from the north, and we must prote—"

"Come on, friend." Stephan cut him off, maybe a little impatiently.

"The council has mobilized troops. They say it's a national emergency. Men, boys, everyone's been conscripted. We have to be ready to defend Eybalen. And that means no civilians, I'm afraid. Your refugees will have to go to Shurbalen or Monard. We'll take any lad of fighting age, though."

"Who decided this?" Stephan fumed.

"No one really decided anything. We all agreed."

Stephan looked left. Small groups of four to five men were leaving their prints in the snow, walking around his convoy, spears pointed at the cerulean sky. Not just picket sentries. Too many of them. Still more of them on the right side, too. He frowned. The High Council had rarely agreed on anything, especially when he wasn't around. Now this. Too organized, too logical.

"Why aren't you in the city, Adrian?"

His friend looked surprised. "Oh, well, I've been appointed to supervise the military preparations. I'm the new lord of tax and provisions." The other man at his side, a thin, nondescript fellow, preened, which probably made him a top clerk, and one who counted every silver coin twice.

"Interesting development," Stephan admitted, trying to keep rancor from his voice. That would be childish.

The delay was making everyone fidgety. The soldiers were becoming impatient, but no one was going to be a hero when staring at two huge camps full of armed men. Boots crunched behind him, and soon, Sebastian stepped to his side, looking concerned.

"Councillor Adrian," he whispered cautiously.

"Master Sebastian," Stephan's nondrunk friend commented, tone and eyes warm. "I haven't seen you in a while now. But

I guess the northern threat has forced everyone home, even the more reluctant among us."

The guild master pressed his lips thin, but said nothing.

Stephan wondered how the council would take the man's allegiance with Emperor James. Some had definitely endorsed it, others had openly sponsored it, but now that the Athesian man was dead, and the Parusites had spoiled everything, they might want to blame it all on someone, and no one was a better candidate than Sebastian.

"Stephan, did you accomplish what you wanted?"

He had not expected that question. Not like that, not right now. But Rheanna was not a threat anymore. It should be safe to mention her name. "In a manner."

Should be safe.

Almost as if summoned, Lady Rheanna stepped out of her own coach. Unlike the two of them, she had a pair of armed men in tow. Her head was covered in a silk veil, which made her look innocent and fragile, but also, more sensibly, protected her ears from the icy wind. Stephan wished he had some sort of headgear.

"Councillor, why are we delayed?" she asked, coming closer, her body still dangerously voluptuous even when hidden by layers of scarves and fur.

Nudd was there, too, eying the other clerk with animosity. Stephan rubbed his temples. The wind, the sun, the cold, too much chatter, things were really slipping out of control now. He was not prepared for this. "Should we not continue on our way? Adrian, can you instruct those men to let us pass?"

"Most certainly. But first, my colleague will detail your convoy. I'm afraid we will have to appropriate ten percent, or equivalent, in war taxes, and all your men will have to report to the recruiter's office within a week, save for the personal guards." Adrian's eyes briefly touched James's widow, but if he had anything else to say, he kept it private.

"Do it," Stephan snapped.

It took them a while to get going. Some of the carriages were too long and wide, and they could not slip past the barricade, so they had to harness a pair of horses and pull them apart. By the time they cleared the barrier and were rolling toward Eybalen, the sun was beating against their backs. A thousand lights came to life in the camps, and they lost some of their ugly, chaotic feel. Stephan only gazed at the sprawl of tents, low barracks and sheds, improvised stables, and field workshops, trying to assess the numbers, the strength, and more importantly, the loyalty of all those men.

He was pleasantly surprised to learn that things were not as sinister as he expected. There was no great conspiracy, and the High Council was just as divided as ever. The next morning, he left his villa and headed to a meeting to find a bunch of rich people frozen in time, trying to outsmart one another. The war was just another layer to their intrigue.

After probing the hearts and minds of his colleagues, he decided to bring Lady Rheanna back into Caytorean society. The lack of any great sentiment toward her almost shocked him. It seemed that everyone had done their share of thinking of the future, and with the beautiful banker and widow cast down from her power, and irrelevant in the greater scheme of things, they all chose to be benevolent and forgiving.

Her enemies merely demanded more money, that was all.

Stephan almost laughed at how absurd it was.

Rheanna did her best to be charming and vulnerable, and she immediately won all the men over. With the ladies, she tried a different approach, trying to portray a picture of grief and suffering. Even Stephan wasn't quite sure what game she played, but it suited him well as long as she helped Sebastian and him gain more influence with the city's traders, merchants, and guild members.

The flood of refugees actually helped. Prices soared. Desperate shop owners and homeless nobles and councillors turned to the banks and greedy investors for help. Almost exclusively, they found themselves approaching Lord Malcolm or his daughter, beautiful, desirable, and very much a widow. Stephan did his best to vouch for his friends, and Master Sebastian gently coerced the guilds to help everyone make the right decision.

Within less than two weeks, Stephan was the shadow owner of many new businesses, even the ones he had once avoided in the past. He also claimed a whole stretch of land in the north, pastures, vineyards, orchards, farmsteads. They were just sketches and scribbles on paper, but if they somehow won against this northern foe, he would have won a quarter of the realm through smiles and handshakes.

He knew this was exactly what Rheanna had been doing while married to James. Sebastian had told him of the young emperor's plans and how he had managed to sway and fool so many councillors, until it was too late. Ironically, no one seemed to make the connection.

The third week, he had a rather unpleasant visit from one Lady Laura and her daughter Daria. It took him a while to figure out that James had gotten rid of her husband and taken over his steel industry. Otis's widow demanded reparations for the wrongs done to her.

In the end, he arranged for a very public reconciliation between the two widows. Lady Rheanna relinquished parts of the industry back to Laura in return for a small percentage of profits. Stephan promised to find Daria a husband even more promising than Lord Bram. He felt immensely pleased by his achievements. He was the architect of the new Caytor. Without any violence, without tension or strife, he was molding the future of his realm.

Wet snows and hail came in angry, biting showers from the sea, tearing shutters and roof tiles off buildings. The price of bread soared. The rumor of the northern threat persisted. Army patrols roamed the streets, recruiting any boy stupid enough not to flee. Homeless people hid in the sewers to avoid getting conscripted.

All the while Stephan counted his new coin and luck and waited for the turn of the year, each day fatter on hope that the storm from the north would pass them by.

Just two days before the year's turn, he went to bed, thinking about the great ball planned at Councillor Helmut's estate. Stephan wondered if he might convince Lady Rheanna to sleep with him.

A vague, half-muted scream snapped his eyes open.

He rose in a flutter of linen and wool, kicking the sheets off him. Barefoot, he padded over to the door of his chamber and cracked it open. The lone guard was frowning, staring down the corridor, fingers hovering above the leather hilt of his short sword.

"What's happening, Taylor?" Stephen muttered.

The guard grunted. "Lock yourself inside, sir. Don't come out until we tell you it's safe."

There was a thud from somewhere down the dark passageway. Glass shattering.

Where is Bader? Stephan wondered. He nodded at Taylor, but the man was busy staring. Stephan edged back and latched the door closed. Heart thudding with excitement and a solid dose of fear, he tiptoed back to his bed. He had a small assassin-like crossbow hidden in his nightstand, and there was a dagger under the mattress. Not that he was any great fighter, but he was no coward either.

He knelt on the carpet and slithered his hand under the mat. His fingers probed, the heavy pad making his motions awkward. He swiped left and right, dug until his shoulder was pressed against the side of the bed, but he could not feel the knife.

Panic rising in his throat, he flicked the nightstand open. The chamber was dark, lit only by the stars and a slice of moon, making everything distorted. But there was still enough illumination for him not to see the killer's weapon he expected to find there.

Stolen, taken away. Gone.

Treachery.

He swallowed a lump and looked around the room for a weapon. Anything. Maybe the fireplace poker. Not there. How had he missed that?

Outside, he heard steps, snarls, curses, the unmistakable hiss of steel, the whisper of blades, the chewing-like sound of meat and bone being torn open, a weak, breathless wail of someone dying. Moments later, the door crashed open, splinters flying, the latch dangling.

A man he had never seen before stepped in. Short, receding gray hair, ashen clothes, a sword in his hands. The yellow cast of lamps washed him in a golden halo, making him look like some monster.

"Help," Stephan croaked.

"Pointless, Councillor," the gray-haired killer said, his voice sad and deep.

"Bader!" Stephan tried to shout. *No, wait. Maybe Bader is behind this treachery,* his mind gibbered. Maybe Lady Rheanna had organized all this. Or her father. For an instant, the list of his enemies became endless.

Sebastian? Lady Laura trying to avenge her husband? Was Rheanna already dead? Did they kill Sebastian? His friend Adrian? Who? All of them.

The killer moved forward, lithe, efficient, confident. Stephan knew he could not fight him. "Gold! You'll get gold! Anything you want." He hated the sound of his reedy, frightened voice.

"Pointless, Councillor," the man countered. Closer.

"Who betrayed me?" Stephan pleaded.

"What does it matter, Councillor? Really." The man lunged.

Stephan tried to avoid it, but the man was an expert. There was a flicker of sharp black pain somewhere in his chest, and then, the night turned completely dark.

CHAPTER 45

Nigella stepped out of her cabin, eyes full of tears. If she had kept count correctly, the year had turned its page last night as she had been busy turning pages of *The Book of Lost Words*, trying to figure out her future. The Sirtai might argue about the calendar, and how the years were numbered, but it didn't matter.

She now knew what Calemore wanted.

Until that morning, she had been terrified to let Sheldon step out on his own. No longer. He would not be harmed. Not according to the book and its message.

Her boy was not far, busy trying to roll the biggest snowball ever made. It was taller than him, and he was grunting and panting, red like a beet, but the huge thing just wouldn't budge anymore. His hands would slip, slapping chunks of snow off the ball, and his small face would sink into the powder. Not one to give up, Shel would merely dust his cheeks, huff off the pain, and keep fighting the ball.

Several Naum soldiers were watching him, grinning, laughing, thoroughly entertained. Their breath misted and curled around their windburned cheeks. They did not look like evil invaders. They looked like simple men tasked with the duty of guarding some woman and her child, and they did their best to pass the time. For a moment, Nigella was almost inclined to ignore the warning she had read in the book.

"Mom!" Sheldon called. "I need help."

Nigella smiled weakly. She stepped into the snow, the cold seeping through her boots.

Sheldon straightened, adjusting the woolen cap on his head. "Are you crying, Mom?"

"No, it's just the wind," she mumbled. "I'm fine, Son."

"Good," he panted. "I need to get this ball rolling down the hill."

She brushed some snow off the massive thing. "You need to compact the snow, Son. You need to make it denser and smaller."

Sheldon bent down, scooped up a handful more powder, and slapped it back where she'd touched. "No, Mom. I want to make it big. I want it to be so big it can crush the houses in the city."

Nigella sighed. Her boy didn't deserve her pain. He should not know. He would not understand the message.

"Let me help you." With her hands jabbed into the ball, it started moving, but soon, it was skidding rather than rolling, and new patches of snow just fell off it like old bark. She started patting the snow, her fingers freezing. Sheldon started doing the same, but soon he was vigorously punching the ball, causing more damage than good.

"Mom, maybe they can help?" he huffed.

She looked at the northern warriors. "All right."

The boy turned and spoke in their language. A shiver crept down her spine. Even now, months after meeting these foreigners, she felt uneasy hearing their tongue, especially when Sheldon spoke it. Somehow, it did not feel natural to her. Children learned quickly. Nevertheless it was eerie.

The soldiers were almost too keen to join. Two remained guarding, but the rest put their swords and axes down and came over to help her son. She stood back and watched gruff, whiskered adults become children again as they put their shoulders into the ball and started rolling it again.

After a while, the ball was almost as tall as they, and they were struggling with the same concept as her son. One of them used his shield to smooth the ball, pressing against the snow and shaving off lumps. Another was clearing a path ahead, stomping the powder flat.

"We are going to roll it down the hill, Mom," Sheldon shrieked, ecstatic.

"I'm glad," she told him. The tears had frozen on her skin, making her smile wooden.

With a throaty cheer, the men and the boy nudged the ball toward the slope and then pushed it. Their voices followed it as it rolled once, twice, then broke in two, then stopped. The crumpled halves wobbled a little and then joined the vast sea of white in silence. Only tiny lumps continued on their journey toward Marlheim, leaving behind a hundred snaky trails.

Sheldon raised his hands and shouted, "Mom! That's not fair!"

"You will do better next time, Son. Remember, smaller and denser."

"But that's no fun, Mom," the boy lamented.

The soldiers grimaced their disappointment for a while, then walked back and picked up their weapons, becoming bored, uncomfortable sentries once again. Nigella's mind drifted back to her evening's reading, to the sleepless night that had followed.

Calemore would probably visit her any day now. She was convinced he had enjoyed a great success in his war and that his worries were diminishing by the moment. No one could stop him. So he might decide to take a brief respite from the killing and return to her, to his lover, to his future queen. The book promised that. Of all the details that the book might conceal, it had chosen to show her that one.

A part of her soul still yearned for his company, for his touch, for his flattery. Another part, the one she couldn't really control, demanded that borderline terror, that uncertainty, that feeling of self-worthlessness that he invoked in her. She would never admit it, but she couldn't hide from her own feelings. She wanted to be loved and desired. She craved attention and approval, and she would like to wield the power and control that she had once only dreamed of as she had watched the rich councillors with bitter envy and fear.

Best if she fled. Glory and glamor were not for her. She was just a humble witch, a half-breed, and the best she should hope for was a quiet place to live her life and practice her craft. When little worms like her wriggled out of their dark holes, they got crushed mercilessly.

But Calemore liked her. He was the only man who had ever shown her true affection.

Last night's reading had cleared her mind somewhat, but not enough. Even flight demanded courage—or extreme cowardice. And she wasn't even that much of a coward.

So she waited, frozen. Like a little mouse stunned by the screech of a bird of prey.

Calemore would show up at her doorstep any day now. She must be ready. This time, he would want all the answers. He would brook no delays. He would have no more tolerance for her trouble deciphering the future. She had to be prepared.

Well, she knew. She knew everything. She knew what he wanted. More importantly, she knew what she wanted.

That knowledge was liberating, and frightening. To finally have a clear objective in her life other than raw survival. It was as if she were drowning in her magic, and the more she gasped for air, the more she made her situation desperate. She was floundering, breathless with knowledge that belonged in some other time, and she wasn't certain how to cope.

The Book of Lost Words was a dangerous artifact. It should not exist.

Sheldon had recovered from his failed attempt at utterly ruining Marlheim and was now busy fighting the Naum men with snowballs. Another soldier had joined his side, and they were hiding behind an old tree, throwing missiles at the four other troops. Men laughed and cursed and taunted each other, an unmistakable rhythm to their voice, even if she could not understand the words. Her son tried to emulate them, and she was almost happy.

The question of her identity, the question of what she wanted in life, the answers were clear now.

Nigella felt it was safe to leave her son with the soldiers.

Reluctantly, she went back into the cabin, toes tingling with soft numbness. She kicked the snow off, dusted herself clean, and stepped into her tiny, warm world. On the small table, the book of magic stared back.

She wanted to burn that thing so that no one would ever read it.

No one deserved its cryptic, ugly truths.

Her hand rose, reached for the unblemished cover, and trembled. She couldn't. What would Calemore do when he learned she had destroyed this artifact of ancient power? Well, she knew exactly what he would do. She knew what he expected of her, what he wanted, how he perceived the future.

She could tell it all. She no longer needed the book. Not for him, not for herself.

If only life could be easier. If she were prettier, if she didn't have her bastard heritage, if she had somehow avoided all those men who'd abused her and betrayed her. Nigella wanted to blame them, but it was her fault, too. She had allowed them to deceive her with their false promises, with their flattery, with their feigned affection for a homely mongrel living on the outskirts of society.

The White Witch of Naum was doing the same thing, really. Using her like a tool.

Only he was not going to discard her. She had hoped he would stay. She had hoped their fragile, mad relationship could flourish into something more meaningful. For the first time in her life, she was right. He was not going to abandon her. He planned for them to stay together, and she would be his partner, as equal as a human could be to an immortal.

To someone who aspired to become a god.

The lunacy of that idea almost made her kneel and weep, but she managed to stand, hand still hovering inches from the book. She should be grateful that she knew the future. Who else could claim such privilege, such power? She held the world's fate in her hands. Of all the people, she had the knowledge to steer the lives of untold thousands toward destruction, or salvation.

The worst part was, she didn't care. The world could burn as far as she was concerned.

If only it didn't include Sheldon.

The future that Calemore sought was utterly simple. He intended to defeat the people of the realms, to kill them to the last, until religion crumbled and all the gods were killed. Then, he would become the one and only deity.

She could even tell him how he could achieve that. His triumph relied on a single soul. He just needed to kill a single soul, and he would never be stopped. Just one soul. That was all that stood in his path.

In the world that would be after his victory, the Naum people would settle the land of the old gods, returning after countless centuries of exile. Their loyalty to the White Witch would be vindicated, and they would usurp the land from their enemies. She was going to become his concubine, a queen, a lover, the one woman he could desire of all his subjects and slaves.

Nigella almost shed a tear at that thought.

As a god, he would not rule the people on his own. He would install a king in his name. But that could not be one of his Naum men. They had long lost their own free will, had become so deeply obedient to his wishes that he found their servitude dispiriting. He needed someone with a young, fresh mind, someone who would rule with passion.

Her son, Sheldon.

A tear rolled out of the corner of her eye and dripped onto the table.

At first, Sheldon would be trained in politics and military affairs and economics. He would become a skilled, intelligent ruler, and he would bring prosperity to the people. However, time and the dark shadow of his new god would begin to corrupt his soul, almost imperceptibly.

It might be the ultimate power, or boredom, or maybe the sense of invincibility. It might be the slow eroding of empathy, the hardening of his soul against the terror of Calemore's vision, or maybe even his character. But Sheldon would steer away from what his mother had tried to teach him all these years.

More tears, and they coursed freely.

Sheldon would begin to indulge in little sins, in small, meaningless horrors. He would bed women for the sheer fun of it, then abandon them. He would begin to sponsor cruel games of violence, where soldiers would fight to the death in large arenas, surrounded by screaming, cheering crowds. He would taste human flesh. He would punish trivial crimes with atrocities. Her son would become a monster, and he would forget his own mother.

The book promised he would become a great prince. At the price of his humanity.

There was only one thing in this whole world that mattered to her. It was her son. And she would not allow anyone, not the gods, not their sons, or anyone, to harm him.

Perhaps she would never be beautiful or rich, and she didn't care for any of that. As long as she had her boy, he was more important than all else. He was the only person she cared about. He was the reason why she lived and why she wasn't fleeing this cursed cabin. Sheldon was her life. All she cared for was his safety and happiness. She would protect him with her own life.

She would not let him become a monster.

CHAPTER 46

"Gods have mercy!" a Parusite officer shouted.

Gods? Ewan thought sourly. *They won't help you. Tanid's a bloody coward.*

Tanid was watching the enemy mass with naked fear on his ageless face. Not the dignified leadership, nor the spiritual enlightenment he would expect from his creator. Ewan felt he had learned a lot about faith in the recent months.

"You must kill them," the deity hissed.

"Must I?" Ewan said in a low, barely audible whisper.

Cries of despair washed over the line of Parusite troops as they glimpsed the massive enemy force building across the river. Their shoulders sagged. Some removed their helms; others dropped their swords. This wasn't just the army that had chased them all the way from Ecol. This was a new host, coming from the east, huge, fresh, unbloodied.

"Please, Ewan! You must save us!" Gavril's face was only inches away, free of blemishes of war, exhaustion, or guilt. No chilblains, no sunburned or windburned skin, no gashes, no wrinkles of fatigue. Many thousands had died in the realms, but so far, the effect on the one surviving god seemed entirely internal, entirely selfish.

Ewan looked around him. He was surrounded by men of faith: Sergei's troops, Red Caps, some of the god's pilgrims. They were all mumbling prayers and pleas to their gods and goddesses, utterly unaware of the weakling in their midst. Ewan almost considered telling them. But that would just make the humans more miserable. He doubted this god cared about anything except his own sorry life.

"Why don't you save us?" Ewan growled, feeling anger coursing through his veins.

"I have no more power left," Tanid whimpered. "I've used all my strength to create weather storms to slow down the Naum troops. I need more faith. I need more prayer."

Ewan felt disgusted. "These people have given you all they have. What more do you want?"

Tanid shook his head. "It just isn't enough. I will need much more."

Useless, Ewan thought. The god was stalling. He would not use his magic to create violence like the Sirtai did, probably because that would draw attention to him, and then, the witch might attack him personally. But from what Ewan remembered reading in *The Pains of Memory*, Calemore could *not* kill Tanid. Not by his own hand, anyway. So the god was a mere coward. A selfish coward.

"How are we going to win this war?" Ewan asked.

Tanid swallowed. "You. The wizards. You must kill Calemore."

Sacrifice ourselves, Ewan figured. "Calemore may not kill you." He raised his crippled hand. "But he may kill us. Is that what you ask of us? Is that what you ask of me? That I die defending you?"

Tanid hesitated, then nodded slowly. "Yes. I am your god."

Ewan snorted. "You don't deserve to be my god." He shook his head and walked away.

It wouldn't be long before the White Witch unleashed all his might against Roalas. Inevitably, his forces would defeat King Sergei and Princess Sasha, defeat the token forces fielded by Amalia, her Caytorean followers, and the religious fanatics. After that, Calemore would take the rest of the realms almost unimpeded. He might encounter resistance in Eracia or Caytor, but somehow Ewan knew that once this battle was over, it would all be over.

He still could just walk away. Leave this madness behind.

Ewan stopped pacing. He looked at the magical weapon in his hand. Terrible, beautiful. You would not imagine how much death and destruction it could render from its slender, spotless crystalline length. It was only too appropriate that it drank human blood. Nothing else would be deemed a worthy price.

I can use this thing. Risk my own life and use it. He sighed. Why had he ever felt the urge to dive to the bottom of that lake in Kamar Doue? Why had he taken this thing? It could not just be a symbol of chance. He had a calling, something bigger than this misery. More than just watching the realms slowly die, helpless to prevent it.

I have found the bloodstaff for a reason. There must be a reason. There must be. A reason why I can't feel anything. A reason for why I am so lonely. A reason for why I was locked in the Abyss for so many years. I am the son of a god, and that has to be more than just a silly twist of fate.

Must be.

He tried to think like that coward, Tanid. Tried to understand how the god meant to win this war. The ancient thoughts sparkled in his head, telling him snippets of old, forgotten stories. Calemore had planned his revenge ever since his first defeat. His coming back had been inevitable, and it seemed that so his victory would be. Maybe Tanid did not know how to defeat the witch. Maybe he was as desperate as everyone else, clinging to life, clinging to hope.

What would happen if Calemore killed everyone? Would that make Tanid so weak that he just perished? What was his real power? What could a god really do? Affect the weather? Make fireballs explode in the midst of enemy ranks like Jarman and Lucas did? If not, what was the purpose of his divinity except to be an emotional outlet for all those who prayed in his name? Maybe being a god was not a blessing. It might very well be a curse.

Still, no matter what Tanid could do, Ewan was certain the god planned to sacrifice every last human before he risked himself. He would make them pray until they lost their voices, and then he would make them fight until they all died. He would draw strength from their faith and use it to prolong his own existence, and he would not do much to prevent the destruction of all of the realms. The god valued his own life more than any other. Even if it meant the death of all those who believed in him.

That was divinity, all right, he thought. That was morality worthy of a god.

The last shred of his own faith fell apart right then.

If I'm going to sacrifice my own life, I will do it for the people of the realms, not for some selfish immortal bastard.

He gripped the bloodstaff more tightly. There was a weapon that didn't care about his strength. He might crush rocks in his hands, but he couldn't dent the perfect hollow glass rod of the magical weapon.

How do we stop Calemore?

I might have to walk into the enemy ranks and fight him myself, hand to hand.

There just did not seem to be any better option. He would certainly be killed. But it might be worth it.

He should consult with the Sirtai. They might have a better idea. Maybe the three of them together could devise a plan to defeat the witch, or at least wound him so severely that he would admit defeat and retreat. Deep down, though, Ewan knew it would be his battle alone.

He looked across the river, then north. The smoke from enemy camps merged into a low, sooty cloud bank that hid away what little beauty and sunlight there were in the frozen, filthy fields outside the city.

King Sergei had done all he could to prepare for the enemy. Now, it was up to his men.

Ewan was not really sure where the two wizards were. He hadn't seen any of the leaders recently either. Maybe he was avoiding them, uncomfortable with Amalia's crazed stare or the hate in the eyes of Princess Sasha. Above all, he was tired of death and killing.

The finest hairs on his forearms pricked. That was all the warning he had.

He jumped sideways and rolled, under a cart, into a trench. And then he was running, fast, hard, shoving soldiers like they were the errant branches of a pesky tree. The unmistakable sound of red pellets slamming into the ground chased him. Blood and screams engulfed him.

The shower of silent crystal arrows raked down the length of the ditch, but then Calemore lost him, and the cold firestorm swept away, receding. A haze of snow and dust was settling onto the heap of torn flesh. Maimed soldiers were lying in puddles of their own innards, screaming and begging for mercy.

Chaos engulfed the defenders. The words of prayer became curses and shouts, men running everywhere, but mostly away. Everyone had heard the stories about the earlier attack, and no one wanted to be around invisible death. Valor was gone, replaced by terror.

Ewan hunkered down, staring from behind a pile of shaved logs, trying to figure out where the witch might be. He didn't have time to contemplate the man's wisdom or reasoning for this sudden fury. He did not want to learn whether Jarman's shield would hold.

All he wanted was to unleash violence. A well of pent-up fury and disappointment.

Luckily, the snow was a much better killing ground than mud. Ewan could see the spatter, the horseshoe-shaped arc of death, the trail of destruction. Calemore was standing somewhere on the far bank of the Telore, a handful of miles north of Roalas, just before the river curved and hugged the city.

There were no more pellets coming. No retaliation from the wizards. Strange.

Carefully, he inched forward, still trying to hide from a direct line of sight. His fingers itched. He wanted to fire the bloodstaff back at its maker. It might not kill him, but it would wreak havoc with his troops, and that was good enough for Ewan right now.

Tanid was also hiding, he noticed. Hunched like a frightened child, with a dozen Parusite troops holding shields above his prostrate, curled form, a few thin, inadequate wooden buildings separating them from the ruby magic.

Ewan had no doubt the bloodstaff could punch through the boards easily. But Calemore was not firing at the god. He never had, no matter how close the hits scored.

He couldn't kill the god. And still, the coward would not risk his life to protect the people of the realms.

Then...

Ewan saw a soldier coming toward the deity. He looked out of place, because all his comrades were running away or without purpose. This one was marching forward, boldly, unafraid, confident. He was approaching Gavril, and none of Sergei's men and Sasha's women seemed to pay him any heed. Dressed as a Parusite, he was yet another member of the royal army.

Something is wrong, Ewan thought with mounting dread.

Almost effortlessly, the soldier drew his sword and ran Tanid through.

No!

The man didn't even try to defend himself when the other men attacked him, hacking him to pieces. By then, it was too late. The god was bleeding his last syrupy moments onto the snow, a sheet of life almost like crimson silk gushing around the iron blade stuck in his ribs and pooling under him. Tanid's arms moved feebly, and he tried to reach the wet, dripping blade that had him pinned to the ground through his ribs, but he just brushed the red edges and then slumped, not moving again.

Ewan wasn't sure if anyone else felt it, but his soul reeled. His gut clenched, not unlike the feeling he had experienced so often in the past. He gagged dryly.

A god had just died.

The last god in the realms had died.

It had just been a diversion, nothing more.

Hissing explosions erupted among the enemy. Giant showers of silt, gravel, and human bits bloomed across the river. One of the Sirtai magical attacks slammed into the water, and a pillar of steam and mud rose in a gray fountain. The Naum troops were edging back, spreading about.

The whole front was one huge, incessant howl of noise. Bugles and horns were screaming, and the troops were scrambling, some for killing, others for flight.

All too aware he could be killed by the bloodstaff, Ewan crawled from behind his hiding place and dashed toward Gavril's corpse. The Parusites and a handful of pilgrims were milling aimlessly, their faces contorted with panic. Bent low, Ewan sprinted through the crowd, pushing soldiers away, trying not to show his face to the witch.

"He's dead. He's dead," one of the followers was mumbling, tears running down his pocked face.

Ewan knelt in the red snow, staring at the curled form. It didn't look divine anymore. Just a sack of loose flesh and some bones. Gods might have created humanity, but they died like any other man.

Calemore had just assassinated Tanid.

Religion was dead, yet no one seemed to be behaving any differently. They looked just as cold, starved, and confused as they had the day before. Maybe humans could not know their makers were gone. Maybe faith was all about how they felt about themselves.

Even in that small regard, the gods and goddesses had been selfish. They would take from humans, but they wouldn't give back.

"Oh gods, why," someone else lamented. "Please no."

Ewan tried to keep his breath calm, but it was hard with nausea tickling his gullet. *No time for mourning now. We have to win this war.*

"Stand back. Retreat. Now. Take Gavril's body and run. Now!" he shouted.

The soldiers frowned at him, but like any frightened animal, they obeyed a stern voice. Soon enough, all that was left of Tanid's death was a pink stain.

Does Calemore know he's killed the god? Ewan wondered. What would he do now?

But it seemed like he hadn't planned on ending the war after murdering the last of the gods, because the fighting and killing continued. The northern force was pushing. Jarman and Lucas were doing their best, trying to destroy the other army. The Telore was seething, bobbing from explosions, with human bodies scattered on its choppy gray surface like autumn leaves. The Naum troops were milling as only a huge host could, but Ewan saw they were getting ready to cross.

This, too, must be a diversion, Ewan figured, but he couldn't tell what Calemore was planning. The White Witch had very elaborate schemes, and he might be springing another trap. He might be getting ready to kill the wizards after they got tired and dropped their defenses. Or he was keeping them busy until his other troops could advance and crush the defenders.

I hope they can still protect me. He rushed from behind the low barracks, leveled the bloodstaff at the enemy, and fired. Like always, the silent torrent of death surprised him. Red crystals sped away at incredible speed and slammed into the enemy ranks, mowing them down. A gap opened in the Naum units, a deep, crimson wound.

He had that premonition again, the tingling of fine hairs on his arms and nape. Calemore's missiles rained all around him, and he was blinded by snow and debris as he ran madly without looking, sidestepping now and then, hoping his erratic movement made the witch miss.

Then, a red ruby burst at the corner of his eye. He stumbled. *Death, there it is.*

Shards of the blood pellet scattered around him, but none touched him. They grazed around an invisible layer of magic covering his skin. If not for Jarman's shield, he would have been dead right now, a corpse without a head.

Thank you, wizard.

Emboldened, he stopped running and lowered the rod toward the Naum men once more. He let loose a long red tongue of destruction until the last drop of blood ran out. But he didn't have to go far to replenish the weapon. Calemore's earlier work had left him plenty of fresh sources.

He pressed the bloodstaff against a nearby corpse, watching with fascination and disgust as the skin paled. Soon enough, the body was dry, and the rod glistened brilliant scarlet. Calemore was attacking again. Ewan rolled away. He might be protected—for now—but that did not mean he should abuse his luck.

Earth growled as magic hailed around him and clawed against it. Ewan dashed toward the enemy, away from the friendly troops, trying to keep the Athesians and Parusites safe. They need not die for him. He would not demand that from them like Tanid had. He was—

He heard himself cry breathlessly, and he fell hard, his left leg a furnace of pain. Flopping over, his vision blazing silver with agony, his body heavy and ungainly, he saw bone sticking from his calf, punched through. Blood was leaking out, steaming.

Calemore had just injured him again.

Jarman's shield was gone.

Gripping the bloodstaff as hard as he could, he aimed and fired, more, more. The witch responded, and another pellet grazed his arm, spun him around like a mannequin. He could not run away anymore. He would die soon.

The ground shook. A huge column of boiling water and river silt shot skyward, obscuring his view. He dug his left hand into the snow and pulled himself away, trembling like a child. More explosions, more dust and snow swirling almost like a blizzard. He reached forward, jabbed his fingers into the frozen earth, and pulled again, panting, spitting, snot flying from his nose.

I need to get away.

Like a cripple, he rolled over several times, dizzy, and lumped himself behind a rock. A blood trail marked his flight, but he wasn't sure if Calemore could discern such details, wherever he was. At least he hoped not.

His leg needed fixing. Where was Jarman? He wanted to call for help, but there was no one around, just dead bodies. He looked behind him and saw the northern force moving. Soon enough, he would be surrounded by the enemy. They might not be able to kill him, but in his condition, neither could he kill them.

The magical attacks ceased. The Sirtai were probably exhausted. Calemore's armies were moving slowly, inexorably, advancing. Soon, they would crush the people of the realms. No one could stop them. Not even he.

It's over, he figured. *I should never have used this cursed weapon.* If he had only used his muscles, he could have kept on killing the Naum soldiers without end. But he didn't want to make that his legacy.

Your legacy is to die a nameless fool.

He let out a long, shivering breath and slumped against the stone. The cold didn't touch him. Only his ruined leg was on fire, and his shoulder burned. For a moment, he laughed, once, twice, the choked sobs of madness, then started crying. He didn't want to admit it, but he was afraid.

CHAPTER 47

Using too much magic could kill you, Jarman knew. You wouldn't die right away, no, but it thinned your blood. And then you would succumb to simple diseases or the cold. That was why he ate so much red meat and drank goat's blood after engagements with the Naum forces, but it never seemed enough.

Calemore had initiated a sudden strike half an hour earlier with his bloodstaff, surprising them all. After weeks of silent standoff as far as those terrible weapons were concerned, the White Witch had attacked, as if he didn't care that the Sirtai might fight back. No one could guess what an immortal mind might concoct as his battle plan, but the witch was probably trying to kill Ewan.

Lucas and he had the boy shielded.

Jarman had readied to let loose a deadly volley against the witch. With luck, he might kill him.

Only, the enemy troops had suddenly surged forward, both massive camps at the same time, and even Jarman could see they would obliterate the defenders, totally, utterly, that very day. He had been forced to choose between hunting Calemore or killing his troops. Now, Lucas and he were busy trying to fend the huge tide off, to buy time, and each gout of magic cost them more life. They were exhausted, trembling, and what little strength they had was oozing fast. Meanwhile, Calemore was free to sow destruction through the army ranks. Jarman hoped Ewan was fighting back with his own weapon.

Oh, he was so tired.

His friend was much stronger, but even the senior Anada had their limits. The tattooed wizard could fight for hours after Jarman slumped to the ground, weak and shivering and trying to keep bile down, but they just didn't have enough power to stop the foe.

Jarman's strength faltered. He dropped to one knee, dizzy.

The pain that lanced through his temples wasn't his—it was Ewan's.

"The boy is hurt," Lucas rasped, even before Jarman could make his mouth form the words.

"I can't hold the shield anymore," Jarman whispered.

Lucas nodded grimly. His own magic was weakening. Their blasts were much smaller now, less accurate, landing in the water and on the near side of the river. Soon, they would have to stop and rest and let the people of the realms clash with the Naum invaders. They had probably butchered several thousand, but it did not seem to matter much. Not enough to change the course of the war.

"Help him," Lucas spoke. He might be a life slave, but that was an order, from one wizard to another.

Jarman staggered upright, tottered over to a small backpack. Inside, he had strips of goat meat, several blood sausages. Like a madman ignoring the reality around him, he sunk his teeth into the soft, spiced flesh, munching loudly, sucking on the red fibers. He drank water, icy droplets running down his chin. He gulped honey from a glass jar, almost gagging on its sweetness.

"With me," he muttered. Three Parusite men, all metal and fur, jogged after him. They ran through the ranks, heading toward the killing zone. Ranks parted to let them pass. Sergei's men did not like the Sirtai—but they sure feared them.

The forest of men shifted, and then, Princess Sasha was there, in front of him.

She was saddled, armored, her chest and back plate covered in maroon leather, her gloves the color of old blood. The Red Caps were milling, getting ready for the fight. The survivors were all lean, scarred women, disillusioned about the glory of the war to the bone. Many had fingers and ears missing, and others leaned on their spears, pained by half-healed injuries.

Jarman halted, trying to catch his breath. His throat was on fire. He wanted to vomit again. "Your Highness!"

She turned her head, saw him, and her features contorted with distaste. She said nothing.

"I need help, Your Highness. I must rescue Ewan, but I need you to hold the enemy at bay. Please." He wanted to sound important, but his voice was cracking with a breathless chill.

An officer at her side hawked and spat. Someone else muttered, "Freak." The women hated the boy and his magic. They hated him and Lucas, too. The Parusites were all hostile.

"If he dies, we will lose this war," he hissed desperately.

"You may not have faith, wizard, but we do," another nameless face snarled.

Jarman remembered what Lucas had told him only days ago, the way he had spoken to Amalia. He was not yet ready for his first tattoo. He let the frustration subside.

"Please. We do not have much time. Please."

The princess shrugged, an awkward motion in her armor. "Troops, advance."

Jarman slouched with relief. The fact the Red Caps commander had planned to fight back all along did not matter. He was not going to let Ewan die over pride. He nodded his thanks at Sergei's sister, and then he was pushing through the noisy crowd again.

The closer he got to the actual fighting, the worse it got. Men running back, throwing weapons, defeated in spirit even if their bodies were whole. Others, limping slowly to temporary safety. The northern army was crushing the foremost fortifications, flowing over the trenches and barricades like ants. To the east, the second host was starting to cross the Telore in a thousand small wooden rafts. They did not seem to hurry. Lucas's magical blows had ceased. His friend must have been channeling all his power on protecting him—and Ewan.

Maybe just the boy.

Jarman pushed forward against the tide, feeling crazy. The snow had become brown pulp, and you could not tell blood and soil apart. He tripped on discarded gear, walked over bodies. Mutilated corpses, arms, and legs scattered. This had to be the work of the bloodstaff.

He saw Ewan hunching behind a rock, head lolling with pain. He was even pastier than usual, and his clothes were smeared in blood. It was hard telling if it belonged to him, because he still had not shed the rags he'd worn during the butchery some weeks back. Jarman felt a knot of pity for the lad.

Then, he saw the gash in his leg, and he remembered the pain earlier.

Ignoring the threat from Calemore's weapon somewhere to the north or east, he dashed the last stretch across the churned battlefield and dropped to his knees near the Special Child. Ewan only looked at him lazily, eyes glazed with shock.

"Jarman…"

"Where are your wounds?" Jarman panted.

Ewan pointed at his legs, then at his bleeding shoulder. The second wound didn't look serious. Jarman took a few deep breaths to steady his breathing, then started working his magic. He was so tired, and he had to stop twice to rest. But he managed to close the red maw. He scooped up some snow and wiped the red mess away. Sure enough, his healing was sound. The boy might limp for a while, but he would survive this injury.

"We cannot win this war. The witch is too powerful," Ewan mumbled.

Jarman rubbed his forehead. "Let me use the bloodstaff."

Ewan's weary eyes lit up with mistrust, but then the glare faded. "It's terrible."

Jarman wondered about the price of vengeance. He thought about Sergei and his son. He thought about Amalia and her mother. His own reason why he was risking his life in this awful war.

Something snapped, like a twig. He saw a puff of snow to his left, then another. A piece of rock shattered, shards flying. As always, it took him a moment to realize it was the bloodstaff firing. The White Witch must have found them somehow. Or he was just shooting at the last position he had seen Ewan. But he thought he was most likely reacting to magic.

Then, it hit him.

Calemore could probably sense Special Children. And he seemed keen on killing them.

Had Rob been a Special Child, then?

There was no time for investigation now. He had to get Ewan to safety. He had to somehow make the witch stop his attack, before Lucas and he lost the last ounces of their strength.

Once that happened, they would all die, torn apart by silent red crystals.

"…was a god," Ewan was saying, his voice low.

"What?" Jarman snapped, his voice shrill. The pellets were raking the ground, kicking up clouds of dirt and stone and ice. His eyes scanned the scene. Hundreds of bodies, hacked apart, thrown in lurid poses. Even some of the low barracks had been hammered down by the bloodstaff. Dead men, animals, broken lives everywhere. Ewan was still talking.

"Gavril is dead," the boy whispered.

That does not surprise me, Jarman thought, his father's education slithering into his conscience. "Give me the bloodstaff, please."

A red arrow exploded a few paces away, shattered against an invisible bubble of magic protecting him.

"Can you fight?" Jarman asked, his fingers inching toward the slender glass rod.

Ewan blinked slowly. "I don't want to do this killing anymore."

Jarman grimaced. "You must. Otherwise we all die."

Ewan closed his eyes. "Let us die."

"No, please. Think of the people and their families. Think of all the innocent souls. Your friends."

The boy's blood-spattered lids snapped open, oily vigor shining in his eyes once again. He looked at his hands, lingering on the crippled one, as if seeing them for the first time. "I will use my hands. Calemore will not know then."

Jarman's hand closed on the ancient weapon. A tingle went down his spine. "May I?"

Ewan swallowed. "Yes. But you will give it back, wizard. This magic does not belong to the Sirtai."

Jarman lifted the bloodstaff. It was surprisingly light and yet heavy at the same time. Just right. There was still a quarter of the blood left inside the hollow rod.

Noise behind him. Jarman spun, lowering the staff. He saw the standards of the Parusite army and the Red Caps rippling in the wind, moving forward. Not two bow shots away, the Naum white host was churning south. The shuffle of boots and the groan of leather and metal were growing in intensity, becoming a gravely susurration. He could feel the rhythm in his gut.

Princess Sasha was doing her best to protect him. He should not squander her generosity. There was no time for selfishness now.

He turned north and pressed the black dots as he had seen Ewan do. He expected the weapon to twitch, like a crossbow, but nothing happened. No sound, no movement, just a steady stream of crimson death flowing toward the enemy. He realized he was aiming too high, above the heads of the front ranks. He lowered the bloodstaff, and soon enough, a pink haze engulfed the enemy. He spent the weapon in seconds.

Ewan grabbed his robe, trying to stand up. The boy clambered up, nursing his injured leg. Jarman ignored the boy, staring at the red pulp, at the mushy horror he had created. Calemore was probably still firing at them, but he didn't notice. A wave of friendly troops swept past, and the enemy was gone from sight.

Ewan stumbled forward, trying to get pulled into the stream of soldiers. Jarman held him back. "No. Not now. You must rest first. You must recuperate. We have to get back."

Red death rained around them. Soldiers tumbled like broken dolls, missing limbs and heads. Few screamed, if they had time to scream. They died as if wiped away from existence. The storm moved along the front of the Parusite van. Sasha was drawing the fire away. She had bought them some precious time. Maybe Calemore could only sense magic when it was used.

He started retreating, Ewan staggering, eyes still riveted north. The boy was tense, and far too strong to stop. Jarman could only hope he would follow.

His hopes crumbled as Calemore aimed his weapon back in their direction once again. They were running now, left and right, trying to dodge the red pellets. The world turned white and gray, a cloud of debris choking him. He hoped Lucas would have enough skill and stamina to keep shielding them. Jarman had nothing left. Nothing.

His feet landed in a hole, and he fell flat on his face. Something jabbed at his stomach. Turning around, he saw a piece of tack with a rusty buckle sticking through his robe. No blood, but he had almost impaled himself. The witch was still firing at them. The pellets were bursting closer and closer still. Soon, they would be exposed.

I should have listened to the boy, he thought. *That weapon is a curse.*

Ewan hobbled on, not looking back. He was still in shock. Jarman scrambled, legs and hands pumping, his palms burning from scraping the icy ground. The bloodstaff rested in the filthy snow, pristine and perfect. He collected the weapon in his raw hand and moved forward. The ground shook, shards flying again.

I can't protect you any longer, friend. He felt the thought in his head.

Jarman squared his shoulders, waiting for a red pellet to pulverize his rib cage.

"Wizard, here!" someone shouted. Jarman looked through the flurry of rubble and dirt and saw that half Sirtai coming his way. The scarlet storm subsided. Was this man shielding them?

Jarman fell onto his knees, panting. Ewan was standing, looking back, confused.

The other man swept past the boy and knelt at his side. "My name is Adelbert. I will help you."

Jarman snorted mucus onto the ground, gasping for fresh air. "Thank you." A hand closed on the bloodstaff just above his. He frowned. Looking up, he saw a curious grin on the mongrel's face.

"That is—" he tried to say with what little breath he had, his body too slow to react.

Adelbert flew sideways. Hot blood splashed Jarman in the face. Ewan lowered his right hand. It was dripping red.

Calemore's attack intensified.

Jarman looked at the half Sirtai lying dead in the snow. He saw Ewan's chest rising and falling erratically. The boy was staring north. "We have to flee," he told the Special Child.

"It cannot end this way," Ewan spoke. "It cannot." He looked at Jarman. "Keep the weapon safe. If I return, promise to return it to me. Please, wizard. Please, Jarman."

Jarman licked his lips and regretted it. They tasted like salt and metal and human life. He wiped the gore away. "I swear it. On my honor." Ewan probably had not heard it. He looked like an enraged animal, and he started walking back toward danger and death, his gait lopsided with agony.

The red pellets stayed with Jarman.

Oh, I see.

He was running again, but now, he had a whole village in front of him, low, squat towers bristling with stakes, sheds that housed soldiers and horses alike, low walls of stone and wood.

Like a mouse, he bent low and scurried into the maze, and the destruction around him stopped. Calemore fired for a while longer, but the attack eventually ceased.

Jarman bent down and puked. Every fiber in his body burned. His vision was flashing black, and he thought he would pass out. But he did not, the anguish in his throat and belly keeping him away, his stomach heaving like some feral thing was kicking inside it.

As he recovered, he noticed terrified soldiers watching him. Athesians, Parusites, boys with fuzz on their cheeks, and older men with long beards that kept some of the winter cold at bay. *They must be amazed by the weapon,* he thought. No, it was the red mess on his face, arms, and robe.

The battle continued, but he heard it only as one unending groan, the roar of a dying beast, a thunder that belched acid and bile. Gripping the bloodstaff with the same intensity as the self-loathing gripping his soul, he made his way back to Lucas.

They'd won that day. Or rather, they hadn't lost.

Calemore must have lost too many troops to continue his campaign into the night, so he had retreated to his lines, probably confident that his subsequent attacks would be successful. He had no reason to worry. He had no reason to rush. He could not be stopped.

The realms would be defeated, Jarman realized.

He ached all over. He could hardly walk. But he made himself do it. He owed that much to the mourning king.

Princess Sasha had died defending him, after all. Bought him time. Saved Ewan and him from death. All it had taken was one simple plea. True chivalry and gallantry. There was some grim lesson in that, he thought, something his upbringing at the Temple of Justice could never have taught him.

Despite all the chaos and the screams from tens of thousands of wounded, the Parusites were staging a large funeral procession for the king's sister. She would be carried into Roalas and interred next to her nephew.

As he dragged his feet across the cold ground, he saw Ewan sitting on an empty crate, an itchy blanket thrown over his shoulders, not because he seemed cold underneath but to hide the layers of bloody mush covering him. The boy was staring at his feet, and he paid no attention to the noise, to the men walking around him, keeping a safe distance. He was gripping the bloodstaff once again.

Jarman felt his soul tug him toward the boy. He wanted to talk to him. But what could he tell a child who had just killed countless thousands with his bare hands, then limped back to the garrison, dripping red, shunned and hated by his comrades probably as much as by the foe?

Nothing.

"We are invited to see the king," Lucas said.

Jarman nodded. He did not relish the meeting. "Thank you."

Lucas sniffed, his only exhibit of emotion. "Amalia wishes to see you, too."

They passed another group getting ready to bury their favorite. Gavril had been assassinated. So many deaths in one day, Jarman thought. What did it mean for these pilgrims? Would their faith die with their leader? What did they expect from their gods and goddesses? Compassion? Pity? Relief?

"We will lose." Jarman choked on his own words.

"Perhaps," Lucas admitted.

"There seems to be no way we can defeat the witch."

"We will surely not stop trying," Lucas offered, unyielding.

Jarman just wanted to sleep. To shut his eyes, to banish the pain for a while. But he had to see a girl who had lost her realm and her mother, and the king who had lost his father, his son, and now, his sister. What could he tell them that would make their pain go away?

Again, nothing.

CHAPTER 48

Once upon a time, Mali would have dreaded the notion of walking this deep into enemy territory. Not anymore.

The northern army had ravaged Caytor, too. Almost every village and road post stood abandoned, the people and animals long gone. Her little squad was forced to hunt wild game in the forest, because there was nothing left in the frozen fields and musty basements.

They headed north first, toward Bassac, then struck west, following a long stretch of cobbles and gravel, now hiding under fresh snow, aimed straight as an arrow toward Pain Daye. She had secured several maps for her scouts. Some of the charts dated back to the time she had been a young girl starting her career in the military. Others had been drawn more recently, but they all showed the same line crossing the Caytorean heartland.

This was her first time in the enemy land, and it was nothing like she had expected. The terrain looked the same as back home: same hills, same copses of trees, same houses. The snow hid the details, but she guessed no one could really tell Eracia and Caytor apart. Blessedly, it also masked most of the destruction left by the northern host.

Mali met no living soul for almost three weeks. Then, they sighted bandits. Thin, starved men who tried to attack them. But the sorry horde had no horses, so she just spurred forward without incident. Another gang moved on to intercept them not three days later, but once they saw sharp swords and solid breastplates, they wheeled back and headed away, searching for easier prey.

The weather was fair for a while, except for the wind, keening like an old woman in mourning, blasting across the ground in a white haze, making the snow smooth like polished tin. Then it started exposing the bodies, lumps of blue flesh, too hard even for birds and foxes to nibble on.

Most of them did not seem hurt. They had just died of exposure or hunger, lain down and taken a final sleep. Their faces reminded her of Eracia. These Caytoreans were just like the peasants back home. Women and older folk, very few men. Poor and very much fucked when wars started.

She found dead dogs and dead sheep, but all that remained of their carcasses were ivory bones, picked clean. The refugees had scavenged the meat and the skin. At least they had not eaten their fellow countrymen, she thought with some relief.

A fair number of northerners had died, too. She could identify them by their snowshoes and their thick furs, which hadn't kept them alive on their march. They must have died of disease or exhaustion, but she wouldn't let anyone inspect the bodies too closely. She feared ill humors, and ever since the Crap Charge, she was rather wary of infections.

There were no living foes, neither troops nor supply caravans. She was grateful for that.

They spent their time riding in silence, then walking to rest their horses, heads covered in woolen scarves and hunched down to keep the wind from sneaking down their napes. They only spoke when they stopped to eat, which was not often enough. Bjaras tried to learn their language, but he struggled. He could mumble only a few sorry words, and she was in no mood to learn his. He sure did communicate his desire well enough, but Mali refused to bed him. She had made a promise to Gordon.

The road was buried under the snow, and with no carts rolling, it was almost invisible. They guessed where it was by the lack of trees and shrubbery, and the sun rose more or less ahead of them each dawn, which gave them a good idea where they were going. The closer they got to Pain Daye, the more worried Mali became. It seemed as if Caytor had been totally ruined.

What if her son had fought against these northerners?

What if he had been forced to flee south?

What if he'd been hurt?

She did not want to contemplate that.

They figured the old year had died and a new one was born somewhere halfway to Pain Daye.

A fresh blizzard delayed them for a while, and they stayed in one of the ghost hamlets, cold and miserable but at least with a solid roof above their heads. They all slept bunched together for warmth, pressing against one another. Bjaras tried to insinuate his intentions again, but she wouldn't let him. The sky cleared soon thereafter, and it even became pleasant. With the yellow sun beating on them, they took off the filthy scarves and enjoyed a trace of warmth. The world shimmered like it was on silvery fire. Then the road dipped into a valley, and Pain Daye opened before them.

Smoke, human presence, life.

Cautiously, they dismounted and led their horses toward the estate. It was a huge thing, with a sprawling mess of walls and fortifications, designed to be elegant and deadly. The fields around were blanketed in snow or dotted with tents and houses, which looked like temporary camps for the army. The pattern was all too familiar. And that made her slightly worried.

Was there an army in Pain Daye? If so, who did it serve, and would it welcome four strangers, with open arms and no drawn weapons?

Contrasting the sprawl of buildings and canvas was the obvious scarcity of life. There was no traffic on the myriad of tiny access roads leading around the farms and through the surrounding villages and bivouacs. No troops patrolled the area, only a handful of fires and wispy trails of smoke. A perfect ambush or just the remnants of old life and bustle, frozen in place like everything else?

"I don't like this," she muttered, just to hear her own voice.

"This is the reason we came," Alexa reminded her. She fished the oiled paper from her hip bag and spread it open on top of her thigh. "I guess it's the right place."

"Want me to dash over and check, sir?" Suzy asked.

Mali shook her head. "No. We don't want to act hostile. Nothing that speaks military. We are just traders. As lost and confused as everyone else." Explaining armor would be a problem, but it was nicely hidden under leather and fur. They had stripped off any insignia that might betray them as Eracians, but it was still all rather risky.

"So what do we do?" Alexa said, looking at Bjaras.

"We just approach. Slowly, sensibly." Mali turned toward the curly headed northerner. "You do not speak. You are mute. Understand? No speak." She gestured with her index finger pressed against her lips. "Shhh."

Bjaras nodded, smirking softly. "No shpeak."

Mali took a deep breath. Three women wearing sword belts. That was not a common sight in Caytor. The idea of female troops had not caught on in this realm. The locals, if those people out there were indeed locals, would probably be suspicious. But she was not going to walk into this estate unarmed.

Suzy was knocking crossbows and tying them to the outside of each saddle, on both sides. Their group might be small, but the corporal would make sure to fire a dozen bolts at anyone trying to approach them. The burly soldier was a serious type. She reminded Mali of Alexa in her younger days.

"What about him? Do we give him any weapons?" Alexa asked.

Mali grimaced. The Caytoreans would probably not be very tolerant toward northerners, not after they had trampled across their realms and killed so many of their kin and fellow countrymen. If they thought him an enemy, they might attack him.

"An ax will do."

Heart hammering in her chest, Mali led into the valley, toward the speck of civilization. She was terrified. This was Caytor, the old enemy. This was land after war and pillage, and the strangers out there were likely to behave like rabid animals. This was human life after more than a year of isolation. She wasn't sure she wanted to meet people again.

The Caytoreans saw them and came forward from their houses and tents, clustering near the road, waiting. That calmed her a little. People intent on killing usually kept to the shadows, and they wouldn't just wait for their prey. Standing in the open was a sure sign of normal life.

"Who goes there!" one of their lot hailed when they were within earshot—and bowshot.

Mali spread her arms wide. "Survivors. We are just passing through." They had rehearsed their story often enough it sounded like a truth now. If anyone asked, they were heading to Eybalen, where they hoped to find a better life. Everyone wanted a better life, didn't they?

"You bringin' any food or goods?"

Mali glanced back at their mules. The packs were mostly empty. "Some."

"You armed?" the man hailed again.

"Yup." Lies would not do at this point, she figured.

"Come over. We might wanna trade."

Alexa brushed her jaw with the outside of her hand. "Friendly, aren't they?"

Bjaras was looking anxious now. Well, he should be. Mali just hoped he would not open his mouth and doom them all. But she had taken him along knowingly, all too aware of the risks. She had hoped to use him as a shield against his brethren. Now, she would have to shield him against the people of the realms.

"Just keep calm, everyone. Speak slowly and no more than necessary," Mali reminded them one last time.

Up close, the estate looked less majestic, more worn, damaged. Most of the houses had no windows or roofs, and the tents were sagging or torn, left behind because they were useless. Prowling among the ruins was a knot of simple-looking folk. They looked like any peddler or village craftsmen you might meet in Eracia.

They had fires burning, and it looked like they were roasting game. One of them was chopping kindling. A woman showed her face briefly, then ducked back into one of the log shacks. Mali sought courage in her presence. With only men around, it could never be good.

It was a village, all right, she figured. Built on top of the ruins of a large, wealthy mansion.

There were about a dozen and a half souls waiting for them near an old road sign. Another five lingered some distance away, mistrustful. But their gestures did not speak of skilled combat or vile intentions.

"Is this Pain Daye?" she asked.

The one she thought might be their leader pointed with his chin. "What you got to trade?"

"Where you coming from?" another face asked.

"Near the border," Mali lied. She looked at her animals. They were frisky, picking up the human mood. Suzy was standing near one of the horses, stroking its neck, her fingers close to the heavy wood stock of one of the crossbows. "We got skins and pelts." They had hunted their share during the travel.

"What you ladies doing all alone on the road?" a third figure inquired.

"We ain't got no husbands," Alexa snapped back at him, "on the account of the fuckin' war."

The leader scratched his raven-colored beard. "I'm Tim. We fled this northern enemy near Marlheim. We went east to the coast. Then we figured they weren't chasing us no more, so we came here. The whole region was abandoned, and none of the foe were here, so we thought to stay."

A lad standing at the man's side, looking very much like his son, nodded. "The enemy's gone."

"Now, they might come back," Tim warned, "but they is gone south, and don't look like coming back."

"I heard stories like those," Mali shared, trying to sound friendly. "Armies come out of nowhere; then they go away, never to return. Such is life."

"We got folk from all over," Tim continued. "Acer there comes from farther south, but he reckoned he'd come to Pain Daye. We thought we might find some councillors or maybe an army, but nothing. They all fled."

"We haven't heard any news in a long while," Alexa supplied, trying to sound friendlier now.

Tim was silent for a while. "So where you going?"

Mali scanned the crowd. Wary, but not hostile. Just men and women plagued by disaster. "We thought of going to Eybalen, seek our luck there."

Tim snorted. "That ain't good. Didn't you hear?" He waited for Mali to answer as if he hadn't heard Alexa speak just moments earlier. "There's trouble in the capital, too. The High Council is in uproar. Could be on account of this war, could be other things. But they got themselves into a fight like it was with the Feorans years back, and some of them had to flee the city."

Mali frowned, but kept quiet. Any information on Caytor was valuable.

Tim took her silence as encouragement. "It's a mess in Eybalen, all right. We heard this northern enemy is gone to Athesia, but there's war just everywhere. I reckon the safest place right now is Pain Daye. There ain't no people in the wake of that foe from the north, but then there's no war either. Just ask Acer."

Alexa squirmed. Mali followed her sight and saw a couple of armed men show up behind a far cluster of cabins. They looked like hunters, but that did not make her happy. Arrows made for killing deer could kill people, too.

Mali made sure her voice remained steady. "So what happened in Eybalen, Acer?"

The other man stepped forward and spat unceremoniously right between her legs. "Shit, that's what happened. But I didn't wait to get my head cut like the rest of them. Took a couple of horses and rode here. Fast as I could."

The hunters were moving away. They did not seem too interested in the gathering. Mali assumed there were more people in and around the estate than she had initially believed. It made sense. The place was well defensible. It probably had wells, and maybe even stores of food inside. If these people survived till spring, they could work in the fields, maybe even start some small trade.

The same thing must be happening in northern Eracia. The folks had fled the enemy, but once they figured it was not coming back, they had gone back to their hearths. Life was all about self-preservation, and it quickly forgot great armies and majestic military feats.

"What do you have to trade?" she asked. After all, that was why they had supposedly come here.

Tim hesitated, but then he started listing various items, most likely things his men had scavenged from inside the mansion. She listened idly while her mind rolled. Everyone had fled Pain Daye, and that meant her son, too. But she did not dare ask anything yet.

The new inhabitants of the estate started introducing themselves. Mali gave her name. Then Alexa did the same. Finally, Suzy bit off her own. Bjaras kept staring.

"What's with the lad? He ain't got no tongue?"

"Yup, that's it," Mali agreed, almost too quickly. "Mute." Bjaras saw her and nodded. He made a vague sound. She felt another knot of dread in her stomach untie, melt away.

"Let's do some business," Tim offered.

After exchanging some of the really useful stuff back and forth, Mali agreed to stay at the village overnight. Fire was most welcome, and she was glad for the small sense of civilization creeping back into her consciousness. Besides, if they refused, they would rouse the suspicion of the locals.

It turned out to be a strange gathering, men and women who ignored the absolute destruction around them and tried to make some kind of a living from what they had, not quite trusting one another yet cooperating. Deep down, out of a churning cauldron of fears, they had figured that working together was their best chance of surviving the winter, the scarcity of food, the bandits.

Mali watched, with half-deranged fascination, their stilted, brusque dynamics. It was not unlike military life. For Tim's folk, this was normal, but she was on edge, not certain how to respond.

Above all, she was confused.

James was not at Pain Daye. So where was he?

As the evening stretched and her bones warmed, she gathered enough courage to resume talking, asking silly questions, nothing too much. The villagers didn't spare any words. For them, the liberation from law and the authority of the council was almost a blessing, it seemed, and they were willing to forge their own justice and order from the devastation. She wondered if this was how all nations had started, a clump of hardy men who refused to die, creating a life for themselves.

Alexa used the time to sharpen her weapons, which meant she always had a blade nearby. Suzy sat back, chewing on old, lean meat, a crossbow at her side. No one begrudged her that. Bjaras was busy eating and avoiding everyone's faces so they wouldn't know he didn't understand anything.

Mali watched the flames dance, savoring the heat. "I heard a rumor there was some Athesian princeling here at Pain Daye."

At first, no one said anything. She thought she had blundered, and almost touched the hilt of her long knife.

Then, it was Tim who shattered the silence. "Well, you come from far off, no wonder you don't know nothing. But you was near Athesia. Didn't you hear about the fighting?"

Her chest tightened. "No."

"Where's Carran?" Tim asked, looking into the sooty murk.

"Here." An older man stepped into the orange ring.

"Tell the lady about the emperor."

Carran sat down on an upturned log. He rubbed his knees and stretched his legs toward the fire. "I used to be a cooper here. When the northerners came, I said, bugger my knees, and hid in the cells underneath. No one found me. But I know all about them councillors. There was Lord Otis, and then there was this Athesian James, and then Lord Sebastian. Heard them all talk. They all sound the same to me."

Mali swallowed.

Alexa must have felt her discomfort, because she sat closer and took her hand in a firm grip. "So what happened?" Her friend pushed for more details.

The cooper delayed, obviously enjoying this new company. Suzy was watching carefully. The soldier was relentless in her watch.

It was Tim who interfered. "Well, didn't you hear? He went to war to Athesia. Must have come near your town."

"We haven't see any emperor," Alexa said in a quiet tone.

"What place you said you was from?" a short fellow at her right asked, leaning over.

Mali dug for names she had seen on the map, trying to remember them, but her brain was racing with cold fear and motherly premonition. She barely made her tongue move. "Hathbun." Should be a safe choice that. Unless one of the survivors was from there. In which case, they would probably have to fight their way out.

"Anyway," Carran continued, looking irritated by the interruption, "he got into war against the Parusites. Heard Lord Sebastian talk all about it. That lad had quite a following. Lots of councillors and rich folk, got himself quite an army. Alas, he got killed in the war. Lord Sebastian made himself the head of the estate. Then the northerners came, and everyone fled."

The world stopped.

"Killed, you say," Alexa repeated.

"Yup," the man confirmed and spat a thin line into the fire.

"That can't be true," Mali whispered.

"I swear it. Folks saw his body afterward, laid down all princely like, hair combed and pretty."

Mali leaned back against the cabin wall, her head banging into the rough wood. Suddenly, the small shack was stifling. The fire was an orange blur; the air smelled like soot and unwashed bodies. She realized she was going to cry.

Carran frowned. "What's the matter with you, woman?"

"Got smoke in my eyes," she confessed, trying to sound as if she needed to cough. Not a hard thing with that big lump of pain in her throat. Her son, James, was dead. Feeling as if she were watching someone else's life hum its sorry melody, she looked at her dearest friend, a woman who had helped raise James. She was holding her hand in a fierce, trembling grip, her fingers going white.

"Must have gotten some in mine, too," Alexa rasped.

CHAPTER 49

Calemore climbed the hill with slight urgency to his step, the old snow creaking under his boots. His eyes were locked on the cabin where Nigella was waiting for him. He waved his hand. The soldiers watching over his bespectacled prophet moved away from the house. They spread out of earshot, still on guard, still alert, especially with their leader nearby.

Calemore felt anxious. He should not be anxious. But he was.

He had not seen Nigella in months. He genuinely missed her. He missed her body, her imperfections. He wanted her magical talent. By now, she should have unraveled the mysteries of the future from the book, and she should be able to help him decide the last, crucial stage of his campaign.

His foes had lost more than half their number. The surviving god must be awfully weak. Soon, his magic would fail, and Calemore would be able to sense him and send his assassins to finish him off. He had already deployed a number of spies and infiltrators among the enemy, and asked the Naum elders to send their saboteurs and killers into the opposing camp so they could target officers and leaders and cause even more chaos.

The way he knew the gods and goddesses, this last maggot would probably be hiding somewhere, in a small, dark hole. No matter, he would be found and crushed.

From what reports he had, the people of the realms were on the brink of destruction. They would have surrendered long ago if they could, but the total war made them keep on fighting. Ironically, it was his own tactics that were driving them to resist. Well, there was no graceful way he could demand they stop believing in their deities, and then become one himself. That would be a paradox.

Once Roalas fell, he expected the remaining units to fall apart in disarray. With their leaders dead or fled, the nations of the Old Land would become lawless animals, and it would be very tricky for him to keep hunting them down. He needed the enemy unified. He needed them chewing on false hope so he could complete his conquest more effectively. He did not relish years of chasing and butchering lone stragglers through the countryside.

Which meant he had to carefully prepare for the last push. He wanted to encircle the city from the south. He wanted to coordinate the next stage of his campaign smartly. The eastern army would attack the coastal cities in Caytor. The western army would split into two elements, one circling back against Eracia, and the second sweeping through the Safe Territories and Parus. He might need to transfer forces between the two bodies, because his western host had suffered terrible losses. He had to know how he should do that so there would be no ugly surprises, like more ancient magical weapons suddenly coming into enemy hands, or Special Children putting up resistance against him. He also had to avoid any conflict with the Sirtai until the war against the faith was complete.

Most of all, he wanted magical reassurances.

That was why he had come back to Nigella. That and…
well, he did miss her.

The woman should provide him all he needed, he knew.
And it was time to start grooming her son for greatness.

Chance kills more than careful planning. He remembered
the ancient saying as he approached the cabin door. Someone
very wise had uttered those words during the war against the
gods, but he could not tell who it had been. Probably a human.

He rapped gently on the wood. Nigella cracked the door
open, staring at him. She did not seem surprised. He raised a
brow. She smirked, trying to hide her teeth.

"I was expecting you," she said.

Immediately, Calemore felt a change about her. She was
still a frightened little mouse, full of inhibitions and complex-
es, but somehow, she seemed to have mustered some courage.
Standing half an inch taller, her gaze lingering on him a bit
longer, her eyes breaking contact a moment too late. Nothing too explicit. If he were not so keen on seeing her again,
he might have missed it himself. But he liked this. His body
tensed, and he realized he had not bedded anyone in a very
long time. Hardly even seen any women, in fact.

"Good, then you know what I want," he responded.

Sheldon was inside, playing on the cot. "Hello, Master
Calemore," he mumbled, not looking up from his toys.

Calemore inclined his head. "Send your boy out."

Nigella brushed a lock of hair from her forehead. She
licked her lips nervously.

He sniffed, not entirely pleased with her newfound disobedience. Not when it might interfere with his lust. "Send
him out. He will be safe with my troops."

She looked at her son. "Shel, darling, go play with the
guards. And here"—she reached for a wrapped parcel lying on

the table—"don't forget the bread. The soldiers will surely want to eat."

Sheldon accepted the bundle like it was a precious sculpture. "Can I have some, Mom?"

Nigella shook her head. "No, Son. We talked about this. You will have your supper later."

Calemore frowned. She looked nervous all of a sudden. But then, it must be his presence. She had not seen him in a long while either, and she must be feeling confused and excited. He watched the lad walk out, strutting awkwardly. He waited for a moment longer. Then he slammed the door shut and latched it.

He turned back. He was pleased to see Nigella undressing already. His breathing quickened. Muscles taut, he stepped toward her, gripped her shoulders, and guided her to her small bed.

Calemore watched his human plaything prepare a pie for him. She was clothed again, a pity, but he could still guess the curves under her skirt. Whenever she reached for a jar of spices, the skirt hiked up and down, crinkled, teased, hinting at the soft flesh underneath. Despite fierce lovemaking twice already, he was feeling hungry again. But he had to focus. He had many other things to do before leaving for Roalas. Fucking and apple pies were secondary, if more pleasing.

He tried to suppress his emotions, but he could not. He had missed her. He liked being here in this shithole, enjoyed watching her, savored the smell of sweat on the tangled sheet beneath his arm, liked how she worked the lids on and off her jars with mechanical dedication.

"How goes your war?" she asked, eyes focused on the pastry.

"You know the answer to that," he chided without rancor.

The woman turned briefly, flashed him a full-toothed smile. "Yes."

Calemore leaned against the boards behind him. "I presume you have read everything in the book, and you know what those riddles mean?" He wanted to hear her tell him everything, but he liked the suspense. To be on the side with the least knowledge, least power, it was exhilarating, for a moment or two.

Nigella nodded, pushed her glasses up the bridge of her nose with a flour-smeared finger. "Yes. All of them. I have mastered *The Book of Lost Words*, Calemore. I feel so proud."

"Then you know what I must do," he goaded her.

Nigella salted the dough first. Then she answered. "Yes."

Calemore stretched. "Tell me."

She pushed her tongue against her teeth. "First, you must eat the pie."

Calemore realized he was laughing, a rattle of soft hissing escaping through his nostrils. The woman was bantering him! Defying him! Trying to be saucy! A kind of thing that had gotten kings tortured and killed. He had sent men to their graves over much, much less. But now, there was no fury in his heart. In fact, he was blissfully content, even amused. Having human slaves was boring. He liked her attempt at trying to even out the scale of power, to be equal to him in wit. She would never succeed, but just her effort was worth it.

Letting her be on her own had been a very good thing, it seemed. Nigella had learned how to cope with danger, to communicate with his soldiers, men from a strange and terrible nation that did not speak her language. She had been forced to endure uncertainty and fear, and she had been free of his bias and demands and pressure, allowing her to study the book of prophecies with a clear mind. He was not disappointed. In just one early afternoon, she had proved herself worthy of being his lover, of being at his side after the war against the gods was finished.

He liked that very much. She could have been just a toy. But she had grown to accept him, his legacy, the role he planned for her. Few humans would have the strength to do the same, and his little mouse did have it. The old Nigella had been fun, but now, he was genuinely excited.

"All right, I will eat the pie," he ceded, trying to sound vexed.

Nigella seemed to ignore him, and she continued preparing the pie. A pleasant scent of apples hit his nostrils. He slumped onto the mattress and waited, staring at the ceiling, listening to the sound of her culinary work.

An hour breezed by. Finally, Nigella took the clay pan off the coals using a pair of black tongs. Calemore sat up. The pie was sizzling with brown juices. She removed the lid, beat it against the brick enclosure of her little stove to remove the coal dust, covered the pie with a piece of cloth, and let it cool for a while. He was getting rather hungry.

With a marksman's concentration, Nigella cut into the pie and placed a huge slice on his platter. She put it on the table and waited, face contorted with devotion and tension. She was waiting for him to approve of her baking, he knew.

Well, it was his time to delay. As if he didn't care for the apple pie, he sat down in the chair, naked, and sniffed the slice. Then, carefully, he began eating.

It was delicious.

The pie had all sorts of winter spices he had not seen her add before, and they added extra flavor to the fruit. He let the taste slide off his tongue, truly enjoying himself. "Excellent."

Nigella sat at the table beside him, smiling. "Do you want me to tell you about my reading now?"

He ran a tongue over his teeth, chasing crumbs. "Go ahead."

She removed her spectacles and blinked once to adjust to the marred view of the world. Calemore almost felt inclined to fix her sight, but he would not do that unless she asked. She had to learn to stand up for herself in every way.

"I know that you want Sheldon to be the ruler of the realms."

Calemore nodded, biting into the pie. "Tell me something I do not know."

Nigella touched the book, lying just near the plate. "To win, you must kill the man who feels nothing."

He paused chewing. "Riddles again?"

She looked afraid for a moment. "No. He is a Special Child."

Calemore relaxed and resumed eating. That made sense. It must be one of the freaks serving the surviving god. Maybe even that scrawny lad with the bloodstaff. He would just have to make sure to find him and dispose of him.

"Where do I find him? And why him?"

"Because he is Damian's son, too, and he will take your place if you don't kill him."

There, a mortal warning, just like I expected. "How will I know this Special Child?"

"Seek the loneliest man among your enemies; that's what the book says. It does not identify him by name." Nigella shrugged apologetically. "I don't know."

Calemore rubbed his upper lip. He picked a sliver of apple rind from between his teeth. Not as helpful as he had hoped, but good enough. There was a critical threat to his campaign, and it was one of Damian's monsters. It was just like his father to keep annoying him from his grave. Once he killed this man, his victory would be certain. It was a good thing to have come here, he realized. Nigella's words were precious. Finally, she was giving him real, valuable information he needed.

She had earned his respect in every way.

"What else?"

"The book also says you will be blinded twice, once by a god, once by a woman."

Calemore grinned. He thought he could well figure this one out. He would—

He felt a jolt in his stomach.

It was as if somehow had honed surprise to divine perfection and stabbed him with it.

He had not experienced dietary discomfort in all the thousands of years of his life.

Nigella frowned, looking worried. "What?"

Calemore put the fork down. "I don't know." Another jolt. He looked at the woman, at her expression of fear. No. Not fear. Something else. He rose suddenly, feeling dread on his skin. Then, his legs buckled, and he collapsed. What was happening?

There was a numb feeling in his legs, in his arms, spreading through his gut. His sex desire fled him, leaving behind nothing. He looked up and saw Nigella leaning over him, her homely face hovering above him. She was holding her spectacles from falling, her mouth was open, and her teeth showed. That expression still contorted her cheeks. No fear there whatsoever. No surprise. Contentment? Resignation? Determination?

"You once asked me what I want," she said, her voice distant. "I know now what it is. I only want the best for my son. I will not let you ruin my son."

Calemore tried to speak, but he could barely move his jaw. He tried to summon anger, tried to blast this little place apart with magic, but there was nothing left. Just cold numbness, making its way like a slug, crawling up toward his chest, his throat.

"The book knows everything. Even how to kill someone like you," she added.

The sense of betrayal and indignation almost made him scream. But the poison in his blood left him immobile, and the world started to lose color and shape. Nigella began to fade from his sight, replaced by anguish forged in the Abyss itself.

"You will never have my son."

Darkness.

Nigella waited for a few moments, until she was certain the White Witch was dead. Then, she let herself shudder. A whimper of relief fled her lips. Trembling, she sat down on the chair. For just a moment, to steady her nerves.

Sweaty all over, she stood and walked to the door. Sheldon was playing, waving his sword at invisible foes, oblivious to the sight of men sprawled in the snow around him. They would come around in several hours, unless they froze to death, but she had no desire to kill these men who had served Calemore. It wasn't their choice.

"Shel, sweetie, come inside," she called. The boy had done his part well. She had worried he might try the bread, but he was a good boy, and he listened to his mother. In the worst case, he would have fallen asleep like the soldiers, and he would have woken without any ill consequences. But she loathed the idea of having to drag him behind her like a sack of potatoes. "Come."

He lowered his wooden blade, made a mean face at his unseen foes, and hopped back to the cabin.

"Don't touch the pie. Do not touch Master Calemore," she warned, already packing. Gold, food, winter clothing. That was all she needed.

"Why is Master Calemore dozing on the ground?" he asked.

"He is tired, Shel. Come here. Help me." Nigella stuffed another satchel of coins into the bottom of the pack. Luckily, the Naum soldiers had not argued with her instructions. They had brought her everything she had demanded and Sheldon had translated.

Her son kept staring at the body, and she had to keep him busy. Within half an hour, they were packed. They had a pair of mules tied to a post behind the cabin. The animals would carry the provisions. There was the danger of bandits, but she believed she would be safe within Calemore's newly conquered territory. His soldiers would not accost her, and that would be enough until she got to the coast. Then, the gold should do its charm.

It was still terribly, terribly risky, but she had no better ideas. Staying here would be meaningless. She had to get away from the witch's domain, from his troops, from all this madness.

Sheldon pulled the last strap on his bag. "Done, Mom, before you."

"I'm glad," she said absent-mindedly. She was wondering whether to take her herbs. Would she need them ever again in her life? Maybe. Just a few.

Soon, they were fully packed. The boy went around and loaded the mules. She paid the little cabin one last glance. Nothing of value was there, nothing that meant anything to

Igor Ljubuncic

her, that would make her hesitate or stay. As an afterthought, she tossed a blanket over the prone figure on the floor and stuffed his white clothes under the mattress. Maybe she should torch the place? No. Best if it all remained intact. The soldiers would never dare enter and interfere with their master. That would give her a lot of time to get far away from Marlheim.

From the corner of her eye, she saw she had left *The Book of Lost Words* on the table, near the poisoned pie.

That vile thing. She should burn it. Or just leave it behind. But then, someone might find it and take it and read it. And what then?

She grabbed the book and exited the cabin.

CHAPTER 50

*T*ime to kill more people. *Again,* Ewan thought.

He shifted his weight, and winced slightly at the pain in his injured leg. Nothing else hurt, just the parts of his sorry existence damaged by the blood pellets. He couldn't feel the winter's grip, the kiss of the wind, or smell the urine and poor cooking and the metallic stench of fresh blood. The world evaded him by a hairbreadth, except for the pain in his body. It was slowly receding, like any old wound, but when you didn't feel anything else, the agony was monumental.

Worse, he had to summon the courage to do it all over again.

He would level the bloodstaff at Calemore's troops and rain death into their ranks. The witch would respond with his own attack, and Jarman and Lucas would try to shield him. They might distract the enemy with their own blasts of magic. Sooner or later, Ewan knew his luck would run out, and one of the pellets would kill him. He did not relish that. Life might not give him much, but he did not welcome death, not after all this torment. Not after having spent twenty years in the Abyss, among the gods. He wasn't even sure what being dead might mean. An eternity among lost souls? Silent nothingness?

He realized the White Witch was keen on killing whoever wielded the bloodstaff. He must fear the weapon. Ewan could have given it to someone else and just used his brute strength to decimate the northerners. But he did not want to be the man who killed like that. He did not want to live with those memories. He did not want to wade through all the sea of blood and hatred.

I once thought I was a monster. I am now a much bigger monster than I've ever imagined.

His soul begged him not to give up. Not just his cause or the fight itself. All of it. Not to give up the weapon either. If Ayrton were in possession of that terrible thing, he would never hand the burden over to someone else. He would never stoop to such cowardice.

He felt shame at having wanted to die after his injury. A moment of weakness. He would not let himself fail like that ever again. And he was done running and hiding. He would defend the people of the realms as best as he could, and that was all he had to offer the world. That was his legacy. A sad and maybe meaningless one, but it was his.

He swallowed.

The northern army had not attacked them for a while now. They should bless the respite, but there was no joy left in people's hearts. Half the defenders had died; many others were wounded or starving or freezing. The king was doing his best to prevent crime and mutiny, keeping a watchful eye on Amalia and fighting his own sorrow. Two old enemies, eying each other over the corpses of their families. All the while the city supplies dwindled, more people died from disease, and the northern army kept threatening annihilation.

Both sides spent time preparing for the next engagement, digging frantically, mending tools and weapons, beefing up their gear and blades. For the people of the realms hunkering around Roalas, it was the one and only pastime. For the enemy, it was yet another day in a senseless madness. They would soon march south and trample all in their path.

Scouts reported lots of activity that morning. It seemed the enemy was getting ready to try crossing the river at four points, one almost five miles south of the city. King Sergei was diverting his already-worn defenses to try to cover the rear, too. But there just weren't enough soldiers or weapons to maintain an effective perimeter. Even women were forced to defend the walls now, and not everyone had a spear. Ordinary soldiers got promoted three or four ranks just so the armies could maintain their structure.

Ewan did not pay too much attention to the dealings among the Parusites, the Athesians, the Borei, and others, but it seemed the mercenaries were rather loyal to the king. Amalia's Caytoreans had almost all left, heading home to their country. Gavril's pilgrims remained, but their zeal was gone, replaced with the dejected stupor of men without cause and faith.

Ewan still could not tell how the god's death had affected people. They just did not seem to know. They had never really known.

All faith had been was to make the gods and goddesses stronger. Their own blood tax.

Ewan felt like he shared in all their terror, and it seeped through his pores and burrowed through his veins, formed into a black diamond two hands below his heart, making him queasy just by breathing. He almost retched at the image of hot, steaming organs spilling from bodies, and his hands raking through the pulp like it was river water.

A distant bugle wept a forlorn note into the gray world. Somewhere, a unit was moving to engage. It was beginning.

Ewan tried to breathe, but he couldn't. His chest would not expand. He tightened his grip on the bloodstaff, wiggled the fingers on both his hands, what few he had left.

Jarman looked at him and nodded. The wizard had lost weight, and he looked haggard. But like him, the Sirtai was not giving up, fighting a war for the greater good, for the people of the realms. This wasn't their war, and yet, they had made it theirs. Through all the selfishness, they'd made sacrifices.

The troops began to stir, a huge monster flexing its hundreds of gangrenous joints, each a different color, a different shade, a different state of rot. Ewan let the sights blur past him in a nauseating display of color and chaos. The Parusite regiments moved; the Athesians manned their siege engines. Inside the city, the cripples, children, and women lit fires and dipped their arrows in the flames.

Ewan took a deep breath and stepped into a long, elaborate ditch. Calemore knew when he was firing the weapon, so at least he would use thick layers of earth to protect him and help him scurry about unseen. Soldiers on all sides stepped back. They all knew what was coming.

He dragged his injured leg into the trench, placing it down gingerly. The soil was iced brown cake. His foot slipped, twisted, and he bit off a lump of pain.

Then, another kind of pain made him double over. It lasted for a moment and was gone.

His middle hurt, as if someone had kicked him, a memory of pain from when he used to be human. He had no idea what it signified, but he had never seen anything good happen after his guts clenched.

There were no more gods left to die. So who had? Was it his turn now? Time for the monster to be finally destroyed?

Same and yet different, his belly throbbed with the lingering shock of that brief lance of agony.

He waited until he saw the host on the near side of the bank move. It took them a while, like it always did. The huge army never rushed, and their formations uncoiled like a big, fat snake, utterly confident in its sheer size. Soon, though, the huge white mass of troops was marching toward the defenders. Not a particularly coordinated attack, but it had numbers to compensate for every tactical failure.

Ewan aimed the bloodstaff. And fired.

He did not want to watch the death he caused. He closed his eyes and waited a few moments while the magical rod spewed red horror at the enemy. Not waiting for Calemore's own volley, he dashed left, limping and jumping as best as he could. The Sirtai were shielding him, he hoped. He could not hear any concussion from their magical explosions, so they must be focusing all their strength in defending him.

No return fire from Calemore either.

That worried him.

But he was not going to give up. He leveled the weapon at the Naum forces. His whole body gave off an involuntary twitch. His hands spasmed, and he dropped the bloodstaff against the ditch wall. His knees buckled, and he sank into the cold mush. There was pain in his gut again, his old, familiar companion, his only friend. Like earlier, the pain reminded him of all those times the gods had perished. The sensation gripped him, making him nauseated, like he had eaten too much honey.

The White Witch had not attacked him yet. Maybe this was his new strategy? Magic?

The hurting became dull, spread through his limbs, leaving him weak. Then, it began to fade, leaving behind a warm, itchy feeling. Soon, the tingling disappeared, leaving him whole and strong and strangely rejuvenated.

Almost like fog slithering through a forest, understanding licked his mind.

Images started to coalesce, and he saw the witch in a distant place, curled on the floor of a small cabin. He had never seen him, but he knew it was him. Words came on top of those fuzzy pictures, spoken in all languages, but he had no problem deciphering them.

It took him a few moments to grasp the enormity of what he had just experienced.

Swallowing a lump, wiping tears from the corners of his eyes, he gripped the bloodstaff and climbed out of the ditch, into the filthy snow, facing the hundreds of thousands of soldiers coming his way. He thought he could hear the defenders behind him screaming defiance or calling him back. It no longer mattered.

Arms spread wide, he walked toward the Naum troops.

The wind and the noise wrapped around him.

He raised the bloodstaff.

And shouted.

"Thank you for everything," Ewan whispered, extending his hand.

The Sirtai wizard hesitated. Slowly, he reached forward. Ewan could not feel the warmth of his skin. There was just the feel of ridged, paperlike texture, soft underneath.

"Are you certain?"

Ewan nodded. "Yes, I am certain. It's the only way."

Jarman pursed his lips, thoughtful. "It sounds incredible."

Ewan smiled weakly. "It is incredible, but the war is over. There will be no more bloodshed."

Lucas came over. He looked just as tired, but his blue tattoos hid some of his exhaustion. "I would very much like to study you, god child."

Ewan looked behind him. Several Naum elders were waiting patiently. "Maybe in the future, one day. Now, I must save these people. Save the realms. Save everyone."

"Roalas is still in chaos. I believe the king may want to see you, despite his aversion toward magic." Jarman smoothed his robes nervously.

Ewan stared at the city walls. No one inside wanted to believe the incredible story. No one was willing to put aside the grim terror that had held them for so long. Daring to hope, only to have their dreams shattered, that was even worse.

The northern hosts had halted their advance, but their presence still sullied the fields north and east of Roalas, a huge sprawl of men dressed in white furs, stretching into the hazy, snowy horizon. You didn't have to be any sort of military expert to assess their strength, their invincibility. Cautiously optimistic almost to the point of paranoid denial, the Parusites and Athesians were waiting for that massive presence to disappear before they'd let themselves exhale with relief. No one would say anything. No one would smile. Until the Naum forces marched away.

Finally, he shook his head. "It's best if I just leave. King Sergei will not understand."

Jarman grimaced uncomfortably. "You wish no recognition for your effort?"

Ewan sighed. "What would be the point?"

"You are absolutely convinced the White Witch is dead?" the young wizard repeated.

And all the gods, too. "Yes, he died."

"Farewell," Lucas said.

Ewan nodded and walked away. He left behind him the field littered with the dead, heaps of broken gear, and human suffering. He knew that life in Athesia would be hard for many months, maybe years to come. The little affairs between the kings and emperors and lords remained. They would keep fighting and bickering, maybe follow with a war of their own. Selfishness could always drink more blood.

He wanted no part in that. He didn't want to walk among men who eyed him with distrust and fear, who hated him for just being different. He did not want to tread anywhere his presence would invoke terse silence or make mothers send their children inside. He did not want to be a monster, an abomination, a creature of sin.

His feet crunched toward the leaders of the Naum tribes. They spoke an ancient language, unheard in the realms for countless generations, but his mind translated the words perfectly. The elders feared him, too. All of them. In their hearts, the legend of a man who carried the bloodstaff went back thousands of years, and nothing Ewan could do would change it.

But they listened to him. They obeyed.

Stopping a host their size with nothing more than his appearance spoke greatly of what Calemore had achieved during his seclusion in the north. It saddened him to learn these men had traveled so far from their homes just to participate in meaningless carnage so their leader could become a deity. They had left everything behind and come south. They had no idea how to plow and till the fields of Athesia and Caytor. They knew nothing about husbandry. They were sick and weak and hungry, and many of their women and children had died during the journey, left behind, lost, or killed.

Still, their society was huge and remained largely intact. There was hope for them.

Ewan knew he had to provide that hope. Take them away from this madness, isolate them.

They are not my people, he thought. *But then, I am the only one who can help them now. I am the only one who can stop this war.*

The elders cast their gazes to the ground. Their behavior reminded him of the Oth Danesh. The same ingrained fear, the same animal instincts rooted in through the random viciousness of their ruler.

I could send them back north, Ewan figured. They would obey. They would follow the roads north until the roads ran out. Then they would walk through the wilderness until they reached their far, secluded land. Their return would be murderous. The realms had been picked clean, villages burned and abandoned, fields left fallow or trampled dead. The Naum folk would not find any food or supplies along the way, and moving such a large army would lead to more conflicts, more killing against whoever they met.

He could do it. Remain the monster that he was. Or he could try to redeem his blood-drenched soul. His clothes were dark brown, stained with old death he hadn't bothered cleaning, because he wanted a reminder of what he had done.

Ewan looked back one last time, toward Roalas. Jarman and Lucas were standing in the snow, watching him. A sizable body of the Parusite heavy cavalry, led by one of their dukes, was keeping a safe distance from the Naum people. Ewan wondered what they were trying to prove. That they hadn't just been saved from total defeat? Maybe they were making sure no angry mob would storm toward the northerners and cause more grief. It didn't really matter.

Behind the rider, there were still more troops, soldiers collecting rubbish, dragging the corpses away and picking them clean, folding old, filthy tents, taking them back into the city barracks. On the walls, hundreds lined the crenelations, staring dumbly. Maybe one of them was the king. Amalia might be there somewhere, too. He did not care about any of them.

He knew what he had to do. Best if he set about it.

"Follow me." He motioned to the elders. Bent forward, cradling the bloodstaff in his whole hand, he began furrowing through the snow, heading west, into the Safe Territories, the new home of the Naum people.

CHAPTER 51

Sergei sat on Adam's throne, staring toward the entrance. Apart from the old, seemingly immortal adviser at his side, and several royal guards, the vast hall was empty and cold. He had not bothered with fires, and the winter's bite was seeping through the thick masonry.

Sergei wondered how Theo could endure standing in one place for so long, so patiently. He must have tendons made from iron. No matter how long he was required to wait on the king, he did so without complaining.

"When she enters, I must ask you not to speak. Not one word," Sergei muttered, not looking at the adviser.

Theo swallowed noisily, wetting his mouth. "Yes, Your Highness."

Sergei reached for the gilt goblet resting on the floor, by the throne. He groaned as he pushed his ribs against the armrest, feeling blood gush into his head. The goblet was empty. Well, perhaps it was for the best. Servants watched him warily, uncomfortable.

Sergei didn't care.

It had been several weeks since some unassuming youth named Ewan had ended the war. One day, they were all losing, and the next, the Naum forces had halted their offensive and were waiting to be taken away to the Safe Territories. At first, Sergei had been surprised, shocked, but now he just pondered the outcome.

What did it matter where that army was going, as long as it no longer sowed destruction? The Safe Territories had been a homeland for his settlers in the past two decades, but even they had not been able to restore faith to all the holy places. Most of the cities remained in ruins, and the Territories were a shadow of their past glory. Now, with half his troops dead or dying, he didn't have the privilege of sending anyone there. He would need all of the people in the south, to make sure the realm did not starve.

The priests might lament all they wanted, and maybe it was blasphemy, but he did not care. He could not bring himself to summon empathy for the plight of the patriarchs. Their battle was over. The realms had fought their war of religion—and lost.

Instead, they had been saved by magic.

Not that long ago, every Parusite would regard even the slightest rumor of magic with distrust. They would openly dislike the Sirtai, and the priests would hunt down anyone who showed magical skills. Now, even the more fanatic soldiers loudly blessed a scrawny boy possessed of almost indestructible power. Everything their nation had been built upon, churned into mud, like the wet, bloody snow under their feet.

It was good that Ewan was taking the Naum people to the Safe Territories. It was the only sensible option. Going back north would have meant that huge host trampling the realms dead a second time, ruining what little was left. Going into no-man's-land was the best choice. Faith would have to survive. It would have to endure in people's hearts.

Roalas was coming to terms with its near ruin. Soldiers were busy hunting down criminals, subduing riots, and securing the food stores. No matter how grim the situation, men would always find ways to profit, and he would not stand for it.

The mixed armies were recuperating, licking their wounds. Almost every house, every bed in the city had someone wounded lying there, resting or festering. The unity he had hoped to achieve, the unity Emperor Adam had tried to bring to the realms, was happening because of a great, costly tragedy. People were too tired to worry about who followed who, for once. Not that Sergei had any illusions about the future. Once the terror of the war faded, the nations would remember their mistrust and fear of one another. The Athesians would not forgive him the execution of Lady Lisa. The Parusites would not forget the death of their prince.

Spring would be grim, the next autumn and winter even more so. Sergei's head hurt when he tried to grasp the enormity of losses and damages. He had lost an entire cadre of skilled warriors, and thousands of farmers and craftsmen across Athesia had died fleeing the northern menace. There would be a great shortage of labor and experience, and he feared hunger and banditry.

But somehow, this sorry little place would live on. It would seem that Athesia was a special place. It had been invaded and pillaged so many times in the recent years, and yet, it clung to life, stubbornly, like a weed. Despite all the misery and suffering, Roalas would survive. And the land and people around it would follow its lead, crippled and weak, yet alive.

Once, he would have cherished the challenge. He would have embraced the responsibility.

He no longer cared.

His heart had no more room for grief. Losing his father, his son, and now his sister was simply too much. Athesia was the bane of his family. He was tired of all this tragedy. He sorely missed his wife, his remaining children. He wanted to go home, to leave this madness behind.

Which was why the upcoming meeting was critical.

The door of the hall opened. Giorgi stepped in. "Your Highness?"

Sergei took a deep breath, trying to steady his nerves. "Bring her in."

Several armed men in the livery of his house guard stepped in first, holding ornamental halberds. Following in their wake was a slim woman in a silver-white dress. The cursed daughter of the cursed former emperor of this sorry place.

Amalia.

She had surrendered to him. She was his vassal. Officially, she was the governess of Athesia, and that meant she might run this place, if he let her.

She walked with a dutiful, slow step, surrounded by those men. Her face was stern, her gaze locked somewhere above his head. But he could not see any defiance, any rancor. Just grimness. Maybe the same kind of expression that wrinkled his own features.

"Your Highness," she said, bowing.

Sergei waited, watching her. This was the first time he was seeing his enemy. This was the first time he had come face-to-face with the woman who had caused him so much pain. Just a silly girl. "Lady Amalia."

"You have called for me." Her voice was steady. He had to admire that.

Sergei flicked a quick glance at Theo. The old man was staring at the former empress, but his lips were pressed shut. "Were you there when my sister died?" he asked.

Amalia hesitated. "No, Your Highness. She led the troops into battle. I didn't see her fall."

Sergei shifted his weight. "Were you in any way involved in the death of my son, Prince-Heir Vlad?"

The girl lowered her eyes, and their gazes locked. Her eyes looked moist now. "No, Your Highness."

He rubbed his chin. He remembered the day he had walked into this chamber, facing the old adviser, telling him, in that slow, melancholic voice, that his son had been killed. His chest tightened, air coming in a reedy whisper up his throat. He remembered Lisa's execution. She had been dignified to the very end, unafraid, and she insisted on convincing him that her daughter had not been involved in Vlad's murder. Amalia's hands were clean, she had not been involved, the woman had pleaded, even as she stared unblinking, unflinching at the headsman's sword.

Adam took my father. Lisa took my son. This girl hasn't harmed me. Who do I blame for Sasha's death? Myself.

"I am willing to put all our past grievances behind us. As negotiated in the peace agreement between us, Athesia will remain a vassal state of the Parusite kingdom, with rights equal to a duchy or a princedom. You will govern the region in my name. Will you uphold this pledge?"

Amalia tried to stop herself from crying. It was not dignified. She was Adam's daughter, and she could not be seen crying in front of anyone.

But this man had killed her mother. This man had ruined her realm. Destroyed her dreams, her nation, everything.

Amalia knew she could refuse his offer. She could decide rebellion and resistance were better than a lifetime of servitude. The Athesians would rise against the invader, and sooner or later, the Parusites would be forced to leave. True, she would be going back on her word, but what did words mean anyway? King Sergei had killed her mother after signing the peace treaty. He had broken the agreement first.

The Parusites were weak and demoralized. Thousands had perished in the war against Naum, and they didn't have the necessary force to upkeep the king's reign, even bolstered by those religious fools and their Borei mercenaries. Amalia needed only to refuse his offer, and there would be war in Athesia once more. She was certain her nation would win this time. The Eracians were badly battered, fighting their own war against the nomads. Caytor was in upheaval, it seemed, with the High Council in a state of bloody feud. No one would interfere now, and her people would fight against the enemy, and they would defeat the Parusites.

The price was quite small. Her own life.

Sergei was trying to buy off the murder of her mother with peace. Once, she wouldn't even have wasted a moment considering his words. She would have laughed in his face. But this man, this king had tried to make life better for Athesians even after his son had been killed in this very city. This king had offered her peace, not once but twice, having seen his father and firstborn killed by her family.

That galled.

That was wrong.

No one could have such morality.

So why had he not stayed his hand and spared her mother? Weakness? Anger? Revenge? Did it matter? Nothing would bring her back. The only thing left was how she intended to observe her mother's death. Through childish defiance or hard, painful compromise. Like Father did, when he'd offered peace to those who had tried to assassinate him so many times.

And yet…after all he had been through, Sergei was willing to compromise, willing to forgive. He was brave enough to offer a second chance. He had what it took to be a king, to be an emperor, she realized with profound bitterness in her soul. She knew she stood in the shadow of someone better, greater than her. Someone she could never best.

She finally understood the terrible price of authority.

Prove that you're a better person than him, her conscience taunted. *Prove it, you foolish girl.*

But she was Adam's daughter. And she could try.

Her hand brushed over the ropy scar on her temple. The hair had grown over it completely, and no one could see the ugliness.

She thought about Gerald, about all her friends she had spurned and ignored. She thought about Agatha raising her child in this grim world. She thought briefly about Ewan and how he had been willing to die to save everyone. She even thought about Princess Sasha, marching toward certain death. Selfless sacrifice, every one of them, except her.

"I will uphold it, Your Highness," she croaked and had to cough. "Yes."

Sergei's face twitched, and he almost lost his calm composure. "Good." He rose from the throne. "Good." In slow, measured steps, he walked past her. "Then you will know what to do. Please consult with Theodore about the management of the city. I will expect monthly reports."

Amalia spun after him. "Your Highness."

Sergei stopped walking, tensed, then slowly turned toward her. "Yes?"

Amalia clenched her fists hard. "I am sorry."

He nodded once. "I am sorry, too. Now, you will excuse me. I am going home."

Amalia watched him depart. Some of the guards stepped in beside him, flanking him. Others remained in the chilly hall, still as statues. Heart beating rapidly, her emotions a bruised storm of panic, joy, and regret, she looked back at her old adviser, wiping tears from the corners of her eyes.

"Theo."

"Amalia," he said in his familiar tone. "Welcome back."

EPILOGUE

E wan stepped toward the Womb.

It was early spring. Flowers were waking up shyly across the little clearing. Patches of snow clung to the shadows beneath the trees, but the rest of the turf was shining soft green, basking in sunlight.

He had spent the last several weeks leading the Naum people to the Safe Territories, helping them settle in the abandoned places, picking up life where it had stopped two decades earlier with the Feoran invasion. With as much wonder and dismay as he had felt a lifetime ago watching those intruders come and torch his monastery, the northerners filed into the ghost places, overgrown with weeds and shrubbery, teeming with wildlife. Humans had come and disturbed the peace of nature, scattering the animals. There was always someone usurping and someone fleeing, it seemed. Finite land, infinite greed, infinite need for survival.

He had helped them populate the big places, then left them on their own. They would figure out where to send their folk. They would know not to go past the flag markers laid down around the border of the holy land. That was his one rule for this lost nation.

Their life would be harsh, Ewan knew: learning everything in this alien, warm world where snow fell for only a fraction of the year, identifying the strange new trees that withered with the first storms, herding sheep, sowing seeds, establishing law and order.

In the realms, a different slew of tragedies would unveil, but unveil it would.

All the while, people would continue their lives, convinced there were gods and goddesses watching over them.

The Naum people had their unshakable belief in their master with the bloodstaff. For them, belief was in seeing power, feeling power. For the Parusites, Caytoreans, Eracians, and maybe some Athesians, hope was all about faith in divine creatures that had long forgotten about humans.

Finally, a meaning to his life. To become the guardian of the people of the realms, to become their protector, their chaperone, to help them overcome their doubts and grief and fear. A life of solitude, a life of burden.

He was ready.

He stepped toward the pile of pebbles. Dark, opaque, dead like the gods and goddesses.

He picked up one at random, cupped it hard in his palm, and willed life into the little stone. The rock started to glow, becoming translucent. Strangely greenish in color, like the growth underneath piers in a harbor.

The world around him started to change. He noticed the touch of the chilly breeze on his skin.

Ewan gasped with wonder. He saw goose bumps on his forearm. For so many years as a child, he had taken the caress of a cool wind for granted, never wondered what it would be like to be bereft of all smells, taste, hunger, heat, and cold.

It was coming back to him, all of it. Never had the experience been so sweet.

As his body attuned to the early spring morning, his consciousness began to expand. He thought he heard chatter behind him, so he spun, but there was no one there. More voices, barely audible, everywhere, all around him. A silly grin exploded on his lips. He was feeling human life, everywhere, across the realms. Invisible lines of life's energy merged with his soul, and he could sense the realms, like a bird hovering many hundreds of miles above the terrain, seeing everything.

He dropped the shining pebble onto the heap. Oh, he was hungry now and feeling weak. Human once again, vulnerable. A wildcat could kill him now; a stray arrow would drop him dead. He would have to eat to survive; he would have to cover himself with a blanket to ward off the night's chill. The price of divinity.

Of being human.

I'm a god now, he figured stupidly.

Ewan promised himself he would never abandon the people of this land. Not them, not the Naum folk. They all deserved guidance. And unlike their old leaders, he would not hide away. He would embrace their passion and fears and work toward making their lives better. He would pay them back for their prayer and love for him so they would know their god listened to their plight.

He glanced at the graves of Elia and Damian, now overgrown with grass, barely there. In time, he hoped, he might find a girl who might like him for who he was. Break the bonds of his solitude. One day. Now, his task was restoring hope to the realms.

Gripping the bloodstaff, he went back into the surrounding forest.

After all, he had to hunt himself a dinner.

Mali looked at the curly haired northerner with pain in her chest. "We might meet again."

Bjaras did not speak that much Continental, but he figured the gist of her words. "Meet."

She nodded, pointing her chin behind him at the convoy of northerners waiting for the carpenter. Among the last of the invaders and their families to depart the realms. A small, frightened group, mostly the folk she had taken under her custody several months back. Despite all the killing and confusion, they had been spared.

Bjaras hesitated, but then he turned and walked out of her life.

Alexa stepped close and laid a gentle hand on her shoulder. "Well done, I'm proud of you."

Mali pursed her lips, trying to ignore her sadness. "Time to stop being a coward."

Yes, not being a coward. The hardest part was ahead of her. Or rather just behind her. As if some nightmare monstrosity lurked there, she pivoted on wooden legs and glanced at Captain Gordon, sitting in the back of an old army cart, peeling bark from a tree branch. Mostly to keep his hands busy, it seemed.

"I'm right here," Alexa goaded her.

Mali inhaled deeply through her nostrils. "That's not what worries me."

Alexa turned the friendly shoulder touch to a brusque pat. "And what does?"

What does? Mali mused. *A thousand things.* The new monarch frightened her. His campaign against the nomad tribes was turning into the bloodiest feud in known history. He was going to make Vergil's Conquest into a jolly stroll through the wilderness, by comparison.

Surprisingly, Monarch Bart had spared her troops from the march west. He had thanked the girls for their sacrifice and given them six months of leave from combat so they could visit their families, rest for a while, as well as heal their old wounds and prepare for the next phase of his glorified revenge spree. That suited her well enough. It meant she did not need to fake her death again, flee the army, and become a renegade, a traitor, and a plain woman once more. She could retain some of her status until she figured out what she wanted to do with her life.

The future frightened her, the uncertainty of war. She feared being alone at night, crying softly, thinking about her dead son. She feared living in a world that held no illusions for her. Most of all, she feared walking over to Gordon and committing herself to him.

He had waited for her, dutifully, patiently.

She could walk away, like she had done in the past. She could go away from this madness, this war, become nobody and nothing once more. If she were lucky, she had two more decades ahead of her. Long enough not to see war ever again, she hoped. That would take no courage whatsoever. All she had to do was walk away. Ride past Paroth's gate and head somewhere. Maybe the Safe Territories, where no one knew her name, and no one could speak her language. Or maybe Parus, and she didn't mind the religion if it gave her the peace she needed from everything else. One of the ruined places in Caytor or Athesia. Anything.

A simple, straightforward choice. She had done it before. She knew what to expect.

Fuck it, she thought.

Bracing herself for the thing some might call love, she walked toward a very much grinning Captain Gordon.

Jarman enjoyed the pitch of the ship under his feet. He loved the sight of the gray-blue water, the roll of froth on the waves, the caw of birds following the cutter on the swift currents above. Somewhere ahead, just behind the gentle curve of the Velvet Sea, was Tuba Tuba.

Sanity. Home.

He had avenged his third mother, Inessa, after all. He may not have killed Calemore himself, but it did not matter. He had died in the war, and that was good enough. His work in the realms was complete.

True, he was going home with many questions unanswered. He had never learned about Rob, and if he told his father about it, Armin would surely have a few witty remarks emphasizing his ineptitude as an investigator. It did not matter. He had done pretty well in the war, he felt. Not bad for an uninitiated wizard.

Lucas was no longer his life slave. He was now a terrible senior Anada, and it was as if the last decade had not really happened. Nothing had changed, Jarman knew, and yet, it had. In one stroke of luck, he was just a rookie, and Lucas was a dreaded, powerful teacher.

The wind ruffled his hair, made his cheeks stiff as if someone had caked them with mud and let it dry. His fingers were numb on the salt-crusted rail of the front deck. Around him, sailors went about their tasks, not minding the robed men. They were Sirtai, and the sight of Anada was quite common for them. His life was going back to being how it should, clean and logical. Although, he might miss the taste of ugly freedom that the realms had offered him. At least he had learned a valuable lesson.

"Lucas," he said, his voice carrying strangely on the wind. "What's on your mind?"

Jarman pushed himself upright. "I was wondering if I have earned my first tattoo yet?"

The blue-faced man's expression never changed. "No."

Not the answer I had in mind, he thought with some disappointment. "Why? Did I not perform well in the war? I think I did master the subtlety of their culture and communication, and I assisted in the fight against the White Witch."

Lucas blinked once. "You did all that. But that's not the reason."

Jarman rubbed his hands together. "So what is the reason?"

"You keep asking about the tattoo," Lucas preached in a flat tone. "That means you're not ready for one."

"I'll keep that in mind," Jarman said after a while. Should he feel frustrated? Perhaps. But he knew that would not get him anywhere near earning his promotion at the temple. The Anada did not reward sulkiness. So he kept his mouth shut and stared at the offing, waiting for the contour of his homeland to appear. Lucas remained at his side, senior, severe, as grim as the first day he had met him.

War changed some men, he knew. It had shaped him, he was certain.

And some men never changed. For Jarman, that was a relief, knowing that no matter what happened, he could always rely on Lucas. That was his sanity away from home.

He really missed Tuba Tuba, so he stared harder, willing the land to show itself sooner.

Nigella stared at the two wizards with a mix of fear and curiosity. She knew who they were, and that worried her a little. Then she remembered murdering Calemore, and her courage spiked up. Behind her, leaning against one of the masts, Sheldon was playing with a pair of lead figurines, leading an elaborate deck fight against pirates. He had such a vivid imagination, and she was proud of him.

Cradled in her son's lap was that crystal egg, the gift from Calemore. At first, she had considered throwing it away, but she saw no harm in the thing, so she'd let Sheldon keep it. She believed the book would have warned her if there had been any danger.

The book...

It rested in a pouch in her oiled coat, the weight dragging the garment at a funny angle. She had many other useful items in her pockets, all kinds of spices, recipes, gold. Even after paying the hefty price for the travel to Sirtai, she still had enough to see Sheldon and her well through a couple of years in life, long enough until she figured out what she wanted to do.

She would need time before she could hope to find employment for herself, she knew.

Her hand touched her belly. No one could see it yet, but she was with a baby again. That last lovemaking with Calemore. Well, she had stopped taking her special herbs a while back, and her womb turned out to be quite fertile, despite years of poisons in her veins. At first when she had missed her menses, she had felt a deep, primal fear and almost decided to swill laserwort again. But then, she had quickly decided against it. That was *her* baby. Not Calemore's. He was dead. The White Witch was dead, and she alone would decide how her child would grow. Another son, she knew. It would be another strong, healthy, smart boy.

Her hand trailed to the pocket sagging with the book's bulk and fished it out. Heavy, beautiful, evil.

Making sure no one was looking, she hesitated only a moment before she tossed it overboard. It flapped open in the wind, tumbled over, and sank with a small splash into the lead-colored spray. The water covered the pages, and it vanished, lost in the ship's furious wake.

Her eyes went back to the two wizards. Sheldon needed a future.

She had killed the most dangerous thing in the world. She could secure apprenticeship for her son at the Temple of Justice.

Nigella adjusted the spectacles on the bridge of her nose. She ran her tongue over her big teeth. She knew they were big, and did not care. With as much dignity as she could muster in the wailing wind, she stepped toward the two men, the young, lean fellow and the menacing, blue-faced one.

"Excuse me, wizards. I must ask you something…"

ABOUT THE AUTHOR

Igor Ljubuncic is a physicist by vocation and a Linux geek by profession. He is the founder and operator of the website www.dedoimedo.com, where you can learn a lot about a lot. Before dabbling in operating systems, Igor worked in the medical high-tech industry as a scientist. However, he really likes to write, particularly in the fantasy genre, and has been doing so since the tender age of ten summers. You can learn more about Igor's writing on his book series website, www.the-lostwordsbooks.com, or you can find him on facebook.com/thelostwordsbooks.

46083462R00343

Made in the USA
Charleston, SC
03 September 2015